Grant Sutherland was born in Sydney and grew up in Western Australia. He now lives with his wife and children in Herefordshire, England.

www.grantsutherland.net

Also by Grant Sutherland
in the Decipherer's Chronicles

THE COBRAS OF CALCUTTA
THE HAWKS OF LONDON

EAGLES AT
YORK TOWN

*The third volume
of the Decipherer's Chronicles*

GRANT SUTHERLAND

PAN BOOKS

First published 2012 by Macmillan

This edition published 2012 by Pan Books
an imprint of Pan Macmillan, a division of Macmillan Publishers Limited
Pan Macmillan, 20 New Wharf Road, London N1 9RR
Basingstoke and Oxford
Associated companies throughout the world
www.panmacmillan.com

ISBN 978-0-330-50874-2

1 3 5 7 9 8 6 4 2

A CIP catalogue record for this book is available
from the British Library.

Typeset by Ellipsis Digital Limited, Glasgow
Printed and bound by CPI Group (UK) Ltd, Croydon CRO 4YY

Visit www.panmacmillan.com to read more about all our books
and to buy them. You will also find features, author interviews and
news of any author events, and you can sign up for e-newsletters
so that you're always first to hear about our new releases.

The
EAGLES AT
YORK TOWN

Here in the writing of these Chronicles, I am determined to make report of my actions to my own soul as to the king of kings, following truthfulness as close as any man dare. Read it who may, this is the life I have lived, such as it was and is, written for all time on the face of the world.

I, Alistair Malcolm Douglas, have roamed the earth, a spy for the Crown. God's mercy on my soul.

PRELUDE

*T*he news came at midday, but it was near midnight, and the fire dying in the grate, before I had collected myself sufficient to pen the enciphered letter to my superior in London.

New York, 3rd October 1780.

My Dear Jenkinson,

I have till now forborne to trouble you concerning the particular actions I have lately taken in furtherance of the King's cause. Alas, I can forbear no longer. I mean this letter as no extenuation of me, but I send it as an armour for you, and a shield for the Deciphering Department, that a better defence may be made against those gentlemen who await only the weapons to do us harm. My news, you may surmise, is of no sanguine nature.

These past six weeks I have been hardly a day out from New York, except it be to visit some of our outposts and to make a few brief sailings near to the Bar. Yet though I have moved little, my labour has been constant.

General Washington has throughout this time kept his army near to the Hudson, making sure of his defence of West Point even while threatening us here. But though he rattled his sabre yet we have ever felt ourselves secure, both in our own defences and from the knowledge of an imminent naval reinforcement (reinforcement came at last on the 18th September with the arrival of Admiral Rodney's fleet).

The near-proximity of the enemy has brought with it just those opportunities that I had looked for, and, in short, I was able to re-establish that communication with General Arnold that I had opened in the early part of the year. And he, to my great satisfaction, proved more willing than formerly to countenance a defection to our side. However the exigencies of such a defection (which must involve the surrender of Arnold's whole command to our army) necessitated the prior knowledge and approval of General Clinton for the plan, and likewise Major Andre, with whom I had worked closely on these matters. Messages were duly exchanged with General Arnold, and offers made. An agreement seemed possible.

It then happened that General Washington departed the Hudson with a small contingent to travel into Connecticut, there to consult with his French allies. Behind him he left General Greene to command the main Continental army, and General Arnold with a smaller force at West Point. This fortuitous disposition could not long continue. And so it was decided (and decided, I confess, at my urging) that we should arrange a secret parley with Arnold. But at Arnold's insistence it was Major Andre alone who must go up to negotiate in person the final terms of the grand defection.

The prize, you well know. With Benedict Arnold's defection we might have had West Point without loss, broke their army at a stroke, and possibly ended the war. In consequence I put by my misgivings concerning Arnold's demand.

And to say true, though Major Andre was but a young man, I

4

never doubted of his abilities. Nor was it in General Clinton's power, I believe, to overrule Arnold's terms for the parley. We must act, and act quickly; and so we did. Major Andre passed upriver in the 'Vulture' and went ashore under the escort of two colonials sent down for the purpose by Arnold.

That was on the 20th day of September.

The ensuing three days we heard nothing of Andre, but only the discomforting news that the 'Vulture' had been forced to retire downriver without him. One night might pass in such a fateful parley; but that no agreement between Andre and Arnold had been reached by the second night, it strained credulity beyond breaking. By the 23rd we feared the very worst.

And now it was that I received a very questionable intelligence of Major Andre proceeding southward toward New York upon foot, though still behind the enemy lines. General Clinton and some few of his senior officers at once assayed the possibility of sending up a raiding party to his rescue. This appeared to me but a hopeless gesture. And knowing the questionable nature of my information concerning Andre I was very forceful in my opinion that to send a party up through Tarrytown (which they intended) would serve no purpose. I feared it might prove only a provocation to our enemy and a positive danger to Andre should he truly be in that vicinity. The proposed raid was in consequence abandoned.

You will understand, then, both my own feelings and those of Clinton and his senior officers, when we learned on the 24th that Major Andre had been captured as a spy; and, by good report, captured on the previous day near Tarrytown as he endeavoured to cross back into our lines.

What reproaches have been made against me cannot exceed those I have made against myself.

The days since have seen an endless stream of letters passing between our headquarters and Washington's. We assert that Andre having gone into the colonial lines at General Arnold's invitation, there might be no proper charge of spying levelled against him. They in turn assert that the greatcoat Andre wore over his uniform when *he left the 'Vulture' was a deception and a disguise, and that he should definitely be tried as a spy.*

(I must add that to the back of all this has been the hard and indisputable fact of General Arnold's flight from West Point to join us. For after being captured, and that with such papers upon him as I understand to be highly incriminatory, Major Andre yet had the ingenuity and wit to cause a message to be carried to Arnold, who thereby escaped with his life – though, regrettably, leaving his command at West Point still under Washington.)

And today, at last, comes the news we had most feared, and which brings a stark and shocking end to these events. On the 2nd of October, Major Andre was hanged.

Not an officer here but is appalled and stricken, for Andre was a man esteemed by every soldier, and also by the townsfolk who were his intimates. For myself, I will say that in all my dealings with him, and particularly in these recent weeks when I have passed hours each day in his company, I never met a more generous spirit nor had an apter pupil.

Nor can I overlook my own part in his unhappy fate; for most of what he knew of spying I had given him, which was enough to put him into the enemy's hands but not near enough to save him. And as to the proposed raid toward Tarrytown that I forestalled, I think on that now with the bitterest regret.

Indeed, this is all very close, and I do not doubt but that it shall be some good while before I can cast my mind over these days without suffering the sharpest pangs of remorse.

Society and gaiety are what I cannot think on at present, and though it was my intention to return to London this month, I find now that I am thoroughly disinclined to it. Being equally disinclined to remain in New York through the winter, I have told General Clinton that I am wanted by our Indian allies in the south. Upon his agreement to release me (which I expect on the morrow) I shall travel across the Appalachians into the Indian country, whence you shall hear from me by way of our Superintendent. It is possible I may do some useful service there

before rejoining our army on the planned southern campaign in the
new year. I trust that you need no assurance from me that in
whichever quarter I find myself I shall spend all my energies upon
the work of the Deciphering Department, and in furtherance of the
interests of the King.

    I enclose a separate letter for Francis Willes at the Lane.
    Yours in sorrow and respect,
    Douglas.

In the event, there was neither of my expectations fulfilled. For it was three weeks before General Clinton was pleased to allow me release from New York. And it was already summer, and the next year's campaigning almost done, before I finally came away from the bloody troubles of the Cherokee.

Then it was that I recrossed the Appalachians, pursued our southern army up through the Carolinas, and arrived on the tidewater in Virginia at the ripest moment of the war.

CHAPTER 1

I got the fellow in my sights and held him there.

'Militia?' said Campbell; but I could not tell.

The man was coming around behind the rocks on the headland of the cove, his musket held across his chest. He was a hundred yards off from us, advancing cautious and slow. He picked his way about the rocks as though to keep hid from the muddy beach, stopping every few yards to look ahead. But we had made no fire, and the fallen pine behind which we crouched hid us from his view. The fellow came on, looked about, and stopped again. I had a quick suspicion of the reason.

'Alone?' said I quietly.

Campbell at once turned from me. He moved along behind the fallen pine, gained the cover of the scrub, and then rose and went silently into the wood.

There was shade where the stranger was now, so that he was almost invisible. The barrel of my musket still rested on the pine, trained upon the dark shadow. The last week of our journey had sharpened our distrust of everyone that we met with; for Cornwallis's army had but recently come by, and the whole tidewater country hereabouts was under arms. After my sojourn beyond the mountains I was returned now to the front lines of the war.

After ten minutes Campbell returned.

'Alone,' said he, taking up his musket. While he sighted the stranger I fetched my spyglass and turned it upon the river.

The James River was wide at that place, for we were near where the mouth opened into the Chesapeake Bay; but though I studied the quiet water a full minute there was no sign yet of the boat that must take me off.

'Ride on with me,' said Campbell.

I considered it, certainly. I had considered it all the while that he scouted the wood. Our horses were hobbled by a tidal creek but a short way inland, and we might be gone in a trice if we chose. But two days would then be added to my journey, which I baulked at. We had travelled weeks since leaving the Indian country, and I was impatient now to get myself directly around to Cornwallis in York Town and thence north to New York, where my latest instructions from Jenkinson and the Deciphering Department awaited. But as I turned to answer Campbell 'No,' he clicked his tongue in warning.

Out from the shadows the stranger was advancing. I put the spyglass on him again. He was no Continental soldier, but though he wore the buff breeches and the loose white shirt of a farmer, and had also a farmer's broad-brimmed hat to ward against the sun, yet I much suspected the caution of his advance and the ready state of his musket. In the last farmhouse we had stopped at, though they were Loyalists, they were frightened, and only too willing to see us gone. They had sent a message ahead to arrange my crossing, but I wondered now at the chance of some betrayal. As the stranger came nearer, Campbell sighted carefully, put his finger to the trigger, and only stopped when I whispered, 'Hold. Let him come.'

One minute, and then two, and the fellow came on with the same crablike advance. Upon reaching the small creek that ran from the wood across the beach and down into the river, he stopped. Here he must decide whether to turn back, or to go into the woods, or to cross over the creek; which last choice, if he made it, would bring him within thirty yards of us, directly under our muskets.

Campbell settled upon one knee. The heat was thick in the air, and I envied him now the Cherokee headband that kept the sweat from his eyes. I dipped my own face to my sleeve, and when I looked up again the stranger was stepping into the creek. The water went over his boots, and then to his thighs. But the creek was narrow, and after a few wading paces he rose and then stepped again onto the beach. By his movement, he was a younger man than I had first supposed. His hat was low over his eyes, and his face half-hidden.

Campbell took careful aim. And then the stranger put one muddy boot forward, looked up into the woods, and called, 'We are in the next cove!' and I reached to prevent Campbell firing. 'Mr Douglas!' called the stranger, and straightway turned Campbell's musket aside.

A log-canoe is no canoe but a boat native to the Chesapeake, low-cut and shallow-drafted, used by all the oystermen of the Bay. And it was in Cable Morgan's log-canoe that I now set out upon the James River.

'We must put the girls down at home before we go around. You do not mind, Alistair?'

'Only get me to York Town today,' I answered Cable Morgan, 'and I shall not mind any slight diversion.'

Cable hauled up the sail while his son David (who was that young stranger Campbell had nearly shot) took the tiller. Cable's wife Sally, and their daughter Elizabeth, sat opposite me in the bow. It was only by the merest accident that the whole family was there; for my message had found them upon the Portsmouth side, where Sally Morgan visited a cousin.

'Have you left someone?' asked Cable as we came into the river; for he had seen me look back along the shore. But Campbell had stayed hidden while I went down to the Morgans, and by now he must be mounted and riding up toward the Richmond road. Campbell had troubles enough without I make a general announcement of his presence, and so I told Cable no, that I had left no one behind me.

The sail once hoisted, Cable put out the flatboard over the gunwale and sat there to keep the boat trimmed. It was almost five years since I had last been in company with the Morgans. Five long years of the war. And in that time Lizzy had grown from a babe to a child, and David from a twelve-year-old boy into a young man. Cable looked little changed, his face just as dark from the sun, his smile just as broad and open as I remembered. But though he answered me now some few questions concerning Lord Cornwallis's movements about the Bay, and the disposition of the rebel force near Williamsburg and Richmond, I sensed a reticence in him. His several quick and uncertain glances toward his wife soon gave me the reason. I held off then, for I saw that we might talk more freely once Sally and Lizzy Morgan were set down at the farm.

As we went further downriver I turned my spyglass toward the Bay. Two ships stood out there.

'That to the north is the *Guadeloupe*,' said Cable. 'The other is British too, the *Loyalist*. The *Guadeloupe* shall leave for New York upon the night tide.'

After so many months spent inland, and then the hard journey, they were an unexpectedly cheering sight. At length I closed up my spyglass and put it in my satchel. Then glancing up I found Sally Morgan watching me with an expression quite melancholy. I ventured a smile, but she said only, 'You look tired, Mr Douglas.'

'Aye.'

'Shall you stay a time now on the Chesapeake?'

'I should not think so.'

Her hand rested upon her daughter's shoulder. Though I saw there was more she would say to me, she at last forbore and turned away to look out over the water. A strand of silvered hair had escaped from beneath her white bonnet, the breeze moving it about her face till she pushed it behind her ear. She had passed from thirty years to thirty-five since I had seen her last, and though she spoke of my tiredness it was her own looked the deeper. She remained a slight woman, but with nothing of the lively gaiety I remembered, nor in her eyes the clear-hearted joy.

In less than an hour we arrived at the muddy shore the far side of the James, below the Morgans' farm. While Cable and David made some necessary repair to the tiller, I carried Lizzy onto the beach. Then I fetched the baskets up to the leaning pine where Sally Morgan now stood watching her husband and son at work together down in the boat.

'I shall not take them from you for so very long,' said I.

'I would stop them if I could,' said she, which remark surprised me. For she had ever been a help to her husband, not only when I had first recruited him as a spy for us, but throughout the war, as I had learned from Major Andre and others. She faced me now directly. 'Do not receive this ill, Mr Douglas, but I must ask that you keep from our house while you are here.'

Somewhat taken aback, I said that I should speak to Cable on the matter. She shook her head.

'He shall say only that you must not listen to me. He shall tell you that you are most welcome to call on us.'

'And am I not?' said I. She hugged her arms about her and avoided my gaze. 'Has something happened that I should know of, Mrs Morgan?'

'Your work is very important, I am sure, Mr Douglas. But it is work done in passing. Our whole life is here. It is here that Cable and David must live when you are gone.'

'I understand that.'

'You do not understand. You do not understand what the war has done here.'

'I work as your husband works, that the war shall end.'

'It shall not end here, but only for the soldiers. We must live with our neighbours after.'

'Is Cable suspected?'

'All men are suspected who are not under arms in the militia. And only one man in each family may be excused to earn his family's bread.'

Understanding came to me, and I looked down to the log-canoe. 'David is now of an age to join the militia,' said I, and she nodded.

But when I asked had any recruiting sergeant come to demand his service with the Continentals or the militia she again turned her head.

'But they shall,' said she. 'You cannot know what bitterness there is in every quarter, either against the Congress or against the King.'

'And so you fear to have me near your house.'

'I wish to God the war had never been,' said she with a depth of feeling quite remarkable. Raising her eyes boldly to me, she added, 'And though you may despise me for it, Mr Douglas, I tell you truly: I cannot find it in my heart to care any longer who shall win. While you are here now, I beg of you, stay away from my house. And once Cable has set you down in York Town, I would that you ask no further service of him.'

Lizzy came skipping up from the river, calling out to her mother. Sally Morgan took up the two baskets from by my feet, dipped her head to me, and turned quickly onto the path homeward.

'She has read you the Riot Act,' said Cable Morgan, amused as he helped me aboard again; for he had seen his wife talking with me up by the leaning pine, and well knew the meaning of it. 'You must not mind her, Alistair. She likes you well enough. It is the coming here of all the soldiers has frightened her.' He made light of the whole business, though when I told him of her warning that I should keep from their farm, he agreed that it might be as well for our mutual safety. He did not think that he was suspected of spying for the British, but nor did he wish at this moment to invite the closer scrutiny of his neighbours. He spoke all this within earshot of his son, and by some few remarks that then passed between them I surmised that the lad had become a helper in his father's secret business.

Cable raised the sail again, and as we went down toward Old Point Comfort he told me what he knew of Cornwallis's recent campaigning in the south, and of a skirmish nearby between the British forces and Lafayette's rebel soldiers. There was little that I had not heard on my way northward. The one surprise to me was how often he must turn to his son David for confirmation of some number, of either boats or horses or men. The lad was become like a second eyes and ears to the father, and a very close helper indeed.

As we emerged from the mouth of the James River into the Bay, I turned my spyglass once more upon those two ships. The nearer, the *Guadeloupe*, was but two or three leagues off from us.

'What chance you might take me out to her?' I asked Cable.

'It is calm enough,' said he, glancing over the water and then up at the clear sky. 'But you cannot want to leave us so quickly.'

I said that I would write a letter to my superiors in London, and that the *Guadeloupe* might carry it the first part of the journey. Cable made no hesitation then, but reefed the sail and called David to steer for the ship.

The breeze was fresh, and our boat cut clean through the small waves, so that I was reminded of those times I had sailed the Bay with Cable at the start of the war. In those days I had worked with him hauling in his crabpots and dredging with the oyster rakes, and there had been almost an innocence in it; for though I must sketch every landing place and cottage near the shore, and with Cable's help enlist several Loyalist fishermen as the eyes of the British fleet, yet our day's work would invariably end with a return to Morgan's farm. There young David would meet us upon the muddy beach and help his father rope the sail before we took our catch of crab and fish up to the farmhouse. Sally would cook the evening meal, and with one eye always upon Lizzy in the cot. Then we would do nothing very much, but only talk, and the Morgans with some surprise at my travels, and I thankful to be momentarily becalmed in the bosom of a good family. We little thought in those happy evenings how very long and vicious might be the war.

We were soon to the *Guadeloupe* now, and one of her officers hailing us from the quarterdeck as we came around her anchor-line. But no sooner had I called across to identify myself as Douglas of the Board of Trade and Plantations than the familiar face of Captain Symonds appeared at the rail.

'Douglas is it, by God.'

'You are a long way from Jamaica, sir.'

'Stop your fellows messing about there, and come aboard.'

David Morgan having a great curiosity to inspect a ship-of-the-line, he came aboard with me, while his father stayed in the boat and stood off.

'You shall get your pen and paper soon enough,' Captain Symonds told me as we two repaired to his cabin. David Morgan we had left with a midshipman to make a tour below decks. Symonds called back through the open door for his man to bring in the Madeira, then he offered me a chair.

He was a square-built fellow, rosy-cheeked, and though I had never sailed with him, I had often been in his company whilst ashore in the West Indies; for he was a long-serving captain in Admiral Rodney's fleet. By repute, his captaincy answered much to his appearance: nothing handsome or extraordinary, but dependable and solid. When the Madeira came he gave me a short account of how he had come to be in Chesapeake Bay, and he told me of his current intention to sail north to join Admiral Graves. I asked after Admiral Rodney, and he said Rodney was temporarily returned to London and that Hood commanded in his stead. We had some minutes more talk of this kind, each asking after different ones of our acquaintances now scattered along the coast and across the West Indies. He was disappointed to discover that I had been inland for some while and so had no recent news from London. He confessed himself not unhappy to be leaving the Chesapeake. Cornwallis, he told me, was now entrenching in York Town, and might even winter the army there.

'It shall be a dreary winter for some unfortunate captain upon the York River. Thank God it shall not be me.'

At this moment his First Lieutenant entered to report the sighting of a sail off the cape.

On the poop deck, we found the officers scanning the mouth of the Bay. There were two ships coming wide around the cape, standing well out to sea in avoidance of the extensive and dangerous shallows closer in. Seamen now gathered along the *Guadeloupe*'s rail, and some climbed into the rigging; but there were as many more continued their several duties about the deck. Cable Morgan, fifty yards off from us, was standing in his boat with his own spyglass turned likewise upon the mouth of the Bay. As I watched him, he dropped the spyglass and went in some hurry to the tiller.

'Sir, there is another sail to the south,' reported the First Lieutenant. And no sooner had this new arrival emerged fully from behind the southern cape than there came another directly in its wake. 'Sir—!'

'Yes, I see the flag,' said Symonds. 'We cannot get past them now, I think.'

'No, sir.'

'Give the order to weigh anchor. Call up all hands.'

The lieutenant hurried to the rail, crying orders to the junior officers.

'They cannot be French,' said I.

'They surely are, Mr Douglas. And more of them yet,' said Symonds; for trailing those first vessels around the southern cape were more ships appearing, and no longer singly but in twos and threes. It was a French fleet, and a large one. And a mystery, and a shock to all of us aboard, how it should come to be in these waters. Symonds, when he was over his first surprise, decided that it must be Admiral de Grasse come across from the West Indies.

'Sir, they are coming around.'

It was the van swinging leeward, while the trailing vessels held their line, continuing wide, to seal up the Bay. Crossing to the rail I called out to Morgan. He was already bringing his boat quickly in. Then I ran down to the quarterdeck and almost knocked over a lady and her black maid who had come up to see the reason of the commotion.

'You had better stay in your cabin now, madam,' said I.

'The captain has not told me so.'

'He tells you so now!' roared Symonds from above. 'Get below, madam, and stay below till I call you!'

The woman blanched, but she had the good sense not to argue. She turned the maid about and they went hastily below. After sending a midshipman to seek out David Morgan, I returned to the poop deck.

A few leagues off from us, much nearer the French, the *Loyalist* appeared to be about the same urgent business as ourselves. But so sudden and unexpected was the French arrival, and so near to her mooring, that it was doubtful the *Loyalist* could now weigh anchor, set sail, and outrun the French van. There were a half-dozen French ships-of-the-line bearing down upon her, and yet more enemy sail appearing around the southern cape. Further north, those first two vessels we had sighted now barred any escape to the open sea.

Symonds called the local Chesapeake pilot to him. Between them they swiftly decided that the *Guadeloupe*'s best chance lay in a run for the York River, thence a dash up to York Town, where we might gain the protection of Lord Cornwallis's guns.

David Morgan appeared on the quarterdeck, seeming in some confusion at emerging from below into the midst of a great scramble of seamen.

'You must go down into your boat now, Mr Douglas,' said Symonds, 'or you shall lose your own chance to get clear.'

But should the Morgans be overtaken and captured, I knew that they would be much safer without me. So I went down and took David across to the rail. His father had the boat already below.

'Is it the French?' Cable Morgan called up to me.

'It is,' I answered. Then I told David to go down to his father; which when he had done, I called down to ask Cable if he thought he could make Old Point Comfort before the enemy.

'Only if you come away now,' cried he.

'I shall keep aboard here and go up to York Town. Cast off now!'

David cast off upon the instant, and they cut away under our bow, making straight for the safety of the shallows near the Point.

'We have a sporting chance,' remarked Symonds when I rejoined him. 'But it looks not so well for the *Loyalist*. It is mere good fortune we did not anchor with her. And look there – still they come.' The waters about the southern cape were now crowded with sail, and the First Lieutenant called up into the yards for a count of the enemy ships. 'It is certainly de Grasse,' remarked Symonds to his officers. 'And it looks to be his whole West Indies fleet with him.' I asked if our own ships in these waters had the guns to dislodge de Grasse should he anchor; for control of the Bay must be vital to our army ashore. 'That is not a present concern to us, Mr Douglas. Let us only preserve ourselves till York Town, it shall be work enough for today.' And so saying he moved away from me to consult again with the pilot who stood by the wheel.

At the capstan the men bent their backs like oxen, and not a one of them shirking in the labour. The sight of French ships was a goad much sharper than a mere midshipman's order. Aloft, the seamen moved sprightly along the yards releasing the sails, and the count finally came down from them of twenty enemy ships certain.

I stood well clear of the officers now as the anchor came up to be lashed. The first breath of wind caught our unfurling mainsail, and we listed leeward. Far astern of us, three French vessels peeled away from the main fleet to give chase. It was a minute later that a frigate broke from the fleet and appeared to make toward Old Point Comfort. I crossed with some anxiety to the aft rail. But the Morgans had a sharp breeze in their sail, and their log-canoe skimmed over the small waves. They had a good start on the frigate, and they knew the waters and the shallows well. The frigate would quickly close upon them, but I had a fair hope they might outrun her.

After several minutes, and the greater part of the French fleet now spread like a chain across the mouth of the Bay, I asked a lieutenant for another count of the ships. The number returned this time was twenty-four.

'And there must be stragglers yet in a fleet so large,' remarked the young officer who brought me the count. 'There may be thirty by tomorrow.'

'You are not alarmed, Lieutenant?'

'Not alarmed, sir, but struck, you might say. It is a rare sight.' A rare sight indeed, and a very fine and welcome sight it must be for those rebels about the Bay that witnessed its arrival. The breeze ruffled the blue water, and the full white sails of the fleet looked like clouds blown in from the sea. But poisonous clouds they were to us, for that fleet was certainly filled with guns and munitions and French infantry. 'They have got the *Loyalist*,' said the lieutenant unhappily.

Like a fox overrun, she disappeared into the midst of the French pack. Her sails were struck, her flight finished almost before it began. The lieutenant made an oath beneath his breath and then returned to his station near the wheel. The *Guadeloupe*'s three pursuers were under full sail now, but two of them visibly lagging the leader.

'West Indies weed slows them,' said Symonds, joining me at the aft rail. 'They have had no scraping yet. The front ship has perhaps recently joined the fleet. She is the only one may catch us.'

'She does not appear to be closing.'

'She is, but slowly. It shall be a quarter-hour before she brings us within range. You must come for'ard, now, Mr Douglas. These guns may be needed.'

Ahead, the mouth of the York was not easy to discern, the green line of tidewater vegetation being identical both sides of the river. Our Chesapeake pilot kept the wheelman steering straight before the wind.

'One league,' the First Lieutenant reported, peering astern through his spyglass.

Symonds screwed up his eyes against the sun and looked ahead to where the York River and safety must be. 'You are standing us well out,' he remarked to the pilot.

'Sandbar,' replied the pilot, pointing. 'Tack too early, we'll ground.' He must have felt Captain Symonds's hard eye upon him then, for he added, 'Never you fear, sir. I'll not give you to the French from too much caution.'

The wind stayed steady, neither strong nor light, and we carved a clean line through the choppy water. But so too did our nearest French shadow. In a short time it appeared she was gathering speed and closing ever more quickly.

'Half a league, sir.'

All eyes went between the French ship and Symonds, the seamen apprehensive and impatient for the order to tack. But Symonds's gaze stayed fixed upon the pilot. The men at the guns aft began murmuring together, seeming in doubt of the supposed sandbar that kept them from safety. The pilot was unmoved, he continued his quiet orders to the wheelman to hold steady.

At last Symonds broke. 'How long, man?'

'A minute more,' the pilot answered, very calm.

'One minute and no longer.' Symonds then turned to his First Lieutenant. 'As we go about we shall make a pretty target. Prepare the stern and larboard guns.' While the order was passed, Symonds rocked upon the balls of his feet. He clasped his hands behind his back as if to prevent himself from snatching the wheel. But after a minute that seemed an hour the pilot turned to him and nodded.

'Give them a shot from the stern chaser,' Symonds sharply commanded his First Lieutenant. 'Then take us about smart.'

A bellowing of orders cascaded through along the decks and up into the rigging. And it was then that the first French gun fired. A puff of smoke showed at her bow before the clap of thunder reached us. A spume of spray then rose a hundred yards to our stern.

'Fire!' shouted the First Lieutenant, and our two rear guns fired in quick succession. The smoke bloomed about us, the sound of the shots still roaring in my ears as the ship listed sharply and came about. We were becalmed for a moment, but then the wind caught our sail and I clutched the rail to steady myself as we came upright just as easily as we had listed.

Our larboard guns fired next, and the French answered with a broadside. All empty sound and fury. We remained just beyond their range as they beyond ours, and every shot fell useless into the water. As our sails refilled we moved again, and now the French must either risk the shallows and the bar or give up the chase.

'She'll put herself aground,' the pilot muttered, peering astern as if he willed the French to make the rash attempt.

Turning my spyglass toward the Point, I made out the Morgans' log-canoe running close into the shore, and the French frigate standing a quarter-mile off. Should a smaller boat be launched from the frigate, the Morgans might easily outrun them into the James River. And once there Cable Morgan would be certain to elude them, secreting his log-canoe in one of the creeks. With some relief I returned my attention to the nearer danger.

But it was little time the pursuing French captain astern of us now wasted in reaching his decision (indeed, he must have his own

Chesapeake pilot aboard who had warned him of the bar). After a minute he swung her away, and she at once set sail to rejoin the main fleet.

In silence our crew watched her go. Captain Symonds removed his tricorn and congratulated our pilot, which though the congratulation was sincere, it was muted; for we had preserved ourselves, but the *Loyalist* was lost, and the French fleet now held the Bay. A quiet and sombre ship we continued against the tide, ten miles upriver to York Town.

CHAPTER 2

'Who shall tell me now that we should not have stayed in the Carolinas?'

'We might return there,' said O'Hara.

'That is not General Clinton's inclination.' Lord Cornwallis came back from the window and dropped into his seat. The summer's campaigning had given him a leaner look than I remembered. He was in his early forties, much of an age with myself, and his red coat of command, the gold braid and epaulettes all sat very comfortably upon him. General O'Hara, an Irishman and Cornwallis's second-in-command, had said little while Symonds had been present; but now he suggested that Clinton's inclination might be modified by the unexpected circumstance of de Grasse's arrival. Cornwallis dismissed the suggestion with a turn of his head, and then peering at me said, 'Twenty-four, and all ships-of-the-line?'

'More must be expected, my Lord.'

'Yes, I expect they must,' he observed calmly. Then dropping his gaze he remarked again the negligence of Admiral Hood in leaving open the Bay. He intimated that the Admiralty should hear more of it in a private dispatch.

Though Lord Cornwallis was not the senior general of our forces in the American colonies but only second to General Clinton in New York, yet he had by both his breeding and his soldierly exertions become a great counterweight to his nominal superior. From my own communications with London I knew that Germaine, our Colonial Secretary with charge of the war, was continually vacillating between the advice of these two generals. And these men frequently maintaining contrary views on the conduct of the war, Germaine's instructions to the army from London were often confusing and even contradictory. The French fleet had now sailed into the midst of these personal strains and strategic confusions; but Cornwallis, for all that he found himself unsure of the enemy's next purpose, or even General Clinton's, gave no sign of any real dismay. His tone with me was almost chaffing.

'And you, Mr Douglas. I suppose you must regret your arrival among us at such a time.'

'I may be of some service, my Lord.'

'I daresay.'

He leaned back in his chair. His initial surprise at Symonds's report of the French fleet's arrival had abated, and his natural confidence and ease were uppermost again. And now that Symonds had taken his leave, I knew that I must soon follow. This therefore seeming the moment, and certainly my first opportunity since entering his headquarters, I took from my satchel the broad belt of bead-embroidered leather that I had brought with me from across the Appalachians. When I placed it upon the table before him Cornwallis regarded the thing curiously. General O'Hara rose from his chair and came over.

'It is a war-belt, my Lord. From Dragging Canoe.'

'The Cherokee chieftain?'

'Aye.'

Cornwallis turned the war-belt through his hands. The beadwork was as fine as any I had ever seen, and the belt a thing of real beauty. 'I must assume it is not sent to me as a gift.'

'He wants soldiers of us, to fight the settlers.'

'He has the Superintendent and the Superintendent's helpers.'

This was the Board of Trade's Superintendent he meant, who managed our affairs with the Indians. I reminded him that the Superintendent commanded no soldiers. 'It is your redcoats Dragging Canoe requests the aid of, my Lord. Without our help to keep the settlers this side of the King's Line, the Cherokee shall be overrun.'

'He is surely aware that we have our own troubles.'

'I have advised him that there shall be few troops we may spare.'

'It were better you had refused him directly.'

'My Lord—'

'We shall see, Mr Douglas. I will have no dispute of it now.' He leaned forward and very deliberately gave the war-belt back into my hand, that there be no doubt of his refusal of it. 'You shall be fully occupied here awhile, I think. At least till we discover what the French are about. Have you found quarters in the town? No? Then announce your presence to Major Ross. You may tell him that you have my authority for any men that you shall need. I presume that you have some people about the Bay?' I thought of Cable Morgan and inclined my head tentatively. 'Good,' said he. 'Once you have rested, Ross shall give you the names of the few miserable fellows we have taken into our pay since our arrival. Make what use of them you will.'

O'Hara then gestured to the wall-map, telling me that Lafayette's troops were last reported between Williamsburg and Richmond. He remarked that it seemed likely they should now establish some communication with de Grasse by way of the James River. 'We have drubbed them once or twice, so they keep their distance. But any reinforcements they get from de Grasse shall likely embolden him.'

'It would be as well for us to have some notion of de Grasse's intentions,' put in Cornwallis meaningfully. When I bowed my head in acceptance of the implicit command, he asked if I would be able to conduct my business solely from within York Town. I said that I should almost certainly need to range across the whole peninsula.

'You must have a brevet commission then, and a uniform,' said he;

his thought being, I knew, that if captured in uniform the rebels could not then hang me as a spy. When I answered that my civilian clothes should answer better to my needs, he exchanged a glance with O'Hara. I had no doubt then but that they had both heard of my part in the loss of Major Andre. And that Andre's fate was indeed in Cornwallis's mind became certain when he said, 'It was disregard of proper uniform that hanged Major Andre.'

'The case here is very different,' said I.

'You might be captured just the same.'

'It is the chance of war.'

'And you would be hanged just the same.'

'I am content, my Lord.'

'Are you indeed? That is no happy thought.' His look now was penetrating. 'You have hidden yourself away among the Indians too long, perhaps. But you must now put off the sackcloth if you are to be of any use to me.'

'As you wish, my Lord.'

His eye stayed steady upon mine. 'Captain Symonds has invited me and my senior officers to dine aboard the *Guadeloupe*. You shall join us, Mr Douglas. Major Ross shall now see you to your quarters.'

The work of entrenchment then proceeding at York Town was extensive. Our main line stretched in an arc of less than a mile about the landward side of the town, and to the bluffs north and south overlooking the river. In truth, the place was hardly a town at all but more like to a large village, with a score or so red-brick buildings (the best of which was Cornwallis's headquarters) and perhaps a hundred houses and outbuildings constructed from the local pine and cedar. As Major Ross escorted me to my billet, he told me that York Town was intended to serve as a temporary stronghold, and a possible winter quarters for the army. 'Gloucester Point is already secured,' said he, gesturing across to the land half a mile distant on the opposite bank. 'Our ships can now lie between, and upriver, in safety.'

Below us, on the shore at the foot of the bluffs, was an encampment of sailors and marines, evidently come from those few ships lying at anchor off the town. Just along from this first encampment was another.

'Plantation runaways,' Ross said when I remarked the great number of blacks in this second encampment. 'Most joined us in the Carolinas. They earn their keep working on the entrenchments.' He led me then to one of the red-brick houses; we went in through the unlocked door and looked about. Its rear drawing room gave a fine prospect of the river and the ships. There was only one of these, the *Charon*, to match the *Guadeloupe* in size. While I held back the dark drapes from the window, Ross asked what servants I should need.

'A cook will suffice.'

'A cook and a manservant, then.'

'A cook only, if you will.' Facing him, I saw that he thought my refusal a peculiar economy. 'Perhaps a young lieutenant or ensign might serve as my aide,' I conceded.

Ross promised to arrange a fellow for me. He then offered to show me the rooms above, but I assured him of my satisfaction with the place, and so he left me. After making a brief inspection upstairs, I went down again, repairing to the library off the hall to seek out pen and ink.

York Town, 30th August 1781.

My Dear Jenkinson,

I am returned at last to the coast but only to find myself (upon the instant of my arrival) entered into the service of Lord Cornwallis, who, having brought his army up through the Carolinas, is now entrenching here at York Town. Till today his hope was to establish himself in this place, that it might be a base for further incursions deeper into Virginia; or, failing this, that his troops be embarked from here and thereafter transported to New York where General Clinton has need of them.

These fond hopes of his Lordship have these past few hours turned to dust with the unwelcome and unexpected arrival of a French fleet, under de Grasse, into the Chesapeake Bay. There are more than twenty French ships-of-the-line, and it will be no small work for Admiral Graves to have them out from here. Whether de Grasse shall land troops here to make a common force under Lafayette (who commands both French and colonial troops to the number of some three thousand inland of us), or whether he will make so bold as to send some smaller vessels of his fleet directly to attack us from the river, this is more than his Lordship or his senior officers may guess. It is very evident that he is in want of better knowledge as to the French intentions and the current disposition of the landward forces, which want I have agreed to attempt some remedy of by my own exertions. Though this must be some aid to him, without the French ships be expelled, I cannot but think our army must soon make a retreat across the York River to Gloucester Point, and thence inland to a better safety.

There is one matter more, which though it cannot outweigh this present difficulty, yet in some wise stands aback of it and so I trust will not be overlooked or forgotten. That is to say, our support for the Indians against the illegal settlers across the mountains. The viciousness of the battles now occurring between the Cherokee and the Back-Mountain colonials is beyond description, and must leave such a stain upon the earth as can never be expunged. The township of Chota is destroyed, and several more Cherokee villages, and Dragging Canoe is now upon the warpath and like to wreak a bloody vengeance on any settler he meets with to the west of the King's Line. He has sent war-belts to the Iroquois and the Choctaws and the Shawnee, and also one to Lord Cornwallis (by me), which last has been refused. Though I well understand that in this present part of the war we can spare no troops to hold the Line, yet I am certain that without such troops be sent before the Winter, the Line must become a name only, and no security to the Indian allies of the King.

It is a considerable while we have been friendly with these people, and many promises we have made to them, and I cannot accept that all the efforts of our Superintendents, both Johnstone and Stuart, and those who have followed them, will now be set at nothing for

mere want of some few hundred redcoats and muskets. As Secretary
at War, you will know better than any the exigencies of the moment;
but from my place here I may tell you that howsoever the war with
our American brethren be concluded, the battles to the west are like
to continue, and not to the advantage of our native allies. Should
we abandon them so lightly (which I must tell you they have a fear
of), and in despite of our past treaties and promises, it must be to
our eternal shame.

I lifted my head, interrupted suddenly by voices out in the hall; and
it was undoubtedly Major Ross who then called my name. Blotting
the unfinished letter, I slipped it into my pocket before unlocking the
library door. I found Major Ross deeper in the house, at the foot of
the stairs. He was accompanied by a lady and her maid.

'Mr Douglas,' said he, opening his hand toward the lady. 'This is
Mrs Kendrick. She is the owner of the house.'

It was the woman from the *Guadeloupe*, the one I had almost
knocked down in the moments following the French arrival in the
Bay.

'Mrs Kendrick,' said I, and I made a polite nod to her. But she made
no return of it, nor offered me her hand. 'I understood that the owner
of the house had departed,' said I, glancing from Mrs Kendrick to
Ross.

'She has attempted to depart and failed,' said Mrs Kendrick. 'As
you saw.'

Ross, looking apologetically uncomfortable, commenced an explanation of the incorrect information that he had received concerning
Mrs Kendrick's whereabouts. I put up a hand.

'It is a misunderstanding, and no trouble to me. I have left my few
things above. By your leave, madam, I shall fetch them down and leave
you in peace.'

'There is no need, Mr Douglas. Major Ross has spoken for you.
And I am certain you shall find no better accommodation in the town.'

'Then I am obliged,' said I; but she had already turned to give her
black maid some instruction. Though it was perhaps no deliberate

rudeness, it was certainly no courtesy. When she faced me again she added, 'Your presence shall be but small inconvenience. If you want privacy you may have the library for your own use. Francesca shall bring you the key.'

I told her which bedroom I had chosen above, and advised her that its neighbour room must be needed for my promised aide.

'That is acceptable to me, Mr Douglas.'

'Madam, if this is too much—'

'If it were not you it would be another, sir. Or some several others. Only keep from my drawing room during the day and I shall have no reason to complain of you to the General.' She nodded to me, lifted the folds of her skirt and climbed the stairs. And as she went she threw over her shoulder, 'If you are to be my escort to Captain Symonds's dinner, Mr Douglas, you shall no doubt want to wash. Francesca will bring water for you. We shall go down to the ship upon the hour.'

CHAPTER 3

Mrs Kendrick seemed little inclined to speak as we walked along the main street to the head of the small valley that led down to the river. She had changed from her plain travelling dress and now wore something finer, a turquoise silk with a white-laced jacket. Her only jewellery was a small but exquisite diamond brooch pinned to the jacket lapel. After attempting and failing to engage her in conversation, I was quite content now to pass down to the wharf without speaking; but as we proceeded along the path we saw ahead of us Lord Cornwallis's party descending. Major Ross, General O'Hara and some other officers were of the party, but there was a portly civilian among them. The elderly gentleman was rather loud, though somewhat infirm it seemed, for he walked with the aid of a cane.

'It is Secretary Nelson,' replied Mrs Kendrick in answer to my enquiry. 'He is the uncle to Governor Nelson.'

This, I own, surprised me; both the fact and the sangfroid with which Mrs Kendrick had spoken it. For 'Governor' Nelson was no British governor, but a leader among our enemies and one of our prime opponents in Virginia.

'Does he come here as an emissary from his nephew?'

'He does not "come here", Mr Douglas. He is a freeholder in York Town. It is Secretary Nelson's house that Lord Cornwallis has sequestered for a headquarters.'

'Shall he now dine with his Lordship?'

'York Town is not so extensive, you shall find, that we may any of us be quite so discriminating as we might wish in our fellows.'

I glanced at her but she kept her eyes straight ahead; and so we continued the last of our way down to the wharf.

Aboard the *Guadeloupe* the crew had temporarily removed those planking walls separating the quarterdeck from the captain's cabin. Two tables were drawn end-to-end over this space, and it was here that we guests of Captain Symonds took our supper. There was clean linen upon the tables, and two silver candlesticks. But the other candlesticks were pewter, as were the plates, so that there was something of the effect of a good family fallen upon hard times. The food, however, was plentiful, and being the first well-cooked meal I had enjoyed in several weeks, most welcome to me. The sombre air there had earlier been over the ship was soon lifted by the Madeira, and by the easy confidence of Lord Cornwallis and his party. And the naval men had begun to talk now as though they expected de Grasse's expulsion from the Bay to happen just as soon as our Admiral Graves might bring his fleet down from New York.

Seated just above the salt, I took little part in the conversation at the upper table. I spoke, when prompted, with the Commissary's wife upon my left and with the young naval lieutenant upon my right, but I was otherwise content to merely listen. And throughout the meal I found my eye drawn continually to that fellow Secretary Nelson. He had a high place at the table, up by Mrs Kendrick, and near to Symonds and Lord Cornwallis. He had no reticence in this company, but his manner was rather that of a gentleman among equals; and he seemed to lead their conversation just as often as he followed. It was the direction of his leading that was altogether surprising to me. For he made no avoidance of the war, but quite the contrary, he introduced the subject at every opportunity.

In little more than an hour he had touched upon almost every significant event of the conflict. He instructed us on the 'unjust and
rapacious taxation' that had first led to the rebellion; then we heard
of the 'underhand and reprehensible actions' of the redcoats in the
opening skirmishes of the war; similarly noted was the violent push
and shove over Philadelphia, whilst the defeat of our General
Burgoyne at Saratoga in '77 was held up almost as a sign of God's
undoubted blessing upon the rebel cause. But judging well those
places he might not safely venture, he was considerably less voluble
concerning the entry of the French as allies to the rebels. And, likewise, though he openly deplored General Clinton's actions in
Savannah and Charleston the previous year, and positively excoriated
Lord Rawdon's battlefield command, yet he affected to have no clear
information concerning the more recent southern campaign of Lord
Cornwallis.

By the end, however, Cornwallis had but half an ear for the fellow,
though continuing to turn occasionally from his own talk with
Symonds and Mrs Kendrick to give an amused rebuttal to Nelson's
wide-ranging commentary. There was not so much as an eyebrow
raised to any of this by the others at the table, who were evidently
accustomed to Cornwallis's indulgence of Nelson. For myself, I never
thought to hear Thomas Payne quoted so earnestly, and with such
impudent good cheer, at a table of British officers.

Nelson's ruddy cheeks flushed pink with the Madeira, he at last
rested his forearms upon the table and leaned forward to crane around
his neighbour.

'You are with the Board of Trade, Mr Douglas. I trust you at least
have advised them of the great harm the war now does to British
commerce.'

'They need no advice upon that, sir.'

'Indeed. Then it cannot be right what I have heard that they have
requested the British navy to strangle the little remaining trade of our
southern colonies with the West Indies.'

'I have no instructions on the matter.'

'But you have an opinion.'

'What opinion I have, you will understand, sir, is a private opinion.' Then smiling to soften my reply, for I would have no argument with the fellow, I added, 'But when I make my next report, be assured, I shall leave them in no doubt as to the opinion of Secretary Nelson.'

'You may do more than that,' said he, eyeing me sternly and ignoring the several smiling faces about him. 'You may give it as the opinion of most every man between Savannah and Boston.'

He was clearly one of those fellows who must bait his companions and yet always have the last word; and so I dipped my head to him before turning to speak with the Commissary's wife at my side. I was careful, thereafter, to invite no further conversation with the upper table. But once the meal was done, and Captain Symonds's boat had ferried us ashore, I discovered Nelson at my elbow as we came off the wharf.

'My man there has brought a lantern down,' said he, clutching at my sleeve to support himself as he stepped from the wharf to the high beach. Ahead of us, Lord Cornwallis had already crossed to the path with Major Ross. Now they with Mrs Kendrick and some several others were going up to the town, three servants carrying torches to light their way. As Nelson's black came down from the path with a lantern, Nelson begged the favour of my arm. 'Damned stick. Useless in the sand,' he muttered, striking his cane upon the beach as we advanced. He clutched my arm as one obliged to borrow the strength of another man, but against his own will. His black soon joining us, Nelson released my arm and leaned his weight upon the fellow. 'You have come up from the south, Mr Douglas,' Nelson remarked as we turned up the path.

'I have.'

'Then you have observed the results of his Lordship's campaigning.'

'I have been for the most time with our people to the far side of the mountains.'

'Dear God, among the savages? Then you have my sympathy.'

'The country is known to you, sir?'

'I never went there, nor never hope to go. Have we not the finest land in the world already beneath our feet? No, no. Let us cultivate our own garden. It is all yet to do.'

'Regrettably, not all of your fellow colonists agree.'

'Let us only throw the British army out from here, and then we shall sit down peaceably to parley with our heathen neighbours.'

Whether he was sincere in this opinion I could not tell. But certainly the opinion was misguided, and, if sincere, it revealed a monumental misjudgement of the character of those wild settlers now crossing the mountains and battening hard upon the Indian country. He made some further questions of my work with the Board of Trade, which questions I easily turned aside. What information he thought to get from me, I know not, for there was no evident point to his careless enquiries. Nor was it long before he recommenced his lamentation concerning the terrible waste made by the war, and his certainty in the inevitable victory that Washington and the Congress must have over the King. I answered him with a studied silence, which when he perceived that I would not rise, he at last broke off from his jeremiad. His gaze then falling on the party ahead of us, he said, 'I fear that Mrs Kendrick may have cause to regret that she was turned back from the Bay.'

'She takes it calmly enough.'

'She has endured worse, no doubt,' said he; and upon my remarking that it was not every day that a lady found herself fired upon by the French, he continued, 'She has lost her husband this past year to consumption. And she has no children to console her widowhood.'

'I am sorry to hear it.' I looked ahead to the upright figure of the lady, her hand now resting upon Major Ross's arm. It seeming a subject might keep Nelson from further questioning of me, I said, 'She was not long married then?'

'Ten years and more. Her husband was a wealthy man, a merchant. He had several houses all along the seaboard. She often travelled with him. The belief is that he ill-used her on account she was barren.'

'Perhaps the lack was in him.'

Nelson barked a dry laugh. Then releasing his man, he shuffled closer to me, and touched my arm as if to take me into his confidence.

'Mr Kendrick lacked nothing in that sort, I do promise you. There are three of his black bastards not twenty miles from here.' He squeezed my arm, smiling as if I should share in his unpleasant amusement.

This low-mindedness, and the evident pleasure he took in repeating a scurrility that could only be laceration to Mrs Kendrick, gave me a sudden revulsion for the man. And though I attempted to conceal the feeling, I believe he sensed it; for he made no more of the business, but took the arm of his black once more, and we were soon to the head of the valley and in the town.

Major Ross had turned aside to walk Mrs Kendrick to her house, and Lord Cornwallis and his officers had not tarried but were in retreat to their own night-quarters. I declined Nelson's offer to break fast with him the next morning, and once he had left me I went directly after Major Ross.

'You have enjoyed your evening rather more than your morning, I hope,' said Major Ross good-naturedly as he came from the porch and met me in the street. He had left Mrs Kendrick within. The door of the house was closed.

'Is it usual, Major, that Secretary Nelson should be so free with his Lordship?'

'My Lord Cornwallis is much entertained by the fellow.'

'He might be as well entertained at some greater distance.'

'Nelson does not answer to everyone's taste, Mr Douglas. But he pays us the inestimable compliment of looking us bold in the face while he proclaims himself an enemy to our cause, if not to our persons. After all the slyness and treachery we have had practised upon us in the Carolinas, his Lordship is pleased to give hearing to a frank and open opposition.'

'It is surely unwise to allow him a continued accommodation in his Lordship's headquarters.'

'It is Nelson's own house. And it is by Lord Cornwallis's invitation that Secretary Nelson remains there. Nelson has been promised an accommodation for as long as we shall stay in York Town.'

'You will please inform his Lordship of my advice against the arrangement.'

'You shall not persuade his Lordship to break his word to the fellow, Mr Douglas,' said he; and very apparent it was that Ross was tired, and wanted no more discussion of the matter, and he stiffly bade me goodnight.

Inside, the house was quiet, with only a single candle burning in the hall. Mrs Kendrick had evidently gone directly up to her bedroom, so I took the candle into the library, set it into a stick upon the desk, and then went and locked the door. I was weary now, and all the miles of my long journey seemed to weigh on my shoulders. I brought my unfinished letter from my pocket and read what I had written. There was nothing to amend, and but little to add; and so I made the addition quickly, before the candle should fail.

I have dined this night with Lord Cornwallis and his officers, and found entertained in their company a local gentleman of rebel sympathies called Secretary Nelson. (The sobriquet attaching to the man that he may be distinguished from his nephew, the pretended governor of Virginia who commands the rebel militia here.) This Secretary Nelson shares a freedom with our officers that I neither like nor trust, and I think I never saw a man more likely to brave us to our faces and stab us in the back at the first opportunity. I shall urge his removal from the town, though I much doubt that I shall prevail over Lord Cornwallis's rash promise of accommodation to the fellow.

Tomorrow I shall cross the peninsula to the James River and there take the measure of the enemy force gathered near Williamsburg.

I shall write separately to Willes, from whom I am sure you must receive better information of our northern forces in New York, as being under the command of his brother-in-law General Clinton.

You may report to any of my acquaintance that I am well. And I will say of myself that I am recovered now from the blighting melancholy that afflicted me for a time after the hanging of Major Andre. (Your letter to me on the matter was an unlooked-for kindness, and more charitable than my desert.)

I shall put this letter into the hand of Major Ross before my departure tomorrow, that he might send it by the first packet that attempts the French blockade. If necessary, your communications to me may be safely directed through him.

Your obedient servant,
  Douglas

I blotted and sealed the letter before slipping it into my jacket. And then I took up the guttering candle, departed the library, and went thankfully to my bed.

CHAPTER 4

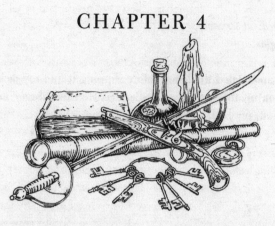

*I*t was by Cable Morgan's help that I got unhindered across the several miles of the narrow peninsula to the James River; for every forest track was known to him, and likewise every farm that we might pass near to without raising militia. But though he had brought his son David with him into York Town, I had sent the lad back to their farm. I had not entirely forgot Sally Morgan's warning to me, and saw no need to bring the lad into any danger. We skirted wide now around Williamsburg, which had been from the first a prime stronghold of the rebellion, and then directly down to the James. Here, whilst keeping ourselves hid among the pines and bushes, twenty yards up the bank, we observed the movement of the boats and men upon the water. The James River was too shallow in its upper reaches for any ship-of-the-line, and so de Grasse had sent up a small squadron of flatboats. These vessels were now drawn up at the landing a quarter-mile from our place of hiding. Many Williamsburg townsfolk had come down from curiosity, and others to sell tobacco and drink to the French sailors.

We watched an hour before Morgan went down among them. An hour more, and he returned to me.

'They mean to begin the disembarkation tomorrow.'

'In number?'

'Thousands. Every farmer is asked after grain, and what he has to sell.'

'A ruse?'

'There is a junior French quartermaster parting with real money. It is no ruse.' He added that the quartermaster's English was very halting, and that the young man might be grateful to hear the French tongue spoken by any local merchant. Though Morgan had no French himself, he well knew my easy fluency in the language (which language I had spoken since a lad, by the accident of a French friend of my father taking refuge and residence in my childhood home).

'Then perhaps I am a grain merchant from the Elk by way of Montreal,' said I. 'Let us see what we may have from the man.'

The Williamsburg folk began to depart shortly after, but we waited till the hour before sunset and then started down from the pines. But as we started, a flatboat launched from the landing and came down-river.

'It is the quartermaster aboard,' said Morgan quietly.

The fellow must be going back to the fleet out in the Bay, and if he went my chance at information of him should then be lost; and so after a moment's hesitation I strode boldly down to the riverside, waving an arm and calling, 'Monsieur!' With some few words more of French I soon drew the flatboat toward me.

As Morgan had supposed, the young quartermaster was only too happy to speak with me. And then to hear from me a promise of grain, and at a fair price, all in his own language – he could scarcely hide either his surprise or joy. I own, my success led me beyond my first intention, and I was soon inviting him ashore that we might better discuss the bargain. He replied with that which I scarcely knew how to answer; for it was an order that I must come with him, out to the senior quartermaster of the fleet. The oarsmen at once brought the boat against the bank, and a French marine put by his musket and reached out a hand to help me aboard. It was done too suddenly for any gracious withdrawal. No right-minded grain merchant would hesitate at the opportunity; and if I was to bring no suspicion on either myself or Morgan, neither must I.

With what deep misgivings may be imagined, I stepped aboard.

'When shall I expect your return, sir?' said Morgan, as if in no disquiet at the self-snaring I had made. '*Matin*,' said the quartermaster, 'morning', and then the marine shoved us off. A minute later and we were riding the ebb-tide, and Morgan falling away behind us, alone on the shore.

As we entered the Bay, I raised my kerchief to my mouth whilst remarking the delicacy of my stomach and the discomfort of the swell. An amused marine called me to the stern, where I might have the liberty to heave my guts into the water. I went, and gained thereby some freedom from the quartermaster's conversation. All the rest of our journey I spent in considering how best to extract myself from my unfortunate situation, and, if possible, with some advantage. I confess, my consideration had come to very little by the time we reached the ships after nightfall.

Though the French vessels had made a fine and clean spectacle under full sail, there was now a strong smell of jettisoned refuse about them as we arrived among them off Portsmouth, near to the mouth of the Bay. And as we moved past the dark silhouettes of their many hulls, the number and size of them were oppressive to me. And daunting too, when I thought on the unfinished work of our engineers and sappers in York Town.

Our boat passed beneath the bow of Admiral de Grasse's flagship, the *Ville de Paris*, a vessel of quite prodigious size, and the quartermaster cheerfully asked me how many guns I thought she carried. A hundred, I guessed. 'And twenty,' said he very proud; and no doubt it was true, for she was almost the biggest ship I ever saw.

Our destination was the vessel lying next to her, the *Auguste*. The night being warm, many of the *Auguste*'s seamen had come up to lie about the open decks, and also many of the infantrymen. These fellows paid us no mind as we climbed aboard, and I saw little else above decks, for I must then follow the junior quartermaster directly below. The usual odour of tar and rope permeated everything below decks, and the darkness was very close. The occasional light of a lantern showed us here and there some men; more often they were but quiet voices in the shadows.

Then as we neared the senior quartermaster's cabin in the stern there came a sudden shouting from within. The cabin door flew open, and the quartermaster drove a man out before him with a most terrible invective. The unfortunate fellow was no Frenchman, but, by his clothes, appeared to be a local merchant. Having banished this fellow into the ship's dark bowels, the quartermaster turned a fierce look upon us. My companion, somewhat rashly, attempted an introduction of me. His superior then opened such a fire of abuse upon him that the junior man shrank back like a cur.

'I have had a parade of these damned scoundrels all day,' cried the quartermaster. 'I have made a finish of them. I must eat. They are a plague, I must have some peace, do you hear? Peace. Get him from here. What does he sell?'

'Grain, sir.'

'He may apply to me tomorrow,' said the senior man and slammed shut his door in our faces.

The junior quartermaster's attachment to me was instantly broken by this onslaught. I was no longer his prize, but had become a nuisance. He called a cabin boy to him and instructed the lad to give me food and a blanket. Then he abandoned me without apology, saying only that I should keep from beneath the officers' feet and stay 'with the others', where the lad would now take me.

It was to the galley the boy took me, and there he left me in company with that same merchant I had just seen driven off by the quartermaster, and two more merchants besides. They were little pleased to have me join them. But I soon discovered that two of them hailed from Portsmouth, to the south of the Bay, and one from Williamsburg. So I gave them a story of having myself just come down from Boston by way of the Elk, and after that they were accepting of me, believing that I must be no real competition to them upon their own

41

ground. They made a place for me at their mess-table, and once we had at length finished our meal of thin pottage and biscuit it was decided that we should take a turn up on deck before sleep.

At the bow were sailors gathered about the lanterns, playing at dice. I propped myself at the larboard rail and ran an appraising eye over the hulls all across the moonlit water. There were three first-rates just by us, and yet more further out; and second-rates aplenty, so that my eye scarcely paused to notice the fifty-gun ships and the frigates. There were scores of men on every open deck. And to judge by the many transports and flatboats tethered by the hulls, and the whinnying and stamping of the horses stabled within, there must be a great disembarkation prepared for the morning.

'Tobacco?' enquired one of my fellows, coming to join me at the rail. He was the Williamsburg man, Traherne, and he held now out to me an opened tin that I might take a plug. I declined, and he took some for himself, and then followed my gaze over the fleet. 'They will do for the British now,' said he.

'You mean to say, sir, that we will do for the British.'

'I'll see de Grasse's money first. After that I may weigh him better against the redcoats.' Traherne spat over the side, and I was on my guard against him, for it seemed he meant to sound my allegiance. I asked him if he had done business with Cornwallis.

'Not Cornwallis, but only Rawdon there,' said he, with a jerk of his head toward the captain's cabin astern.

Now this truly caught me by surprise. 'Lord Rawdon? But he is not here.'

'Butcher Rawdon. And he is aboard most certainly, for he was taken at sea.' Traherne turned a cunning eye upon me. 'You have had some dealings with Rawdon, then?'

'I know him only by his foul reputation.'

He studied me a moment, and then spat again into the water. 'He is very likely the monster they say. He paid me quiet as a lamb, but there's many a one he's strung from the nearest tree.' The doors of the captain's cabin having been left open on account of the warm night, the lantern-light shone out from there. Though I could recognize no faces in the cabin at that distance, I glimpsed several uniformed figures.

'Is he paroled?' said I.

Traherne shrugged, indifferent to Rawdon's fate. He then went on to give me his assessment of the senior quartermaster's character, obliging me with a warning against trusting any French bills. He advised that I accept nothing from the French but their coin. I thanked him for the advice (which had I been a merchant, and followed it, must surely have sunk me) and soon after that he left me to sow the seeds of financial ruin in the ears of the other two merchants.

How Lord Rawdon, whom I had last heard of as marauding freely near Charleston, should now come to be Admiral de Grasse's prisoner, was more than I could properly understand. I glanced several times back toward the cabin, yet I saw no sign of him. I began to doubt the veracity of Traherne's information, and was readying myself to amble astern, there to dispel all doubt, when my three fellows called to me and went below. It were unwise for me to then singularize myself by a separation from them, and so I reluctantly followed them down.

The next morning I lingered beneath my thin blanket while the others took their breakfast at the mess-table. They none of them called me, and seemed all three in ill-humour, for they were men accustomed to resting their heads only upon soft pillows. By their talk, their every concern now was to get themselves quickly before the senior quartermaster, secure contracts, and then remove themselves at the soonest opportunity from the Spartan discomfort of the ship. As for myself, I had no pressing desire for any further dealings with the quartermaster. For he had looked to me a shrewd and able man, and fully equal to any sharp practice or deception that might be tried against him.

'Danby,' said Traherne as they rose from their breakfast – Danby being the name I had given myself – 'Danby,' said he, and pushed me with his boot. 'We shall see you back there.'

I muttered some few words to him but kept my head upon my

folded jacket. And hardly had they started away from the mess-table than there came a bellowing of orders from the stern. A lieutenant hurried past, gathering sailors, roaring at them to look lively. Traherne made bold to ask the meaning of the commotion. The response was a loud oath, the French seamen shoving the merchants aside now in their rush to get by. In the galley, the cook's lad went hurrying to get the pots off the stove. There came the unmistakable 'Ay-yoh' of seamen at the capstan poles, and then I sat up sharply.

'By Christ,' said Traherne in sudden alarm. 'By Christ, will we sail?'

The three of them hurried to crowd about the nearest gun, craning to look out through the gun-port. But when the gunner lashed out at them with a rope, cursing, they retreated, cursing in their turn, and rushed to the ladder. I was up in an instant. Pulling on my boots, I ran after them and climbed swiftly to the open deck.

Seamen raced about in every direction, and some scrambled into the rigging. Officers leaned over the rail, warning off the transports and flatboats. All about us the whole French fleet was weighing anchor, the ships slowly turning toward the sea with the tide.

And now we saw other ships-of-the-line arriving around the northern cape, and yet more standing a short way out to sea beyond the Bay. But they were no part of the French fleet.

'It is the British,' cried Traherne in sudden realization and fright. 'For the love of God, we must get off from here.'

On our poop deck stood the *Auguste*'s captain. Blue-jacketed, and somewhat plump, he surveyed the British fleet calmly through his spyglass; it was only when he lowered the glass that I recognized him as de Bougainville. And very grateful I was now not to have arranged the face-to-face meeting with Captain de Bougainville that I had once attempted in Paris. But now his First Lieutenant was pointing directly toward us four unwelcome passengers, and shouting at the bosun to get us below.

It was at this moment that Lord Rawdon appeared on the quarterdeck. Turning to seek the target of the First Lieutenant's wrath, Rawdon's eyes fell instantly upon me. He gave a slight start of surprise, but quickly mastered himself. He then went to the rail as if to get a better vantage of the British fleet. The bosun was soon herding us unwanted merchants unceremoniously below; and glancing over my shoulder as I descended, I saw Rawdon throw me a look of frank puzzlement and question.

'We must demand to be set down. We'll make a petition. The Admiral shall have our protest. What say you, Danby? Congress shall hear of this. Have you friends in Congress?' This from Traherne.

I took my seat at our mess-table by the galley, and would have given much to be quartered at any other place on the ship. Traherne's false and cowardly instinct, with which the others quickly assented, was that de Grasse might be successfully threatened with the name of a powerful lawyer or some high-placed politician in the Congress. They were determined they must be set down safely before any engagement with the British. And I, by necessity, must make common cause with their low and futile indignation. Though it was soon apparent that no Frenchman would hear their demand, or even take forward their petition to the captain, they continued to air their frightened grievance to each other. We had sailed and complained for almost a half-hour, and the gunner's lad was reporting us just off the southern cape, when the surprising apparition of a uniformed British ensign of the Dragoons appeared by our table.

'My Lord Rawdon's compliments, gentlemen,' said he. 'My Lord finds that he requires the services of a notary. He asks if there be any of you gentlemen so qualified.'

There was a sudden silence, and a general shuffling of feet while each man contemplated his own hands upon the table. There was little likelihood that assisting a captured British officer should help win any French contracts. When after a time I rose, the others looked at me very cagily. They thought me a fool, no doubt, and I to confirm them in their opinion made a hesitation like a fool. But then the ensign thanked me and turned on his heel, and I dropped my gaze and went with him.

'I am Danby, my Lord,' said I, when the ensign had opened Rawdon's door to me. 'I was told you had need of a notary.'

'Come in, Mr Danby.' Rawdon said, and he instructed his ensign to wait outside the door. When the door closed behind me, Rawdon said softly, 'He shall give us warning of any approach. But it shall be as well to speak quietly, Mr Douglas. Are you sent to me?'

'I am here by an accident, my Lord. And I am certain that Lord Cornwallis and the others in York Town have no knowledge of your capture.'

'Has he not moved himself from the Chesapeake?' I turned my head. 'And Washington?' said he.

'He is pressing General Clinton in New York.'

Rawdon looked pained, and said gravely, 'Washington is at this moment marching toward the Chesapeake with General Rochambeau. They mean to join with this damned French fleet.'

'My Lord?'

'It is the common talk of every officer aboard. Must I believe that Cornwallis knows nothing of it?'

'Nothing.'

He touched a hand to his forehead in dismay.

Though not yet thirty years of age, he had won a considerable reputation during the course of the war, albeit he was reviled by the rebels. Though my own dealings with him had been slight, I had found him on those few occasions capable but headstrong, and by no means the worst of our officers. And if he trusted in this story of Washington coming south, there was no good reason I should disbelieve him.

'I feared he should not know,' said he. 'We must pray that Admiral Graves blasts us all to Hell. Sit you down, if you please, Mr Douglas.' He gave me then the story of his capture, which incident had happened by the merest bad luck. After sailing from Charleston, Rawdon's ship had blundered into privateers. These fellows had taken both Rawdon and his ensign, and later passed them on to de Grasse, whose fleet they had met with at sea. Admiral de Grasse had subsequently offered a parole, which Rawdon had accepted and signed. The humiliation of it, I saw, still rankled him. At length he fell silent. He sat upon his narrow bunk, his fists clenched upon his knees.

I remarked my surprise that the French should have been so very free with him regarding Washington's move south.

'What need have they to conceal anything from me? I can do nothing, or so they believe. And Cornwallis must himself witness Washington's arrival soon enough.' When I asked the size of Washington and Rochambeau's armies, he confessed that he had no certain knowledge. 'But I do know this, Douglas: Admiral Graves must maul us now, and badly. For if he fail in that, de Grasse shall hold the Bay. Washington's heel shall then be planted firm on my Lord Cornwallis's throat.'

'Have you ever been in a sea battle, my Lord?'

'No,' said he, looking somewhat surprised at the question. 'But I am sure it cannot be worse than I have seen.'

The ensign tapped a sharp warning at the door. There then arrived a midshipman from de Bougainville, inviting Lord Rawdon to join the officers above.

Rawdon rose and picked his tricorn from the peg.

'I may myself try the extent of the captain's hospitality,' I ventured.

Rawdon raised an eyebrow as he went out. 'As you wish, Mr Danby.'

We were soon on the quarterdeck where the gunners were clearing for action. Behind them the front panels of the captain's cabin had been removed. Bougainville was inside, his senior officers all gathered around him. Rawdon bowed his head to acknowledge the courtesy of being allowed above decks to take a brief view of the British fleet. Bougainville nodded to him in return and pointed to the poop deck overhead. No question being made of my presence, I went directly up after Rawdon.

The day was clear, the wind lying north-north-east. The French fleet was now clear of the Bay, some few miles out to sea, with the British line bearing down upon us from windward. The *Auguste* was part of the French van. Bougainville's high reputation was such that I had no doubt but he commanded these front ships. The rest of de Grasse's fleet made a long, straight tail behind us.

'I am no naval man,' said Rawdon after some minutes' observation of the two fleets through his spyglass, 'but why the devil did Graves not fall upon de Grasse in the Bay?'

'Lack of judgement,' said I, at which bold criticism Rawdon seemed taken aback; and so I added, 'But he may yet make good. The French have the numbers but Graves has the wind.'

Rawdon gave me his spyglass. Behind us the Bay was open again, and several smaller vessels were now taking their opportunity to go freely out and in. My letter for Jenkinson must be aboard one of them.

By the time Bougainville had joined us at last on the poop deck, the British line was coming fast into range. There was a calm intensity of purpose about Bougainville, and no sign of any apprehension in his officers or men. Bougainville neither bellowed nor roared (unlike many inferior French captains) but his orders were each of them given firm and clear, and instantly obeyed, so that I was in no doubt of the fearful harm he might do to us.

'What is it that we are about there?' said Rawdon, narrowing his eyes as he drew my attention to a change in the British line. 'Does Graves split his fleet?'

Something peculiar was certainly under way. For it appeared that only the van of the British fleet, the first several ships, were now bearing down to engage. The others continued on their first course as if to keep themselves off from any action. This strange manoeuvre caused a momentary surprise and bafflement among Bougainville's lieutenants. But then Bougainville grasped what had happened. Striving to keep down his excitement, he turned sharply to his first officer. 'They have missed their own signals. Close with the van, and fire all larboard guns.'

CHAPTER 5

We closed and fired. The shots went high, slashing through the rigging and the topsail of the nearest British ship. The answering British volley fell fifty yards short of us. Rawdon swore in disgust.

'The wind heels them over,' said I. 'She cannot use her lower guns.'

Fore and aft of us, the other ships of the French van now opened upon their opposite numbers in the British line. Though the British van answered, there seemed still that same terrible confusion at the British rear. Half Graves's fleet yet held back from the engagement.

A lieutenant then came to Rawdon with Bougainville's command that we must go below for safety. The *Auguste*'s guns at that moment opening a brisk cannonade, the officer extended an arm stiffly to usher us directly from the poop deck. And in truth, it would now be an idiot obstinacy for us to remain there; for if the British line came nearer we would be within range of musket and grapeshot, and the poop deck must then be the place of greatest danger from the flying British lead.

'Is this the great seamanship Graves boasts of?' burst out Rawdon when we were alone in his cabin. He flourished a hand toward the sound of the guns larboard. 'I might have done as much with a ketch and twenty marines.'

'Have you been allowed your pistols?'

'In my trunk there,' said he.

'And powder?'

'I suppose there is a little.' He regarded me with a sudden curiosity. 'You would not lower yourself by any foul act, Douglas?'

'Danby.'

'What?'

'It is better I am always Danby. And it is no dishonour but a duty that we give all possible assistance to His Majesty's Navy.'

'You shall not tell me my duty, sir.'

'How much powder have you?'

He was but a moment standing on his dignity; then a fresh barrage from the *Auguste*'s guns, and a following cheer from the gunners, moved him to open up the trunk. There was a great tearing of timber somewhere above us. And screaming. 'I cannot arm myself,' said he as he gave me the pistol-case. 'I have signed the parole. But you may have the pistols, though I cannot think what good they may do you.'

I removed the powder-horn and returned the case to the trunk. Then unsealing the cap, I examined the contents of the horn. It was full. 'Have you a flint?'

'Shall you tell me your intention?'

'You are paroled.'

'I cannot take up arms. But I am under no obligation, I believe, to make an impediment to my own countrymen in their dutiful actions.'

'The flint then, if you have it.'

He soon brought the flint out from the trunk, and gave it me. But as he did so he warned me that Captain de Bougainville had been a very gentleman to him. Further, he forbade me to do that good man any personal harm.

'It is not Bougainville's assassination I intend. But I will sink his ship from under him if I can.'

'That is impossible.'

'Let me put a grenade into his powder room, and we shall see then what is impossible. Now, I must have something for a fuse. And a shell.'

He hesitated, as if considering the propriety of my intention. But after a moment he decided in my favour and quickly busied himself with rummaging again in the trunk. 'Here is your shell,' said he, bringing forth a hip-flask. 'There is a finger of brandy may serve to soak your fuse.' He then brought forth a white cotton shirt and tore off a long strip. We felt the shock of the *Auguste*'s guns all this time, and the shudder of the hull each time she was hit. Rawdon's cabin being on the orlop deck to starboard, we could still hear each other speak. But now came the first screams from just outside his door, for it was there the *Auguste*'s surgeon had his table. I exchanged a look with Rawdon. Then I took the cotton strip and coiled it into a pannikin. As I poured the brandy over it, Rawdon asked how I hoped to get forward to the magazine.

'I shall make myself useful to the surgeon. I must take my chance as it comes.'

'And I, Mr Danby?'

'The surgeon would not refuse your assistance.'

'The surgeon may go to Hell.'

The screaming outside the door now rose to a dreadful pitch. Setting the flask and the powder-horn down by the pannikin, I removed my jacket and went out. On the lantern-lit table was a single wounded seaman, the injury to both his legs truly as awful as any injury might be. His legs were crushed almost to mince below the knees, and a loblollyman was trying to pin down his thighs. Two others held the injured man's shoulders while the surgeon readied scalpel and saw.

With all the brute strength of his agony the seaman twisted and bucked, seeming about to send himself violently to the floor. I went directly over and grabbed the man's head and pulled it down to the table. There was no getting grog into him, or even a leather into his mouth, for he was crazed and absolutely unreachable. So the moment the fellow was properly pinned, the surgeon cried, 'Hold him there! Hold him!' and set straight to his labour. But hardly had the knife-work begun than the seaman's body gave two tremendous jolts, and he went limp as a rag beneath our hands. While the poor fellow lay motionless, the surgeon continued with his knife. And so crushed was the lower leg that it came away without the need of a saw. The surgeon dropped the foot and the attached pulp into a bucket and then looked up.

'Well?'

The loblolly brought a lantern up near to the patient's stilled face. After a moment's inspection, he declared, 'Dead, sir.'

'Get him off from here then.' The surgeon turned aside to wash his hands and his scalpel in the water-bowl. Without looking at me, he continued in French, 'You are not Lord Rawdon's man.'

'I am a Montreal merchant,' I answered in the same language. 'Captain de Bougainville has sent me down with Lord Rawdon. If I can help, sir, I am at your service.'

'Keep away from the table unless I call you. There are sails cut there, ready,' said he, nodding toward the bulwark. 'Wrap the dead when they come to you, and then put them aside. Be sure they are out of the way.'

I went and spread a piece of the cut sail on the deck, and then they brought the dead seaman across. After wrapping the sail like a shroud around the body I set it to one side. The roar now of the *Auguste*'s 32-pounders directly over us was tremendous. I crouched in the dimly lit corner, with my hands now to my ears, while another injured seaman was carried down to us, shouting for his mother. As they set him on the table, I looked all about me. Though we were below the waterline, and so had some protection from the British shot, I had no comforting illusion of safety; for the sea pressed close, and seemed no cradle but only a vast and watery tomb.

In the next hour I wrapped fifteen more men, the pile of bodies growing like cut logs where I stacked them by the bulwark. When at last there came a lull in the firing, I quickly crossed the blood-slickened floor to Rawdon's cabin.

'Is it over?' said he, sitting up from where he had lain braced upon his bunk. The *Auguste*'s guns answered him with a fresh cannonade, and he swore.

'The powder and flint,' said I, extending my hand.

'Having considered of it, I cannot see how I may in good conscience indulge you.'

'What?'

'There shall be no grenade. It would be a foolishness. You would be stopped before you were halfway to the magazine.' When I reached past him in irritation toward the trunk, he said, 'The powder is not in there.' Then I followed his glance to the floor. The powder had been tipped from the horn, and beside it lay the empty pannikin. And the powder was no longer powder, but a useless mud made by mixing with the brandy. I raised my eyes, scarce trusting myself not to strike him.

'I gave Captain de Bougainville my word as a nobleman,' said he, and his cheeks now glowed crimson. But though he saw my fury at what he had done, and felt the shame of his own change of heart, yet he did not flinch beneath my gaze.

'That is not a reason,' said I. 'You knew my intention.'

'It is reason enough. But if you would have another, I could not let you kill yourself to no purpose. You must surely have died, whether or not you reached the magazine. And I must surely have answered for that. Both to Lord Cornwallis and to my own conscience.' He looked defiance at me now, his confidence in his thwarting action growing even as he spoke. 'And you, Douglas, must be content that you have more important business yet to accomplish than to kill yourself.'

'That judgement was mine to make.'

'I might have reasoned with you, only that I saw you were not to be reasoned with.'

There was nothing now I might do to repair his obstruction of me. And I did not yet trust the restraint of either my tongue or my fist. When a blast from the guns swayed me I clutched at the handle of the door to steady myself before turning my back without a word and departing the cabin.

*

53

While the fighting continued, the bodies mounted; till after an hour I had made a pile three deep by the bulwark (which pile, though a tribute to the British gunners, was a sight that no Christian might look upon with equanimity). The orlop deck was soaked now, both from the spillage of blood and from the frequent swabbing ordered by the surgeon. When the firing at length slackened, it seemed at first a lull, of which there had been several since the opening of the engagement. But after several minutes more, the firing ceased altogether; and then Rawdon came out from his cabin.

He stopped, and stared in some horror at the appalling scene. There was a seaman upon the table, and this fellow unconscious, but with his stomach cut open, and the surgeon's hands searching the entrails to dig out the grapeshot. I quickly stepped into the lantern-light where Rawdon might see me, and I jerked my head above. Rawdon regathered himself then, and called across, 'Come aloft with me, Mr Danby.' And no question being made of Rawdon's move to the steps, I followed him up.

As we passed up through the decks, Rawdon looked continually about him with a bewildered disbelief. For the *Auguste* was holed in several places to larboard, and the daylight came in at the torn timbers to illuminate a wreckage and destruction quite remarkable. Not every injured seaman and dying seaman had been carried below, but many had been bandaged by their fellows at the guns, and others roughly stitched by the sailmakers. These poor wounded fellows now lay propped like bloodied and discarded marionettes against what remained of the smashed mess-tables and gun-carriages. Exhaustion was etched upon every face. I confess, the sight of the destruction gave me some small hope of a British victory.

But on the quarterdeck, that same lieutenant who had taken us below now swept his hand north-east toward Graves's fleet a league distant, proudly announcing that the British had been compelled to disengage. When he left us we went to the rail. The sun, to landward, was just setting; and the eastern sky had turned salmon pink above the sea. Two British ships billowed smoke, and the worst of them clearly in some real difficulty. Astern of us the French line was reforming. Many French sails appeared torn and shredded, but none of de Grasse's ships was burning.

'Graves has disengaged too early,' said Rawdon quietly.

'Or perhaps not early enough,' I returned; for though it had evidently been a rough mauling on both sides, it was unquestionable that the French had come off the better. Not an outright victory, but Bougainville's officers on the poop deck appeared sufficiently pleased with their work. Bougainville himself now called down to Rawdon, who went up at once to join him.

'You cannot remain here,' that lieutenant came to tell me. Then noticing the blood on my cuffs, he enquired the reason of it, and whether I was injured.

'I have assisted the surgeon.'

'Then I must thank you, sir. But you must now return below to your friends.'

'Shall there be a further engagement tonight?'

'Only if the British are fools.'

'Then we may expect it,' said I, at which he smilingly clapped a hand to my back. With a final glance across the water to the continuing disarray of the British line, I went unhappily below.

There was no further engagement that night. Nor was there any on the following day and night either, but the two fleets sailed continually south-east with the wind, keeping each other in sight. The *Auguste*'s carpenters seemed everywhere about the ship, effecting repairs both above and below decks. The sailmakers were likewise kept busy, having the exclusive use of the foredeck to make good the torn sails. The mood aboard the *Auguste* (and, I suppose, in the whole French fleet) was exceedingly cheerful during this time. And no more cheerful than after the first morning when the worst-damaged of the British vessels (the *Intrepid*, I later learned) was abandoned and scuttled to prevent her capture by the French.

Among my merchant acquaintance much ridiculous speculation arose over the meaning of the mutual shadowing practised by the two fleets. Feigning illness, I kept myself from these idle and querulous ruminations. Most of the time I lay quietly beneath my thin blanket and calculated the small possibility now remaining for Graves to get control of Chesapeake Bay. My concern was to get quickly ashore, and take some warning to Cornwallis of Washington and Rochambeau's march southward. But my concerns were not Admiral de Grasse's, or even Captain de Bougainville's, and so the French fleet continued to sail away from the Chesapeake, leading on the British.

It was after two days of this tedious sailing, and no sign of any further engagement, that Rawdon's servant came for me. His master, he said, required me again as a notary for some papers. Rousing myself, I muttered a complaint of the summons, and went.

'Sit, if you please, Mr Danby.' Rawdon had set a pen in an inkpot and two sheets of paper upon his trunk. I sat upon the end of his bunk and looked at him curiously. He had his arms folded, his back against the wall. 'We have little time. Copy out what I have written. It will serve if you are questioned later concerning your presence here with me.' When I looked down at the written sheet, he said, 'It is supposedly some instructions to my people in London. All nonsense. Take it with you when you go, and you may show it to any French officer who asks it of you. Burn it when you are safely ashore.' He gestured to the pen and so I took it up and began to copy out the written paper as instructed. While I wrote, he told me that which he had really summoned me to hear. 'I am to be moved to another ship before the next watch. That other ship sails for France with their badly injured officers. The greater part of the French fleet, however, will put about and return to the Chesapeake.'

I lifted my head in surprise. 'Shall the French offer no further engagement? It looked that they had the advantage.'

'They have never intended an engagement while we have sailed these past days. Not since that first battle. It is a trick they have played upon Admiral Graves. Their intention – which they have succeeded in – was only to lead him ever further out from the Chesapeake Capes.' Rawdon spoke in restrained agitation now, and I glanced between him and the paper that I wrote upon. 'It seems they were expecting another of their naval commanders, Barras, at the Chesapeake. Admiral Graves came instead. This Barras has a number of ships carrying siege guns and artillery. Bougainville's officers appear very confident that Barras must have arrived there by this time.'

'And de Grasse shall now return to the Bay?' said I.

'I fear Lord Cornwallis little understands the force now converging upon him. When you are put ashore, Douglas . . . Danby, you must get word to him at once.'

'What more?'

'That is for Lord Cornwallis to decide. Were it me, I should take the army inland.'

'I meant, sir, what more have you heard? How many ships has Barras? What is the artillery he carries?'

Rawdon did not know. He seemed annoyed that I should expect it of him. But I saw the great impression the loose talk of Bougainville's officers had made upon him, and also his disappointment at his own impending transportation to France. He told me some few other matters he had heard mention of among the French officers, but there was nothing to equal this first.

When I had finished copying out Rawdon's worthless sheet, I asked him if there was anything more he might have for Cornwallis. There was nothing, he said, but only a private message to his fellow officer and friend, Colonel Tarleton.

'You may tell him that I am confident we shall dine together before next summer,' said he, to which idle bravado I made no remark, but simply blotted the paper. He studied me anew. 'I shall not apologize that I prevented your attempt upon the magazine, Danby. In fact, I find that I am very glad of it.'

I wished him a safe voyage, and a speedy parole; and then I did not linger but came directly away from his cabin.

It was but a few hours later, and I seated at a desultory game of dice with my merchant companions, when we heard a flurry of orders on the upper decks. The *Auguste* slowly listed to starboard. The cook and his lad hurried over from the galley to peer out the nearest gunport, talking excitedly together. We were going about. I rose with the other merchants and went up to the foredeck.

The whole French line was coming around, peeling away from the British fleet; and the British ships looked unwilling to shadow the French fleet any longer. After ten minutes the new course was set, and it was clear that the French vessels were returning to the Chesapeake Bay. But still the British stood off. And when they too finally came around several minutes after, it was not to make a pursuit of us. They set their own course now directly north. They would bypass the Chesapeake and make instead for New York.

'What say you, Danby?' said Traherne. 'Shall we see them again?'

'The British have missed their best chance,' said I. 'But they may make another.'

'They have their tails between their legs. We shall not see them again.'

Over on the quarterdeck, Captain de Bougainville issued the order for an extra shot of rum for every man aboard. My undeserving companions and I soon joined the general move toward the barrels.

We sailed into Chesapeake Bay on the eighth day of September, meeting Barras's small fleet there, already lying at anchor off Portsmouth. Barras had several transports beside his nine ships-of-the-line; and when de Grasse brought his own fleet by them, colours flying, cheering and huzzahs broke from every deck and yard. Barras fired off a cannonade to salute our arrival, and there was no doubt in my mind but that a vessel had gone ahead of us with news of the drubbing Graves had taken off the Capes.

It was shortly after this salute that I swallowed some of that dried Appalachian herb that I kept in my satchel. Its effects I well knew from previous unhappy experience among the Cherokees. Within a half-hour I was before the *Auguste*'s surgeon, perspiring heavily, trembling, and generally showing every sign of a malarial contagion. He did not hesitate, but asked me where I would be put ashore; for he would have me at once from the ship and well away from any possibility of spreading an infection aboard.

So it was that I was lowered into the first French flatboat that passed up the James River toward Williamsburg. They set me down at

Burwell's Ferry, just below Williamsburg, and very glad they were to be rid of me. For the native purgative had by that time begun to put alarmingly dark blotches upon my skin. After making my way with some difficulty to that place in the woods where I had hidden with Morgan, I finally dropped. The worst effects of the drug then came over me, which were an intense coldness, and a complete and violent purging of the stomach. Strange creatures stalked through my mind, and a thousand mites upon my flesh. I clutched my jacket tight about me, shivering feverishly till exhaustion at last carried me into a troubled sleep.

It was night when I woke. The half-moon was bright, and shining directly upon my face through the pines. After a minute I somewhat tentatively sat up. My limbs ached, but the fever was past. I sat there a minute and more to let my head clear. By the landing, two hundred yards upriver of me, the French soldiers' campfire had burned very low. There were voices, but very few. It must be that most of the soldiers there slept. At length I rose uncertainly to my feet. And so light-headed was I that I must briefly lean upon a pine to steady myself. But soon I could move my head left and right with no effect of giddiness, and then I pushed off the tree. Turning my uncertain step into the forest, I started out along the track that must lead me across the peninsula to York Town.

CHAPTER 6

'*T*here are others I had sooner given them than Rawdon.'

'He is treated well, my Lord.'

Cornwallis tapped his fingers thoughtfully upon his table, weighing all that I had told him. Cable Morgan having long since reported to Major Ross the blunder that had put me into the French fleet, Cornwallis made no question of it now. My dishevelled arrival at the headquarters in York Town had surprised Major Ross, but he had soon found Lord Cornwallis out by the earthworks and brought him back to hear my story. And after hearing me now, Cornwallis did not rebuke my carelessness in being taken aboard the French fleet; for the news I had brought him of Washington and Rochambeau's march was all his concern. He asked if I could really be sure that our own fleet would make no second attempt upon the Bay.

'Admiral Graves took a knock from the French that he had not expected, my Lord. He is undoubtedly sailing for New York to make some repairs.'

'You need not dissemble, Douglas. You are telling me they have run.'

I inclined my head, keeping my eyes on his. One corner of his mouth turned upward in contemptuous annoyance at Graves's flight.

'As I came past Williamsburg,' said I, 'there were French soldiers encamped in great numbers. It cost me some trouble to go around them.'

Major Ross, who had stood all the while behind Cornwallis's shoulder, now broke in. He told me that de Grasse had put a regiment ashore the day before sailing to fight Graves.

'They are joined now with Lafayette's rabble,' Cornwallis added. 'They have kept off from us, and so I have kept off from them.'

At this surprisingly pacific remark, I glanced from Cornwallis to Major Ross. I knew already, from the conversation of Ross and some officers at Captain Symonds's shipboard supper, the high regard the soldiers had for Cornwallis's martial qualities. Whilst coming up through the Carolinas, Lord Cornwallis had ordered all the baggage wagons burned, including his own, so that the army might suffer no impediment in its pursuit of the rebels. He had fought and marched and fought again, month after month, till at last fetching up here on the Chesapeake. It seemed unaccountable that here, of a sudden, the desire to be at the enemy's throat had simply left him. But Major Ross was too loyal a servant of Cornwallis to now make any question of this unwonted passivity. When I looked at him, his bland expression offered me nothing.

I then asked Cornwallis if he intended to attack the French before Washington arrived.

'I shall not waste my men on futilities. General Clinton has put us here with an assurance of safety. It must be for him to get us off from here, if it comes to that. Till then, we rely upon our engineers for some better entrenchments.'

'Colonel Tarleton has made raids upon the French,' said Ross. 'And also on the Gloucester side. They are not so many there.'

Cornwallis opened his arms in mock despair. 'You see how I am beset by my own officers, Douglas? They cannot quite bring themselves to trust in our orders.' Cornwallis's tone was light, and there was an obvious mutual regard between the General and his aide; but

I could see that Ross bridled now a little at this indulgent dismissal. Cornwallis continued. 'Also, should I order a withdrawal to Gloucester Point and a retreat up into Virginia, we must soon be met by Rochambeau and Washington. We should then have succeeded only in removing ourselves from any hope of reinforcement by sea.'

'While de Grasse commands the Bay—'

'I am aware of the situation, Mr Douglas. And I like it very little, as any sensible man must. But it is our orders have placed us here, and my duty now is to secure the town as a stronghold while we await reinforcement. And you shall serve me best by keeping yourself in future times from going aboard any French vessel.'

Cornwallis delivered the instruction with an amused glance from me to Ross, who now smiled in his turn. We talked then of the disposition of his forces about the town, and of the preparedness of the inner and outer defences, which was a great concern to Cornwallis. Gloucester Point, across the river, having received the first attentions of the sappers and blacks, could now boast a single-line entrenchment, redoubts, and some few batteries of guns between. But a want of the necessary entrenching tools – picks, shovels and sundry implements – meant that the works around York Town were not nearly so advanced as Cornwallis might have wished.

'My engineers give me a hundred reasons for the tardiness. It is only the blacks who can work through the heat of the day, and even they must be constantly chivvied. But it goes on. We shall have both an inner and an outer line completed before long.'

I wondered did he fear no attack in the meantime.

'Lafayette knows he would not carry our position. It is why he sends out patrols to surprise our people in the woods. Tarleton is out there now, returning the salute. We need fear no proper attack unless they have reinforcement. And even then they cannot carry us without siege guns.'

An ensign knocked at the door and put his head in to announce the arrival of the two men that Major Ross had sent for. Ross, at Cornwallis's nod, ordered that the men be sent in.

'You shall have other concerns than our entrenchments, Mr Douglas,' said Cornwallis. 'And these fellows may assist you.'

It was a young lieutenant of the Fusiliers came in, a lad of seventeen or eighteen years, and behind him a captain of the Guards, and this second man little older than twenty. The lieutenant had an impish look, and a light freckling upon his face. The other was a handsome young fellow, fair-skinned and fair-haired. Both held themselves stiffly upright as they stood before Cornwallis. 'Be at ease,' Ross told them, and then he introduced me to the junior man. 'This is Lieutenant Harry Calvert. He shall be the aide that you asked for.' And then to Calvert he said, 'This is Mr Douglas, who I told you of. You are to answer to him as to me.'

'Sir,' said the lad and dipped his head to me.

'You shall take quarters with Mr Douglas in the Kendrick house.'

'Yes, sir.'

Lord Cornwallis then spoke to the captain, gesturing toward me as he said, 'I believe that you know this gentleman here?'

'Yes, my Lord.'

'And Mr Douglas, I believe you have met Captain Stuart before now.'

After studying the young man a moment, I said that the captain must accept my apology, but that I could not recall that I had met him.

'It was some years ago, sir,' said he, and an amusement came to his eye. And at my remark that some years ago he must be only a boy, he grinned and said, 'I was eight, sir. And you were a guest of my father.'

'In London?'

'In the Appalachians, sir.'

I stared at him. The realization of who he was struck me silent a moment. Captain Stuart. But who else must he be but the son of the late John Stuart, Superintendent of our affairs with the southern Indians. John Stuart, a man who while he lived I had been proud to call my friend. 'Jonathan? You are John Stuart's son, Jonathan?'

'Yes, sir.'

It was so unexpected that it was yet another moment before I stepped forward and gave him my hand. He smiled broadly.

'This young man,' said I, smiling myself now as I tapped Stuart's chest and looked back at Cornwallis, 'this young man once tried to kill me with a tomahawk.'

'I had hoped you had forgot that, sir. I have not thrown one since.'

'But, my God, look at you,' said I, standing off. He was tall and lean like his father. And now that I studied him better, there was something also of his father in his face. It was more than ten years past that Jonathan had been sent away for his education in England. And though I knew the heartache that had come from the decision, to both the boy's parents, when I looked at Jonathan now I could truly believe it a decision well made. I started to ask Jonathan after his mother, but Cornwallis broke in upon us.

'You must reminisce another time. But shall I take it that you have no objection to Lieutenant Calvert as your aide? Very well.' He explained that there was a patrol going up to the head of the York the next day, of which Captain Stuart would be a part. Cornwallis suggested that I might wish to join the expedition, and take Calvert with me. 'There shall be marines go ashore there. We hope they may intercept the messages now passing between Lafayette and the militia on the Gloucester side. If they succeed, they shall of course make the messages available to you, Mr Douglas.'

Major Ross opened a map across the table. He pointed out to us the places upriver where our sloops were positioned, and the overland route at the head of the river where the enemy messengers were known to pass. I noticed that we should be set down just two or three miles south of the Pamunkey Indian reservation. Campbell must be there yet. A thought was forming in me, but nothing so definite as a plan, and so I let Ross talk and made no interruption to his instruction of us.

The next morning as I buttoned my breeches, the door of my room opened and Mrs Kendrick's black maid, Francesca, entered with a steaming pitcher of water. I gestured to the bowl upon the dressing table, and she poured the water, though avoiding my eye. I asked was her mistress below.

'She is in her room, sir.'

'Mr Calvert tells me that she means to stay here in the town, in spite of the French.' The maid glanced up as she finished pouring, but made no answer to me. I nodded to the door and she slipped quickly away.

I was soon shaved and dressed, and found Calvert below, seated upon the staircase steps. He rose as I descended, and began a report of the patrol's preparations for embarkation. I asked had he eaten.

'A little, sir.'

I turned him toward the dining room, for I would spare us both the ship's biscuit. The widow and her maid were already in there, and the widow seated at the table's head. She invited us to take our breakfast with her, gesturing to the places already laid for us.

'I understand that you are away again, Mr Douglas. Upriver this time?'

'I am away, madam,' said I, taking a firm pinch-hold of Calvert's sleeve. And much to his surprise, I prevented him taking his seat. 'And so we must bid you good morning.'

'But you shall breakfast with me before you leave.'

'That is a pleasure we must put off till our return. We are called to the boat directly.'

'I cannot accuse you, Mr Douglas, of leaning too heavily upon my hospitality. I had feared an idle lodger.'

'That is a strange compliment, madam.'

'It was not meant for a compliment.' She looked at me with that frank directness peculiar to the native-born women of the American colonies. Her youth was gone, but there was yet about her an undeniable handsomeness of face. She was perhaps thirty or thirty-five years. Her cheekbones were somewhat wider than the usual, much like a Cherokee's, and her auburn hair intertwined with a white ribbon and spilled over her shoulders. But in her eyes was no pliancy, much less any feminine softness. 'But I cannot insist, Mr Douglas. If you must go straight down to the river, then I must abide your absence.'

I made her a small bow and retreated with Calvert.

Once from the house and on the path down to the wharf, I said, 'You informed Mrs Kendrick that we would be going upriver.'

'She asked why I fetched your pistols, sir.'

'In future you shall refrain from any such discussion of my affairs.' I glanced at the lad, and his face flushed red. 'We shall say no more of it, Mr Calvert. I think you understand me.'

He pressed his lips together and nodded. He was sharp enough, but still young.

Upon weighing anchor, we made directly for Gloucester Point and there set down the chief engineer, Lieutenant Sutherland, with his assistant and some blacks; for there having been a question raised of the quality of the initial earthworks, these fellows must now make a repair. I took the opportunity of our short stop to disembark and let Calvert give me a brief tour of the four redoubts, which were considerably slighter than I had expected. For a certainty, they would not long withstand a well-directed cannonade from one of de Grasse's ships-of-the-line. A young Hessian officer joined us on our tour, and with halting English and a withering contempt for the engineering works, he gave it to us as his opinion that the chief engineer did not know his own business. Though the poor quality of the sandy soil thereabout seemed to me a more likely cause of the necessary repairwork, I took it as instructive (and no good sign) that such discontents should be openly voiced by a German officer.

There was barely a score of buildings standing between the river and our landward entrenchments, and the hamlet of Gloucester was not to be compared with York Town upon the opposite bank. The place would evidently be to us just what it must have been to the local inhabitants: a bridgehead to the Virginian hinterland. Once I had satisfied myself of the layout of the place, I paid my respects to Colonel Simcoe who commanded there, and then reboarded the sloop with Calvert.

As we drew away, I stood with Calvert at the stern. Gloucester Point was to our left side, York Town upon our right, and on the river between was anchored a small fleet of barques and transports. The

40-gun *Guadeloupe* and the 60-gun *Charon* were the only ships of any real size, and neither one of these likely to trouble even the least of de Grasse's ships-of-the-line.

'I cannot understand, sir, why the army is not crossed over.'

'Lord Cornwallis is no more his own master than you or I, Mr Calvert. He has made what preparations are possible. General Clinton has given the orders.'

'General Clinton is not in York Town.'

'Though that may be a just observation, you would be unwise to repeat it.'

I sent him to fetch my spyglass, and then I leaned upon the rail. A hazy mist of heat seemed to thicken over the water and the boats, and also over York Town and Gloucester. A minute more, and nothing was distinct, neither building nor tree nor shoreline. All seemed blanketed now by the same enervating miasma. The masts of the *Guadeloupe* and the *Charon* broke briefly from the wavering heat; but they seemed things insubstantial, washed strokes on a pallid canvas, and the next instant dissolved into air.

The York River was navigable almost the full extent of its upper reaches, twenty miles above York Town. Every few miles of our way we passed the sloops that Captain Symonds had stationed as patrols upon the river. (These kept Lafayette's men from any short crossing, and at the same time secured York Town against any attack from the upper river.) At the head of the York were two primary tributaries, which were the Pamunkey and Mattaponi rivers; and we were nearly to the mouth of the Pamunkey before we stopped. Having made an arrangement with the captain that he should return for us in two days, our party then rowed ashore. In a muddy cove just east of the Pamunkey we disembarked, and three marines stayed to hide the boat and maintain a guard over it while the rest of us went at once up into the cover of the brushwood. Though we had seen no sign of any people yet, it was well known that the necessary foraging of Simcoe's Rangers had set many of the local people against us. We surely knew enough to go forward with care.

The marine lieutenant had made a reconnaissance of the place several days earlier; and so within twenty minutes he had led us to that narrow trail where he meant to ambush Lafayette's messengers. He next showed us to a small clearing, a hundred yards distant from the narrow trail, where he expected us to camp. But before any man could settle, I said, 'We shall meet you at the boat tomorrow, Lieutenant.'

'Sir?'

'Captain Stuart and his party are not needed for this ambush.'

'But Major Ross has instructed me—'

'He instructed you to accommodate me, Lieutenant. And Captain Stuart, Mr Calvert, and these two gentlemen' – I indicated the two redcoats who had come with Stuart – 'they are none of them needed here. They shall accompany me a little further on.'

The lieutenant looked not a bit certain about this. But then Stuart said to him, 'I shall answer to Major Ross for it'; and Stuart being his senior, and the marine lieutenant therefore hesitating to make any objection, I called Calvert and the redcoats to me. With a final assurance to the marine lieutenant that I should bring these men safely to the boat the next day, I started with my party toward the Pamunkey River.

CHAPTER 7

*T*hough the land all about there was very flat, and though we were shaded by the thick woods, yet was the heat so oppressive that even a short march was uncomfortable and fatiguing. We advanced with great caution, wary of an ambush by the local militia. In truth, we must have been very unlucky to have encountered any organized enemy soldiers in such a place, but the Virginian militia might be anywhere, and even a farmer or fisherman might have reason to raise a musket against us. But the soil was poor, and no homestead had been planted among the tidal creeks. In an hour's march we saw no one. Stuart at last raised his hand to halt us. When I came up beside him, he pointed to several threads of smoke rising from the trees ahead.

'We might find a track wide of here,' said he.

'No. That is the place.'

'What place?'

'The Pamunkey reservation.'

While I looked ahead, Stuart asked in surprise what business we could possibly have with the Pamunkey Indians. Before I might answer him there appeared a cart on a nearby track half-hid by the woods. The cart was but fifty yards to the right of us, and an old Pamunkey man stood in the tray. He held the reins in his hands while his horse ambled along very leisurely. The old man looked directly at us across the scrubland between. Though he saw us he gave no sign of recognition, but nor did he turn away.

His grey hair hung to his shoulders. He wore deerskin breeches and a white cotton shirt. In his cart was a load of sawn cedar.

Raising a hand, I hailed him. He made no response. He watched us a few moments more, and when his cart followed the track into the next trees he faced forward again, slipping from our view. He seemed in no hurry, as if to see redcoats in that place was a thing as natural to him as the presence of deer.

The cart once gone, I told the others what I had told Stuart: that it was the Pamunkey reservation we had come to. 'I expect no trouble of them. Nor shall we make any for ourselves.' I next instructed the two redcoats to keep their muskets ready, but not to fire except at my order.

We crossed to the track down which the cart had gone, and went forward cautiously. After a few hundred yards we came out from the trees. The Pamunkey village was right before us.

There were perhaps twenty houses, most of them clapboard, and built in the European style. But here and there in the midst of these houses were native constructions of wood and bark, and these something like upturned boats, only taller. They were open at one end, so that the high platform within each one was visible as we approached. The smoke we had seen, and which hung like soft mist over the village, came not from the houses but from a row of fires that smouldered to one side of the track. The few people about the houses and huts eyed us keenly, but all kept their distance.

The old cartman had stopped by the fires and he was now unloading the cut timber. When we approached his cart the fellow ignored us and continued with his unloading.

'Old man. We are thirsty.' He still paid no heed to me, and so I said, 'Is there water?'

He paused in his work and looked at me; and then he looked at the two redcoats and their muskets. When I ordered them to ground the weapons they hesitated and turned to Stuart. He repeated the order, and they finally set the musket-butts upon the dirt. Once this was done the old fellow called something in the Pamunkey tongue to the woman at the first house. She rose from her haunches and went inside. The old man jerked his head toward the village, indicating that we might proceed and get water.

As we neared the first house the woman brought out a pail and set it down outside her door before retreating inside.

'Dip your kerchiefs in the water, gentlemen, and splash your faces,' I said quietly. 'But do not drink a drop.' Gathered about the pail, we refreshed ourselves in this way while the half-naked Indian children came out and stood ten yards off from us, watching silently. After a minute, the first of the young men appeared. I nodded to the fellow, and he to me, and soon there were more of them. Like the old man at the cart, they were most of them dressed in some motley mixture of European and Indian clothing. Most wore moccasins, and many also sported beaded headbands that kept their long and unkempt hair from their eyes. But so different in appearance were these Pamunkey men to the Cherokees with whom I was more familiar that I must work hard to believe them of the same race of people. For there was nothing of bold ferocity about these fellows, but they observed us now with a mild curiosity, and with an evident hesitancy to question our purpose in coming amongst them. A few had clay pipes clasped firmly between their teeth. They puffed on these pipes and watched us, and sometimes spoke quietly to each other as if speculating our intentions.

I singled out one of these bovine fellows.

'I am looking for a Cherokee. His name is Campbell.' The young man answered me nothing, nor gave any sign that he knew the name. 'It may be that he would want to see me.'

'There is no Cherokee with us.'

'My name is Douglas. I am certain that he shall want to hear of me.' I dipped my kerchief into the water again and put the kerchief to my

71

neck. The young fellow watched us a minute more. When I at length signalled to Stuart and the others to rest in the shade of the house, the young Pamunkey broke off from his friends and slipped away. And then we waited.

After fifteen minutes he returned. He beckoned me out from the shade where we had settled, and I rose and followed him down to the river. There was but a small bank, ungrassed and sandy, and Campbell sitting upon the highest part, with his back to a persimmon tree. He was alone, though a campfire was burning further along the bank, nearer the water. Several Pamunkey were gathered at the fire, and some children played close by. Campbell glanced up at me then returned his gaze to the river.

'I feared you had already gone,' said I.

'Your friends got you safe to York Town.'

'Yes.'

'He says you have brought redcoats,' said Campbell, gesturing toward my Pamunkey guide.

'Brought them, aye. And I must take them back with me to York Town.' Campbell craned to peer at me. He saw that I hesitated to speak in the presence of the young Pamunkey, and so he waved the fellow off. The young man went down to join his fellows at the camp-fire. Alone now with Campbell, I said, 'Cornwallis did not take the war-belt.' Campbell said nothing in reply; but in his eyes was a heavy weariness and disappointment. 'But I have not given up hope that I shall have soldiers from him,' I quickly added. 'Only that it shall not be tomorrow, or any day soon. He must first throw off Washington and the French, and then I think that he shall not deny me.'

'Dragging Canoe expects my return.'

'He shall not complain of a delay that brings him redcoats.' I sat myself down then and made my proposal. I explained the great help that Campbell and the Pamunkey might be to me.

While I talked, Campbell stayed silent. He wore a necklace of coloured stones, and buckskin moccasins and breeches. But the day was hot, and he had taken off his shirt and headband which now lay beside him. He was just past thirty, and in recent years had become an important diplomat of the Cherokee, and an envoy of the chieftain Dragging Canoe. Though Campbell's father was a Scotsman he had been raised after the Indian fashion, by his Cherokee mother and her brothers. And though at his father's insistence he had received some European schooling, and spoke English as well as a few native tongues, yet there could be no doubt of Campbell's allegiance to his mother's people. In blood and manner he was half European; but in heart he was fully Cherokee.

Campbell's father having been an assistant to our Superintendent of Indian affairs in the south, John Stuart, and a friend to me, I had known of Campbell since he was a lad. And in later years, following his father's death, the son had become a frequent companion to me in my travels through the Indian country. After hearing me out now, he made no hesitation in pointing out the flaw in my proposal.

'Look at them,' said he, lifting his chin now toward the Pamunkey men over by the river. A flagon was passing among them; more than one of the fellows was visibly drunk. 'What use can they be?'

'Shall none of them return south with you?'

'A few.'

'They seem not unkindly disposed toward us.'

Campbell then told me that a young Pamunkey woman had been murdered but a fortnight since, by a troop of Virginian militia. She had been raped repeatedly before they killed her.

'They may be avenged by any help they now give us,' said I.

'They cannot fight.'

'I do not require them to fight. They may move freely about the peninsula and no one question them. They can do what I cannot. Let them only keep their eyes open and report the movements of the French and the militia to us. To you.'

Campbell thought awhile. 'They shall want money.'

'They shall have money just as soon as they give me a better understanding of the enemy's disposition. And also any changes in that disposition.'

Campbell's head fell back against the tree; he closed his eyes a moment. And I own, I had some sympathy for him. For he had not travelled so far to now be pushed into a war that was not his. Those Indians he had recruited as we came up through the Carolinas had most of them by now gone over the mountains to join with Dragging Canoe. But there were others who now awaited Campbell's return, that he might lead them over to fight against the settlers. Here in Virginia was the furthermost point of his journey, and he was more than ready to turn now for home. It was no small thing that I asked of him, to stay with me and have his Pamunkey recruits work in aid of me.

'These shall make a feast for me tonight,' said he.

'I feared as much.'

He smiled at that. It had become an amusement to us as we travelled how much food and drink we were plied with in every Indian village on our way. He asked me how long I would stay now at the reservation, and when I expected an answer of the Pamunkey.

'I must leave tomorrow.'

He turned and looked down at those Pamunkey by the river, and at the flagon going around. The dismal scene was no different here than at most of the Indian villages we had passed through in the Carolinas. This side of the mountains, the Indians had made their accommodation with the European settlers. But it was not this side of the mountains that Campbell thought on now. His heart was on the far side, with his own people, in the Indian country.

'Let me speak with them,' said he at last.

Resting a hand upon his shoulder, I stood and brushed the dust off my breeches. 'One thing more. John Stuart's son is now a captain in the British army at York Town. I have brought him here with me.' Campbell looked up in surprise. 'You remember him,' said I.

'The boy who was sent to England.'

'I have just now told him that it is you I have come to see here. He remembers your father.' I did not say, as I might have done, that Captain Stuart had evinced no interest in meeting with Campbell. And squeezing Campbell's shoulder now as I left him, I said, 'Speak for me to the Pamunkey.'

*

Among the Indians, there is no celebration can be accounted either proper or of any great importance unless there be both an enormous fire and a very large quantity of drink. So before nightfall there were many logs brought by the women to the open ground behind the village, and the men went from house to house gathering flagons. There seemed no orders given, but only some general guidance from the older people (that fellow the cartman proving to be a chief among them). The lighting of the fire at sunset was all the signal needed to bring most of the people out from their houses. Beyond the fire, and nearer the river, was a burial mound of a Pamunkey chieftain long dead; and before settling to the night's entertainment the villagers went down there – and I too, with Calvert, from curiosity. The old men made a small ceremony and poured a libation of grog onto the mound. An old woman sang a Pamunkey prayer-song to the dead man's spirit, and then another made a Christian prayer, till after a time they seemed well satisfied and returned up to the main fire.

Stuart had taken the two redcoats to post as sentries along the track leading into the village; for though the Pamunkey assured us their village was unregarded, and that the nearest farm was some miles off, yet it must be mere stupidity to take no precaution. While awaiting Stuart's return I sat by Campbell, with Calvert to my other side, the three of us upon a log drawn before the fire. The drinking had already commenced. There were some old fellows had produced hand-drums, which though they looked like toys, the expert wrists of the men soon set the suspended leather wads flicking to and fro. Once the beating rhythm settled, a few more old fellows joined the drummers in making a nasal and incomprehensible singing. The older women had places on logs near to the fire, but the younger women stayed further back with the children in the night shadows.

I had made sure to warn our redcoats against any attempt upon the women. But I well knew that should the women prove forward and willing, then my harsh warning must go for nothing. Now I kept the women in the corner of my eye; and it was a relief to me to see that the flagons did not go back to them.

'How long shall they continue, sir?' said Calvert after a minute, and with an unhappy glance at the singers.

'You would not rather be making the entrenchments in York Town, Mr Calvert?'

'No, sir.' A flagon then coming to us, I swigged a little and passed it to him. He took a mouthful, which made his eyes water. 'I did not think any Indians should treat us so friendly, sir. In the Carolinas we were ordered to keep away from them.'

I asked had he heard of the Indian princess Pocahontas, famed from the early days as a saviour of the British settlement. He said that he had heard of her.

'These are her people,' I said, gesturing about me. 'This is her tribe.'

'These?' said he in surprised disbelief.

I appealed to Campbell for confirmation of the fact.

Campbell nodded gravely. He reached by me and clapped a hand on Calvert's knee. And then with a deep seriousness that I recognized for jest, he related a vulgarity concerning this Pocahontas such as might turn a maiden's hair white. The story once done, Campbell lifted his hand and returned his attention to the fire. I saw that the whole proceedings had caused Calvert some real astonishment (as I suppose it might have done to any man unaccustomed to the blunt talk of the Indians in these matters). But I had not expected what came next, which was that Calvert called out Campbell for the ungentlemanly remarks. Campbell wisely ignored him. Calvert then began to rise, and he seemed about to make the veriest fool of himself till I put my hand upon his shoulder and pressed him down.

'Perhaps it was, as you say, Mr Calvert, uncivil. But we are not in a drawing room here. And if you rise to every bait that Campbell offers you, you shall have little time for any other occupation.' I took the flagon from Campbell, who was smiling now, and gave it to Calvert. And very pleased I was when Calvert blushed in confusion and at last took the flagon and drank. The Indians neither like nor trust a man who will not partake with them; and I daresay they are right.

It was an hour later, and I beginning to feel the first effects of the drink, when I noticed that Stuart had not returned from his posting of the sentries. Withdrawing myself from the increasing rowdiness by the fire, I wandered up toward the track to discover what kept him there. But hardly had I reached the village than I saw him seated upon the porch of that house the Pamunkey had given up to us for the night. His jacket was unbuttoned, and his boots were off. His stockinged feet rested on a neighbouring chair. A lantern shone at his elbow, and there was a book open in his hand. He raised his head from the book at my approach.

'We have missed you.'

'Not overmuch, I think,' said he; and nodding behind me, he remarked the Pamunkey fondness for noisy celebration.

'What is that?' said I.

He turned the book. 'Nothing. A manual given me by one of the Hessians.'

'Does he mean to teach you soldiery?'

'He thinks we have made our entrenchments at Gloucester very poorly. I believe he has some notion I shall convey the correct Hessian method to our engineers.' Stuart set down the manual, and I put my foot upon the bottom step. 'When shall they finish?' he asked, looking down now toward the fire.

'You know how long these things may be, Jonathan.'

'I do. But we cannot wait days here while they debauch themselves.'

This startled me, not only the words but also the tone of them. 'They shall not be hurried. Come down with me now.'

He set a hand upon the manual. 'I feel there is much good sense to be had from Chapter Four – Abatis, Fascines, Gabions and Fraising. At the very least, I shall sleep well on it.'

'You do not wish to come?'

'No. But I thank you that you have thought to fetch me.'

'Is something wrong, Jonathan?'

'Nothing that you may put right, Mr Douglas. Enough to say that I am disinclined at this moment to any merriment.'

This admission of low spirits was almost the firmest obstacle he might place before my curiosity; for it was the selfsame defence I had made for myself in the weeks following Major Andre's hanging. 'Then I will not trouble you further. The sentries—'

'They are in place, sir.'

I might have pressed him, I suppose, but that my wits were already a little dulled by the drink. Instead, when he took up the manual and opened it, I bade him goodnight, and came away from there. It was only as I drew near the fire that it occurred to me that the sound of the hand-drums and the singing must remind Jonathan of his dead father. For many were the nights of his boyhood that he had fallen asleep to these sounds at his father's side. And when Campbell the next hour asked after Stuart's absence I gave this as the reason, which Campbell understood, and I thought no more of it.

The night was both longer and harder than I had feared. The roasted venison was dug out from beneath the hot coals at midnight, the cooked meat being shared out by that old cartman (and he all the while looking lordly, dignified, and drunk beyond the power of speech). Having paced myself steadily, I retained at least part-ways my wits, though confessedly within a general fog of stupefaction. But certainly enough to observe with a genial indifference the several bare-knuckle fights that started up among the young bloods near the fire, and also the laughter and cheering of the women before they retired with the children to the houses. I joined in, too, with the whooping acclamation when young Calvert staggered drunkenly to his feet and went into the midst of the dancing men who must several times tug at his open jacket to keep him from falling into the glowing embers.

And all through this disordered entertainment Campbell brought me those young Pamunkey men who had sworn to travel south with him, and join the fight against the settlers in the Indian country. There were six of these fellows, and whether from fealty to Campbell or to get some revenge for the raped and killed woman, they were every one of them willing to work in aid of me. Not a word did I say to them of what they must do, but I only ate and drank with them, and so in the Indian fashion they came into my service, though under Campbell's direction.

A short time before sunrise an old woman came down from the village and set about her drunken husband with a club. While they tried to put her under restraint, I rose and stepped over Calvert's motionless body and continued up to the house to get what rest I could before our departure.

The reservation lay on a great bend in the river, and a large part of the reservation being wetlands it was little wonder that the Pamunkey should be expert upon the water. But as they canoed us down the Pamunkey toward the York, their skill in paddling and manoeuvring (and the fineness of their canoes) made a more considerable impression upon me than I had expected; for it was only among the northern Iroquois that I had seen paddlers their equal. Campbell had distributed some small amount of silver among the six Pamunkey who had joined with him. Now his intention was to proceed to a place above York Town before leading them over the peninsula toward Williamsburg, where the enemy troops were mustering. Campbell and his fellows were in the three canoes a short way ahead of us, with our three canoes following close behind.

As my canoe came near to Stuart's, I enquired after Calvert's present state. Stuart glanced down to where Calvert lay near his feet, hid from my view. 'He is green in his appearance, sir, but alive. It looks that alive may be as much as we should reasonably hope from him today.'

'It may have been as well, Jonathan, that you last night kept quietly to your book.'

'Aye,' said he, and smiled. He seemed about to say more but then a musketshot sounded somewhere downriver. The paddling stopped. The water whispered softly along the sides of our canoes. When a second shot followed the first, Calvert sat up groggily. We drifted on a few moments more in absolute silence. At length I signalled ahead to Campbell, and at this signal our canoes veered toward the bank.

'Get down here with your men,' I told Stuart quietly. 'You also, Mr Calvert.'

'Is it the French, sir?'

'If it is, they are not firing upon themselves.' As Stuart disembarked I told Campbell not to linger, but to carry on down to the York River and do just as we had planned; for three Pamunkey canoes must be nothing to the French or to the Virginian militia and should get peacefully past any trouble that lay ahead of us. 'If it is our marines you find there, do not stop to give any assistance to them.'

He relayed the order to his fellows and they were soon paddling fast downriver, standing well clear of the bank, and were fast lost from our sight. We waited some minutes, but no sound came back to us, neither voice nor musketshot. Finally I ordered Stuart to take his two redcoats and Calvert forward along the riverbank.

'I shall keep the canoes alongside of you. If we meet with nothing in the next mile, then you must re-embark.'

He moved his redcoats and Calvert around behind the rocks onto the higher bank, and once there they spread into the pines. He kept himself nearest the river, anchoring the line within call of me.

Our three remaining canoes pushed off and we moved slowly downstream. The stillness of the river, which had been so pleasant, was now become like a threat. My pistol lay primed in my lap. As we nosed around the riverbend I raised my spyglass and squinted to see through the dazzle of light on the water. In the far distance Campbell's canoes were passing out from the Pamunkey and into the York River and safety. My two Pamunkey paddlers then spoke with quiet urgency to each other, and I asked what they saw.

'Soldiers,' said the fellow to my front, and he pointed.

I turned the spyglass shoreward. 'It is the marines,' I then called up to Stuart on the bank. 'They are two hundred yards ahead of you.'

'Engaged?'

'It does not appear so.'

We went forward cautiously. As we drew nearer they saw us, and so I waved my arm and hollered, that the marines might not mistake us. I also called out to warn them of Stuart's approach, for I knew by bitter experience the accidents that might happen with primed muskets and fearful men. Coming to the shore, I saw that the marines were not alone, but they had with them a French soldier. This fellow was propped against the base of a rock, his white uniform stained with blood both about the waist and over his breeches. There was little sign of life in him, but only a gentle moaning.

I walked up the muddy beach and crouched by him.

'It is little good that fellow shall do you now, Mr Douglas,' said the marine lieutenant.

'Courier?'

'He had this.' The lieutenant handed me a satchel. Opening it, I found a number of letters and papers in French plain-text, and two letters in cipher. I asked which direction the lad had come. 'From the west, sir. It must be Williamsburg.'

'Alone?'

'Just him and the horse. When we dropped him, the horse bolted.'

Stuart then arriving with his redcoats and Calvert, I took myself aside and sat down to make a first perusal of the French messages. Those in plain-text seemed to be addressed to various ones of Lafayette's officers who must be on the Gloucester side. There was nothing extraordinary in these, but they were just such orders, encouragements, and replies to complaints and requests, as was to be expected from a military headquarters to weary officers in the field.

The two ciphers, however, gave the promise of something better; for though I had not the key by heart, I was as certain as I might be that I had seen the final sequence on one of these enciphered letters several times before. And just as certain that it was Lafayette's own name written there. But the final sequence on the other message was not remotely the same. I wondered was it perhaps from de Grasse. Or it might even be Lafayette again, but unsigned.

At last I returned the papers to the satchel and went and joined Stuart and the lieutenant, who were standing aside from the others and discussing quietly whether the young Frenchman should be left to die in his own time or if the greater mercy were to shoot him and be done.

'We shall take him with us,' said I.

'He shall not live, sir.'

'I daresay, Lieutenant. But while there is some small chance of having some information from the fellow, I want him by me. Have him put in my canoe, if you will. And I would be obliged if you did not kill him while you are about it.'

CHAPTER 8

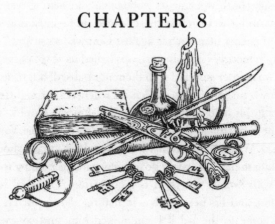

*O*ne man pricks his thumb upon a thorn in his own garden, goes peacefully to his bed, and is dead of a poisonous infection before the morning; another man courts every danger and yet walks whistling and unmarked from the bloodiest fray. God only is the cause. And surely it was God preserved that young French soldier's life; for though the marines were very careful putting him into the canoe, and the sailors equally careful in taking him aboard the sloop, yet the lad was unmoving all the while, with his eyes closed, and nothing but the feeblest beating of his heart to signify his continuing presence this side the Hereafter.

At my order, Calvert sat by him on the deck to make sure of the shade-cloth's protection, and to put a flask of water occasionally to the lad's lips in the hope that the moisture should at least prevent him choking upon a dry and swollen tongue. Calvert made no complaint of the duty, and seemed himself much improved from that wretched figure of the morning. But though much improved, he was still fragile, as I saw by his pallor and by his bloodshot eyes each time that he came to report to me on the Frenchman's condition.

We saw no sign of Campbell on our way down to York Town, for we kept to the midriver, and very likely the Pamunkey had turned their canoes aside into one of the many creeks on the York. Campbell had learnt that there were several dozen Pamunkey spread about the peninsula, both working as woodsmen and netting waterfowl in the creeks. And it was such as these whose aid he must now enlist to get word of enemy manoeuvres against Cornwallis's army.

Captain Symonds's patrolling sloops hailed us as we passed downriver, but we neither stopped with them nor paused, but rode the tide directly down to York Town, which we reached after nightfall.

'You want this fellow to live?' asked the surgeon, Gould, when we brought the Frenchman into his hospital (which was the York Town courthouse). When I replied that I did, he told me that I should then not leave him there. 'We have a dozen new patients coming to us each day now with swamp fevers. It is a contagion. The shot has gone through him, and his best hope is in nature, and in prayers.' Gould agreed to come to the lad if I summoned him, and so we left the hospital and took the Frenchman along to the Kendrick house. Here the men set down the stretcher in the library, and then left me, Stuart going to report to Major Ross.

'You need not stay, Mr Calvert,' said I, lighting a lamp upon the desk. 'You many find out your messmates, or retire to your bed, or what you will.'

'Shall you want anything, sir?'

'You may send the maid to bring me a pillow and blankets. I shall sleep here on the sofa tonight.' I sat at the desk and opened the Frenchman's satchel. Taking out the two enciphered letters, I spread the sheets before me.

'Shall you want food, sir?'

'No.'

'But I think that you must,' said another voice, and I turned sharply to the door. It was the widow Kendrick standing there and looking in upon us. In the next moment she saw the stretcher and the Frenchman.

'He is a French soldier, madam,' said Calvert. 'He is shot.'

'Is my house now an infirmary, Mr Douglas?'

'He is here by a singular necessity. You need not fear to be overrun.'

'Is he badly hurt?'

'He shall likely die.'

She came in and leaned over the stretcher. And then she did what few English women would have done, which was to kneel by the stretcher and put a hand on the fellow's face. 'Can he take food?'

'If he lifts his head in the morning, we may try.'

She glanced up. 'Was it your shot?'

'No.'

'He is very young.'

'He is a like age to Mr Calvert. And I am told that he was offered the opportunity of a peaceful surrender.'

'That is weak.'

'The lad is here now, madam. And in such a condition as neither accusation nor regret may mend. It is quiet he is now in need of. Quiet and rest, which I had hoped to give him here.'

She took his hand from his face. And though she would say more, she refrained and went out and fetched blankets and pillows. Returning, she covered the lad with a blanket, and with great gentleness put a pillow beneath his head. She left bedding on the sofa for me, and very civilly bade me goodnight.

I worked upon the ciphers till almost the morning, but broke only the first.

My Dear Weedon

 Though General Washington must be satisfied to learn that you have not suffered the loss of a single man under your command, I cannot agree with you that he shall be pleased. It has been now more than a month you have been on the Gloucester side, which I think must be sufficient time for a force exceeding a thousand men to have made some bolder and better strokes against Simcoe.

 Can it be true that even yet you hold your men fifteen miles distant from the first British defences? So it is reported to me; but I will not chastise you for what must surely be reported either in error

*or in malice. However, it is little to be expected that you shall
properly threaten the British (as you were sent to do, and must do)
from a distance such as that. I trust that I shall receive a more
satisfactory information of your position by the next report of it.
(You make bold to remind me of the men lost at Green Spring by
'a certain rashness of command'. Whatever may be said of
General Wayne – or of me – none may accuse us of torpor; and
a vigorous action must ever seem a rash one to men concerned
only for safety.)*

*As to the guns you have requested, I have made enquiry of
Admiral de Grasse. It is entirely possible that some 6 or 8 pounders
may be spared you, though I make no promise of it. Nothing shall be
finally decided till Generals Rochambeau and Washington have
arrived here and given their orders for the siege. We look for their
arrival within the week, and so you shall not be long in doubt of the
further supplies that may be afforded you.*

*You may put your mind at rest concerning the several ships that
you have seen proceeding north up the Bay. It is no British attempt
to land men to the rear of you, but the ships are some of Admiral de
Grasse's vessels gone up to the Head of the Elk (and to Baltimore),
there to meet with your comrades in the Continental Army. It is
hoped that the troops may then be ferried the more speedily with
their heavy guns down here to Williamsburg, and so no time to be
lost in waiting for them after.*

*I acknowledge your advice that Admiral de Grasse should attempt
to get some ships up into the river above York Town. I may tell you
that a similar advice has gone to him from several persons here. It
has, till now, been met with a sharp refusal.*

*It is left only to tell you that though the British continue building
their entrenchments and earthworks at York Town, there is yet some
doubt that they are in earnest in remaining there. And if
Cornwallis decide to remove his army off from that place, then it
must now happen by water, either upriver or over to the Gloucester
side. In such a case, you must be with your men the first obstacle
that prevents his escape into the backwoods of Virginia. A first and*

valuable obstacle, I trust; which will be the more likely the closer
and the sooner you move your men up to face the British line.

    I am yours respectfully
    Marquis Lafayette

'There is another I understand?' said Cornwallis, once he had read the decipherment. He handed the paper to O'Hara.

'It is in a different cipher, my Lord. I have not yet broke it.'

'It may interest you, Mr Douglas, to see a note that I myself received early this morning from New York.' Cornwallis beckoned Major Ross, who at once brought the note to me. It was dated the 6th day of September.

My Lord

    As I find by your letters that de Grasse has got into the Chesapeake, and I can have no doubt that Washington is moving with at least 6,000 French and Rebel troops against you, I think the best way to relieve you is to join you as soon as possible, with all the force that can be spared from hence, which is about 4,000 men. They are already embarked, and will proceed the instant I receive information from the Admiral that we may venture, and that from other intelligence the Commodore and I shall judge sufficient to move upon.

    I beg your Lordship will let me know as soon as possible your ideas how the troops embarked for the Chesapeake may be best employed for your relief, according to the state of circumstances when you receive this letter. I shall not however wait to receive your answer, should I hear, in the meantime, that the passage is open.

    I have &c.,
    H. Clinton

I looked up from the note and found Cornwallis was observing me closely. I asked him how the letter from General Clinton had come.

'The French cannot seal up the Bay completely. It is not the means of communication upon which I want your opinion, Mr Douglas, but the substance.'

'Any reinforcement must be welcome, my Lord.'

'So it must. But is it your opinion that the letter promises me reinforcement?'

'It shows a clear intent.'

O'Hara spoke without looking up from Lafayette's letter. 'We have had some experience of General Clinton's clear intentions. Regrettably, there seems an estrangement between his intentions and his actions.'

Cornwallis then rose from his desk, and with his hands clasped behind his back turned to consider the map on the wall. He made some speculative musing upon the movement of de Grasse's ships northward, as revealed by my decipherment. He wondered if Admiral Graves might know of it, and whether our ships might now return to challenge the depleted French fleet and retake the Bay. I gestured to the deciphered letter. I said that Lafayette's greater fear seemed to be that our army might abandon York Town and break north through Virginia.

'He would fear it the less if he considered it the more, Mr Douglas.' Cornwallis turned from the map. 'I cannot move an army onto the water in secrecy. De Grasse would have his fleet up the York within hours. Lafayette would move his men instantly over from Williamsburg to attack us. It must be a folly to attempt any flight from York Town while we have any fair hope of Admiral Graves and General Clinton.'

This was delivered almost as a statement to himself. And I could not help but notice that it was received by both O'Hara and Ross in silence, and with the distant looks of men who had heard the argument before. Heard it, I surmised, and remained unconvinced by it. But they made no open objection now against their commander.

Cornwallis retook his chair. 'Major Ross tells me that you have been among the Indians.'

'I believe they shall be useful to us, my Lord. They may move freely all about the Chesapeake.'

'Have you paid them?'

'A few shillings.'

'And for a few shillings more they shall leave you. Do not mistake these for those other Indians of your acquaintance. These are no Mohawks or Cherokees, Mr Douglas. I am told they are considered the tinkers of the Bay.'

'Only let the Washington and Rochambeau think that of them, my Lord, and they shall serve us very well.'

He leaned back in his chair and studied me. At last he said, 'We can offer them no protection here.'

'They shall not need it.'

'You may draw ten pounds from Major Ross. Nothing more till I have some better evidence of their usefulness to us.'

I asked him if I might call directly upon the services of Captain Stuart, should any such need arise. I explained that Stuart's familiarity with the Indians could be useful to me. Cornwallis agreed to this, and then receiving the decipherment back from O'Hara, he perused it thoughtfully. He asked me how long I might be about the decipherment of the other letter.

'There are ciphers unbroken after fifty years, my Lord.'

'Then we must not detain you longer.' When I hesitated to leave, he raised an eyebrow in question.

'My Lord, I could not help but notice as I came in Secretary Nelson's man upon the stairs.'

'Major Ross has mentioned to me your advice concerning Nelson. I am grateful for your concern, but he causes us no trouble.'

'My Lord—'

'Mr Douglas. You will allow that I am the master of my own headquarters. I have obliged you with your Indian tinkers. Now your time must be better spent upon the second decipherment than upon any concern for my judgement.'

After leaving the headquarters I made no prompt return to the second decipherment, for I had been closed in the library all the night, with only pen, paper and the ailing Frenchman for company. Instead I went along the main street a short way and then turned west by the white clapboard church. But a stone's throw to the rear of the church was a party of blacks working with shovels and picks; and they directed by a German officer who spared them nothing in their labour. Wooden stakes had been planted in several places by the engineers to show the extremities of the redoubt now under construction, and similar stakes made lines north-west and south-east, away from the redoubt. The ditch here was very shallow as yet; for the work had just begin upon this line, which was clearly intended for the inner entrenchment, and the town's last line of defence.

I followed the markers south-east and soon came to another redoubt. Here were no blacks, but only some loosed poultry scratching in the open earth, and so I continued on to the Hornwork, jutting out from the main line and commanding the southern approach. Out to the front of the Hornwork the land fell away gently. It was undoubtedly the best ground near the town, being neither marshy nor cut by small ravines like the ground to the north. And here, equally undoubtedly, must be the favoured point of attack for any enemy approaching from landward. A dozen blacks were at their work here, and when I climbed onto the loose foundations they had made for the parapet, I found Captain Stuart directing some sappers and soldiers at the far side of the ditch. The sappers were stripped to the waist like the blacks. Wielding axes and machetes, they were busily engaged with sharpening the ends of pine-logs to make palisades and fraising.

'Would you try your hand as a woodsman, Mr Douglas?' called up Stuart. 'There is an axe for any man who wants it.'

I remarked that it might be of use to those soldiers standing idly about, upon which one of the sappers good-naturedly told me that I should hope for nothing from those lazy bastards but only the pox. There was a general laughter from the sappers and soldiers, and then Stuart left them and crossed the ditch and scrambled up the wall to me.

'There is much work to do yet,' said I.

'Weeks,' said he, and pointed several hundred yards across the open ground to the two Pigeon Hill redoubts that made the best part of our outer defences to the south-west. The engineers' time had not been entirely wasted; for nearly every pine and cedar between the town and the outer defences had been felled, and the fallen trunks were now positioned to make obstructing abatis that might impede the enemy infantry.

'They shall palisade the beach both ends of the town,' said Stuart. 'It is not badly done.' He led me then to the northern side of the Hornwork and pointed out (fully a mile from us, and half a mile beyond the northern edge of the town) the Star redoubt of the Fusiliers. Of all our outer defences, this was the largest. Overlooking, and almost abutting the Williamsburg Road, it had the river at its back. That same work of clear-felling to make abatis and palisades was proceeding to the north-west of us, with several teams of bullocks and blacks engaged in dragging and positioning the fallen trees.

Like many of the younger officers, Stuart was much taken by all the proceedings attaching to the works; for the American war, in which they had seen most of their training and all of their action, had till now been mostly a war of skirmishes and field-battles. The sieges at Boston and Charleston had been neither of them typical, or fitting demonstrations of the regular European mode of entrenchment. He was some minutes more instructing me before I finally interrupted.

'I have a favour that I would ask of you, Jonathan.' He cocked his head, smiling pleasantly, and waited. 'Campbell is now with those Pamunkey upon the peninsula. He shall need to communicate with me here, and it is likely I shall need an intermediary to go out to him.'

'You have Calvert.'

'Your understanding shall serve me better. I have Lord Cornwallis's agreement on it.'

'May I think on it, sir?'

I was, I confess, more than a little surprised by his hesitation. 'You may. But I own, I had not expected a refusal.'

'I have not refused.'

'Neither have you accepted.'

'Am I ordered to it?'

'Jonathan—' said I, and then stopped. For in his face was more emotion than any simple refusal of my request might have engendered. And it suddenly came to me the reason. 'When you did not come down with me to the Pamunkey fire, I thought it must be that you remembered your father.' He looked away from me, and I said, 'And perhaps your mother also?'

'I remembered many things.'

'Is she well?'

'Well enough.'

'When you next write to her—'

'I shall send her your respects, Mr Douglas. Though in truth, she does not like to be reminded of those days.'

'I see.'

He forced himself to look at me. His face was flushed. 'You must know that my father had children of a Cherokee squaw.' When I inclined my head, he turned away again.

'I think no less of him for it,' said I.

'He was not your father.'

'He was my friend, Jonathan. A good and a true friend. If your mother would not stay with him in his work – and she would not—'

'You shall not blame her.'

'Here is not the place for this,' said I quietly, and I cast a glance toward the soldiers and sappers the far side of the ditch. He nodded, and apologized that he had forgot himself, which I waved aside. 'I shall not insist upon your aid of me. Only think on it, Jonathan.'

As he went down from the loose-piled earth to rejoin his men, it seemed that he carried the world; but neither I nor any man but only himself could throw that weight off from him. So I returned to the widow's house, and my own silent work, which I did but poorly, and full of distraction.

CHAPTER 9

'How is your patient this evening?'

'Once the lad wakes, and I have spoke with him, he shall be removed from the house.'

'Pray, not on my account.'

'I do assure you, Mrs Kendrick, your wishes were not considered. They have made a place for him at the hospital. They may tend to him properly there.'

'Is it by some order, Mr Douglas, that you must make yourself disagreeable?' I looked up from my soup. Calvert, across the table from me, kept his head down. 'I feared lest my house became a barracks,' said she. 'Shall you continue to chide me for that?'

This seemed almost a peace offering. But before I might accept it, there came her maid into the room saying that the Frenchman stirred. I tossed my napkin onto the table and went out, Calvert following close on my heels.

'Shall I send for Major Ross, sir?'

'Not till I instruct you. Stay here in the hall, and let no one in unless at my order.'

When I passed into the library I found that the young Frenchman was indeed stirring, and I drew up a chair by his stretcher. His eyes remained closed. There was the perspiration of a light fever upon his brow.

'Monsieur?' said I.

He answered me, but so feebly that I could not hear his words. I bent closer, and he murmured, '*Maman.*'

In French, I said, 'No, my lad. I am but a doctor. You need have no fear. The British have shot you, but you are safe now. You are returned to us.' His head went from side to side as if he dreamed. 'You are in the hospital in Williamsburg. Do you understand? You are safe here.'

'*Maman.*'

There was little strength in him, and there must be but little time I should have him in this state. I went out and ordered Calvert to fetch Gould from the hospital. 'Tell him to bring an opiate for the Frenchman. Warn him that he is to speak no English.' Withdrawing again to the library, I returned to the chair by the stretcher. The lad was in some small distress now, and I took his hand. He clutched mine with a force I had not expected.

'Do not fear, lad. You shall live. Do you hear me?'

'You,' said he with his voice but a whisper. 'I—'

'Yes?'

'Water.' He grimaced now, and his body twisted sharply, as if he felt for the first time the wound in his belly.

'Do not move. It shall be easier for you. Only listen, and try to answer me. You have been brought in here with a satchel. There were letters in the satchel, and we must now return the letters to the authors of them.' His free hand came up and grasped the air, which movement I did not at first comprehend. But then he whispered, 'Satchel.'

'Yes. And letters.'

When he grasped at the air again, I took up the empty satchel from by the desk and gave it into his hand. He clutched it against his chest, which seemed done by some professional instinct of protection.

'You have saved the letters. But they must now be put back into the hands of those officers who wrote them.'

'Marquis—'

'His has been returned. But the Marquis did not write all of them.'

'*Maman.*' His perspiration flowed ever more freely. He began to speak in a manner quite incomprehensible. He turned his head from side to side, but his body remained still, and he gripped my hand with the strength of a seaman drowning.

And though I questioned him more, my attempts to guide his fevered imaginings proved useless. Minutes passed, but I could not bring him back to my purpose. He was evidently in some considerable pain now, and the pain increasing. At Gould's arrival I went out into the hall.

'Once you have given him the opiate, how long shall I have?'

'It must take him almost instantly.'

'And how long shall he sleep?'

'A good while. A day or more, but it sounds that it is necessary.'

I told him to speak nothing while he examined the lad, and then I opened the door and ushered Gould in.

The examination was brief. The lad still gripped the satchel with one hand, but the other I took hold of to prevent him pushing Gould off. But Gould was quickly satisfied of the necessity of a full dose of the opiate, and while he opened his medicine box I got my arm beneath the lad's shoulders and gently raised him,

'Oh,' said the lad, and I thought I had hurt him, but when he said it again I wondered if it was '*eau*' he wanted, water.

Gould put the cup to the lad's lips. The lad drank it, and then murmured something scarcely audible, and I said, 'Yes. Water.'

'. . . beau,' he said, as Gould took away the empty cup. '. . . chambeau.' And he clutched hard to the satchel.

'Rochambeau?' said I. 'General Rochambeau?'

'You may lower his head now,' said Gould.

'Is it the letter, lad? But it cannot be from Rochambeau.' His eyes were distant, and his weight grew ever heavier upon my arm. A thought struck me, and I said, 'Is it not from Rochambeau, but to him? Is it a letter to the General?' I lightly slapped the lad's cheek.

'He cannot hear you, Mr Douglas.'

One word may break a code, if only it be the right word and in the right place. And with a letter there is no word more useful than a name; for men have habits so deep they seem almost nature, and a name is ever signed as the last word upon a letter without thinking. But once match the correct name to the last figures of a ciphered letter, and the key is halfway turned in the lock.

But to have the name and not its place in the letter is to suffer the agonies of Tantalus. And so did I, after I had seen Gould out, and for some hours.

Rochambeau? General Rochambeau? Comte de Rochambeau? Mon Général le Comte de Rochambeau? If I guessed right, and the letter was indeed intended for the French general, then somewhere in the opening lines of the cipher must be a match. But the possibilities were far too many, both the exact name and the placement of it, and once I had wasted hours in trying endless variations, I did what Francis Willes, my first tutor in the art of deciphering, had ever advised me. I put down my pen and walked away from the desk.

They had not yet taken the young Frenchman to the hospital, and he slept upon the stretcher with an unnatural soundness. In the lamplight his face was serene, as if he might be sleeping in his own bed in Paris or Lyon, and nothing to disturb him on the morrow but only the smile of his sweetheart. What he knew, I could not; for it was sealed up in his dreams. And so I stepped by him and moved about the library shelves.

It was no great collection of books, but only the usual tomes that must furnish any gentleman's house in the colonies (which is mainly histories, belles lettres, yearly almanacs of the country, and numerous London magazines). Running a finger idly over the spines, I occasionally drew out a volume. There was an edition of Paine's *Common Sense*, with the pages uncut, and further along I found several novels tucked discreetly beside Thucydides. My hand alighting upon

Sterne's *A Sentimental Journey*, I was soon browsing the opening pages by the light of a wall candle at my shoulder. A soft knock came at the door, at which I raised my eyes expecting Calvert. But it was the widow Kendrick stepped in. She said nothing, but gestured to the shelves at my side.

'You may speak, Mrs Kendrick. The lad shall not be wakened.'

'I came only for my book. I had not meant to disturb you.'

'Please,' said I, and stepped aside from the shelves to allow her by. She came across the room, and directly to that place where were the novels. Crouching, she touched a hand over the slim volumes. There was a hesitation in her search, and I said, 'I trust that I have not stolen your reading.'

'No.' She took a volume and then rose. 'I am only surprised that you should have selected Mr Sterne for your amusement.'

'You are well acquainted with your shelves.'

'My husband was not a man for social entertainments. I am perhaps better acquainted with my shelves than I ever expected to be.' I made no remark in reply, and she glanced down at the French lad, and then up to me. 'Francesca is afraid for her safety here. I have told her that there is nothing to fear.'

'I am sure that you are right.'

'That is only as much as I may expect from any of the officers, Mr Douglas. From you, I would in this instance welcome your plain speaking.'

I considered, and then I said, 'You shall be safe here till any siege begin. It is no certainty yet. But if it happen, Lord Cornwallis shall not want the burden of the local townspeople inside his entrenchments.'

'We shall be ejected.'

'The chance to leave shall be offered you. And if it comes to that, you would be unwise to stay.'

'How likely is a siege?'

'That must be only an opinion.'

'And that is an evasion.'

'Very well. In my opinion, it is very likely. But you shall have fair warning of it. For the present, you are quite safe here. You may give Francesca my assurance.'

She dipped her head to me, and thanked me that I had not dissembled.

'It seems you are a Stoic, Mrs Kendrick.'

'I fancy myself a thwarted Epicurean, Mr Douglas. And I would not be so presumptuous as to venture an untutored opinion on your own philosophy. I shall leave you to your Sterne.' With this sally she crossed to the door, where she paused and looked back. 'Your Mr Calvert seems a pleasant young gentleman. I hope you may give him some occupation to take his mind from the conquest of Francesca.' She held my look steadily. And when I at last inclined my head, she bade me goodnight, and then dipped her own head to me and withdrew.

After she was gone, I turned a few more pages of Sterne; but my attention soon wandered and I returned him to the shelves and laid myself down upon the sofa. The light of passing lanterns came in at the window, and the talk of the men; for work on the entrenchments was not stopped at sunset, but the parties of blacks and soldiers were as busy by night as by day now, digging by lantern-light and using the cooler hours to industrious effect.

My mind turned then on Jonathan Stuart, and on his boyhood spent in the Indian country, his several years at school in England, and now his first years of manhood in the American war. His mother was a decent woman, and I much doubted that she had poisoned the lad's mind against his own father. But his loyalty to her was very strong. And though in boyhood he had been always at his father's side, and almost a shadow to the older man, it seemed that this earlier affection and respect he had now quite consciously put by. In those early days when I had been so often in company with the family, I had frequently wondered what it must be to have a son such as Jonathan. Indeed, I wondered it still, and sometimes most powerfully.

Just why a mind released from conscious labour should then labour to better purpose undirected, I know not; but so it was with me that night. And as my eyelids drooped in tiredness, and I continued to think on Jonathan and matters unconnected with the decipherment, the name Lasceaux came into my mind. The suddenness with which it came to me as I half-dozed was something peculiar. After a moment I rubbed a hand over my face and sat up.

The French lad had not stirred. Rochambeau, he had said. And who should write to General Rochambeau directly but only one of the most senior officers? By which reasoning I had already tried the names of de Grasse, Lafayette, St Simon, the duc de Lauzun and some several others as a match for the last ciphers of the letter. But, fully believing him to be in company with Rochambeau and Washington, and nowhere near Williamsburg whence the ciphered letter had come, till now I had not thought to try the name of Lasceaux. But once allow that the senior Intelligence officer of the French was not to the north, allow that he had gone on ahead of the generals to Williamsburg, and then what could be more likely than that he should write to Rochambeau?

Upon the instant, I was returned to the desk and at work with my pen. First I wrote out Lasceaux's name and tried it upon the last figures of the cipher. When this gave me nothing I turned my attention to the triple in both names, 'eau', and with this I made another assault upon the opening and closing of the letter. It was scarcely a minute and I had found matching ciphered triples in the opening and closing lines. My heart beat a little faster; I was fully awake now, and I wrote the three letters above, then quickly verified the match of the 'c' from both names. This done, it was all done, and the key at last found. I filled in the remainder of each name, which gave me half the ciphered alphabet, and from that I wrote out the entire decipherment almost directly, with hardly an amendment or correction to stop the flow of my pen.

In half an hour it was finished.

Williamsburg, 9th September.

Comte de Rochambeau, I have been at Williamsburg three days, and yesterday went out to our ships and delivered to Admiral de Grasse your congratulations and your letter. The fleet is exactly that strength reported to us, and the Admiral in control of the whole Bay, and the York River blockaded in its lower reaches. The Admiral has not let his fleet sit idle, but everywhere are such signs of industry and dispatch as I am certain shall meet with your approval and approbation, and as must gladden the heart of General Washington and his officers.

Of the three thousand troops brought from the West Indies, nearly every one is now ashore and (to my observation) they are suffering no ill effect of the journey. They appear in good health, and are well equipped and in full readiness to fight. (St Simon commands them, from whom compliments, etc.)

De Barras has brought nine ships down and joined with de Grasse. There has been already a quantity of heavy artillery put ashore, and all unmolested by the British, who keep themselves safe in York Town. There is a want of good carriages for the guns, and transport is lacking, for which reason most of the ships' carpenters have been landed. But the work proceeds steadily, and I think shall make no impediment to us.

The Admiral has sent several frigates and transports up to the Head of the Elk, there to fetch down that part of our forces no longer marching with you. There is a universal expectation of their imminent return, which I shall instantly inform you of when it happens. None here fear any interception of these transports by the British, whose own few ships remain sealed within the York River, whence they dare not venture into the Bay lest they put themselves beneath de Grasse's heavy guns.

Lafayette has about three thousand useful men mustered here under his command, and General Weedon a thousand more on the far side of the York River, sealing off the British garrison on Gloucester Point. It is common talk here that Weedon should be either reinforced or replaced upon your arrival. I make bold to recommend a reinforcement. For I fear that to remove one of the American generals at such a time might instantly open that rift between our two armies that you have studied so hard to avoid. Even if it be done at General Washington's order, Lafayette has with his usual indiscretion made his unhappiness with Weedon a public matter, and it must be that we (that is to say, you) should get the blame of any such open slight to the Americans.

General Greene is also here. By a foolish accident he was shot in the leg by one of Lafayette's men as he came into our lines. However, he makes nothing of the injury and gives something of his courage to our soldiers as he goes about the encampments with the aid of a stick.

The British preparations at York Town I shall go to see tomorrow. By report, Cornwallis makes both an inner and outer line, the outer consisting of earthen redoubts where his best artillery shall make a warm welcome for us. Lafayette sends patrols daily to harass the British sappers, and I shall join myself to one such patrol in the morning (and an engineer with me) that we may make a fair survey of the British defences. All being well, both a map and my own notes shall be ready to put into your hand at your arrival.

The local people are thoroughly our allies (and even more so than most others in the American colonies), but they show a great concern for their crops and stores, which are already much depleted by the aggressive foraging of the British (Tarleton's Legion, I understand, to the fore). The British army having been here the longer, they are presently judged the harder on this particular matter; but the larger our own numbers grow here, and the longer we must stay, the more we must expect the same judgement against us. Therefore the siege, after you are arrived here, should not be long delayed.

My respects to General Washington, and my assurance to you both that no preparation is neglected here, but our noose tightens daily upon the British.

Yours in good hope, Lasceaux.

P.S. There are in the town a dozen or more deserters from the British, but these are the scum of the earth, and beyond some petty information we have got from them, they are quite worthless to us. I am working to discover those few people here who remain loyal to the British Crown, and have already had two farmers, a father and *son, identified to me as British spies. I shall see to them upon my return from York Town.*

A father and son.

Chilled to the heart, I called Calvert down from his bed to watch over the Frenchman; and then I went myself to find Colonel Tarleton.

CHAPTER 10

*T*arleton would make no move from York Town till the hour before dawn. But once I had Tarleton's word that I might then accompany his patrol, I quickly went to the headquarters where an ensign roused Major Ross for me. I gave Ross the decipherment, which after he had perused we agreed that Lord Cornwallis need not be wakened on account of it, but that it might wait till the morning. I told Ross of my intention to go with a foraging party out toward Old Point Comfort, but I made no mention to him of the Morgans. Returning then to the Kendrick house, I snatched a few hours of troubled sleep upon the library sofa. When I finally rose to dress, my movement disturbed Calvert in his bedroom above, and he came down.

'Sir?' said he, looking in.

'I am out from the town until this evening, Mr Calvert. You must arrange this fellow's removal to the hospital,' said I, indicating the Frenchman. 'You are then to remain here and receive any messages that come for me.'

'Yes, sir.'

'Have you lain with Mrs Kendrick's maid?'

'No, sir.'

'When you speak with Doctor Gould, you shall not waste the opportunity to procure some prophylactic for yourself.' He seemed about to protest, but then saw my look and stopped himself. I finished buttoning my jacket. 'The pox shall be the least of your concerns if Mrs Kendrick discover you, lad. Do not take her for a fool.'

To the south end of Main Street I found the horses already brought from their stables and standing quiet as they were tacked up by the grooms. Most of Tarleton's Legion was encamped in a field a few hundred yards outside the town's entrenchments, but his officers kept a mess in the blacksmith's barn by the inn. A few of these cavalry officers now wandered out from their breakfast to make a casual inspection of the grooms' early work. There were torches on every side of the cobbled yard, and the gold buttons on the officers' green jackets gleamed in the flickering light.

Colonel Tarleton was seated by the barn entrance, his man kneeling before him and fixing the spurs. 'Shall you come with us alone, Mr Douglas?' said Tarleton, looking up at my approach.

'I cannot need more defenders than this,' said I, opening my hand about the yard. He then pointed out three horses, saying that I might have my pick of them, which when I had done, he called his men about him.

'Mr Douglas joins us today. He has an enquiry to make at a farm out by Old Point Comfort. My column shall proceed in that direction, the usual orders and formation applying.' He gave to various ones of them some more particular instructions, and also to those officers who would lead out the other foraging parties. He had a few jesting words, too, for the young fellows standing with muskets; by which words I understood that these were the juniors of the Legion, and designated as the drivers of the carts. In the next minute the men were to their horses, the hoofs clacking over the cobbles as they filed past us from the yard.

I complimented Tarleton upon the good condition of his horses.

'There are two hundred more fed only on hope,' he said in answer to my remark. 'It awaits only the General's order to slaughter them. Let us mount now, Mr Douglas, or these shall leave us in their dust.'

Openings had been left at a few places in our entrenchment as entry and exit points, and it was through one of these that we now proceeded from the town. We went out toward the Pigeon Hill redoubts, the felled pines lying to either side of us, and a soft grey light now began to spread across the eastern horizon. There came a flight of ducks up from the Bay; they went over us and disappeared across the river toward Gloucester Point. Out at the redoubts, the sappers exchanged jocular profanities with the column as we passed, but then a quiet descended as we traversed the last quarter-mile of open ground to the wood. Though there had been no enemy harassment of our foraging parties this side of the town, the landing of the French troops had emboldened the local militia, and Tarleton and his men were wary.

But after a mile travelling through the wood, and the dawn light growing stronger, these first apprehensions lifted with the darkness. There was then some quiet talk among the men, and Tarleton took the opportunity to ask me what I had witnessed aboard the French fleet. He would have from me the details of the sea-battle, and I gave him what little enlightenment I could, adding, 'Captain de Bougainville has almost the fairest reputation in the French navy. If Lord Rawdon must have a gaoler, he could have done very much worse than Bougainville.'

'In truth, Mr Douglas, I had feared they might do him some harm. Rawdon's reputation with the enemy is scarcely better than my own.' Tarleton was of an age with Rawdon, not yet thirty, and when he smiled now he seemed even younger. He had the fair skin of the Irish, but months of riding beneath the American sun had tanned his face, so that there appeared a stark line on his neck beneath his opened collar. His reputation was long since made in the war, and his Legion become the sharpest weapon in Cornwallis's armoury. There was not a man in our army more despised and feared by the rebels than Colonel Banastre Tarleton.

'There are no Americans in the French fleet.'

'For which he may thank God,' said he. 'But I must be glad that Rawdon is not ill-treated. I shall take it as a good omen for the day.'

The woods opened in several places into wide clearings where tobacco had once been planted; but the ground was mostly exhausted and rank with weeds or lying fallow till the next season. There were a few small farmhouses we passed, but these had already been visited by earlier foraging parties and so we made no stop at them but continued until we came to a track leading toward the James River. And along this track we turned off at the first farm entrance, and found a small clapboard farmhouse in a cleared hollow. The farmer was seated on the steps of his porch as we rode up, almost as if he expected us. He did not rise, but looked over to where one of our carts was drawing to a stop by his barn. Tarleton bade him good morning.

'You'll be Tarleton,' the fellow said, chewing a plug of tobacco.

'I am, sir.'

'And you'll be wantin' my grain.' When Tarleton drew a letter of requisition from his pocket, the man said, 'I don't need to see no papers. I got three sons, but they're all in Williamsburg. And you got more 'n enough fellers here to burn me out.'

'We have not come to burn anyone out, sir.'

'What you payin'?'

Tarleton told him.

'Guess bargainin' won't do me no good.'

'It is a fair price, and what your neighbours have had.'

'Man with a hoe likely got a different idea what fair is than a feller with a sword.' The farmer's sleeves were rolled up his lanky arms. His hair and eyebrows were bushy and red, and he let his elbows rest on his knees, with his enormous fingers linked loosely together. At my estimation and by his voice, he must be only a generation distant from Ireland, which was Tarleton's own country. But in the colonies, one generation is more than sufficient to stiffen a man's pride. He looked at Tarleton directly now, and had no fear of him. But after a time he spat out the tobacco plug, and then rose and walked across to the barn.

Inside the barn was a main floor and a loft; and upon inspection, both places proved surprisingly empty. There were only ten sacks of corn below, and in the loft but a few forks of hay. Tarleton's look darkened when he received the report from above. He turned to the farmer and asked after the horse-feed, and where it was kept.

'Don't have no horses.'

'Then how do you plough?'

'Hoe.'

'Do not try me, sir.'

'You want my grain, there it is, an' I'll take your money. If'n you don't want it, you don't.' He shrugged like he cared very little either way.

Tarleton fixed the fellow with a steely gaze. It was quite clear what had happened: the farmer had been told of Tarleton's calls upon the neighbouring farms, and had taken the precaution of securing his own stores against a similar depredation. His grain and hay was likely sitting on his own wagons, hidden in the woods nearby. But at last, and somewhat to my surprise, Tarleton's gaze slid from the fellow. Without further argument, he instructed one of his officers to pay the farmer for what was in the barn.

'Load it, and let's away.'

This was soon done, and no word more spoken between Tarleton and the farmer. As our column came up from the hollow I remarked Tarleton's composure in the face of the farmer's obstinate cunning.

'It was not my good temper spared him,' Tarleton replied. 'But only that it may be useful to have some supplies outside our entrenchment. That fellow shall keep his stores hid from the French as surely as from ourselves. If the need arise, I shall have them from him at gunpoint.' Glancing at me, he added, 'But we shall not need a second such outlying supply. I trust that your friends the Morgans shall understand that.'

'And if they do not?'

'Then you must help them to a better understanding.' By his look, I could not mistake his absolute resolve to have the Morgans' grain from them, whatever their loyalty or service to us. He flicked his horse and drew on ahead of me.

The Morgan farm straddled a creek that ran down a broad valley into the James River. Near the head of this creek stood the two-storey farmhouse, a place built of pine and cedar by Cable Morgan's own hands. Thirty or forty acres of cleared land lay by the house, but there was much heavy woodland above. We left two infantrymen up by the woods to stand sentry, and then our column went through the top field where one of Morgan's blacks worked to repair a stretch of broken fencing. I recognized the fellow as Caesar, a slave who had been with the Morgans for many years. He stood and watched us go by.

The James River was but a half-mile distant, a small part of it visible through the lower pines as we went down. We soon passed into the farmyard, and as Tarleton and I dismounted, Sally Morgan came out from the house.

I bade her good morning, and she said nothing and returned me no kindly look. Tarleton put his hat beneath his arm and we went forward to her.

'Madam,' said he, introducing himself; and though she gave him her hand, there was little friendliness in it.

I at once asked after her husband, and if I might see him directly.

'He is gone into Williamsburg,' said she.

'And David?'

'He has gone with his father. Why have you come here, Mr Douglas? And in despite of my request that you keep away. You are not welcome.'

'When shall they return?'

'Not today. I have had a message from Cable just this morning.'

I now feared the worst. 'What manner of message?' At this, she looked at me askance, hearing some meaning in my voice that she could not quite decipher. 'Did he say when he should return?'

'They want me to go to Williamsburg tonight. I expect that we shall return here together.' She was unsettled now, for she had sensed my fear, even if she knew not the reason of it. 'You must go now, Mr Douglas. I have things I must attend to before I leave.'

'You cannot go into Williamsburg, Mrs Morgan.'

'You shall not order me.'

'Sally,' said I; but the words died in my throat. Then I simply opened my hand toward the door, indicating that we must speak further inside. When she hesitated, Tarleton stepped forward and opened the door for her, and she looked from him back to me. I said nothing. With her fingers now playing over the button at her throat, she at last went in.

Her girl Lizzy was inside, and Lizzy came and clutched her mother's skirts and looked with suspicious curiosity up at Tarleton. His silver scabbard first drew her eye, and then the feathers of his hat beneath his arm. Seeing this, he plucked a feather from the hat and crouched to offer it. But she would not take the feather from his hand, and so I took it from him and gave it to her. All this while Mrs Morgan called to the slave-girl in the kitchen out back, telling her to come and fetch Lizzy away. When this was finally done, Mrs Morgan closed the door and facing me said, 'You have put a fear into me, Alistair.'

'I hope without reason.' I directed her to a chair at the table, and myself took a chair opposite. Tarleton remained standing near the door. 'When did they go into Williamsburg, Sally? And what called them there?'

'They set out Monday morning. It was to keep the boat that they went.'

'The log-canoe?'

'The same that you crossed in. The French are taking every boat they can find along the James. We never thought that they should come this far. Or that they should want a small boat such as ours.'

'When?'

'They came Saturday. They landed below and marched up from the river.'

'French or Continental?'

'French. And few words of English could we get from them either. But very civil. They gave Cable a written demand for the boat. That was in English. Either he must surrender the boat to them at once, or present himself in Williamsburg to plead his need of it.'

'Plead before whom?'

'A French officer.'

I asked did she recall the name, and when she shook her head, I prompted, 'Lasceaux.'

'I cannot remember.'

'They might have had the boat without asking Cable's leave. You could not have stopped them.'

'They had no present need for the boat. Cable believed it was our permission for its use they mainly wanted. They sought to know if they might have it when they willed. They made no threat to us. Once Cable agreed to go into Williamsburg, to explain his need of the boat, they were satisfied.'

'But he did not go at once.'

'The next day was Sunday. And Cable and David must hide the boat.' She told me that the log-canoe was now in the first creek east from the farm, drawn onto a bank fifty yards up from the main river, hidden there among brush and reeds. 'Cable did not see he should bother you, Alistair. Not till he was certain that they might take it.'

'I am not angry.'

'Nor are you pleased.'

'Was there some reason he took David?'

'If they could not be persuaded in Williamsburg, then David would go to York Town to tell you of it. Cable would return here to find a better hiding place for the boat.'

'How came the message that you got from him today?'

'It came by Caesar. You have passed him in the top field.'

'It is the black repairing the fence up by the wood,' I told Tarleton. 'Fetch him down.' Once Tarleton was gone, I asked Sally if I might see her husband's letter.

'There was no letter. The message was that I should return with Caesar to Williamsburg before dark. And I was to bring a payment for the miller.'

'Was that usual?'

'Not the payment. We generally pay him in the Fall. But he would not ask if he was not in need. He is a friend to Cable.'

Through the window now we saw Tarleton give his orders, and

then two of his men rode out from the yard and up the track toward the top field. Even when they were gone, I kept my eyes upon the window; for I hardly dared now to face Sally Morgan. Every part of what she had told me gave me such misgivings as were compounded now to a cold and icy dread.

A father and a son. The time of the French party's arrival at the Morgans' farm agreed exactly with the intention expressed in Lasceaux's letter. And to have got Morgan into Williamsburg on such a pretext as the requisition of the boat, and completely unsuspecting, was a stroke fully worthy of Lasceaux's reputation. That David had gone too was a dreadful misfortune, and one I could not repair. For I had little doubt now but that both were fallen into Lasceaux's hands, and that their lives must be suspended by the slenderest of threads.

'Alistair?'

'We shall hear what Caesar has to tell us.'

'They cannot be in any danger. The boat is nothing.'

'Let us wait for Caesar.'

It was a heavy few minutes we must wait, and I with such discomfort now in her presence, and beneath the shadow of my fears, that I met Sally Morgan's every attempt to get some further understanding from me with a polite but unworthy dissembling. It was a relief to us both, I think, when we heard Tarleton's riders at last return into the yard. The relief, however, was brutally short-lived.

'Your fellow Caesar is gone,' said Tarleton, coming in. 'Our sentries saw him leave the field and go into the woods soon after we came down. They thought nothing of it. Two are now in search of him.'

'They shall never find him,' said she. 'The wood is thick. Caesar knows every part of it. But I cannot think why he should run.'

'Because he saw me arrive,' said I. 'And because he would not be questioned concerning the message that he brought you.'

'We cannot stay much longer,' said Tarleton, making a glance through the window toward the barn. She noticed the glance, and turned to me in question.

'Colonel Tarleton and his men have not come out here only as my escort, Sally.'

She did not at first comprehend my meaning; and before I might explain it to her, Tarleton stepped forward, taking from his pocket Lord Cornwallis's order for the requisition of supplies. With a flush of shame upon his cheek (which was to his credit as a man, but which would not impede him as a King's officer), he presented the order. As she ran her eyes over the paper, he told her that he undertook personally that there would be no delay in the payment, nor any under-pricing of the Morgans' grain. Though he undoubtedly meant well by these words, they seemed, in the present circumstances, something worse than the veriest insult.

She made no answer to begin, but read a while more, though it could not have been to the end of the order. Then she returned it to his hand, saying quietly, 'Of course,' and, 'Thank you'; but altogether with an air of complete distraction, as if both the order and his words were matters so slight now as to be nothing against what was in her mind. And then she said to me quite suddenly, 'I must go to Williams-burg.'

'You cannot.'

'It is my husband and my son.'

'It is not they who have called you. And if you were to go there now, I fear it would be much to their harm.' Her sharp protest I fully expected; and once she had made it, I told her firmly, 'You must allow me to make my own enquiries of them. Which I may do the better, and with an easier mind, once you are from here and back with us to York Town.'

'Cable expects me.'

'You cannot help them, but only by coming away with us now.'

'You should not have come back.'

'Sally—'

'When Cable told me you had returned, I knew it must end badly. I knew that something would happen. You would not keep away. Why would you not keep away?'

'Mrs Morgan,' broke in Tarleton, 'you must pack a trunk for yourself and your daughter if you would come with us now.'

She said nothing in reply to him. But she gave me a look that went through me, and then rose, defeated, and went to pack for York Town. All the while that she packed I thought of Cable and David Morgan. Whatever I must do, I determined that they should not join Major Andre and make two further indelible black marks upon my conscience.

CHAPTER 11

*A*s I came with Calvert from the widow Kendrick's house that night, and walked along the bluff with him, he drew my attention to the furthest fires on the lower beaches at both ends of the town. 'They have made a start there on the palisades, sir. There is talk that Captain Symonds shall sink a line of boats. That must give us some defence against de Grasse.'

'In my experience, Mr Calvert, there are a hundred plans talked of for every one that is carried.' I asked him what else had happened in my absence and he told me of some small reinforcement ferried over to Gloucester Point, and of a party of townspeople calling on Mrs Kendrick to request her name upon a petition protesting against the petty thieving by the soldiers and the blacks.

'Major Ross was very grateful to her that she did not sign.'

I had, at that moment, a fair reason of my own to be grateful to Mrs Kendrick, for she had taken Mrs Morgan and the child Lizzy into her house with no objection. Indeed, once I had told her something of the circumstances, she had taken them in with a genuine concern.

The bluffs above the river were not particularly high, and were certainly no cliffs, but they made a stout wall perhaps twice the height of those several houses erected on the bedrock behind the sandy beaches. The shingle roofing of these places was just below us as we made our way along the path on the bluff above. At length we entered the southern valley leading down toward the river.

Lanterns and torches were clustered in several places along this valley, and yet more lights moved up and down like so many fireflies. The sounds of men scraping and digging came up to us, and their voices, for scores of men were at work there, cutting caves into the steeper slopes. Once Calvert had pointed out my destination I sent him back to the house; and I was soon standing with Major Ross and Lieutenant Sutherland, the chief engineer, and peering into the brightly lit cavern that was to be Lord Cornwallis's headquarters should any bombardment drive him from the upper town. The cave was about seven feet in height, fifteen in breadth and fifteen deep. Sappers worked on the timber props to the rear (which were like to miners' pit-props), while a pair of blacks laboured with picks on the stony earth of the walls.

I remarked the good progress of the sappers, but Sutherland seemed ill-satisfied. With some small grumblings about the want of better picks, he went to supervise at the magazines being dug across the valley.

'I have not yet met an engineer who did not want more tools,' said Ross to me quietly once Sutherland was gone. 'But I own, there is something in it. General Clinton has failed to send down what tools we have asked for. We shall now be hard pressed to have everything done.' Then turning from the cave we went together down toward the river. For we were again invited aboard the *Guadeloupe* to dine with Captain Symonds and Lord Cornwallis, but this time more privately, and I would speak with Ross now before going aboard. My whole concern was centred upon the Morgans; and it was Ross, I thought, whose aid I might most profitably call upon.

After recounting to him briefly my long connection with the Morgans, I told him also of the unfortunate accident of Cable and David Morgan's presence out by the *Guadeloupe* when de Grasse had first entered the Bay. I concluded with the decipherment of Lasceaux's letter (which he had read), my visit to the Morgans' farm, and my bringing of Mrs Morgan and her daughter back to York Town. Though he commiserated with my troubles, it was a much more businesslike commiseration than I had hoped for.

'From what you say, Douglas, there was little more that these Morgans might have discovered for us. Their farm is some distance from Williamsburg. That is where we must now look for information.'

'My concern is not for any further use they might be to us. They have shown us a real fealty.'

'As have these,' said Ross, gesturing to the encampment of blacks below. 'But if a dozen die, it shall not turn the war.'

'These have our protection.'

'For the present,' said he, which equivocal remark somewhat surprised me. But his mind ran on a different matter, and he said, 'If these Morgans have been taken as you fear, should we have any apprehension of what they may tell Lasceaux?'

'Their sole connection with us has been through me. Or through men in my service.'

'Then no other is in jeopardy.'

'They are in jeopardy, Major. And of their lives.'

Ross bade me to silence then, for we were approaching near to the blacks' encampment. Some hundreds of these plantation runaways milled about the tents, both men and women, and even a few score children. And many of them had gathered by the fires and were singing, as blacks in any number are wont to do. It was the men mostly who sang, a deep and sombre harmony that carried over the river and into the night. We passed in silence. And then with the encampment at length behind us, Ross said, 'Had we more tools, those fellows should not then waste their time so.'

'I would get the Morgans out from the hands of the French. I would get them free, and back here to us.' He made no reply to me. We walked along the sandy track toward the wharf now, and Major Ross kept his gaze upon the ships in the river. After a time, I said, 'I would go to Williamsburg, and I had hoped for your aid in it.'

'If you would have me apply to Lord Cornwallis—'

'No.'

'Because you fear a refusal.'

'Lord Cornwallis has but a single purpose here, which is the preservation of his army. I cannot throw the responsibility of the Morgans upon his shoulders. He must only shrug them off, as you know very well.'

'You cannot call him to answer for that.'

'Tomorrow Dr Gould shall take the wounded Frenchman to Williamsburg in the early morning. I would go with Gould as his helper.' Ross glanced at me, but did not dismiss my suggestion out of hand. I made bold to add, 'An order from you would suffice, Major. I would present myself at the hospital and inform them of what I intend. And if they send to the Headquarters for confirmation of it—'

'Williamsburg is now behind the enemy lines, Mr Douglas. If you were caught there, no quarter would be given you. You would be hanged for a spy just as surely as was Major Andre.'

'The Morgans are already caught. And what quarter shall be given them?'

Ross locked his hands behind his back and strode toward the wharf, his head down. I saw that he was out of temper, and that my request now preyed upon his mind. He was not an unfeeling man, and knew we must have some obligation to the Morgans. There was a heavy silence between us, which I at last must break.

'I have presumed upon you, Major.'

'If I am intemperate, Douglas, the fault is mine entirely. The day has been a long one indeed. Your request comes as the last of all too many I have had before me.' He lifted his chin toward the *Guadeloupe*. 'It has not helped that Captain Symonds believes our navy shall soon come to our relief.'

'You are doubtful of it.'

'Whatsoever my own thoughts, it is only Lord Cornwallis shall decide the army's disposition. For the present, he decides us to stay. I am content.' But he was evidently very far from content; and it was into this discontent that I had so carelessly introduced my own troubles. When we came to the wharf, he stopped and faced me. 'Is there truly no other who might go to their aid? Or no other means by which these Morgans might be brought to safety?' When I turned my head, his lips tightened. One of the boatmen sent for us from the *Guadeloupe* then called out to us. Ross left off from his thoughts and stepped onto the wharf. I put a hand upon his arm.

'I shall go to Williamsburg tomorrow, Major. With the help of your order or no.'

'You shall not go anywhere if Lord Cornwallis's order prevents you.'

'I have opened myself to you in good faith, Major Ross. I trust I have not been mistaken.'

Risen before the sun, I pulled on the dark breeches and dun jacket that Mrs Kendrick had the previous night brought me from her late husband's wardrobe. The shoes were likewise an old pair of her husband's, and when I put them on they fitted me without pinching. I tied back my hair carelessly, and then turned myself before the full-length mirror.

'When shall I look for your return, sir?'

'I cannot say. How do I appear to you now, Mr Calvert?'

'Not much like a gentleman.'

'Good. And you have my letter safe?'

'It is here, sir,' said he, touching his breast pocket nonchalantly. I was glad now that I had not told him what it was, which was my last will and testament. He would do as I had ordered and pass it to Major Ross in the case of my failure to return, and so I gave him no more instructions now but sent him back to his room.

Once he had left me I checked the sheathed dirk strapped against my chest, beneath my arm. Then reordering both shirt and jacket, I made a final inspection of myself in the mirror before snuffing the candles and going down. From the hall, I noticed a light already lit in the rear kitchen; and thinking it must be the maid, I went back there to put some bread into my pockets for the journey.

It was not the maid but Mrs Kendrick; and she bending to the newly lit fire by the stove. She glanced over her shoulder and saw me paused in the doorway. 'Do not stop there, Mr Douglas. Either come in, or go through to the breakfast room. In a few minutes, the water shall be hot. We may have tea together.'

'You must excuse me, I cannot wait. But if there is any bread you may spare me, I shall take it.'

'The jacket sits well on you,' she said very pointedly (for when I had asked for the clothes, I had told her they were needed for a patient at the hospital). 'And the shoes,' said she, glancing down. When I made no answer, she left the stove and went and fetched a pie out from the larder. 'There is a napkin in the drawer behind you.' She took up a knife and set the pie upon the table. While I fetched the napkin she said, 'I suppose this concerns Mrs Morgan's husband and son.'

'I would not have you tell her so.'

'Oh?'

'It is important, Mrs Kendrick.'

She cut the pie and wrapped a large slice in a napkin. 'It is no business of mine, Mr Douglas.'

'She is in need of kindness. I would not have a further weight put upon her.'

'Are they really in the danger that she fears?'

'What did she tell you?'

'Only that she fears for them.' She glanced at me and at my borrowed clothes. 'As to the reasons for the danger, I believe I may guess at them.'

'You would do a great service to me if you would be a friend to her. And to the child.'

She proffered the wrapped food and I took it from her hand. Then as I went to the door, she said, 'Does Mr Calvert go with you?'

'He shall be no trouble to you here.'

'That is as may be. But I wondered only if you should have any aid or companion with you, where you go.'

'No. It is better alone.' She looked that I had said more than I intended, and so I quickly thanked her for the care of Mrs Morgan and the child, and then departed.

At that early hour there were few people about the streets, though as I crossed to the hospital I heard the sound of the work-gangs, the voices and the rhythmic thumping of hammers driving palisades into the earth out by the entrenchments. The main door to the hospital lying open, I discovered in the lobby a sergeant of the 23rd sitting upon a stretcher and buttoning his jacket. At my enquiry after Gould, he pointed me to a side-room, saying that the doctor had just gone in to prepare the Frenchman for removal.

Gould soon came out. He appeared harassed, and displeased to have been given the duty of the Frenchman's transfer. But at the sight of me, and of the manner of my dress, his scowl turned to something more doubtful. I briefly explained my intention to accompany him into Williamsburg under the white flag, which he seemed to accept at the first (I think from surprise). But when I added an instruction concerning how he was to call me, and behave toward me as my superior, he became more wary. He said that he could agree nothing with me, but that I must speak with the senior surgeon, Carruthers. And so, in spite of my protest, Carruthers was sent for. It was a short while before he could be found; and when he came he seemed preoccupied, and gave Gould but half an ear. Eventually he faced me and asked the question I had most feared. 'Have you an order for this, Mr Douglas?'

'I have spoken with Major Ross.'

Carruthers instantly sent the sergeant to the Headquarters to get confirmation. Further protest must now avail me nothing, and so I held my tongue and watched the sergeant go out.

The wait seemed long, for I was left alone in the lobby while Carruthers went to busy himself about the hospital, and Gould to fetch the cart and driver. Indeed, the cart had already drawn up near the main door, and the prone Frenchman was being stretchered out to it, before the sergeant returned. Carruthers then came out and consulted with the sergeant before beckoning Gould across. They spoke briefly before Gould went and tied the furled white flag to the pole on the cart. Carruthers approached me, and I upon tenterhooks now to hear Ross's answer.

'Do the patient no harm as you go, Mr Douglas,' said Carruthers, and he clapped a hand on my shoulder as he walked by me into the hospital. I must strive then to keep the relief from my face as I climbed into the cart.

Gould rode with the driver, and I upon the tray with the Frenchman. As we passed the Headquarters I saw through the window Major Ross with a lamp at his elbow, hunched over his papers. He must have heard our cart, but he did not look up.

Once we were out through the northern opening of the entrenchment, and onto the Williamsburg road, we carried on a quarter-mile to the Star Redoubt which the Fusiliers, under Captain Abthorpe, had built into a substantial stronghold. They had an encampment just by it, and their campfires were being stirred into life as we trundled past. The ground upon this side of the town offered not the same fair prospect as that further south. Being traversed with ravines, and the main woods encroaching much nearer the town here, it must be easier to defend with bayonets than with guns. But the same work of tree-felling had been done here as to the south, and close by the redoubt an abatis was laid against the prospect of attack. But the Williamsburg road was clear all the way out to our sentry post beyond the creek.

The officer of the sentries volunteered two of his men to go with us, which Gould sensibly declined as being a possible incitement to any militia we might meet upon the road. Instead, Gould declared, we must trust to our white flag, and at his order I stood and unfurled it from the pole. There was no breeze, and the flag hung limp as we left our lines and crossed into the no-man's-land beyond.

We did not speak. From time to time I glanced up at the white flag, but mostly I kept my eyes on the woods and my hand firm upon the Frenchman's shoulder. The fear and dread in me threw superstitious lines of hope into the future. If the Frenchman survives – thought I as we rattled along – if the Frenchman lives, so too shall the Morgans.

CHAPTER 12

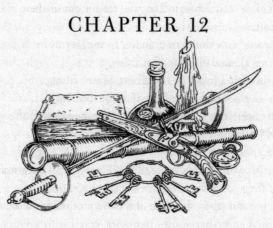

*I*t is little understood how many small civilities may pass between enemy armies in the field. Though they make none of the substance of war, yet by these do soldiers prove themselves men and not beasts; and as bitter as had been the campaigning through the Carolinas, there remained yet some badly worn threads of decency between Lord Cornwallis's officers and General Greene's and Lafayette's. And so it was that by means of a drummer boy a message had gone from our surgeons to the French officers, explaining that one of their men had been wounded and had fallen into our care. By the same means they were forewarned of our intended return of him. It was this previous understanding as much as our flag, I believe, that kept us safe upon the road; for two miles beyond our sentry post, uniformed Continentals in buff-and-blue began to show themselves in the wood, and also some white-uniformed Frenchmen. Several of these French called out to know how their wounded countryman fared, which I left Gould to answer with what halting French he could muster.

But these enemy soldiers being few, and scattered, there were long stretches of our way when I might focus my attention solely upon those points of the road vulnerable to ambuscade. Similarly, I took note of the small bridges, the branching tracks and any such military observations as I might report to Lord Cornwallis upon my return to York Town. It was along this road that the enemy artillery must be drawn, and very necessary that we should cause them the greatest obstruction and mischief before they came near to our line. This study, I confess, was a welcome distraction to me; for none but a fool goes without trepidation into the lion's den.

We continued slowly, the best part of two hours.

'They have a sentry post ahead,' said Gould at last, and he craned around to me. 'It is likely the French surgeons shall offer me some hospitality. Shall you wait with the driver?'

'I shall look to myself.'

'When I have done with them, there can be no long delay in our return.'

'If you do not find me with the cart, you must go at once, and without me.'

'Shall I meet you upon the road?'

'Possibly,' said I; which though I saw that he much doubted of, he made no further question, and before long we were arrived at the enemy sentry post before the town.

The French sentries saw at a glance that I had neither pistol nor sword. After a brief inspection of the wounded patient they bade us '*Merci*', thanking us for our care of him. Then one of them climbed up to sit with Gould and the driver, and on we went into Williamsburg.

It was a considerably greater place than York Town, having been till this past year the capital of Virginia, and a very fine collection of public and private buildings graced its better avenues and streets. Lafayette had evidently refrained from any reckless military occupation of the town; and though there were both officers and common soldiers abroad, they mingled at something like an equality of number with the local townsfolk then going about their daily business. Indeed, it was a thing quite remarkable to see how the usual daily life of the place continued, and what a stark and unhappy contrast it made to our own situation in York Town.

A golden fleur-de-lis was displayed upon the banner outside the William and Mary College where we halted. This handsome red-brick building was one of the largest and finest in the town, and from its broad doorway a French surgeon emerged to greet Gould. A stumbling exchange then commencing between the two medical men, I climbed down and looked for an opportunity to slip away. But no such occasion presenting itself, I must then assist the three fellows who came to bear their wounded comrade inside. The patient was soon upon fresh linen, and the French surgeon swiftly cut the bandages to make his first inspection of the wound. While this was doing, I looked along the line of beds to where another surgeon was engaged in conversation with a patient; and at the sight of that second surgeon I had a very great fright. For who should it be but the naval surgeon from the *Auguste*, the fellow for whom I had wrapped in sail all those lifeless bodies. He must have accompanied some of his patients ashore, and a vile piece of luck for me that he should be so unusually assiduous in his care of them. Finishing his conversation, he started toward us. My alarm gave me sudden voice.

'Shall I go now, Dr Gould, and buy those few things for you?'

Gould looked at me askance. The French surgeon offered that if any medical necessities were required, he might allow Gould some furnishment from his own supplies. And Gould seeming then in perplexity how to answer him, I said directly to the Frenchman, 'It is things of a private nature, sir,' and waiting no longer I turned my back and departed. Once outside, I bent my head a little to avoid meeting any eye; for though most of Bougainville's people must surely be aboard the ship, yet the shock of coming upon the surgeon so unexpectedly was a warning to me of the greater care I must take. And a reminder, should I need it, of the possibly fatal consequence of a haphazard unmasking.

But once clear of the hospital, and after passing several people in the street and raising neither interest nor comment, I breathed a little easier and began to look about me more freely. There was an undoubted gaiety in the townsfolk, and a certain liveliness in their faces, as if the arrival of so many military people, and the near presence of war, was a mild intoxicant to them. Having seen the like before, I well knew that it would not long last, and that the inevitable abrasions of a close proximity to soldiers must quickly take a toll. There would soon be resentments bred that only the army's removal might cure. But for now there seemed a general air of conviviality abroad in the town, and so I passed on my way as just one more stranger among the many newly arrived there, an object of neither curiosity nor suspicion.

In truth, I had expected a much greater military occupation of the town's buildings, and Lasceaux's headquarters, therefore, to be easily discoverable. But along the main street was no sign of any building occupied by French officers. If Lasceaux had not established himself in the town then he must be encamped with Lafayette and St Simon's men half a mile westward, among those troops we had seen as we came in. And wherever Lasceaux was, there the Morgans must be; and the more time wasted till I found them, the smaller their chance to get free.

At the bottom of the Green I paused, hesitating whether to go up toward the Governor's Palace (which though a fine building, and once the residence of the British Governor of Virginia, was certainly no palace). But then ahead of me on Duke of Gloucester street appeared a pair of mounted French officers. I at once turned aside onto the Green. Catalpa trees shaded the new-mown grass there, and people crossed the Green in front of me on their way to the house of Mr Wyeth, a leader of the first rebels against the King. Whether Wyeth was in residence, or now kept himself in the new capital Richmond, I could not tell; but certainly there appeared a considerable activity about the place, the reason of which I soon discovered when a self-important fellow loudly berated a servant girl that she must look more lively when General Washington came there.

I proceeded almost to the Palace gates, which was at once the same and yet very different from the time of the last British Governor's flight a few years before. Those British subjects he had then alarmed and angered by his removal of powder from the town's magazine were now the acknowledged masters of Williamsburg, and the Governor's

Palace was now indisputably theirs. But by the appearance of the Continentals' flag near the main door, I deduced that the place was given over to some military purpose. Besides the Palace's extensive gardens, there was also an orchard, and from this orchard a maid now came with a basket of early apples perched atop her head. I crossed over from the Green.

'Ha'penny apiece,' said she in answer to my question, and she put the basket down by her feet. I remarked the fine quality of the apples, which she agreed.

'You must put some by for General Washington then.'

'An' maybe I will.'

We chatted amiably while I made my selection. I discovered that the Governor's Palace was designated as a hospital for the Continental soldiers and militia, and that the College would serve for the French. I gave her tuppence, and while she delved into her apron, I said, 'I was sent by my ship's captain with a message for Lafayette's aide, Lasceaux. I had thought to find him here.'

She shrugged; the names meant nothing to her. 'You must ask at Mr Wyeth's house,' said she. Then she gave me my change and hoisted the basket again.

I did not linger there, for it seemed to me unlikely Lasceaux should quarter himself at the hospital of the Americans. And if the Wyeth house was to be General Washington's headquarters, Lasceaux would not be there either. I sorely regretted now the hasty retreat I had been obliged to make from the French hospital, for it was there that I might most easily have learned what I must now be at some trouble to discover.

I was to the end of the Green, and at Duke of Gloucester street, when I espied a wagon arriving at a general store across the way, and a number of townsfolk gathering to see what new supplies had come in. I soon joined myself to the rear of them, turning an ear to their conversations as I watched the unloading. The wagon-driver complained of his back, the storekeeper's two slave-boys shouldered their burdens in silence, and the storekeeper made a tally while keeping up a friendly banter with his neighbours.

Though there was some talk of the goods, the greater subject was the expected arrival of Washington and Rochambeau, which the wagon-driver promised would happen on the morrow, swearing that he had seen both of these fine gentlemen in Richmond where he had just come from. There were several women asked after the Continental army regulars, and whether he had passed any of these fellows on the road. It seemed, by the women's talk, that there were many local husbands and sons enlisted in the Continental army, and that the return of these men was now looked for with an anxious hope. But the driver had seen none of these upon the road. Instead he recounted the rumour he had heard that Washington's men were mostly to be brought down the Bay by the ships. He had heard that there was but a small band travelling with the generals, who had themselves taken a diversion to Washington's Mount Vernon estate in their coming down. 'But they're not a day behind me now,' he concluded. 'And when they comes, then God help Cornwallis and Tarleton, and the whole redcoat scum.'

There was some low and vulgar rejoinder made, at which I must laugh with all the others. The fellow's credible information being soon exhausted, his audience began drifting away, and I with them.

But to wander then, aimless about the town, was almost the worst thing I might do. For the longer I wandered, the more I must be seen; the more seen, the more noticed, till at last someone must enquire my business of me. The excuse of my errand for the surgeon might suffice for a time; but should I be compelled to its use I might likewise be compelled to return to the French hospital, and thence to York Town empty-handed.

So I passed down by the old Magazine toward the Capitol building, a place long the centre of the rebels' political opposition to the King, and now serving I knew not what purpose. It was, however, just such a building as might be given over to the allied armies. At either side of the street stood a number of taverns, coffee houses and shops. And it says much for the allied armies that the taverns were not filled with soldiers. Even the officers inside these places appeared quite sober. But as I drew nearer to the Capitol I saw neither flags nor officers about the place, but only some local gentlemen coming out and going in. My hope of it as Lasceaux's quarters died.

I then removed myself from the main thoroughfare, which when I had done I sat myself down on a carved cedar-log bench. Here I ate my apple pensively, looked about me, and considered of my situation. The French encampment was a half-mile to the west of the town, beyond the French hospital at the College. To get there I must either pass back through the town, or else make a wide detour around the outskirts, a thing I was loath to do on account of the soldiers upon the road.

While I weighed these unhappy thoughts, a clanking of iron drew my eye to the building opposite. I knew the place for the town's Public Gaol (indeed, I had once questioned a fellow in his cell there before he was hanged), but I confess, till I saw the two French officers coming out from there, it had not occurred to me that the place might be put at their disposal. But the sight of them brought a new thought into my mind; for of a certainty, it was no social call that they had made there. But then a hand suddenly clamped my shoulder, and I froze to the heart.

'Danby?'

Traherne. That damned fellow, the garrulous and untrustworthy merchant from the *Auguste*. I reordered my expression as he came around to the front of me.

'I thought it was you,' said he. 'But what has happened to you, man?' He flicked the lapel of my cheap jacket with an impertinent familiarity. Then he creased his brow, as though concerned to find me in such a condition. 'Surely you do not remain unwell.'

'I fear that I do, sir,' said I, seizing upon his suggestion and drawing my jacket close about me. Instantly there was a change in him, and he stood off from me as if he now regretted his approach.

'That will not do,' said he. 'I know a doctor here—'

'I have consulted with a doctor. He has advised me that I keep myself alone, as much as I am able. It is fair advice. I would cause no infection to those about me.'

'But are you in some want?' said he.

'It is low spirits only, sir. Once I am recovered, you shall find me more minded to dress myself as I should, and to keep company. Till then I shall keep myself quietly.'

'If the climate here ill-suits you, Danby, the cure must be to get yourself away.' When I conceded the good sense in that, he added, 'Then you must take my advice to your bosom. But if you are sure you are in no need of help—'

'I need only the help of time, sir. But I thank you for your kindly advice.'

'Then I beg pardon I have broken in upon you.' He dipped his head to me, wishing me better health, and then got himself from me as quickly as decency might allow.

Neither did I linger there, nor congratulate myself on being so easily rid of him; for I had by this unfortunate meeting got a name attached to me, and a story that would not sit easily with what the apple-girl knew of me, or with my pretence to be Gould's assistant. In less than an hour I had left three contradictory traces, and my luck seemed to run so ill that I had a foreboding how those traces might accidentally ravel to my own undoing. So wasting not a moment longer in considering the possible routes out to the French encampment, I struck for it directly, setting my foot upon the backstreet leading by the gaol and toward the Palace Green.

Upon each side of this street stood single cottages, a few of brick but the others clapboard, and all with poultry scratching in their yards, and dogs lolling in the shade of the outbuildings. The people were fewer here than upon Duke of Gloucester, and I walked briskly, as a man about his master's business. But so intent was I upon my own ends that I at first missed the significance of the several horses tethered beside a large corner house on the opposite side of the street. The place was clapboard like its neighbours, painted white, but considerably larger and finer than the other houses in the street. I noticed it, certainly; but it was only as I went over the crossroads and glanced back that I saw the French banner with its golden fleur-de-lis. The banner was upon a makeshift pole planted by the side-door.

Here was a piece of good luck to overmatch the bad that had dogged me since my arrival. For the Palace Green and Washington's intended headquarters at the Wyeth house were but a short way distant; and so I had no doubt but that this large house with its several outbuildings and golden fleur-de-lis must be the headquarters intended for Rochambeau and his senior officers.

I made no pause but continued on my way, and only at the corner glanced back. Any one of the several outbuildings might make an appropriate separate quarters for Lasceaux. As to the Morgans, they might be held in the main house or any one of the outbuildings, though with the Public Gaol so near at hand it must be possible that they were kept there. I went on to the Palace Green, intending to turn northward and circle about by way of the backstreet near to the Palace, and so approach the French headquarters from the rear side. For I had noticed a small mill there, and what looked to be the miller's storehouse, backing onto the yard of the French headquarters. And this storehouse, I thought, might be the best vantage from which to discover and observe Lasceaux and the Morgans.

But I had hardly taken ten paces on my new course when my ill-fortune returned. A pony and trap had come up past the Wyeth house to the far side of the Green, and the two fellows riding the trap were none other than Gould and the French surgeon with whom I had left him. They could not fail to see me. Nor could I make any avoidance of them when they stopped, and the Frenchman hailed me.

'I have not bought them yet, sir,' said I, gesturing vaguely about.

The Frenchman again made enquiry of Gould what it was that I sought to purchase. And Gould was thrown into such a confusion that he straightaway ordered me to desist in my search, saying that he had no pressing need of the articles. 'Get you back to the French hospital now,' he instructed me. 'I shall dine with my good doctor at the Governor's Palace before you and I make our return to York Town.'

What might I do then but only be silent and obey. I touched my brow, and turned from my purpose with the blackest heart in Virginia.

At the Duke of Gloucester street I turned west toward the French hospital at the College, all the while considering how I should best go on. I took a great care now to look no one full in the eye, lest I invite another unwelcome recognition. But after a hundred yards I became aware of a fellow who seemed to shadow me, though he walked upon the far side of the street. He kept a fair distance between us, and so apart from his clothes – which seemed as poor as my own – I could tell nothing about him.

I was noticed, just as I had striven not to be, and my heart started up a fierce clamouring. But I strove to quiet myself, and I kept my pace steady as if in ignorance of his presence behind me.

How I had drawn myself to the fellow's notice I could not tell; but my coming into the town was recklessness enough to invite discovery, and I did not long dwell upon bootless self-recrimination. I was noticed, and nothing for it now but to draw the fellow off to some quiet place and hope to God that he put up no hue and cry before I might silence him.

As I passed through the College gates I made a careless push of my hand into my jacket pocket, making sure of the dirk sheathed there by my ribs.

A path led rightward from the gates, across the grass and into a grove of cedars and low bushes. I walked down this path, and only once I was behind the cover of the first thick foliage did I stop and look back. He was behind me yet, within the gates now, and coming after me down the path. I could still not make out his face, but he appeared in some hurry, as though he feared to lose me in the grove. And yet he had set up no cry against me. Praying that his silence continue, I stepped off the path and crouched down to hide in the bushes. And I must work now to quiet my breathing, and to steady my hand. I unsheathed the dirk and waited.

Seconds seemed minutes; minutes, hours. But when my hand began to ache from its fierce grip on the dirk, it came to me just how long it was that I had waited. But even yet there was no sign of him, nor any cry raised against me. Had he, I wondered, turned aside to the College. Or perhaps he had stopped at the edge of the grove. Finally daring to move, I stood up very slowly. Then as I peered through the foliage toward the path there came a sharp sound behind me. I went rigid. But no second sound followed the first. Though no word was spoken, and though I heard not a breath, I had no doubt but that the fellow was behind me. Slipping the dirk into my sleeve, I forced myself to slowly turn.

He was but a few paces off, and simply watching me. In his hand was neither dagger nor pistol nor weapon of any kind, but only the stick that he had broken to make that sharp sound of warning. His straight black hair fell to his shoulders. His skin was dark, and his cheekbones broad and flat. He was an Indian, and most likely a Pamunkey.

'Campbell?' said I warily.

He walked by me onto the path. When I hesitated, he turned and beckoned. With no better track before me I at last followed him out from the grove and away from the town.

CHAPTER 13

*A*xes stood propped against a stack of sawn cedar planks, and besides these were adzes and saws. Scattered over the ground were wood chippings, sawdust and bark, and the sweet smell of cedar, rich in the air. I took all this in, and the bark shelters erected in the centre of the clearing, as Campbell pointed out to me a grey-haired fellow. 'That one was near the road when you came into town.' I remembered the old man, but vaguely, from the Pamunkey reservation. Campbell then lifted his chin to the younger man who had just led me out to the woodcamp from the town. 'I sent him in to fetch you.'

Tinkers, Cornwallis had called the Pamunkey; and had he seen those fellows about me now I daresay it should have confirmed him in the opinion. Campbell explained to me that the camp was temporary, and that the men would move back to their reservation before the winter. There were no Pamunkey women in the camp, and when I enquired the reason Campbell told me they had sent their women back to the reservation after the arrival of Lafayette's soldiers at Williamsburg. He made no mention of the Pamunkey girl who was raped and killed, and his eyes warned me to a similar silence. The absence of the women from the camp must be of some several weeks' standing, and in consequence a look of comfortable shabbiness had settled upon both the camp and the men. Few of them kept themselves clean-shaven, and their clothes were stained from the cedar and covered in sawdust. Campbell's clothes, however, were clean, and he was properly shaven (he being very particular in such things). Indeed, as he stood there he seemed a very prince among them.

Through the pines a few hundred yards to the south-west I could clearly see lines of tents, and French soldiers moving about. I asked why the soldiers had not driven off the Pamunkey.

'The French buy the cut timber. What the Pamunkey do here is useful to them.' Campbell then told me what he had discovered, which was that Washington and Rochambeau were expected on the morrow, and that French ships would soon arrive in the James River with yet more Continental soldiers from the north.

This was such information as Cornwallis needed; but my mind was still on the Morgans. And so I asked Campbell how far we were from the York Town road, and how easily and safely I might be brought back to the woodcamp; for I intended to return into the town, leave with Gould's cart, and then get down a mile past the sentry post when there could be no doubt I had departed Williamsburg. Campbell questioned the grey-haired fellow, who answered that there should be no difficulty in it.

'Then have him wait for me there,' I told Campbell. 'I shall leave the town before nightfall.'

Campbell was not one for idle enquiry, and he made no question of me. So I at once left the camp, that same fellow who had led me out now taking me back to the French hospital. There I sat by the stables with the driver and awaited Gould's return.

It was late afternoon before the trap drew in through the hospital gates. Gould was half-drunk, and I had little trouble convincing him of our need to instantly depart. In the general air of fellow-feeling and good will he shook the French surgeon's hand, as did I, and we soon rattled away from there, and out to the sentry post. There we stopped briefly to be marked in their logbook before proceeding on the York

Town road. I was well satisfied by this time that neither the French surgeon nor the sentries could doubt of my removal from the town.

About a mile past the sentry post, I leaned forward from my place in the tray and said to Gould, 'I must leave you here, but do not stop. And be sure to tell Major Ross that I have remained here of my own volition.'

Gould turned with a look of fuddlement. I clapped a hand upon his shoulder and then leaped from the side of the cart. A short way into the woods the old Pamunkey found me, and we turned our backs upon the road.

'It is the two men that ferried me across the James,' I told Campbell. 'If I cannot get the men from here, they shall hang for spies. They must be held at the French headquarters, or in the gaol.'

Campbell reflected awhile on what I had told him. Then he leaned out from the bark shelter where we had retreated and called to one of the Pamunkey. This fellow proved to be the same man who had followed me in the town. Campbell made a place for him in the low shelter, and he came and sat before us cross-legged. He held a clay pipe clamped between his teeth, puffing smoke all the while that Campbell told him of my search for two captured friends. But at last he removed his pipe to cough before saying, 'I have seen them.' My scepticism was almost equal to my surprise. But he then described the Morgans exactly, and named the day of their arrival in the town. He said they had been taken several times between the gaol and the French officers' quarters at the Peyton house. (The Peyton house being, by his description, that very place I had suspected was marked for Rochambeau's headquarters.)

'It is them,' said I. 'It can be no one else.' The fellow drew upon his pipe again, nodding as he watched me, and with no more sympathy for the Morgans than if they were stones. I asked him who it was took them from the gaol to the Peyton house, and whether they were hurt or ill-treated. A pair of French infantrymen were the escort, he told me; and though the prisoners' hands were tied, they walked unaided and seemed healthy enough.

There was no more that he knew. It was clear to me that I must send him back into the town to make a proper reconnoitring of the Peyton house, its outbuildings, and also the mill-yard behind. I dare not show my own face there again, at least till I had some definite plan for the Morgans' rescue. But hope was now kindled in me. I thought on the disruption to the regular course of the town's affairs that must happen the next day when Washington and Rochambeau arrived. With all attention diverted, then must surely be the best opportunity for some bold action or ruse.

After I had sent the fellow back into the town, I remained with Campbell in the bark shelter and rehearsed to him my first thoughts on what might be attempted. He said little, and it was very plain to me that he did not share my new hope.

'These Pamunkey cannot fight,' he said at last.

'If it comes to any fighting, the Morgans shall be already lost.' I looked out to where the Indians worked the felled trees with their axes. A few of the young men wore French jackets. When I remarked this, Campbell told me that the jackets were sometimes given in payment for the cut timber.

'How difficult might it be to put together a uniform?'

'Officer?'

'Officer or common soldier. Anything must be better than this,' said I, touching my own dun jacket. 'When the generals come down, there shall be new troops come into the town with them. Only let me find myself a uniform, I may pass muster as a new arrival.'

Campbell, though he seemed little taken with my notion, crawled out from the bark shelter to make enquiry of the fellows without. When he returned some minutes later it was to tell me the Pamunkey had only those few badly worn and scuffed French jackets that I had seen. Their recent attempts at barter had apparently been refused, nor had they any French breeches to match the upper garment. Campbell left me to my disappointment, crawling by me to lie down on his blanket.

I kept myself hidden within the shelter till nightfall lest I draw the attention of any soldier who might pass through the woods nearby.

And even after darkness descended I made sure to keep back from the campfire, staying in the shadows while I ate stewed venison from a wooden bowl. The French had dug their latrines at a place midway between their own tents and the Pamunkey, and though the smell thickened on the night air, yet I was grateful for the barrier the latrines made between us and the French. Without the Pamunkey women to draw the soldiers across, there was nothing to bring them from their own campfires at the far side of the pines. Even so, I kept my eyes open.

I understood much of what passed between the Pamunkey, for though they spoke an Algonquian dialect peculiar to the Chesapeake, and unrelated to the Iroquois of the Cherokee, they used also a good deal of English. And the thing most remarkable to me in their conversation was just how little of it concerned the great actions now unfolding all about them. The British occupation of York Town, the French fleet in the Bay, the imminent arrival of Washington and Rochambeau; none of these concerned them anything so much as the blight that had spread through the young pines that summer, or the poor fishing now to be had on the York River. The raiding of their crabpots by a local farmer merited more weighty debate than any edict of the King or the Congress. They owned no part of these lands save only their small reservation, and yet their lives were immovably deep-rooted in the country. What once they had, they had lost; and the mightiest army or fleet could now hold no threat for them.

The venison stew finished, and a pipe or two shared, they took themselves severally into the bark shelters and there drew their blankets about them. For myself, though I tried to follow their good example, I slept but poorly, and thought continually on the Morgans, and on our soon-to-be-encircled army in York Town, and on Campbell, who had left the Pamunkey camp at sunset and had not yet returned. Twice in the night the guard changed in the French camp; and twice I startled awake to the sound of distant French voices before returning to an uneasy rest.

At dawn I opened my eyes wearily and found Campbell wrapped tightly in his blanket near the opening of the shelter. Setting down my hand to raise myself, my fingers alighted on a small heap of clothes.

They were just by my side, and had not been there when I had first lain down. Atop the heap was a blue French jacket; underneath that, the white shirt and breeches of a French infantryman. I looked toward Campbell, and then it was I noticed the musket propped against the shelter near his feet. The musket was French too, just like the powder-horn slung from its bloodied bayonet.

Though I donned the French uniform I made no unnecessary excursions from the shelter but waited all the morning for some word of the generals' approach to Williamsburg. Toward midday, the grey-haired old Pamunkey returned from the Richmond road to report that the first of Washington's northern troops were upon the road and must be arrived in Williamsburg within the hour. He had seen no sign of the generals.

In the French camp there had been much beating of drums and parading all the morning; but now came both pipe and drum, as if they readied to march out in celebration and welcome. I delayed no longer, but took up the French musket and set out with Campbell toward the road.

Two hundred yards inside the French sentry post, he left me to go and find that Pamunkey fellow he had sent to watch at the French headquarters. My own concern was to keep hid from the French officers passing along the road, lest I find myself put under orders. When Campbell returned it was with the best news that I might hope for: the Morgans had been seen at the Peyton house, they were kept incarcerated in the outbuilding nearest the mill.

'Guards?'

'One infantryman in the main yard.'

'One only?'

'Another outbuilding is used by the quartermaster. There are soldiers always passing by.'

I determined that I must go down at once and make my own reconnoitring. But Campbell then telling me that the townsfolk had already begun to gather on the Palace Green in expectation of Washington's arrival, I agreed that he should go along there and wait.

We could not enter the town together for fear of inviting attention, so after he left me I stayed till the road was clear and then climbed out from the ditch and hurried to the cover of the cedars on the far side. Next I turned and made my way down toward the Peyton house.

It was not long I had the cover of the trees, and as the woods thinned I came onto a track with ahead of me the white mill-sails clearly visible. Soon the rear of the Governor's Palace gardens was to my right, and finding no soldiers about I pressed boldly on till at length I came almost to the railed fence by the mill-yard. There I turned aside from the road. The miller's cottage was quiet, and no dog being present I slipped quickly between the rails and crossed the yard to the storehouse. From here I looked across to the outbuildings of the Peyton house, the French headquarters. A single guard sat with his back against the wall of the house, shaded there from the sun.

It was a very different scene from that busy one of my imaginings, and for certain to go there directly must be to invite my own capture. With no body of French soldiers about the place, my uniform was a worthless disguise. Indeed, to stand – as I then was – openly and unoccupied by the mill storehouse must call to me an unwelcome attention. Snatching a look in at the storehouse window, I saw that the place was empty. So I went along to the door. There was no lock fixed there, and I let myself inside and bolted the door behind me. The storehouse was of clapboard construction, like the mill, and its floorboards white-powdered with a dusting of flour. But there was not a single sack of flour stored there, the reason for which must surely be the extraordinary demands of Lafayette's men and de Grasse's fleet. Moving the small tally-table across to the high window facing the Peyton house, I climbed up and looked out.

There was now a pair of French officers in the Peyton yard. They spoke together a while before parting, one to the house and the other to the outbuilding nearest the road. The door to that outbuilding stood open, and hardly had the officer gone in than another came out, and in the next quarter-hour there was a constant traffic between that place and the house, both officers and servants. It seemed to be a quarters for the officers. And the outbuilding opposite was evidently the cookhouse, for a black soon came there with several newly killed ducks strung from a pole, followed by another black with a tub of steaming water. These two settled themselves by the tub and commenced to pluck the birds.

There were but two other outbuildings. After a half-hour more, the guard came and looked in at the window of one of them, and then he took a key from his belt and called the two slaves to him before he unlocked the door. It must be the gaolhouse. Confirmation came upon the instant; for the door once was opened, and young David Morgan emerged with a pail in his hand and fetters about his ankles. He moved awkwardly, his feet spread wide to keep from stumbling. With a shuffling movement he went around to the rear of the outbuilding, escorted now by the blacks, and he emptied his pail into the ditch there. All this while, the guard stood near the gaolhouse door, his musket ready. He spoke with someone inside who – though I could not see him – must be Cable Morgan. David soon returned with that same painfully awkward movement. He went into the gaolhouse and the door was closed and locked at his back. The guard resumed his seat by the house and the blacks crouched by the tub to recommence their plucking of the birds. I set my hand upon the wall and dropped my head. The Pamunkey had reported the Morgans unfettered, and it was this had given me a fair hope of their rescue. Fettered, the difficulty of any rescue was compounded tenfold. Greatly troubled by this turn, I let myself from the storehouse and went to find Campbell upon the Palace Green.

A crowd had gathered before the Wyeth house, both townsfolk and soldiers, and there was an atmosphere very festive in that happy throng, the French bandsmen playing some sprightly airs to amuse the people while they waited beneath the green shade of the catalpas. But before I could discover Campbell, the music stuttered and died away. A cry came from down on Duke of Gloucester street. The cry was taken up by the crowd on the Green, and then the bandsmen struck up 'Yankee Doodle' as a troop of horsemen came into sight.

Amidst these horsemen was a carriage and four, the whole column now coming up to the Wyeth house. The leading horseman carried a standard, the motto of Washington's personal guard, 'Conquer or Die', clearly legible. (This motto had caused a wide ridicule among the British soldiery when it was first heard of, which ridicule had long since been silenced by the undeniable bravery of these fellows.)

A mighty cheer went up when the carriage stopped, and a greater cheer yet when the door opened and onto the footplate stepped General Washington. He sported a jacket of buff and blue, which colours he had become known for during the war. As he stepped on the plate the carriage listed, for he was truly as imposing a figure as I remembered. Though there was nothing of triumph or joy in his expression, he allowed a quick smile to break across his stern features as he acknowledged with a nod the exuberant reception. The natural gravity of the man seemed to quiet the crowd a little. Nor did he attempt any ingratiating words, or practise any flattery upon them, and he came quickly and unceremoniously down from the carriage. The people for their part made no press upon him but they stepped aside to let him go unimpeded into the house.

Next from the carriage came General Rochambeau, alighting with even less ceremony than Washington. And though he was not nearly so imposing a figure as the American, yet the same respect was accorded him, with the people making way to let him go across to his officers who waited in the middle of the Green.

Espying Campbell at last, I indicated with a quick sign that he should follow me at a distance, which he did; right away from the Green, and up behind the Governor's Palace, all the way to the woods.

'If they are in irons you cannot help them,' said he, when we had converged in the woods and I had told him how the Morgans were kept.

'I cannot help them as I thought.'

'You cannot help them at all. They cannot run. They would be caught, and you with them.'

I was so far from accepting this that I made no response but went fifty yards deeper into the woods, where he followed me. There I went down into a hollow, laid my musket beside me and looked back toward the town. The Palace chimneys and the mill-sails were visible over the undergrowth. Campbell asked what I now intended.

'The officers shall dine tonight with Washington and Rochambeau. They shall most of them be in drink. If they continue to keep only one guard on the Morgans, then we may get them from there.'

'They cannot move in irons,' said he.

'We must secure a boat down on the river. In a boat we may carry both the Morgans and their chains.'

Campbell looked doubting, but he answered me nothing.

Throughout the afternoon we stayed quiet in that place, undisturbed but by the woodland birds that flitted through the leaves and branches overhead. Pipes and drums sounded frequently to westward, as Continental troops arrived after the generals. But at last the evening darkness descended, and we roused ourselves and skirted about the eastern edge of the town.

Insects abounded in all the ponds and creeks of the tidewater, and now a great chorus swelled as we came near to the river. A campfire burned on the shore, and behind this were several tents. A dozen or more French seamen directed blacks in the gathering of firewood.

There were guns drawn up on the bank just above them. Very large guns, but only a few of them yet mounted upon carriages. 'Siege guns, I think,' said I in answer to Campbell's question. 'They must be brought off the ships.'

We lay low and observed the seamen awhile; and then we saw lanterns being lit upon a schooner a hundred yards out from the landing. The schooner seemed a local vessel, making no part of de Grasse's fleet. After a minute Campbell touched my arm and directed my attention to a small boat drawn up on the sandy beach just below and to the left of us. There was no one about, and so we went quickly down and found the boat tied to a tree-root high upon the bank. The schooner was now directly out from us. It looked to be that some fellows had come ashore from it to drink the health of General Washington. But however that might be, the boat was perfectly suited to my purpose. After a brief inspection of its soundness, we withdrew.

I told Campbell, 'If you would not come with me to fetch the Morgans, you might wait here.'

'You shall fetch a rope for your own neck.'

'Perhaps,' said I.

He looked at me a moment; and then he stepped by me onto the path leading back to the town and the French headquarters.

CHAPTER 14

We kept to the rear side of the Capitol, and then went around behind the Public Gaol and along by the brick kilns till we came to the storehouse that I had used for my reconnoitring. The night was very dark, and so our greatest fear now was not that we should be seen but that the town's dogs should set upon us, or worse, summon up their masters. But not a cur stirred as we crept along by the storehouse wall and looked down to the headquarters outbuildings. The Peyton house yard was much as I had last seen it, but with a lantern now suspended from a central post, and a bright light shining out through the open door of the officers' quarters. A lone sentry was seated on the rear steps of the main house, his musket propped by him.

'The sentry has the key,' I told Campbell. 'Once we have put him by, we shall have but a short time to get them out from there. We shall first bring the Morgans over here. And from here down to the river.' Campbell nodded. 'Are you ready?' said I. He nodded again, and we crouched and ran from the storehouse to the railing fence. Climbing through the rails, we soon passed that ditch where David Morgan had emptied his pail.

In the shadows of the cookhouse we stopped. The sentry was now but ten yards off from us. He had not moved, but still sat upon the step with his musket propped against the wall beside him. But then we heard voices in the yard, and smartly pressed ourselves against the cookhouse wall. A clattering of boots now joined with the voices in the yard, and after a moment I shot a careful glance around the wall. French officers, and several of them; dress uniform, wigged and hatted and with swords at their sides. They were passing by the sentry and discussing what ladies there might be at General Washington's dinner. The last of them turned with a parting instruction to the sentry, whom he addressed as Noailles.

The officers once gone, the yard fell silent. The sentry soon relaxed, propped his musket against the wall once more, and seemed about to retake his seat upon the step. I tapped Campbell's shoulder in warning and he unsheathed his knife. Then I called gruffly, and in French so that he might mistake me for one of the recently departed officers, 'Noailles. Lend a hand here.'

The fellow made not the slightest hesitation but came off the steps and along toward the side of the main house. I moved from the cook-house wall, and almost met him as he crossed into the shadow.

'Sir?' said he.

'Here,' said I sharply and he came nearer, peering into the darkness. In the next moment Campbell was upon him.

It was swiftly done, and silently; and Campbell then dragged the fellow back toward the ditch. I stopped him there, and felt along the belt of the dead sentry for the keys, which I removed as quietly as I could.

All was now at the hazard, for I must go into the lit yard, release the Morgans, and get them clear, and they in iron fetters. Should any Frenchman come into the yard while I was about the desperate business, my own life must be forfeit along with the Morgans'.

Forcing myself to walk with a calm I did not feel, I went into the light and across the yard directly to the gaolhouse door. Steadying my hand, I inserted the key. And found to my horror and alarm that the key would not turn. I joggled the handle, but still the key would not move, and the sound of it seemed shockingly loud. But I could neither give up nor withdraw, and so once more I joggled the handle and pressed the key. And this time, though the key did not turn, the door suddenly opened. Surprised, I hesitated; and then I went in, whispering urgently, 'You must come away quickly. Pick up your chains. Make no sound.'

But in the small room were two chairs and a table, a pail that was lit by the lantern-light spilling by me from the yard, and that was all. It was some few seconds I stood there, stunned, while my mind took in the awful fact of their removal from the place. Finally I went out and closed the door. Fighting back an almost ungovernable urge to flee, to get myself clear and preserve my life, I crossed the yard and went in through the open door of the officers' quarters.

I could not leave now without I first make some plausible reason for the murder of the sentry. For if Lasceaux suspected an attempted rescue of the Morgans, he would be certain to hurry them straight to the gallows. Inside the officers' quarters I knelt by the first chest that I came to. With the point of my dirk, I scored the brass lock. Then I slid the blade beneath the lid, prised it open a crack, and levered the blade to and fro. With one eye upon the open door, and with my heart almost driven into my throat with fear, I kept myself kneeling and worked the blade behind the lock, till at last the lock gave. Opening the chest, I rummaged quickly and carelessly through the clothes and linen, pulled out a few pieces and dropped them on the floor. Then I rose and walked out.

Nothing was changed in the yard. The lantern still shone; the sentry's musket still rested upon the wall; there was a distant noise and laughter from the taverns. But my luck could not hold for very much longer. The night air was growing cold, and colder yet the perspiration that ran down my neck and into my shirt as I walked across the yard and into the shadows. Campbell rose to meet me.

'The Morgans are gone,' said I. 'Where is the sentry?'

He took me to the ditch and I scrambled down and drew the body up from the muck. There was a noise from the house.

'Quickly,' said Campbell, and I clipped the keys back on the sentry's belt, lowered him, and then climbed up from the ditch.

We moved then, hurrying away from the house; but once we had clambered over the railings of the fence, I paused and looked back. A French officer had now come from the main house. He glanced down at the musket leaning against the wall, and then he stood upon the step and looked about the yard. The lantern-light was fully upon his face, and I startled at the sight. Indeed, I stood transfixed a moment. But when Campbell grabbed my arm I came to myself, and I turned and hurried after him past the brick kilns. The officer called for the sentry Noailles, though in no alarm yet; and at the sound of the officer's voice all doubt fell from me. For the voice was unmistakably that of Sebastian Cordet, and no different than when I had last heard it half a world, and half a lifetime, away.

Through the brickyard we ran, but at the road we forced ourselves to slow to a walk. The next open ground was fifty yards off, and we had gone not half that distance when we heard the voices back at the Peyton house calling, 'Noailles!'

Somewhere behind us a dog barked, and then another.

We reached the open ground and ran again, turning down toward the river, and I with a sudden wild thought at the strangeness of it should Cordet be the man to hang me.

We arrived at the river just in time to see our carefully selected boat shoving off toward the schooner. I looked at Campbell, and he at me in despair. The fellows aboard her were three sheets to the wind, but too many for us, and so we crouched in the bushes, struggled to get our breath, and forlornly watched them go.

When I suggested we return to the Pamunkey camp, Campbell firmly shook his head. Our presence there now, he said, might prove a danger both to them and to ourselves.

'We cannot stay here,' said I, lifting my chin toward the French seamen gathered about their campfire further along the beach. The dead sentry Noailles must have been found by this time, and the alarm raised. It must be only a short time before that alarm was carried here. For messengers would be sent to the sentry posts about the town, and down here to the river, with word of the French soldier's murder. The sentries would be redoubled at every road and track. 'Come,' said I rising, and then I led Campbell along the path going east, away from the town, along the James River.

There was no talk between us now, and we went with what speed we could in the darkness. We put our hands before our faces, shielding our eyes from the branches and leaves, and we stepped high to keep from stumbling over the roots and stones. There was no horse might follow us upon so poor a track, but we kept on to make sure of out-distancing any foot-patrol that might come out, and evading any cordon that might be thrown about the town.

We had gone barely a mile when the moon came up. It was almost instantly hid by the gathering clouds; and soon the insects and frogs started up a chorus from by the river, and then came a splashing through the foliage of the first heavy drops of rain. Onward we pressed through the darkness.

The path took us sometimes a hundred yards inland, and then suddenly back to the river, and the rain came steadily now so that the ground was soon slicked with mud. After a time we slowed to a walk to keep our footing, but made neither stop nor pause. Several times we saw lights up on our left side through the pines; and though each time the lights were unmoving, as if shining from a farmhouse window, yet we took warning from them and never turned aside from our way. We pressed on for an hour and more, our clothes as sodden as the ground beneath us; but by slow degrees we grew less fearful that we were followed from the town.

At last our way took us along by a small cove on the river, which I might not have recognized but that I stopped a moment to rest, and noticed then the leaning pine just by me. I waited, soaked and exhausted, till Campbell came up.

'This is the Morgans' beach. Their farmhouse is a few hundred yards up the valley.'

'Empty?' said he.

'Their slaves are not to be trusted.'

'We have come far enough. We should rest till the morning.'

I told him of the Morgans' boat, the log-canoe, that was hidden in the next creek. Agreeing that we should strike for it, we went on till we came to that creek and then we turned inland a short way. But the brush and reeds were very thick there, and we soon gave up any thought of searching for the boat before morning. Campbell set to breaking branches and stripping bark, while I hacked at the reeds with my dirk. After a half-hour we had made a small shelter, and I spread the reeds inside. We then stripped off our jackets and shirts, and hung them on sticks at the rear of the shelter to dry. Cold and wet and hungry, but grateful for our lives, we sat and listened to the lashing rain.

We found the Morgans' boat soon after daybreak. It was secured above the tideline, and we were an hour dragging it down the bank and onto the muddy creek-bed where it lodged immovable. But the tide was coming in, and so we sat on the bank and waited as the water trickled slowly up to us in narrow channels. Though we considered walking the few miles across the peninsula to York Town, we decided in the end that with so many French and Continental soldiers now arrived, the boat remained our better hope. (Though Campbell might have gone where he willed, even back to the Pamunkey, yet he would not abandon me.)

It was two hours we waited, and the tide almost risen to the boat, when we heard the sound of voices. Very faint, to be sure, but we looked instantly at one another, and then Campbell pointed toward the river. We moved up the bank to the higher ground and there pushed our way forward through the undergrowth. When it thinned, we dropped to our bellies and crawled forward to the crest.

A French ship-of-the-line was riding up the James River on the tide. The mainsail was set, but there was no wind, and the vessel seemed almost to drift as it went leisurely by. Two smaller vessels, single-masted, went up in the ship's wake, and these likewise in no great hurry. They were all three of them undoubtedly de Grasse's, and we watched them proceed very stately from our sight.

Campbell then said what I only thought: that had we been out on the river at that moment, they would certainly have taken us. We could now dare to go nowhere but under cover of darkness.

We floated the Morgans' boat by the late morning, but we had a further hour of struggle to move it through the thick tangle of reeds and low-hanging branches to a place of hiding fifteen yards short of the James. Once satisfied, we took the spyglass from the boat's locker and went again to that observation point above.

Only a handful of boats went up toward Williamsburg before the early afternoon, when the tide turned; and from that time till the evening only a handful of boats came down. But just near sunset came down that same French ship-of-the-line we had seen in the morning, its progress no less measured and stately than before.

Through the spyglass I saw that they kept no lookout aloft, which was a nonchalance quite vexing to me; for it showed that they feared nothing from Admiral Graves, and gave no credence to the possibility of his return to the Bay. And when I turned the spyglass upon the quarterdeck I saw something else that I had not expected. For the large figure standing there was dressed in buff and blue; and beside him was a smaller figure in a blue jacket with much gold braid lit by the setting sun.

'Washington and Rochambeau,' said I, handing the spyglass to Campbell. 'No doubt going to call upon de Grasse.'

'To send him up the York River?'

'God knows. It is a noose closing about us. I fear Cornwallis shall refuse to feel it till it prickle his neck.'

We watched the ship from our sight, and then went down and broke up our shelter. After wading out through the reeds to our boat, we climbed aboard and poled ourselves out into the empty river. There we raised the mast and sail, and in the twilight rode the slackening tide down to the Bay. The French fleet lay many miles to starboard as we came around the Point. By then the darkness was fully closed upon us, and their lanterns shone like a very bright constellation, low in the eastern sky.

Ahead of us, and less than a mile out from the shallows at the mouth of the York, were more ships' lanterns, which must be the French vessels blockading the river. We stayed close in to the Point and watched these lights carefully, but found as we went on that there were two ships only, and both riding at anchor. And now I saw how it was that Cornwallis continued to receive General Clinton's missives from New York. For though the main channel was sealed, and neither the *Charon* nor the *Guadeloupe* nor any heavy British ship could come into the Bay, yet all the shallows lay open. By day, the French gunners would make short work of any boat passing near; but by night, almost any small vessel might pass safely out.

It was a peculiar neglect. To keep almost the whole of his fleet over near the mouth of the Bay, and to put only two ships-of-the-line by the York River, showed a caution quite remarkable in Admiral de Grasse. But whatever the reason of the French caution, Campbell and I made full use of it that night. We sat out the slack tide off the Point, and then entered the York River over the shallows at the turn, and no challenge was made to us till we were far upriver. The lights of York Town appeared off the port bow, and a minute later a boat rowed down menacingly upon us.

'Declare yourself!'

'Douglas, Board of Trade and Plantations, in the service of the King!'

'Pass, an' welcome, sir.'

CHAPTER 15

'I f you receive any hurt, Mr Douglas, or if you fall ill, you would be unwise to place yourself under the care of Dr Gould.'

'He was merry enough when we parted.'

'He was very far from merry when he came to see me. No doubt he had passed some time by then in a sobering reflection.' Major Ross, I was pleased to find, was so relieved at my safe return that he did not care to hear of any perils I had been in, though he commiserated with me upon my failure to free the Morgans. He had been asleep when I attempted to call upon him directly we arrived in the night, and so I had retired to the widow Kendrick's house, to be received there by Calvert with an unaffected delight. Mrs Kendrick's welcome, too, was surprisingly sincere. She warned me not to go up to see Mrs Morgan, but to wait a while yet; for there was some nervous complaint she said had stricken Sally Morgan since my departure. Mrs Kendrick made no objection to my introduction of Campbell into the house, and so Francesca had put a mattress on the floor of my room and made up a bed for him. Campbell was sleeping there yet when I had come out to find Major Ross on his morning rounds about the lines.

'And what have you told the Morgan woman of her menfolk?' Ross asked me.

'I have not seen her.'

'You have done all that you could, Douglas. And I all that I could,' he added with a quick glance.

'For which I am obliged to you.'

'You may repay the obligation by making no more such requests of me.' He took a notebook from his breast pocket as we entered the battery on the bluffs overlooking the river. The naval officers had supervised the throwing up of the earthworks here, and now they oversaw the ships' carpenters building platforms for the guns. There were but ten platforms finished, and these supporting 12- and 18-pounders brought up from the ships. While Major Ross went to get a report from the lieutenant as to the progress of the works, I climbed onto the earthen rampart.

The sun was not yet risen, but dawn was in the sky, and from the beach rose the sound of pots and kettles clanking. A bracing smell of pine-smoke came up from the new-stoked fires. The *Charon* lay at anchor directly under the battery, and the *Guadeloupe* lay off the Fusiliers' redoubt a few hundred yards further upriver. These, and a few frigates and sloops-of-war, comprised all Captain Symonds's fleet.

Over at Gloucester Point, half a mile across the river from us, fishing boats and transports were huddled close in to the shore. Downriver, two of our schooners were anchored to keep watch for any incursion into the York by the French. To look down from the battery was to see how vulnerable we must be if any one of de Grasse's ships got by us into the upper river.

'Let the enemy give us but a little more time,' said Ross joining me, 'and we shall give such an account of ourselves as neither the French nor the rebels will quickly forget.'

I asked what news there was of General Clinton. Ross said that there had been nothing heard since that letter Lord Cornwallis had shown me. 'It must take something more than a letter to remove de Grasse from the Bay,' said I.

We came down from the earthworks, and I quite unsettled by what

I had seen. For though our preparations were but a continuance of those undertaken before I had gone down to Williamsburg, yet against what I had now witnessed of the massing of the enemy armies – to say nothing of de Grasse's great fleet – our work seemed all too makeshift and slight. If General Clinton could truly do as he had written and get a British fleet into the Bay, our situation might then be retrieved; but to believe that we might overcome the steadily increasing enemy force on the peninsula, and with the limited guns and ammunition at our disposal (and those mostly borrowed from Symonds's ships), it seemed almost to invite our own destruction.

I continued with Major Ross along all the length of our inner line; and though the entrenchments were certainly far advanced, there was yet no single section completed, not even the redoubts or the great Hornwork. After an hour Major Ross finished his inspection of the night's work on the inner defences, and he pocketed his notebook. He told me he must now ride to the outer redoubts, where I was welcome to accompany him. When I declined, he said, 'I cannot blame you. But my Lord Cornwallis shall expect you after he has break-fasted.'

'I can tell him no more than I have told you.'

'Even so, he expects you. And you need not try to hide from him my small part in your rash venture after the Morgans. I have confessed all.'

'He has forgiven you?'

'I was to be forgiven upon your safe return. So, you see, I am in your debt.'

'It is Campbell you may thank for my safe return.'

'You would not bring that fellow here, I trust, Mr Douglas, in order to make a further plea for soldiers to aid the Cherokee?'

'I had not thought of it.'

'I am sure,' said he, and smiled. 'But if you will be advised, do not press his Lordship upon it. Your fellow Campbell's presence must be reminder enough. Press your case now, and you shall certainly be refused.'

'I suppose that Secretary Nelson remains in the headquarters.'

'He does. And I would not press that either.'

A lieutenant then arriving with a message for Ross, I dipped my head and departed.

Returned to the house, I found Mrs Kendrick seated at her dining table with both Calvert and Campbell; and when I stopped in the doorway I felt the awkwardness of the silence among them as they ate. Calvert stood when he saw me, and Mrs Kendrick gave me a look not altogether cheerful. Campbell ignored me and continued to eat.

When I jerked my head toward the hall, Calvert followed me to the library. I sat at the desk and took out a paper and blotter. 'You must take a message to Captain Stuart for me. Do you know where he is?'

'I shall easily find him, sir.'

'Good.' I inked my pen and commenced writing. 'Is Mrs Kendrick displeased now to have Campbell here?'

'She has tried to make some conversation with him.'

'She no doubt finds him disinclined to her pleasantries.'

'Very disinclined I should say, sir.'

I smiled at that. Having been schooled with the sons of colonials, Campbell was consequently fully at ease with European men; and yet I had more than once been witness to his extreme discomfort in the company of any white woman. His unease showed itself in a moroseness quite remarkable, and which Mrs Kendrick was evidently now witness of. I asked Calvert, as I continued to write, after the health of Mrs Morgan.

'I have hardly seen her, sir. She has kept to her room almost since she came here.'

'And the child, Lizzy?'

'Francesca and Mrs Kendrick tend to her.'

'I am glad to hear that Francesca is well occupied.'

'Yes, sir.'

We were interrupted by a knock at the door. Mrs Kendrick came in.

'Shall you be joining us at table, Mr Douglas?' she enquired, with a look somewhat strained.

'Presently,' said I; but that answer seeming to give her no

satisfaction, I added, 'You have perhaps found Campbell not quite as convivial as the gentlemen you are accustomed to at your table, Mrs Kendrick. I hope you shall have the good grace to look past that.'

'And if I do, Mr Douglas, what then shall I see?'

'I would rather have Campbell by me than any number of courtly gentlemen.'

'But can the man not speak?'

'He speaks well enough when he has something to say. For myself, I have always found his silence quite companionable.'

'How long shall he be with us?'

'The house is yours, Mrs Kendrick. And Campbell is quite accustomed to receiving no benefit of any doubt. If you would evict him—'

'I have not suggested it. And is that the opinion you have of me? That I am unthinking and brutal? Am I a savage?'

This outburst could not have been worse timed; for, in the doorway behind her, Campbell had just appeared. He could not have failed to hear her. But now he looked right by her and said to me, 'Spyglass?'

I pointed to the ceiling, the bedroom directly overhead, and told him that he might take the spyglass from my satchel.

He withdrew. We listened in silence to his step as he climbed the stairs, and Mrs Kendrick then cast a look of pure womanly fury at me before she turned sharply on her heel and went out. As I sealed the note that I had written to Stuart, I glanced up and saw the amusement in Calvert's eye. I gave him the note. Then I put on my jacket and went to take my breakfast with Colonel Tarleton and his officers before proceeding to the headquarters.

News of Washington and Rochambeau's arrival had already come to Lord Cornwallis by way of a deserter from Lafayette's infantry. The deserter was in fact one of our own Fusiliers, captured by the enemy during the southern campaign. Whatever the truth of the man's claim to have served under Lafayette only while awaiting the opportunity to escape back to his comrades in the Fusiliers, Captain Abthorpe had given him a good character; and so no deep enquiry was made into the circumstances of the fellow's service with the rebels. I therefore found myself conveying little that was new to Lord Cornwallis and General O'Hara when I came to the headquarters, though I was able to corroborate much of what the deserter had reported. Additionally, I told them of the siege guns that I had seen at the landing below Williamsburg. But this information, considerably to my surprise, I found they treated in a manner quite sceptical.

'It was already night when you saw these guns,' said Cornwallis.

'Yes, my Lord.'

'And at a distance?'

'Perhaps seventy yards.'

'Perhaps seventy – and perhaps more?'

I conceded that the distance might have been greater. 'But they were undoubtedly heavy guns brought up from the fleet.'

'Heavy guns, I grant you they may be. But I cannot surmise that they should have any siege guns so readily available to them.'

'Your survey was no leisurely one, I presume? The guns were not your main concern,' said O'Hara.

'No, sir, they were not. But whatever the darkness, or the distance – and despite that it was incidental I got my sight of them – in my best belief, they were siege guns.'

'De Grasse might have a number of carronades at his disposal,' remarked Cornwallis, turning from me now to address O'Hara. 'And were I Rochambeau . . . yes, I well see the reason he should ask for the carronades ashore.'

I held my tongue. And not only because I saw that there should be no convincing them, but also, I confess, because this mention of carronades had put a small doubt in me. The carronade being an unusually short and bulky gun, it was just possible that across that distance, and in the darkness, my eye had deceived me. And yet it concerned me to think that I, who had seen the guns, might allow of some doubt, whilst Cornwallis, who had only my report to guide him, was quite pertinacious in his quickly decided opinion.

They then enquired of me what I had seen of any field-pieces coming down from Richmond; which when I could give them no good information, they were much disappointed. I then mentioned the careful study that I had made of the road into Williamsburg. 'Every artillery piece they put ashore they must now bring up the road. The few bridges between are weak. Our sappers and engineers might with small effort make them weaker.'

'Rochambeau is no novice. He shall surely try any bridge before he draws a gun over,' said Cornwallis. 'But I may tell you, Tarleton has suggested much the same action as yourself. He urges that we should impede them there on the road.'

'So we should, my Lord.'

'The road can be easily repaired. It must take them but a day or two. It is waste of effort unless we know the precise day they mean to march.'

'I shall know it.'

'Shall you indeed?' Cornwallis looked up at me from behind his desk. 'Is this your tinkers, Mr Douglas? I am told that you have brought one of them into the town.'

'He is not one of the Pamunkey.'

'Then I am misinformed.'

'His father was Donald Campbell, who worked with the Board's Superintendent in the south, Superintendent Stuart. Captain Stuart's father. But Campbell's mother is a Cherokee.'

'I see,' said Cornwallis, after turning this over. 'And this Campbell would be the fellow you travelled with from the Indian country.'

'Yes.'

'You evidently trust the man.'

'I do.'

'Then I shall not put him out.'

'Thank you, my Lord, but I shall put him out myself.' I gestured to the wall-map behind him. 'Even if we are besieged, we shall still have the freedom of the upper York. A few Pamunkey canoes passing behind the enemy lines shall not be regarded. And Campbell has some few of the Pamunkey men loyal to him.'

'Are they to be spies for us?'

'Spies and messengers, though I know it is little enough they may do.'

'I shall not stop you, Mr Douglas. Though, as you say, it is little enough. Be sure that Captain Symonds is informed of your intention. It would be a pity to have your tinkers blown from the water.'

O'Hara interjected that the officers at the Star redoubt should likewise be told, that they too open no accidental fire upon the Indians; and also the officers at the northern battery overlooking the river.

'Of course they must be told,' said I, 'but by your leave, my Lord, I would not have them told yet. Let us wait till any siege happens, else word of the Pamunkey's help to us may get to Washington and Rochambeau.'

'You allude to any spies we may have in our midst?' said Cornwallis; and when I nodded, he went on, 'Our entrenchments and gun emplacements are no secret, Mr Douglas. The size of our force is well known. Let them have what spies they may among us, what can they hope to learn that the whole of Virginia does not already know?'

'Your intentions,' said I.

His eyelids drooped at this blunt rejoinder. 'Suspicion is a poison that I will not administer to my own men. Unless there is some particular information that you have, I must forbid you make a question of any man's loyalty within our line.'

'Secretary Nelson's loyalty is very plain, my Lord.'

'He is an old man, and as honourable a Whig as I have ever met with. We have occupied his town and his house,' said Cornwallis, with a wave of his arm about the room, 'which occupation can hardly give him the happiest view of us. Yet he has made no complaint of it. In fact, he has treated us with the rarest courtesy. He is a gentleman. And what would you have, that I should put him from the town? No, sir. Whilst he desires to remain here, he shall do so.'

'If I may be so bold, my Lord, it is but prudence you should put him from your table.'

'You may not be so bold.'

'His presence is too high a price for mere courtesy.'

'What company I keep is my own affair,' said he, and now in some real annoyance. 'Look to your tinkers, if you will, Mr Douglas, but allow of my judgement for their betters. Major Ross shall show you out.'

Captain Stuart was not so easily found as young Calvert had supposed; for every new order from the headquarters sent a cascade of lesser orders through the regiments, and it was officers like Stuart who must finally reconcile these orders with their limited materials and men. The same lack of tools which had so troubled Sutherland's engineers had apparently now taken Stuart over to the Gloucester side scavenging for unused picks and shovels. Calvert reported this to me when I came into the library. He offered to cross over the river to Gloucester with my note.

'No, he cannot be long over there. Stay here, Mr Calvert, but keep an eye out for his return. Inform me of it directly.' I asked if Mrs Morgan was about, or if she still kept herself in her room.

'Mrs Kendrick has fetched a doctor to her.'

About to seat myself, I suddenly stopped. My sharp look unnerved him.

'They are in her room now, sir,' said he, and I at once pushed aside the chair and went out. I was about to mount the stairs when I saw Dr Gould starting down with his apothecary box tucked firmly beneath his arm.

'I suppose I must congratulate you on your safe return to us,' said he, though to judge by his expression he had much rather see me hanged.

'Why were you called, Gould?'

He made no answer, nor did he pause at the bottom of the stairs but carried on by me and out the door. I called after him, demanding to know what had happened to Mrs Morgan. 'There is nothing wrong with the woman but only her nerves,' said he, turning in the porch. 'And I tell you, as I told Mrs Kendrick. You are not to call me here again unless from a real and urgent necessity.'

I strode out and almost breasted the damned fellow. 'If Mrs Morgan has need of you, sir, I shall summon you. And if you do not come, I shall fetch you.'

'Bloody foolery,' he muttered.

'Do you doubt me?'

He did not doubt me. The retort that I saw was in his mind died on his lips. He turned away, and then back. In some dudgeon, he perched his apothecary box on the porch rail, and then took out a small bottle. A red liquid medicine. He thrust the bottle into my hand. 'If Mrs Morgan should become in any way distraught, you may give her a good spoonful or two.'

'I am not her nurse.'

'I did not know if I should trust Mrs Kendrick with the medicine.'

'In future you may trust her, upon my word.'

'Keep Mrs Morgan resting. And do not trouble us at the hospital.'

'I am no doctor.'

'Can you not do as you are told, sir?' he broke out with a startling vehemence. It was so fierce, indeed, that I was instantly in no doubt but that it had risen from a much deeper trouble than his petty annoyance with me.

As he snapped closed his box, I said, 'How poorly is she?'

'Unlike you, sir, I have many other patients besides Mrs Morgan.' He made to move off, but I took his elbow. And when he looked at me now I saw the tiredness in his eyes, and the dark pouches beneath them. It came to me that he had not slept in some good while.

'Gould?' I tilted my head, squinting to read him. 'What is it?'

He pulled free his arm. He pursed his lips and seemed to consider a moment, and then he leaned toward me. 'Keep yourself from the hospital. The smallpox has taken hold among the blacks.'

CHAPTER 16

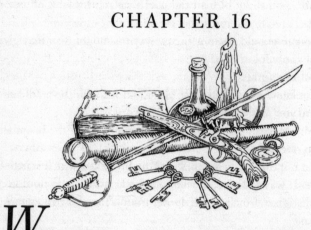

Within York Town were some seven thousand British soldiers, two score townsfolk and fifteen hundred or more blacks; and what chance in a space of a thousand yards by six hundred, which comprised the whole town, that a horror such as the smallpox might be kept long a secret?

Once Gould had departed I made no hesitation but sent Calvert to fetch Francesca and the cook to me. And when they came I gave them the most forceful and threatening admonition that they were to keep from the black encampments on the beach, and to stay clear of any person they suspected of a fever. I asked them if they felt themselves poorly, but they at once declared their good health (their insistence upon it making me suspect that they had already heard some rumour of the contagion). Next I took Calvert aside and gave him the same warning, and also the reason of it, which he took steadily enough after overcoming his first surprise. Then I went upstairs and looked in at my bedroom, where I found Campbell seated with his feet upon the window ledge, studying the ships on the river with my spyglass.

'Have you been down to the blacks' camp since we came here?'

'No.'

'There is smallpox among them. You shall leave the town tonight.'

He received this news with so little change in his expression that had I not known him I might have thought he had not understood me. He gave a small lift of his head, and then returned his attention to the ships.

I then went along to Mrs Morgan's room, and as Mrs Kendrick stepped out I glimpsed Mrs Morgan lying abed within. Lizzy Morgan was at the dressing table near to her, and with a hairbrush in her hand. I drew Mrs Kendrick a short way along the hall, and then told her what Gould had told me.

'But the man said nothing to me,' she protested.

'He has no doubt been ordered to silence by Carruthers.' I explained to her that I had already warned the others in the house, and that the rest of the town would certainly hear of it before very long. 'I expect there shall be transport provided for the civilians who wish to leave.'

It was much for her to take in. She put a hand on her hip, and the fingertips of her other hand touched her forehead. 'What of Mrs Morgan and Lizzy?'

'They must stay.'

'Because you say so?'

'If they were to go down to Williamsburg, they would be used in the interrogation of their men. And there is every chance that Mrs Morgan would be charged alongside of them. Once Mrs Morgan is recovered, I shall get them both to the Gloucester side. It is very little you think of me, madam, but I am no monster to wantonly endanger the life of a woman and her child.'

'It is poor enough security you have been to her menfolk,' said she, which was a stab at my very heart. 'Though I do not doubt your good intentions, Mr Douglas, while Mrs Morgan and Lizzy remain here, I must stay with them.'

'That is not necessary.'

'In my own house it is I that shall decide what is necessary. You will excuse me,' said she.

'Madam,' said I, putting a hand upon her arm to stop her.

She looked down at my hand, and then raised her eyes slowly. There was something in her gaze implacable. 'You will excuse me,' she said again, and very quiet now.

I lifted my hand from her arm, and she stepped by me and went on down the hall.

Colonel Tarleton sat alone by the wall of the stable-yard, and tapped his crop pensively upon his boot. There were a few officers and grooms about the yard, but there seemed such a pall cast over them, and they so visibly downcast, that I was in some wonder at the cause of it. Indeed, had I not been so much in need of Tarleton's help at that moment, I might have forborne to approach him.

When I came near, he continued staring down. I remarked that I trusted they had suffered no loss. He glanced up, seeming not to comprehend me, and so I gestured about. 'I hope you have suffered no casualties among your fellows.'

'No, no.' He rose, taking up his hat and putting it under his arm. 'We have hardly been out from the town since you came with us. But I must go out now to the southern beach. You may join me if you wish.'

Two of his officers fell in with him, and both wearing the same grave expression as their commander. It being necessary that I should speak privately with Tarleton, I must then walk out with them through the southern opening in our entrenchment, but with some puzzlement that they should go unmounted. The strangeness deepened when we passed between the two redoubts under construction near the river.

There were twenty or thirty horses corralled just above the beach, each with a white cross marked upon its shoulder. And though corralled, they were hobbled in the same fashion as our few hundred horses that grazed the land between the town and the woods. Below the corral were two high posts set into the sandy beach, and a sail slung between them like a partition. As we neared, the several dragoons by the corral busied themselves with bringing down more ropes from a nearby cart. Tarleton stopped above the beach, and I with him, while the two officers went to take charge of the dragoons.

It was evident that Tarleton meant to offer no explanation to me, and evident too that this was no moment to be burdening him with my concern for the Morgans; for his hands were clasped behind his back, his gaze fixed before him, and he was absolutely intent upon the scene. A halter was put onto one of the corralled horses. It was then led down the beach and behind the sail-partition, where it was hid from the herd, and from us. What was done I cannot say, but certainly the means were swift, for there was hardly a sound came from there but only a sudden heavy thud, which could only be the horse's dead weight falling upon the sand. The dragoons then appeared from behind the sail, dragging the horse's body the last of the way into the river. A minute more and we saw the new-slaughtered creature floating downriver on the tide.

I glanced at Tarleton but he neither moved nor showed any emotion beyond a clenching of the jaw. The next of the herd was chosen, and then haltered and taken across the beach behind the sail. The second dispatch was no less swiftly effected than the first, though this time a spray of sand kicked up against the sail, which sound caused a few of the corralled horses to whinny and look over; but seeing only the sail and not the shambles behind, they bent their necks again to find out the last blades of grass.

Though there was now some quiet cursing from the dragoons at work behind the sail, and an increased milling of the corralled horses as they scented their fellow creatures' blood, yet it was now evident that the whole slaughter should pass with no panic. Tarleton ordered his officers to remain to the last, and then he turned and I walked with him from the beach. As we came up toward the main encampment of his Legion, Tarleton's gaze went over the hobbled horses there. A sergeant was passing among them and marking those in the poorest condition with a white cross upon the shoulder.

'But shall these all be slaughtered?' said I, astonished at the sight, for they were at least a score. And though I understood the necessity of preserving our supplies, yet so wilful a destruction of our cavalry must tie us more firmly, and perhaps inescapably, to York Town.

Tarleton's answer scarcely reassured me. He said that this was only the first culling, but that he feared worse must follow. He told me that he had made request to Cornwallis that the cavalry be crossed to Gloucester. 'Simcoe promises me that there is still forage to be had there. And I have had a hint from Major Ross that my appeal is not entirely dismissed. Pray God I am crossed over before I have every horse here slaughtered from under me.'

After Tarleton had finished his brief discussion with the sergeant concerning the next horses to be culled, he walked with me back toward the town. And as we went, I told Tarleton, and very frankly, of the great difficulty I was now in with regard to the Morgans.

'As you see, I am responsible for the both of them,' I concluded. 'Just as you should be if any of your dragoons were lost by a blunder of your making.'

'Does Mrs Morgan accuse you?'

'She does not think me entirely innocent. Nor am I. And while Cable Morgan and his son have life, I must work to get them back to her. I shall not let my own pride prevent me from begging any favour that may help them.' He glanced across at me, aware now of where my whole conversation tended. 'Would you hear it?' said I.

'I have not stopped my ears. But whatever my reputation, I should warn you, I am not fool enough to try any rescue of them.'

'When Washington brings up his army, when they first come near York Town, there shall at first be some considerable disorder. It is likely your dragoons shall be sent out to harass them.' Tarleton confirmed this, telling me that he was ordered to go out at the first sighting of the enemy by our sentries. I said, 'There is but one thing can save the Morgans now. We must make an exchange for them.'

'For which you first need a prisoner.'

'Just so.'

'Not any mere prisoner, I presume.'

'It must take more than a captured infantryman.'

'An officer? Allow that I take such a one. Whether he is then kept

166

or exchanged shall not be at my disposal. It must then be for my Lord Cornwallis to decide.'

'Only deliver me a prisoner, and I can ask no more of you. I must answer for the rest.'

'I can promise you nothing.'

'But you shall think on it?'

We neared the line of entrenchment now, and Tarleton looked back toward the hobbled horses. Whether they scented the blood spilling at the river, or from some other cause, these horses had gathered together now and were moving in a hobbled herd toward the wood. But they could not escape the sergeant who still moved among them, marking for the next cull.

'I shall think on it,' said Tarleton. 'But I promise you nothing.'

On the sand by the wharf a flatboat was beached. As Campbell and I came down we saw a party of seamen manhandling an 18-pounder out from the boat onto a waiting cart, and other seamen at the boat's stern unloading heavy shot. Campbell directed my attention to another unloading then proceeding a short way north, under Stuart's command, and we went along there. Neither gun nor shot came out from this boat, but instead a great pile of planks and lumber; and this wood was being loaded onto the cart, near which Lieutenant Sutherland stood making an inspection.

'It is a fair haul you have got there,' said I to Sutherland, to which he answered dourly that it would be enough to make decent platforms for six guns and no more. In truth, and in spite of his sombre look, I could see how very pleased he was with Stuart's enterprise in fetching the wood across from the Gloucester side.

Leaving Campbell by the water, I went up with Stuart to the pair of caves cut into the bluff above the beach. There was a campfire outside the caves, but none of his men were about, for they were all down at the unloading. Once he had fetched out his tally-book from the table inside the first cave, we stood by the fire and looked down toward the boat. I asked him about the conditions the far side of the river, and what trouble he had faced in fetching the load, which questions he answered while his gaze stayed on Campbell by the boat. At last he said, 'You have not come down to enquire the results of my scavenging.'

'No.'

'Is it Campbell?'

'He is leaving us.'

'When?'

'Just as soon as we are done here.'

'Done?' said he.

'I hoped you might have given some consideration, Jonathan, to what I asked you the other day. Campbell has volunteered to stay behind the rebel lines to help us. He shall send Pamunkey down to us in their canoes. You are based here by the river' – I indicated the campfire and the caves behind us. 'I cannot know where I shall be when the Pamunkey come down. I must trust in someone here who must meet them and bring their messages to me.'

'You might send Calvert down.'

'If a siege commence, he shall return to the Fusiliers. And he does not understand the Indians.'

'You are asking me to do it, Mr Douglas.'

'I am.'

'And if I do not agree, shall I be compelled by an order?'

'No. I shall be disappointed. But no, I shall not have you ordered to it against your will.'

His eyes stayed on Campbell, who had now wandered from the boat a short way along the shore. Though Stuart had certainly considered of our earlier conversation, yet it seemed that he had decided nothing till this moment. But now he conceded, though with no great joy, 'Very well. And what must I do?'

I called Campbell up to us. Then I stayed with them only long enough to tell them that I relied upon their cooperation and good judgement to arrange how the coming and going of the Pamunkey should happen. After that I left them together and went down to rejoin Sutherland at the boat.

Sutherland, I now discovered, had been given that map of the

Williamsburg road that I had drawn for Lord Cornwallis, and my sketches of the bridges and other places that might usefully be mined ahead of the enemy's advance. He had from me now a brief sketch in the sand, and an opinion on how many sappers might be needed. Then he asked me what I had seen of the enemy's guns in Williamsburg; and though I mentioned the possibility of siege guns being landed there, I told him that I could not be certain. Yet the mere possibility seemed to cause him no little consternation, and well it might; for such guns proved frequently the Nemesis of an engineer's best works. But also he requested from me a more surprising thing, which was that I should make some proper drawings and sketches of all our entrenchments.

'You have a better hand than me, or any of my fellows,' said he. 'And I have a mind to make some good record of what we do here.' He told me that it was just such field-sketches which were lacking back in Woolwich where the young artillery officers and engineers underwent their first training.

This suited me, I own, very well; for without I had some daily purpose in York Town, there was ever a danger that Lord Cornwallis might send me to the relative safety of Gloucester. And so I told Sutherland that if he would send paper and materials to Mrs Kendrick's house, I should spare him what hours I might. But all the while that I talked with Sutherland, I kept one eye upon Campbell and Stuart, who remained in uneasy conference up by the caves.

In the dim evening light, their dark silhouettes were the veriest copies of their respective fathers. Both were tall men, Campbell the stouter of the two, and with a blunt pugnacity in his stance that made Stuart seem almost slender. The years dropped away as I observed them. Indeed, I might be by the Mississippi and watching their fathers, both now gone from the world, their heads then together and scheming some scheme against the French. It was a fond remembrance, though touched with sadness for times past and friends lost; and, I confess, also for the childlessness of my own life. A man is not meant for solitude; and whatever his ties of friendship and society, it is only a woman or a child may properly join him to the main.

After a time I left Sutherland and went up to the caves. They had already made their arrangement for how the Pamunkey canoes should come in, but there was no warmth between young Stuart and Campbell as they parted. They gave each other the briefest of nods, which though it pained me to see, I refrained from any lecture upon the friendship I had hoped for them. Campbell and I then walked up to the Williamsburg road, where I gave him some last instructions before he disappeared like a spirit into the woods.

CHAPTER 17

*T*he third night after Campbell went out, his first message came down with a Pamunkey canoe. Campbell confirmed that the Morgans were not yet hanged, but that they were now kept in the Public Gaol.

With this heaviest weight lifted from my shoulders, I found myself better able to make proper use of the papers and materials Sutherland had sent me, and for a time almost lost myself fully in the recording of the engineering works that he had requested. I became quickly a familiar presence on the entrenchments, and the sappers in particular took an interest in my work. I in my turn found them very useful; for once they understood what I did, they made sure to fetch me when any unusual or important work was about to be undertaken. I was glad, too, that I had some occupation to take me from the house where Mrs Morgan remained always in her room, and Mrs Kendrick grew ever more watchful of her patient, and obstinate in her intent to keep me from intruding there.

And yet I frequently shared a meal with Mrs Kendrick and Lizzy. The poor girl remained always cheerful, knowing only that her father and brother had extended their stay in Williamsburg, but not the reason; and that though her mother was unwell she might trust in the care of Mrs Kendrick. And Mrs Kendrick showed a real affection for the child. Concerning Mrs Morgan's poor condition, I heard of that only after Lizzy was taken up to bed by the maid, and Mrs Kendrick then came to read for an hour each night in the library.

I was gone out from the house alone one evening, and sketching on the northern rampart overlooking the river, when General O'Hara happened upon me. He stood at my shoulder for a time as I continued my work. Then he stepped up beside me, rested his forearms upon the parapet, and looked out at the ships.

'If our works be as well made as your sketches of them, Douglas, we need not fear the French guns.' I acknowledged the compliment, but did not welcome the distraction. He seemed to sense that, and made no further remark but stayed there looking out quietly across the river till after five minutes I was done with the embrasure and I put my sketchbook aside. Then I followed his gaze across to the far side. Above Gloucester there was no clearing in the woods, for the ground there was too poor to be farmed, so that the country that side had been left largely virgin. It looked now as it must have looked to our first settlers, and to the first Pamunkey, untouched since Creation. 'I shall not be sorry to leave this wretched place,' said O'Hara. 'Not in the least.'

'Do you continue to believe, sir, that General Clinton shall come?'

'Whether he come or not, we shall not winter here.'

He seemed tired, and almost resigned to whatever should now unfold. And after studying him, I ventured a question I should not have dared but for his familiar approach to me. 'Sir, is there something ails Lord Cornwallis?'

'Is there some rumour of it?' said he, frowning.

'No, the thought was mine.'

'Then you may dismiss it. Nothing ails him, but only our situation.'

'If I may be so forward as to make the suggestion, sir, it is his Lordship's tardiness to act upon our situation that has caused me to wonder if he is entirely himself. It is quite contrary to his reputation.'

'He is only flesh and blood, Mr Douglas. The southern campaign was no leisurely walk. And if General Clinton has ordered us here, and promised reinforcement, what else must his Lordship do?'

'General Clinton has no such near view as his Lordship of Washington and Rochambeau's approach.'

'We must keep patience. You know that our morning counsels remain open to you, Douglas. You shall have no reason to complain to Mr Jenkinson of our treatment of you.'

'Be assured, General, that Mr Jenkinson has only my regular reports of me. I would not trouble him with complaints of any imagined slights.'

'Your reports have not dissuaded the King's friends from continuing this unwinnable war,' said he; and eyeing me shrewdly, added, 'Or perhaps I mistake you.'

'You mistake me, sir, if you think that I shall ever break the privacy of my communications with Mr Jenkinson.' General O'Hara was a sufficiently good-tempered man; but though he smiled at my reply, there was a definite strain in it. A brigadier general is little accustomed to being so unapologetically turned aside. But not wishing him for an enemy, I then said, 'I cannot think that the right is entirely on the rebel side or on ours, sir. But something is self-evidently wrong in either our policy or its execution, that after five years of fratricidal war we have not yet reached either an accommodation or an answer.'

'You must tell them so in Westminster and Whitehall, Mr Douglas,' said he emphatically. 'We must all tell them so.'

But in spite of O'Hara's words, and the determined slap of his hands upon the parapet, I knew him for a man too genial, and too fond of convivial good company, to make any open dispute with superiors who were also his friends. Though he might share these private thoughts more openly, and to better purpose, with Lord Cornwallis, it must be idle waste of breath for me to tell him so.

'Indeed, sir,' said I; and gathering up my sketchbook, I took my leave of him and came down from the rampart.

On the night of the 26th three deserters came into our lines, crossing over to us from a black regiment of the Continental Army. Each of these fellows had a tale of grievance against his officers, and each had for us an account of how the French and American troops were now being marshalled and drilled outside Williamsburg. They believed this to be in preparation for an imminent march across the peninsula to York Town. I got confirmation of their information the same night, by a Pamunkey canoe that came down from Campbell; and under this weight of evidence, Cornwallis gave the order for the mining of the Williamsburg road.

Arrived at Lieutenant Sutherland's quarters in the hour before sunrise, I found the junior engineers gathered, and they in some high spirits, which I saw was partly fear; for it was these who must now go out with the sappers to mine the bridges and roads ahead of the enemy's approach.

Sutherland had my drawings spread out on his table, and one last time he talked the young officers carefully through his expectation of them. When he had done, he wished them luck and dismissed them, and they filed out to join the sappers at the two carts already loaded with powder and tools.

Tarleton and his dragoons were to be the sappers' guard, and I mounted with them by the northern gate. Our motley column was soon moving out beneath the Fusiliers' redoubt, and on we went past our sentry post, down the Williamsburg road into the woods.

The dragoons were very thorough in their sweeping of the woods near the road, and with only a few pistol-shots quickly chased out a few dozen Virginian militia from their hiding places among the pines. The enemy kept themselves well clear after that, and took only sporadic and quite useless shots at us through the trees. Wary of Tarleton's dragoons, they fell back continually before our slow advance. We went four miles before we reached the furthest extent of our march, and then the engineers and sappers commenced to mine the first of the bridges. There was no fine skill in the task. The sappers dug the ground by the piers, the engineers planted their bombs, and then everyone stood off while the fuseman did his work. After this first bridge was exploded there was some small increase in the enemy fire; but Tarleton's men soon chased them off again, and our withdrawal along the road to the next placement of powder was unhurried and orderly.

So it went on through the day, a very deliberate and laborious drudgery; and though the sappers did the work well and uncomplaining, yet it was evident from the first that the destruction we wrought could not long delay any competent engineers. For the creeks were low, and their beds not nearly as soft as we had expected; nor was there sufficient rock beneath the road to make our powder blow open any sizeable craters. The sappers felled trees in several places to make obstructions, which they would not have done but for the poor results of the powder. And by the time we had come back to within half a mile of our sentry post, we knew that we had bought at most a short delay, perhaps a day or two, in the advance of the enemy's guns.

Drained by their day's work and the heat, the sappers at last stopped the carts in a shaded place on the road. Some then lay upon the trays while several of their fellows went down to cool themselves at the creek. Being so near to our own line, and not having received even a desultory fire from our enemy the past hour, we little expected any trouble. So when the shouts of anger and alarm came from down by the creek it took those of us above unawares. I looked to Tarleton, who then drew his sabre, shouting to the nearest dragoons, 'About me!'

Those sappers resting in the carts leaped up, turning to where their fellows now hurried up from the creek. Several of these had stripped off their shirts, and others had wet their heads and faces. Every one of them wore a look of raw fury.

Tarleton called to their leader, Baker, 'Are you attacked, man?'

Voices broke out angrily upon every side, but Baker at last got his own voice heard over them.

'The creek,' cried Baker, flinging an arm out behind. 'Come down, sir, and see.'

Tarleton rode down, and I after him, with the angry sappers close at our heels.

There was a fallen branch across the creek, and a debris of twigs and leaves piled high against it, partly shielding the lower creek from our view. But as we neared, we saw over this dam, and the reason of the sappers' fury became instantly clear. There were four dead bodies in the creek, all blacks, three men and a woman. The bodies were naked, and the pale blisters of the smallpox covered every part of them from their faces to their feet. The creek eddied around their limbs and dragged upon the woman's hair.

Cart-tracks led up from the place toward York Town. The bodies had quite obviously been dumped in the water by our own people, with the hope to poison it before the enemy's arrival.

'Who has drunk here?' I demanded of Baker.

There were none had drunk from the creek below the bodies, he said. He told me that he had come down this way to relieve himself. It was he who had found the bodies and put up the first alarm.

'Gather your men from the woods,' I told Tarleton. 'Warn them against the water.' Then I said to Baker, 'Collect together all those men who came down here. Take them up to the road and wait for me there. Warn the others above, and send them directly away from you and into town.'

Turning my horse savagely, I rode upstream along the creek. I rode a quarter-mile, fearing upon every pleasantly shaded bank to find more infected bodies. But I found no more of them. The worst of my fears abating, I came at length upon a pair of dragoons, and I led these fellows back to Baker and the sappers who anxiously awaited my return.

'It is clear a quarter-mile upstream,' I told the sappers, 'and I much doubt that there are any more bodies beyond. It is most likely you are none of you infected.'

'That is no thanks to the damned doctors,' cried Baker, in a manner at once furious and relieved. 'They never gave a blind bloody thought to us,' said he, to which several others of the sappers added remarks very much worse.

'You will hold your tongue,' said I. 'All of you.'

'We are not dogs,' cried one bold fellow.

'They think more of the dogs than of us,' called another; and I own, there was so fierce an anger among them that I was glad they were only a dozen. Though I felt no personal threat from them, yet I was in no doubt that this accident – that we had not been forewarned of the creek's poisoning – had tapped a well of resentment already very deep in the sappers. They had been worked like blacks these past weeks, done much hard labour and got no thanks for it, and they knew it very well.

I ordered Baker to take his men in past the sentry post and wait there for me. 'I shall make enquiry in the town if there are any bodies higher in the creek. When I am satisfied, I shall come out and fetch you in.'

The notion that they might yet carry the infection had a sudden quieting effect upon them. Tarleton brought his dragoons onto the road and I passed the sappers into his care before riding on ahead into York Town.

In the drawing room at Cornwallis's headquarters was no senior officer, but only two ensigns, one of whom directed me to the rear dining room. In there I found Major Ross, and he engaged in amiable conversation with that fellow Secretary Nelson.

'Major Ross?' said I, with a jerk of my head to bring him out.

'You are very welcome to join us, sir,' said Nelson. 'I would not put any gentleman from my table.' This was my own private advice to Cornwallis that was now being used to taunt me. I looked thunder at the man, and he seemed well satisfied with the hit he had made against me. But thankfully Major Ross then rose between us, excusing himself to Nelson, and followed me out.

'You must not mind Nelson,' said he as we entered the front drawing room. 'He causes no trouble to us.'

'I have just come in from the Williamsburg road with the sappers. There are dead blacks dumped in the creek there. The bodies are riddled with the smallpox.'

'But the bodies were to have been put into the southern creek.'

'That is as may be. But they are in the northern creek, I do promise you. And some of the sappers have drunk the water.'

'No.'

177

'Yes. It was the first water that they came to. Neither Tarleton nor I were informed the creek would be poisoned.'

'The order was for the south,' said he defensively. 'There were to be none put into the northern creeks till tomorrow. The dragoons—'

'None of the dragoons has touched the water.'

'Thank God,' said he; and the crimson flush upon his face began then to subside.

'Major, the sappers have taken it as a slight against them that you should be so indifferent to their safety. They are in no good temper. I must confirm with Gould what number of bodies he has put in that creek. Till then, I have ordered any who drank from it to stay out near the sentry post.'

'And what men may they be, Mr Douglas?' said Cornwallis, overhearing my last words as he came into the room. 'I was not aware of any men put under your command.' He tossed his tricorn onto a chair, unbuckled his sword and handed it to the ensign. As he settled behind his table, I recounted to him, somewhat bluntly, the whole incident out at the creek. His face grew grave. 'When you are certain they are none of them infected, Douglas, then you may bring them in,' said he when I was done. 'Major Ross, you shall warn Dr Gould, or whoever it is has made the foolish error, that orders are not intended for guidance only. They must be more careful of a strict obedience in the future.'

'My Lord,' said I in disbelief at the leniency, 'the doctors' negligence has come close to making an end of the sappers.'

'And what would you have me do, Mr Douglas? Rebuke the doctors that they have worked now for several days and nights, till they can hardly stand, much less think? And they always themselves in some peril of infection? If they have made some small error in their orders, then they have done no more than many good officers before them. And with much better reason. It is not a hanging offence. And if none of the sappers have been infected, then let us account ourselves fortunate, and so pass on. Our position here does not allow of every military nicety.'

This was spoken, I must confess, with a manly directness; and, in some wise, with a patience toward me that I hardly deserved. For as the commander of the army, there can be no doubt but that Cornwallis's mind was now under the most tremendous and awful strain. He must hold in balance the needs of every officer and regiment, and Captain Symonds's men too; and even the remaining townsfolk, and the blacks, must make some demand upon his time and his thoughts. Against all this, the indignation of Baker and the sappers at a near-poisoning must have seemed scarce worthy of notice.

It says much that when he then asked me, 'Are you content, sir?' I hesitated only a moment before I bowed my head to him. For though the bitter anger of the sappers had deeply affected me, yet in Lord Cornwallis's presence I felt the touch of the greater shadow that was over him, and the threat of the storm that might soon break over all of us.

Chastened, I went to speak with Gould; and he confirming that there were no further bodies in the northern creek, I rode out to the sentry post and fetched the sappers in.

The whole British army now being brought within the outer line, three carts were set to the dreadful service of removing the smallpox-infected corpses from the hospital, and from the ragged encampment that had sprung up alongside. There were more than enough bodies to poison all the creeks, save only the Ballard Creek from which the Fusiliers drew their water. Nor was it only the dead blacks, but a slaughter was made of thirty more horses, and this time nearer the woods, so that the few bullocks that remained to us could more easily drag the horses' bodies into the standing pools of clear water.

I witnessed most of these dismal preparations from upon the ramparts of the Pigeon Hill redoubts, where I sat an entire day sketching the fascines, which are bundles of sticks laid on the outer earthworks to spread the blow of the shells, and the gabions, which are wicker baskets filled with stone. A party of blacks made the fascines, and a party of sappers the gabions; and each kept its distance from the other.

Nobody talked, but every now and then one of the sappers would stand upright, stretch his back, and look out toward the woods where the enemy must soon appear. And I looked out too, and often; for in that first arrival must lie Tarleton's best chance of a prisoner and my own best hope of an exchange for the Morgans. But the woods were quiet, and nothing disturbed the sweltering stillness but only the sound of those corpse-filled carts going by, the scrapings of insects, and the call of birds rising off the pools of newly infected water.

CHAPTER 18

*O*n the night of the 27th of September, Stuart brought me Campbell's fateful message: the allied armies would commence their march upon York Town the next morning. I took this message to Lord Cornwallis, who studied it very soberly, before putting it aside. 'Let them march as they please,' said he. 'We are ready.'

But just how far from ready we were was discovered in the early hours of the next morning, and before any appearance of the enemy. For a Return being finally made of the provisions remaining in the town, and upon our ships, a significant shortfall from Cornwallis's best expectations was at this late hour brought to light. There was only one course open to Lord Cornwallis, and he ordered that we must put all the useless mouths out from the town. The tents housing the sick blacks near the Courthouse hospital were consequently struck; and from the black encampments down on the beach, the women and children, and the infirm and sick, were all now brought up. A few carried small bundles, but most had nothing but only the rags they stood in. These were then given some pitiful provisions before being sent out from the town with a warning against drinking the poisoned water in the woods.

There was no general marshalling of these people, but throughout the morning there were bands of them sent out from our lines and into the woods. God knows their fate, or how many of these wretched souls survived. The intention of most of them seemed to be that they should hide themselves till the expected reinforcements arrived with General Clinton; and though they buoyed themselves with this hope, the fear in them was very plain as they passed out the gates. They were most of them runaway slaves, and they well knew what harsh retribution would be visited upon them if recaptured by the rebels.

A further decision was then made by Cornwallis to cull more of our horses; and there were a hundred and more killed that same morning, on the same beach where I had witnessed the first slaughter.

With no sign of the enemy by the early afternoon, I went down to the beach to find Tarleton. I found instead a heavy red foam drifting along the tideline, and dead horses like a fleet of upturned coracles floating just out from the shore. But a few hundred yards inland was a company of mounted dragoons, and in their midst I spied Tarleton's tall hat and feathers among the skittish horses. When I joined him, he told me that he had sent out several patrols the past hours, and that the latest had returned with reports of enemy columns upon the road.

'I confess, I had doubted your man Campbell's information,' said he. 'But it seems they are almost upon us.'

'Has there been skirmishing?'

'No, but it cannot be long. They have been little detained by your sappers' work.'

'We shall not see their heavy guns for some days yet.'

He stroked the flank of his horse, bending then to run his hand over the fetlock. The horse raised its hoof, and Tarleton gave the shoe a brief inspection before setting the hoof down. All about us now his officers were talking quietly together, sometimes laughing, and ever with a hand resting upon their horses and an eye upon the woods. 'I presume you have come to remind me of your request,' said he.

'I understand that you can make no promise.'

'If Washington has any sense, he shall keep his men well back in the woods till he has the guns forward. If he does that, we shall see no proper action today.'

But hardly had he spoke these words than away to the north, somewhere up by our sentry post on the Williamsburg road, musketshots sounded. It was but a few rounds, less than a dozen shots, and at that distance (which must be a mile or more) we heard nothing of any voices or shouting. But once the shots had died, there came from the Pigeon Hill redoubts, and from the inner-line redoubts nearer us, an excited whooping and hollering from our soldiers at this first contact with the enemy. Drums suddenly beat in several places in the town. Tarleton leaped into his saddle.

'I am under my Lord Cornwallis's orders,' said he, as his horse danced beneath him and his officers mounted. 'But if a chance present itself, then very well, Douglas, I shall not let it go by.'

'I can ask no more.'

Wheeling, he rode away, and I hurried across to the first Pigeon Hill redoubt.

There were thirty or forty soldiers within the redoubt, and they mostly clustered about the northern side, their captain with his spyglass raised. Apart from muskets, they had but a pair of light guns, 2-pounders, and the gunners now loaded these with grapeshot. In the midst of the redoubt was a magazine cut into the ground, with a roof of pine-logs, and covered in earth. The parapet had been raised to about six feet in height, and I quickly joined the others on the rampart.

Firing came again, but far to the north. When I opened my spyglass, I saw nothing in that direction but only the scrubby wood around the morass made by the many small creeks there. Some of our soldiers were running out from the town toward the unfinished redoubt in the midst of it; but in truth the morass was the better protection to us in that quarter than any guns.

It was half an hour before we sighted the first enemy infantryman in the woods to our front. A blue-jacketed Continental, he was there and then gone. The redoubt's captain called to his men to hold off from any firing, and in the next minutes a score of these blue-jacketed fellows appeared. They made no advance upon us, but moved swiftly about the woods just beyond range of our muskets.

And yet for all that we had seen the enemy, and they had seen us, another quarter-hour passed before any man fired. It came from their side, a single musketshot, and we replied nothing to begin. But after a minute there came a more concerted firing from one part of the woods, their lead pattering harmless against our redoubt wall.

Our captain turned to his gunners. 'Let them know we are here, lads. Advise them to stand further off. First gun. A single shot only.'

There was a run of barked commands, the powder lit, and the gunners turned aside and held their ears. There came a single boom, a judder beneath our feet, and the cracking and slashing sound of the grapeshot spraying through the woods. A moment later, the gunsmoke still drifting over us, a single cry of agony came out from the pines.

'Reload!' cried the captain.

Through my glass now, I saw enemy infantrymen falling back into the woods; and though a few of them fired their muskets, it was with no properly directed intent. The wounded fellow suddenly ceased his tortured wailing, but the silence that followed was almost equally unnerving.

I stayed another two hours on the redoubt, till near sunset. Though the occasional exchange of musketshot continued, it was clear that there would be no bold frontal attack upon our outer line that day. The enemy's purpose, and a wise one, was evidently to scout our defences before they moved in earnest against us. More than once I saw parties of their mounted officers surveying our lines, but these fellows kept themselves well back from our guns. And though I might fervently wish to see Tarleton burst in among them, I well understood the reason he made no attempt. For their infantry were arrived in number now, spread all through the woods, and more than ready to fight.

As the sun set behind the pines, smoke rose from their campfires further back; and our own campfire then being lit behind the redoubt, and piquets being sent out to keep the first watch, I at last came out from the redoubt. I wended my way through the felled trees of our abatis, and walked the several hundred yards back into town. The night Reveille was being beat as I stepped tiredly onto Mrs Kendrick's porch. Major Ross hailed me from the street and then came over.

'We have these for your perusal,' said he, putting a satchel into my hand. It was the twin of that satchel carried by the young French messenger the marines had shot. 'It was taken by one of the Fusiliers this past hour.'

'Taken or found?' said I.

'I am told it was dropped as the Frenchmen fled.'

'Then it is useless to us, Major,' said I, attempting to hand the satchel back to him.

'We are aware of the ruse, Mr Douglas. His Lordship bade me bring them to you only that we may understand what misdirection Rochambeau means to give us.' After considering of this a moment, I inclined my head. I said that I should bring the decipherments across to the headquarters just as soon as I was done.

Ross then told me something of how the afternoon had passed elsewhere on our outer line, and of Lord Cornwallis's satisfaction at the enemy's hesitation to launch any meaningful and direct attack. 'It appears they have brought no heavy guns across with them. Our sappers perhaps did better work than we knew. And yourself, of course.'

I replied that I was little surprised that their infantry had outmarched the carts bringing over the guns. 'But be in no doubt, Major, they have heavy guns in plenty, and they shall not long delay upon the road.' He made no contradiction of me, and I asked him then what we knew of the disposition of the enemy forces, mentioning that I had seen no French uniform all the day.

'It looks to be Washington's men that make the southern part of their line. Rochambeau's Frenchmen are to the north. We shall know better what they intend tomorrow.'

'Their intention is very plain,' said I. 'They shall now entrench and lay siege to us. It is our own intention that I wonder at.'

'An escape by way of Gloucester is not entirely dismissed. Nor is it dismissed that we may hold our position and await General Clinton. There shall be a council held tomorrow night to decide it. I might propose to his Lordship that you have a place of observation with us?'

'I would be obliged, Major.'

As he made to go, I enquired after whether Tarleton's dragoons had been engaged, and whether any enemy prisoners had been taken. Ross had not heard of any engagement; but he was certain that we had taken no prisoners.

The next day was equally fruitless to me, and mostly a waiting time for our gunners; for the enemy established their encampments far back in the woods, beyond range of our shot. Their engineers and officers were occasionally visible in mounted parties, and at a distance, making a survey of our defences; but there was very little we might do to impede them. Within the town, our sappers and the few hundred healthy blacks that we had not put out now worked solely upon the inner entrenchment; and with them now were any soldiers who might be spared from the redoubts and batteries. Sutherland strode about with a fierce look and a harsh word for any junior officer who neglected to keep the men to their work.

I had completed the few inconsequential decipherments during the night, and once I had returned these to Major Ross in the early morning I might go where I pleased. It was, though, but a poor freedom; for wherever I went about our line, my eye was drawn continually to Tarleton's dragoons as they passed between our inner and outer lines. But not once did I see them go into the woods, which was the only place where they might have captured a prisoner.

The previous day I had been disheartened, but this second day was worse. I came back into the town from the Fusiliers' redoubt at sunset almost despairing that I should ever find the means to save the Morgans.

I took my supper with Mrs Kendrick, and a very thin gruel it was. The rationing now imposed by the Commissary, Perkins, was very strict, and no exceptions made for either officers or ladies. And though

I was no better company to Mrs Kendrick at table than Campbell might have been, there was much perception in the woman; and so once she had taken my mood by the first distracted answers that I gave her upon the enemy's preparations, she allowed me my silence. More than that, she let it make no impenetrable wall between us, but instead told me something of her own day. At Gould's request, she had got the linen collected from all the town's houses, and had then set Francesca and some other servants and slave-girls to making bandages.

'Lizzy has helped them. It is almost the only amusement she has had since she came here.'

'How much does she understand?'

'She may hear the guns as well as any. I have told her it is the army at practice.'

'And her mother?'

'Little changed. She is hardly from her bed. I have been careful that she is never long alone.'

'I am in your debt, Mrs Kendrick.'

'It is no chore to me, Mr Douglas. What else might I do here while we wait? And Lizzy is delightful.' There was in her tone, and in her look, an unexpected gentleness. She touched her napkin to her lips.

'I shall arrange to have you all sent over to the Gloucester side,' said I.

A line formed on her brow, and she set down the napkin. 'But Mr Calvert has assured me that we are quite safe here.'

'You are safe only till they bring up their heavy guns. It may take them some days, but they shall do it.'

'And I trust that you shall tell me when they do.'

'I would not let you all remain here till it is a matter of urgency.'

'Let us not dispute the question tonight, Mr Douglas. I think neither one of us has a mind just now for argument.'

'I must insist that you have a trunk packed and ready. Both for yourself and for Mrs Morgan.'

'That is done,' said she; which profession she made calmly, and with no abrasive tone, truly as if she meant me no provocation. I confess it quite disarmed me. I bowed my head to acknowledge her good intention. Then she said, 'Mr Douglas, there is something Mrs Morgan has asked me that I hardly know how I should answer.'

'Yes?'

'I had hoped you might be a guide to me for it.'

'And what is that?'

Mrs Kendrick hesitated. And then she said with a rush, 'She would know whether her husband and son have been hanged.'

I felt the blood drain from my face. But then recovering myself, I said, 'The truth, Mrs Kendrick, is that I do not know. But I have no reason to believe anything is altered in their situation since Campbell's last message to me.'

'What shall I tell her?'

'I cannot put the responsibility of it on to you. Does she think that I have forgotten them? I shall go up to her,' said I, and I made to rise.

'No,' said she, and her hand shot out to fix my hand to the table. 'She is sleeping now. And she does not think that you have forgotten them.'

'I must assure her of it.'

'I shall give her your assurance,' said she. 'Furthermore, I shall tell her that her husband and son have not been hanged.'

'We do not know that.'

'We do not know otherwise. And in her present condition, Mr Douglas, it is what she must hear.'

CHAPTER 19

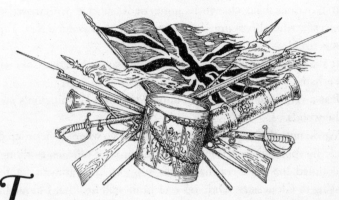

*T*hat night there was such a variety of new-washed uniforms at the headquarters it seemed more like a meeting at the Horse Guards in London than a council held at the front line of the American war. Colonels Abercrombie and Dundas were there, and Fuchs for the Hessians; Sutherland, of course, for the engineers, but also Rochfort for the Artillery, and a good many others, both headquarters and field officers. There was a preponderance of red jackets, and much gold braiding; but this was diversified by the Hessian blue, the green of the Legion, and some few more colours besides. The officers milled about, talking, and as Ross led me in I felt a drab moth among butterflies.

Lord Cornwallis sat at his table with O'Hara to one side of him and Captain Symonds to the other. As I passed, O'Hara raised a finger from the table to acknowledge me.

'You shall not mind to take a seat at the back, Mr Douglas,' said Ross, indicating the seat that I should take when the council was begun. Ross left me with Colonel Hamilton of the North Carolina Volunteers, who was the commander of our loyalist pioneers. With no weight at headquarters, he had been told very little of what would transpire in the council. And once he understood that I should be no help to him, he moved on, and Tarleton then joined me.

'And what shall be decided here?' said I, with a glance over the room. 'Has the arrival of Washington caused a single man here to change his opinion?'

'It has caused no change in mine, at least. Had we crossed to Gloucester when I first urged it, we might be approaching New York by this time.'

'It shall do your argument small good to say so tonight, Colonel.'

'Perhaps.'

'It is a very wide freedom you appear to afford Washington's men in the woods.'

'We do not all have your liberty, Douglas. I go where I am ordered.' While he spoke his gaze moved over his brother officers, as though he counted the numbers that might support his argument for the crossing to Gloucester. 'Did you ever hear,' said he, 'that I trained at the bar?'

'Is that true?'

'It is. And you may take it from me, in the Inns they are rogues to a man, and both sides of the bench. I never thought till now that I might be grateful for the low tricks they were then at such pains to teach me.'

Cornwallis signalled to Major Ross, who rapped his knuckles upon the table, calling us to order and requiring us to take our seats.

Once we were settled, O'Hara made some preliminary remarks on the day's incidents, ending by reading out the short list of our casualties, and giving an estimate of the likely casualties of our enemy. Captain Symonds then gave a brief report on the disposition of our ships, and of de Grasse's continuing blockade of the river. Near the front of the room, I noticed Tarleton's boot jiggling beneath his chair.

At the close of Symonds's report, O'Hara looked to Cornwallis, who sat impassive, arms folded as he stared at the floor. But he was fully aware of every eye upon him, and at last he raised his head and told O'Hara to proceed.

'I think we are all aware of the question under our consideration here, whether to remain in York Town and wait for General Clinton, or to cross over and break out by way of Gloucester,' continued O'Hara. 'Major Ross has with great thoroughness made tallies of all the estimates of the enemy's strength brought in by our patrols. We need not quibble the exactness of the figures, it is by way of our best understanding.' He then took up the paper before him and read the estimates. On our northern side there were more than five thousand Frenchmen. The morass about the centre they had not occupied. To the south were the Continental soldiers, Lafayette's men and the militia, to a total of more than seven thousand. 'On the Gloucester side Colonel Simcoe informs us that the Duc de Lauzun's cavalry are less than a thousand, and the worthwhile part of Weedon's militia scarcely more than that. But in the past hour I may tell you that we have had further news from Colonel Simcoe that there have been some hundreds of de Grasse's marines disembarked a few miles up the Bay above Gloucester. It must be to reinforce their poor containment of us there. Yes, Colonel Tarleton?'

'When were they disembarked, sir?'

'Today.'

There was a murmuring among the officers as each turned to his neighbour to remark this unwelcome news. But then Cornwallis unfolded his arms and leaned forward. 'A few hundred French marines more or less shall not direct my decision. Lieutenant Sutherland, if you please.'

Sutherland rose and went across to the large plan of our defences that he had earlier fixed to the wall. He pointed out the weaknesses that he feared still existed on our inner line. And then beyond our redoubts, he traced with his finger his expectation of where the first French works might begin.

'And how soon might they commence?' interrupted O'Hara.

'Tomorrow.'

'But it shall be some time before they shall have any positions for their guns.'

'Four or five days, sir.'

'That is fast.'

'They shall labour under no shortage of tools,' answered Sutherland, as though O'Hara's remark were accusation against the tardiness of our engineers upon the York Town defences. 'What they can do in five days with proper tools, we cannot do in ten.'

The Hessian, Ewald, then stood; and awaiting no invitation, and with words and accent barely intelligible, seemed to make some question of the whole engineering works that Sutherland had done. Indeed, I think it was only the allowance made for him as a foreign officer prevented it escalating into a matter of honour between him and our chief engineer. As it was, Sutherland, to my consternation, produced one of my drawings (which he had to hand, almost as though he had expected some trouble from this fellow Ewald), and bluntly challenged the Hessian to discover any defect in the works. Ewald seemed about to step forward and oblige him, but then Cornwallis with some annoyance directed Ewald to retake his seat.

'There shall be no further interruption to Lieutenant Sutherland,' said Cornwallis. With a roll of the finger he ordered Sutherland to continue.

In the next fifteen minutes Sutherland made plain the many difficulties we must have in holding our outer line. It was not only that we faced thousands more infantry than were ever expected when the work commenced, but that our own numbers had been reduced by illness, and not merely swamp-fevers, but also by the smallpox, which had now spread to dozens of the soldiers. 'We have not the men necessary to make a prolonged defence of the outer line,' he concluded. 'Nor can I answer for the inner line till we have completed the work. As to the ability of our embankments to withstand their guns, we must first see what they have to bring against us. But the soil – as we all know, and as Captain Ewald has so kindly reminded us – is sandy, and not such as we would have built with by choice.'

O'Hara thanked Sutherland, who then retook his seat. There was a general murmur of conversation followed as the officers considered among themselves what they had heard. In the midst of this, O'Hara raised his voice to say, 'I am asked for our own numbers. I have it from Major Ross that we are five thousand able-bodied ashore, and some eight hundred seamen.' The officers already knew the wastage from sickness in their own regiments, and so there was no sudden alarm; but the announcement of the numbers cast a pall. O'Hara went on, 'We are come then to the main question, whether or not we should remain now in York Town. I understand you would speak to the question, Colonel Tarleton?'

Cornwallis folded his arms and fixed his gaze upon the table as Tarleton rose to speak. When Tarleton faced us I saw how well he had chosen his place, for he had command of the whole room.

'Gentlemen, I must confess that I had intended to come before you in the person of a lawyer,' said he, and he opened his hands as if in apologetic confession. 'I hope you shall forgive me the disgraceful intention.' He raised an eyebrow and had some small laughter before he continued. 'But now that we have heard Lieutenant Sutherland and General O'Hara, to say nothing of Lieutenant Ewald, I cannot see how I may better make the argument for an evacuation to the Gloucester side – which I think every man here knows has ever been my inclination – than by simple plain speaking.

'Not to dissemble, but to begin with what is nearest me, and which I must know best, we have yet a cavalry at our disposal. It is no small thing, gentlemen, as the enemy learned to their great cost as we came through the Carolinas. But in our staying here in York Town, in our long wait for General Clinton, there has been of necessity – and I make no complaint of it, for I agreed the necessity – a cull of our horses. We are thinned. We are weakened perhaps, and perhaps more than I should like our enemy to know, but I say again, gentlemen: we have yet a cavalry at our disposal. It is no small thing.'

There was a murmur of 'hear, hears', which Tarleton feigned not to notice.

'But a cavalry trapped within a siege line, I fear, is a thing so small as to be scarce worthy of mention. It is a fish from the water. It is a lion caged. While it cannot move, all its strength is nothing. Its swiftness, nothing. Its power, nothing. Its courage, nothing. But worse than this, and very much worse, is the harm that may be done to a cavalry so circumstanced. It is no exaggeration if I say that it makes me quake to think on it. For I know, as you know, that what cannot be fed within a siege line must surely die. By degrees imperceptible, by a continuing necessity, a cull once begun shall continue till by mere inadvertence we destroy our own cavalry—'

'Your horse are not the whole army, Colonel,' broke in Cornwallis. 'Nor are they yet entirely useless to us here.'

'My Lord, that is but the lesser part of my argument.'

'Your argument is that the whole army should cross over and break out by way of Gloucester.'

'Yes, my Lord.'

'Now, that is plain speaking at least,' said Cornwallis, which raised some laughter.

'My Lord,' said Tarleton, the colour now rising to his cheeks, and he no longer playing to the gallery, 'as it starts with your cavalry, so shall it be with your army. We have it in our hands now to make the attempt. Once let the siege wear out our strength, that chance shall be lost.'

'It is not Middlesex we shall find on the far side of the river, Colonel Tarleton, but only Virginia. And yet more of the enemy. And to ferry the whole army across – Captain Symonds?'

'It is no light undertaking,' said Symonds. 'Our preparations would be seen. And if de Grasse come upriver against us at such a moment, then only our shore guns might serve us. I should not wish to rely upon them for it.'

Cornwallis let these words hang over the room. And then O'Hara said, 'Mr Douglas has perused some communications of the enemy. Sir, might you tell us briefly what you earlier reported to Major Ross?'

The officers craned around in their chairs. I did not stand to address them, but said, 'They were communications intended to be discovered by us, and meant to obscure and confuse. I told Major Ross there was a notable omission in them, which was that they had made no mention of the river, or of their ships.'

'From which we are to conclude that they may mean some attack against any crossing?' prompted O'Hara.

Now I understood his purpose in calling on me. But this was such a blatant attempt to enlist me against Tarleton, that I said firmly, 'I conclude nothing from it, General. And certainly nothing that should carry any weight in this room tonight.'

O'Hara looked to Cornwallis, as if in question whether I should be pressed any further. Cornwallis studied me a moment and then turned his head. At this moment there came suddenly the sound of boots from the hallway, and then the ensign posted outside the door came in. He whispered to Major Ross, who rose at once and went to whisper in Cornwallis's ear. Cornwallis, in turn, whispered with O'Hara and Symonds, and then all three of them rose from behind the table.

'What is it, my Lord?' Tarleton dared to enquire.

'It may be that Major Frear has brought a letter from General Clinton. You shall all remain here, gentlemen.'

Speculation broke out in every quarter before the three men had exited the room. I approached Major Ross, but he genuinely seemed to know nothing but only the bare fact of Major Frear's reported arrival. He was quite adamant that this was no arranged piece of theatre, but that Frear really had just now come up through the blockade to York Town. Tarleton then joined us.

'If there is a letter, it shall be only another false promise. And yet another instruction to wait.'

'We do not know that, Colonel,' said Ross.

'I know it,' said Tarleton. 'And so does every man here.'

'It may be that some others shall speak for your plan.'

'And you?'

'That is not my place here.'

'You are a King's officer, Major Ross. That you are also his Lordship's aide does not excuse you.' There was a belligerence in Tarleton now, for he knew how slight any argument must be when measured against a new instruction from Clinton. He felt himself outmanoeuvred, and clearly suspected something more than chance in Major Frear's timely arrival. But though I saw that Tarleton's words went home to Major Ross, he would not be baited. He nodded stiffly to us both and retreated to wait by Cornwallis's table.

'I believe Major Ross is not unsympathetic to your argument,' I ventured.

'It is not his sympathy needed, but his voice,' Tarleton threw off angrily.

Lord Cornwallis soon returned with O'Hara and Symonds; and trailing after them came Major Frear, who touched Ross's shoulder in greeting as he went by. Once we had all retaken our seats, Cornwallis said, 'To the point directly, gentlemen. Major Frear has delivered a letter into my hand from General Clinton. I shall read it to you now that there be no misunderstanding how we are ordered. It is dated the 24th, which is the same day that Major Frear received it and departed New York.' Cornwallis cleared his throat and then read.

> *My Lord*
>
> *At a meeting of the General and Flag Officers, held this day, it is determined that about 5,000 men, rank and file, shall be embarked aboard the King's ships, and the joint exertions of the navy and army made in a few days to relieve you and afterwards cooperate with you.*
>
> *The fleet consists of twenty-three sail of the line, three of which are 3-deckers. There is every reason to hope we start from hence 5th October.*
>
> *I have &c.*
>
> *H. Clinton*
>
> *P.S. Admiral Digby is this moment arrived at the Hook with three sail of the line.*

'And there it ends, gentlemen.'

Cornwallis looked up. There was no mistaking his change in temper: he was visibly heartened by the letter, and buoyed, to my thinking, far beyond the letter's desert. All notion of crossing to Gloucester was now quite obviously dismissed from his mind. Clinton's letter had rendered the council voiceless. And to all appearance, Cornwallis had seized fast upon the letter not only in honest hope of his army's rescue, but also as protective shield for his own reputation should Clinton fail to arrive.

But I was not the only man stunned when Cornwallis then turned to O'Hara and said, 'It would surely cost us too dear to attempt any long holding of the outer line. We shall bring the men in from there secretly tonight.'

After the first astonishment at Cornwallis's rash order, there were some few officers professed to consider the new tactic a wise one. And certainly there was a genuine fear that the enemy numbers to our south might turn our left flank, and the outer redoubts then prove themselves only burial grounds for our men. But there were many more officers agreed with Tarleton, who openly voiced his doubt of the decision, both to me and to several others, till a warning word from General O'Hara sent him brooding to his quarters.

What this sudden alteration in our outer defences might mean for my efforts to retrieve the Morgans, that I could hardly tell. But as I stood with Calvert upon the inner line at midnight, and watched our guns and soldiers coming into the town from the outer redoubts, the slender hope in me wilted. All about us the sappers and soldiers (and what remained of our blacks) worked by lamplight to strengthen our earthworks. But they saw the withdrawal from the outer line as well as I; and it was their own hard toil of the past several weeks being so precipitately abandoned. They had worked like oxen, but must feel the waste of it like men; and not a one of them now worked at the inner wall with a will.

'Shall you need me tomorrow, sir?'

'It is unlikely, Mr Calvert.' I glanced at the lad and tried to recall to myself what I had felt all those years before in Calcutta, when I had first been besieged. I was then much of an age with Calvert now. 'You would like to return to the Fusiliers' redoubt tomorrow, I suppose.'

'I would, sir.'

'To be shot at.'

'Yes, sir.'

'Are you are a fool, Mr Calvert?'

'I expect so, sir.'

'Go and sleep, lad. You may serve with your Fusiliers in the morning if you must.'

He bade me goodnight and went down. I looked again out from the town, and there were a few flashes of musketshot out near the woods, but these I knew were only our piquets making a distraction to cover the main withdrawal. Glancing behind me a short time later, I saw that Calvert had reached the house. He stood now upon the porch with Mrs Kendrick, who had come out with a lantern. They talked briefly, and he pointed out toward me, but I was in the shadows of the sappers' lanterns and invisible to them. When Calvert went inside, she lingered on the porch. More musketshots sounded near the woods. I turned and watched the flashes of flame in the far darkness, and when I next looked back she was gone, but had left her lantern hanging on a peg by the door.

CHAPTER 20

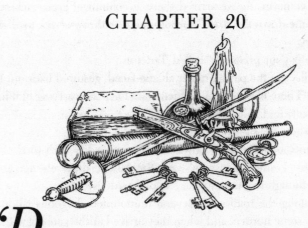

'*D*ouglas!' I lifted my head from my pillow, jolted instantly awake. 'Douglas!' I recognized the voice as Tarleton's just before he burst into my room. 'Where are you, man? I have got your prisoner.'

'An officer?'

'Of course an officer. Get your breeches. I am downstairs.'

It was but a few minutes later that I joined him, and as we hurried out he told me the story. He had sent a patrol out to the woods by the northern creek just before dawn. The dragoons had been moving in silence through the darkness when a blundering enemy officer had become detached from his own men and accidentally fallen in with ours. I looked at Tarleton sceptically, and he laughed and clapped my shoulder. 'I have only the cornet's word for it yet, but I am sure it is God's truth. Though whether Washington shall care to have such a halfwit exchanged back to him is another question. Were he one of mine, the enemy might certainly keep him. We must hope that Washington is not so particular.'

It was just gone daybreak, and the smell of the smouldering pine and cedarwood hung over the town. Reveille was beating, calling those soldiers who had been rested in the night, and now the first of these were coming up the valley from their tents on the beach. The refreshed redcoats hurried by us to take their places upon the ramparts while Tarleton and I continued to the northern gate where he expected his patrol to come in. As we arrived there, a column of green-jacketed cavalry came down the road. The slip-rail was thrown back to allow them entry.

'Where is your prisoner?' called Tarleton.

The officer of the patrol, rather shame-faced, gestured back out to the road. 'There has been an accident, sir. They are carrying him in.'

'What accident? Has he taken a fall?'

'He is shot, sir.'

Tarleton's look darkened. 'I was told he was safely with you.'

'Sir, may I speak privately,' said the fellow, dismounting; and Tarleton, though much annoyed, stepped aside with him.

Then along the road came several unmounted dragoons labouring under some burden, and when they arrived at the gate I saw that they carried the shot enemy officer. A Continental, in buff-and-blue, and he seemed scarcely conscious. Indeed, I feared that he might be already dead, till as they went by me a piteous moan escaped the fellow. The breeches of the dragoons were spattered with his blood.

Tarleton came over, and spoke to his men with quiet fury. 'Get him to the hospital. And pray God he lives. Go on then!'

They hurried away toward the hospital with him, none of them daring to meet Tarleton's eye.

'The fellow is a lieutenant,' I said. 'Washington shall want him returned.'

'He is not my prisoner.'

'An exchange must be possible.'

'You did not notice the nature of his wound? I tell you, the man is not our prisoner.' Tarleton started toward the headquarters, but I checked him with my arm.

'I did not think I should have to beg him of you, Colonel.'

'He is not mine to give you,' said he, and with his gaze upon his retreating men. He spoke very evenly then, and measured, as though he struggled to contain his fury. 'They captured him as I told you, by an accident. But after the cornet was sent in to tell me, something more happened.'

'Then he is your prisoner.'

'He was our prisoner, Douglas. But while he was held a prisoner and as they set out to bring him to me, one of my men took it into his empty head to shoot the fellow. Shot him in the back. A defence-less officer, and our prisoner, and we shot him in the back.'

'An exchange—'

'There shall be no exchange, sir. The fellow must be patched and sent back to his own lines. We are not murderers.'

Appalled by this unfortunate turn, I reached for some argument and found none. The blind stupidity of a cowardly and unnecessary shot had snatched from my hands the only weapon I might use to help the Morgans. Tarleton could not fail to see my disappointment.

'There shall be other chances,' said he, though by his look I saw that he little believed it. He promised that he should inform me at once should another prisoner be taken, and then he left me and went to confess the disgrace of his men to Lord Cornwallis.

The cup seemed so suddenly dashed from my hand that I hardly knew which way I should turn, or what I might do next to help the Morgans. I did not go at once to the house, but went along our line, considering all the while what might be done.

By the sheerest chance I found myself in the Hornwork with O'Hara and Major Ross just when the first enemy soldier climbed atop the parapet of our distant abandoned redoubt. I broke off from my thoughts and took the spyglass Ross offered me. There came a second blue jacket, and a third; and very soon a whole line of the fellows came up, raising their muskets above their heads in triumph, their jeers reaching us but faintly. They had taken our outer defences and hardly a shot fired, and their surprise must be almost equal to their gladness. O'Hara laconically suggested to the waiting gunnery officer that now might be the time to find his range. The fellow had an 8-pounder ready, and he made no hesitation but launched into his orders.

'To – linstock! To – wedge! Match! Front face! Linstock match! Make ready! Fire!'

The gun roared, the recoil jarring it back along the contrary slope of its platform, and the smoke belching upward. At the distant redoubt, the Continentals scurried down to find better cover just as our shot hit the earthen wall beneath them. A cloud of dirt and dust went up. When it cleared, there was no man dared to climb again onto the redoubt parapet.

More of our guns then opened, though with no great ferocity. It seemed but a warning to the other side that they should expect to have no easy work in the construction of their siege line.

After departing the Hornwork, I went to breakfast with Mrs Kendrick, who for the first time since I had met her seemed a little unnerved. I well understood her discomfort, for even in the dining room to the rear of the house the sound of our guns on the line was uncommonly loud. By way of reassurance to herself, she quickly told me that she had spoken with Lord Cornwallis in the street but a quarter-hour past, and that he had promised her that the enemy lacked the siege guns to harm us. 'He said it must take them a week and more to erect any siege line. I suppose a siege line shall be useless to them without guns, Mr Douglas?'

'They have guns.'

'Some of the townsfolk are moving down to the beach,' said she. 'I wondered if I should move Mrs Morgan down.'

'You are quite safe here for some few days.'

'Secretary Nelson says that all the town's houses shall be destroyed.'

'I would not trust the word of Mr Nelson.'

'Everyone expects General Clinton's arrival. Lord Cornwallis told me himself there are five thousand more men he shall have.'

'General Clinton has not yet departed New York. If he finally does so, he must then get his fleet into the Chesapeake Bay. Then he must defeat de Grasse. And once he has defeated de Grasse, he must then get his men upriver to us, disembark them safely, and all under the fire of the enemy's heavy guns.'

'You are sceptical.'

'I am more than sceptical. But it is a certainty that Rochambeau has the heavy guns to make good, if he wishes, Nelson's threat to you.'

'It was not said as a threat to me.'

'It was not said to give you comfort, Mrs Kendrick. But however it was said, within the week you and Mrs Morgan must be gone from here. You shall cross to the Gloucester side.'

'I am not your servant to be ordered so.'

At that moment there came a volley from our guns on the line, and Mrs Kendrick instinctively flinched. Though I felt for her, I own that I was not sorry to see the fright that it gave her. And that sound of the guns would now continue all the day, sometimes the more, and sometimes the less, but pressing upon her constantly, and with a force greater than mere reason. She bore a minute more of it now, and then excused herself and went up to look to Mrs Morgan.

'If he die—'

'If he die it is because he was shot by one of your men, Colonel. To judge by the wound, shot in a most cowardly fashion. You would do better to arrange some means of returning him across the lines than to make trouble for my surgeons.' Carruthers, after addressing Tarleton in this peremptory manner, then flung a hand toward me. 'Your friend Mr Douglas here may help you. He has had some previous experience of such a transfer. But you must understand, no doctor may be spared to accompany the fellow over.' A pair of infantrymen then arriving with a comrade who had taken a musket-ball in his shoulder, Carruthers went to them.

As we came from the hospital, I consoled Tarleton that he had done all that was possible for the wounded lieutenant.

'We have perhaps killed him,' said he. 'And we have lost you your prisoner.'

'You may get another.'

'Not this side of the river. We are hemmed in now. But over on the Gloucester side they have not yet sealed us inside our entrenchments. There I might take my men out against Lauzun and Weedon.'

It was a fresh hope he offered me, and one I had not thought of;

but before I might respond, there broke out an intense musketfire to the north, from the direction of the Fusiliers' redoubt. A gun then sounded from the same direction, and the drums started up to signify an attack. We parted without a word, he to his men, and me to the northern battery whence I might gain a vantage of the Fusiliers' redoubt.

Nor was I the first to have the notion, but when I arrived at the battery several Guards officers were upon the ramparts with their spyglasses trained upon the Fusiliers' redoubt a few hundred yards off. And when one briefly surrendered his spyglass to me, I saw the cause of their evident consternation. Scores of French infantrymen had pressed forward almost to the very ditch of the Fusiliers' redoubt. But being stopped dead in this frontal assault by the Fusiliers' muskets, they were now working their way about the left flank, where a number of redcoats had now turned tail and begun to run. French musketmen picked them off as they fled.

'Stand,' muttered the grizzled captain beside me. 'In the name of Christ, why can they not stand?'

But even as he spoke, the guns of the *Charon* opened from the river. It was brisk, and deadly accurate; and it broke the white wave of advancing Frenchmen at a stroke. The courage went instantly out of them, and they fell back in disorder while a party of Fusiliers rushed out from the redoubt to hurry the retreat. From the *Charon* came the taunting cheers of our seamen, the gunners in the battery joining in with them.

I was still watching an hour later when the French showed a white flag to the Fusiliers, who allowed them forward as far as the redoubt ditch to collect their wounded and dead.

Our light shelling of the enemy was stopped briefly in the late afternoon, and that officer so cowardly and foolishly shot by the dragoons was taken over to their lines. Though he lived, it was only by a thread, and Tarleton and the doctors were well pleased to have him gone. Upon the return to us of the fellow's escort, the shelling recommenced. There was much speculation, shortly after, concerning two mounted enemy officers who then rode up to join the French engineers at the edge of the pines. It was thought they might be Generals Washington and Rochambeau, come to make a personal reconnaissance of our entrenchments. But whoever they might be, a concentration of our guns upon the place soon saw their whole party retire deeper into the woods, and from our sight.

Once darkness fell I went down to Stuart beneath the bluffs by the river. Here the sound from our guns in the town above was muted, and the dozen men under Stuart's command sat about the campfire, talking quietly and taking their rum. The ships' lanterns threw long reflections upon the water toward shore, and a lone voice sang a plaintive air from the *Charon*. It was a scene altogether tranquil, and somewhat surprising to me, who still had the cloying smell of burnt powder in my nostrils. Stuart had the northern of the pair of caves for his quarters, with the larger cave given over to munitions and stores. I found him alone at his table, with a lantern at his elbow, and reading aloud to himself some words from his notebook. Though it was but a few words I heard as I approached, those words were undoubtedly Algonquian. He then heard my approach, fell instantly silent, and closed his book.

'I have interrupted you, Jonathan.'

'It is a welcome interruption.' He came out, and as we walked along beneath the bluffs toward the wooden palisade that stretched across the beach further north, he had from me everything that had that day happened above. It was no consolation to him that only our gunners had yet been called upon, and that his brother officers were as inactive above as was he here below.

'Had the *Charon* not opened this morning, you might have had the French on your beach here,' said I.

'You shall tell me next that it is necessary work that I do.'

'And so it is.'

'A sergeant might do it just as well.'

'I think a sergeant would not take the time to teach himself the Pamunkey language.'

I looked at him, and he understood that I had overheard. He

dismissed his efforts lightly. 'It is just a few words. I asked one of Campbell's paddlers to help me. I wrote the words down just to see.'

'To see what you still remembered?'

'It is very different to Cherokee.' He picked up a stone and threw it into the river, and seemed disinclined to talk any more on the matter; but instead he asked me questions of our gunnery above, and of the action of the Fusiliers.

We walked all the way to the palisade, and I was pleased to have his company, both for the remembrance he brought me of his father, and also for his own sake. He had a great deal more sense than most young officers, and consequently a just apprehension of the enemy siege lines about to close us in. But he was not fearful. His only service had been in the American colonies, and till now he had seen no proper siege, and so our conversation was soon of Sutherland's preparations, and of what Washington and Rochambeau might do with their sappers by way of reply.

While we talked, the guns sounded sporadically above, and I did not hear the noise that made Stuart stop. He cocked an ear, and turned to look into the darkness on the river. After a few moments there came a low hooting, like an owl. Stuart cupped his hands to his mouth, Cherokee fashion, and gave an answering cry before leading me down to the water. We waited but a minute more, and then the Pamunkey canoe came toward us, out from the darkness.

Campbell's message was enciphered with the same simple key that I had taught him before we left the Indian country. I took it up to Stuart's cave, and, by the lamplight there, read it directly.

The import of the first lines was simple: the Morgans were alive, and still kept in the Williamsburg gaol.

But my profound relief at this first and best news was soon checked by what followed. It was a list of the heavy French guns now setting out upon the road toward York Town. In accord with my instructions, Campbell had given an estimate of the size of each gun. By his reckoning, there were at least a dozen siege guns, 32-pounders and above.

'Is it the Morgans?' said Stuart from the cave-mouth.

'They are alive,' said I, folding the message into my jacket. When I came out, the Pamunkey messenger stood waiting with Stuart, barely reaching to Stuart's shoulder. 'There is no message for Campbell,' I told the fellow, and the Indian wordlessly turned his back and went down to the canoe.

'I think that he and the others want to be away now, to the Indian country,' said Stuart as we watched the fellow into the darkness by the river.

'They cannot get there without Campbell.'

'There is nothing that holds Campbell here.'

'His word holds him.'

'And what word is that? His word as an Indian?'

'Your argument is not with me, Jonathan, but with yourself.' He could not hold my eye, and I left him and went up to the headquarters, where I might enlist Campbell's information as the necessary lever to get Tarleton's cavalry crossed over the river.

'I understand that I must thank you and your Indians that I am finally ordered to Gloucester,' said Tarleton, and when I bowed my head to him, he continued, 'It seems that even my Lord Cornwallis hesitates to have his cavalry destroyed by siege guns.'

'You know how best you may thank me.'

'If there is a prisoner to be taken, Douglas, you shall have him.'

'How soon shall you cross?'

'When this is done,' said he, and lifted his chin to the slaughter proceeding just below us. It was upon the same beach as before, but was nothing like the same careful business. The dragoons used swords and bayonets, with all the killing, and the bloody bodies going into the river, happening in open view of the corralled horses higher up the beach. In the corral, the horses stamped and screamed, rolling their eyes in white terror. 'God knows,' said Tarleton, tightly, 'it cannot be over soon enough.'

Then walking back with me to the town, he invited my inspection of the distant earthworks that the rebels had thrown up in the night. The entrenchment wall was low, but already a few hundred yards long, and reaching out in both directions from our abandoned Pigeon Hill redoubts. 'They are not men, but moles,' said he.

'I shall cross with you to Gloucester, Tarleton.'

He shot me a quick glance, and then said, 'Did you fear I would stop you?'

'You would not stop me.'

He hesitated how to answer this, and finally answered me nothing.

We had entered the town through the southern gate, and were nearing his quarters at the inn when Mrs Kendrick met with us in the street. By her look, it seemed that Calvert had given her my message, that she was to be crossed over with Mrs Morgan to Gloucester. Tarleton raised his hat to her.

'Colonel,' said she with a nod; but at once turned to me. 'Pray a word, Mr Douglas.'

'Colonel Tarleton shall take his men over both today and tomorrow, Mrs Kendrick. It may be as well to make your arrangements with him now.'

'I have not agreed to go.'

'Madam—'

'Sir,' said she. 'It is a presumption.'

'You are unsettled.'

'I am sufficiently settled to know my own mind.'

Tarleton then excused himself, gallantly offering that he would make places in the boats for any woman who would cross. 'Mrs Kendrick. Mr Douglas,' said he, and he raised an eyebrow to me as he passed by. But in her eye was nothing like amusement.

'What do you mean, Mr Douglas, sending Calvert with an order for me? Much less an order for Mrs Morgan? He has had Francesca begin to pack.'

'Your maid was to prepare for Mrs Morgan's departure. Mrs Morgan is ill. You cannot hold her here any longer by an unreasonable obstinacy.'

'Obstinacy,' said she, falling in beside me as I started for her house.

'Yes, madam. Obstinacy. Or do you think it an agreeable meekness that you have continually opposed me?'

'You talk as if you are the one reasonable. But it is you who demand an unthinking obedience.'

'You have taught me how unlikely the hope.'

'I might box your ears,' said she quietly.

'And I, Mrs Kendrick, must be less than a gentleman to tell you what I might do in return.' The colour leaped into her cheeks. I knew at once that I had overstepped the mark. For though American, she was yet a lady; and whatever her provocation of me, I was quite wrong to speak to her so. But it had the effect of silencing her a short while, though I felt her sharp glance several times upon me on our way to the house. The guns were firing from our line, not a hundred yards distant, but very little that firing then mattered to either one of us.

She found her voice again as we reached her porch. 'I must ask you one final time that you not attempt to force our crossing to Gloucester.'

'Then it is only this final time that I must refuse you, Mrs Kendrick. And I hope you will now excuse me.'

'Mrs Morgan is carrying a child.'

Caught with my hand upon the door, I steadied myself a moment and then faced her.

'Yes, Mr Douglas. And you have now, by your own obstinacy, made me break my promise to her. For she would not have had you know it.'

'Her illness—'

'She is truly unwell. It is only partly the child. Dr Gould blames the strain upon her nerves.'

She was about to say more, but then a troop of soldiers passed near and we went into the house. We passed into the library, and I walked to the desk before facing her again.

'Surely Mrs Morgan may be moved,' I ventured.

'She fears for the child.'

'There are more certain fears than that to consider.'

'She fears with some reason, Mr Douglas. She has miscarried several times before this.'

'Gould knows all this?'

'Of course Gould knows. Only it seems that he has kept his word to her much better than I have been able. Nor is that the prime question. You have said that we are safe here for some days yet. We are safe till the French bring up their guns.'

'You shall not be safe after.'

'I have taken Gould's advice. He says that even just a few days more undisturbed, and lying quiet in her bed, might be the difference between whether Mrs Morgan keep or lose the child.'

She was calm now, and met my look square. This was no wilful feminine obstinacy, but something so unexpected that I was in some quandary which way to turn. For I had fully intended – till the last few minutes – to remove every person in the household across to Gloucester with me and Tarleton. Mrs Kendrick's hands were clasped together before her waist, her eyes remaining steady upon mine. It was not a challenge, but neither was it supplication.

'You may stay here with her till the French guns come up,' I decided at last.

'Thank you, Mr Douglas.'

'Not an hour longer, Mrs Kendrick. And we shall see then if you still have any gratitude toward me that I allowed of your staying.'

CHAPTER 21

*T*he main crossing of the Legion to Gloucester was done in flat-boats and under cover of night; and just why Captain Symonds should fire into the enemy lines from his ships as we crossed, that I never discovered. But so he did, as if it might afford us some protection. We were ourselves never fired upon by the enemy, and the whole of the ferrying went otherwise peaceably and without incident. By midnight Tarleton's Legion (and a mounted section of the 23rd) had put up their tents in Gloucester and turned out their hobbled horses onto the open ground beyond the entrenchment. Even at that hour it was evident the lesser urgency prevailing this side of the river; for the York Town guns made but a distant booming, and most of Simcoe's Rangers slept on throughout our arrival, as did the Jaegers.

'Let them sleep,' said Tarleton when I remarked upon it. 'Once we have stirred the hornets' nest tomorrow, they shall not get another night so peaceful.'

There were not twenty houses in Gloucester, which in truth was more a hamlet than a town; and these houses being either occupied by the local people or given over to Colonel Dundas and Simcoe and the officers, I needs must bed down in a tent. But a more restful sleep I had there, I confess, than I ever did in Mrs Kendrick's house in York Town. And when the Reveille sounded at daybreak I was soon dressed, and quickly found my way to Colonel Dundas's quarters where the officers were converging.

Dundas was a man approaching his middle years, and with the reputation of a dependable but uninspiring officer. He sat behind his table, a dozen of us standing, and addressed a few words of welcome to Tarleton. This done, he went directly to the day's business.

'There is no change to the orders. Eight wagons shall go out in file, preceded by the foot of my brigade and Colonel Tarleton's men. Hessians to the rear with the Rangers, and the mounted 23rd. There has been movement reported of the duc de Lauzun's cavalry, and also of Choisy's marines. It shall be no surprise to me if they are putting some backbone into Weedon's men at last. We believe there are no heavy guns with them, but only a few field-pieces. If they wish to press forward toward Gloucester, there is nothing shall impede them but only our patrols.

'As to the necessity of our foraging today, I need hardly remind you of it, gentlemen. It may be our last opportunity of an expedition out from Gloucester. What I shall remind you of – and that most emphatically – is the necessity to keep our wagons secure. We are not going out from here with the intention to harass the enemy. We are going out for one reason only, which is to forage supplies that we might sustain ourselves in any siege. It shall be honour enough for any man if we bring back the wagons full-laden.'

There was no particular officer Dundas looked at as he spoke these last words, but every man present understood that they were directed at Tarleton. Though Tarleton, when I glanced at him, kept his face impassive, and almost childlike in its innocence. Then Dundas gave a few more instructions relating to the blacks and the Jaegers before bringing the flats of his hands down upon the table.

'If there are any questions – No? Then I believe we are done, gentlemen. Let us waste no more of the morning.'

As I walked down toward the Legion's encampment, Tarleton came up beside me, and I said, 'There is little chance of a prisoner if we must only stay with the wagons.'

'I understood Dundas to say that we should keep the wagons secure,' he replied mildly. 'It is not the same as to stay with them. Be sure to bring your sword and pistol.'

Our defensive line at Gloucester was nothing so considerable as that at York Town, being comprised of four redoubts placed at a few hundred yards' distance each one to the next, and with a line of wooden palisades between. Also there were three batteries, two in the line and one overlooking the river. A single road came up from the river landing and past the houses, and it was upon this road that our column formed before going out through the palisade gate.

Once beyond the abatis of felled pines, it was open ground for almost a mile to the front of us and so our march proceeded in good order, and I might say even jauntily; for the soldiers this side the river had yet to feel themselves in any way pressed by the enemy. These past weeks they had roamed the hinterland unmolested, and their easy confidence communicated itself now to Tarleton's men, who held themselves very upright, much pleased to have some better work to do than the slaughter of their horses.

We were soon into the woods, and the sandy track took us by a clearing where was an abandoned cottage with its roof fallen in, and tall weeds and bushes growing over its fallen porch railings. It was the first of several such old cottages and shacks we saw in the next hour, with sometimes only the stone foundations of the walls to mark out the wreck of some poor colonist's best hopes. There seemed not half the number of creeks and watercourses as upon the York Town side, but nearby each creek that we came to was invariably a farmhouse, a barn, and some few outbuildings for cattle. Earlier foraging expeditions from Gloucester had emptied the nearer barns, and it was gone eight o'clock, and nothing yet gathered, when Dundas broke the column in two. He sent Tarleton with four wagons up the left fork of the track and himself took the right. I continued with Tarleton.

At the next creek were two farmhouses, and they at no great distance from each other. And at both places we found neither owners nor servants, but only some slaves, and the barns filled almost to the rafters with fodder and corn. Tarleton sent an advance guard of his dragoons further up the road, and then he set the remaining men to loading the corn. Our blacks he directed into the neighbouring fields, ordering them to bring out the sheep and cattle, which when they had done, they commenced herding the animals back to Gloucester.

I watched the fast-filling wagons with an increasing concern.

'Shall you send the wagons back?' I finally asked Tarleton.

'I cannot take them further once they are filled. I had not expected Lauzun should allow us such an easy plunder. If we must go back so soon, Douglas, I am sorry for it. But I cannot break the order.'

I turned my horse and rode a half-mile forward to join with the advance guard; but the road ahead of them was clear. I stood in my stirrups and raised my spyglass, but I could not deceive myself that there was either smoke or dust rising from any place to the front of us. We had reached the outer limit of our expedition, we were plundering at will, and there was no sign that the enemy meant to prevent us, or even come near. And without they made some attempt upon us, there could be none of them captured. Their timidity was galling beyond endurance. And yet there was nothing I might do to provoke them while they held themselves off.

After twenty minutes a cornet rode up with Tarleton's order that we must now cover the laden wagons' retreat to Gloucester. Spurring back down the road, I found Tarleton upon the veranda of a cottage not two hundred yards behind. As I reined in, he touched his hat to the woman of the place and then came away from there and remounted.

'We cannot leave yet,' said I. 'We might push forward another mile or two.'

'The wagons are full, Douglas. And this woman here has seen neither Lauzun nor the militia.'

'I might take some of your men and go on ahead.'

'You know that is impossible.'

'And you know that the Morgans shall hang.'

He made no reply, but turned southward upon the road, and I was soon alongside of him. He was clearly vexed himself that we had encountered no enemy troops, but it was a vexation that availed me nothing if I could not turn it to my purpose. Then as I racked my brains for some good argument, there came a shout from behind us, and we turned to see one of the advance guard riding down.

'Sir! It is Lauzun with the hussars!'

'Get down to the wagons,' Tarleton ordered him sharply. 'Send up every dragoon and Fusilier. Half the Rangers to stay with the wagons and continue toward Gloucester. The rest to come up, and smartly about it.'

As the fellow spurred south, Tarleton turned his own horse upon the spot, studying the ground on every side. 'Your luck is changed, Douglas. Hold the men here when they come up,' said he, and then he went from the road to make a better scouting of the woods and the cultivated field opposite.

The advance party of dragoons fell back to me, and Tarleton soon returned from his scouting to order them from the road and onto the field. Minutes later, the Rangers came up from the wagons, and more of his dragoons; and these Tarleton sent into the woods and the cover to the far side of the road.

All this swift and decisive movement happened with great efficiency, Tarleton's orders passing through his officers, and the horses wheeling with no entanglement or crush. And now to the north the dust of the enemy became visible, as ours must be to them, and Tarleton rode by me and with voice lowered said, 'If Lauzun offers, I shall chance my arm against him. Keep yourself back in the woods till this is done.'

He rode with another fifty dragoons into the open field, and I went back to the cover. As I reached the woods there came the sound of pistol-shots from the north, and opening my spyglass I saw that the shots came from the French hussars who now came into view half a mile up the road. What they fired upon I never saw, but soon they had broken an opening in the railing fence there, and they came filing through just as more of Lauzun's cavalry arrived. Among these new arrivals were twenty or more lancers, their blue-jacketed officers riding to the front of them. Once they were all through the fence, they swung into a broad line and started down the field toward Tarleton.

'We appear to have the numbers over them,' said I to a captain of the dragoons just by me.

'The Colonel should make the best of it while he may,' replied the captain, and he pointed to another dust-cloud coming down from the north-west.

Upon the field, Lauzun had advanced so far now that there could be no safe turning back. Fifty yards in front of us, in the field out from the woods, Tarleton drew his sabre, but he held his men steady. And now a French officer rode out in front of the French line, and by his epaulettes and sash, it could only be their commander, Lauzun. The front line of French cavalry levelled their lances and came menacingly forward.

Lauzun made no pause, but raised high his arm. The French bugles sounded, and Lauzun swung forward his sabre and charged.

CHAPTER 22

'At the bastards!' broke from the captain beside me, and then all about the woods the British cries and shouting sounded, urging Tarleton to action. And finally our own buglers blew, Tarleton's sabre cut a swathe through the air, and the dragoons surged forward in unleashed fury.

The shouting was upon every side of me, as though it might be the Derby they witnessed, but the Derby under arms, and death or glory the prize. 'Ride in and cut them!' cried the captain by me. 'Go on there! Cut the bastards down!'

Pistol-shots cracked across the field, the charging lines quickly losing their good order, and now they were at the gallop, and the French lancers to the fore with Lauzun.

Tarleton angled now across his own line, appearing to position himself for a personal engagement with Lauzun. They closed, and closed; and they were scarcely twenty yards apart when the horse alongside of Tarleton's stumbled. It plunged directly into Tarleton's horse, which instantly fell, spilling him hard onto the ground. The two thundering lines clashed together, and Tarleton disappeared beneath them.

Swords and lances flashed, pistols sounded, and the captain beside me bellowed, 'He is down!'

Tarleton was surely down, and in the very midst of the scrambling hoofs. The lines opened a second, and Tarleton was visible to all, upon the ground and unmoving. The captain was from the woods the next instant, calling his men after him. I spurred out from the wood. A riderless horse was galloping from the first shock of the fight, and I cut across the field and turned it, and then brought it to a stop. Getting hold of its bridle, I led it after me back to the melee. The captain now had a score of dragoons about him, and they shouting wildly as they made a disorderly charge forward to drive off the French from their Colonel. I rode in behind them, and they pushed back the lancers from near Tarleton, who now rose groggily upon one knee.

The captain and his fellows slashed viciously, and clear ground opened before them. They pushed further forward, and I rode in, shouting, 'Tarleton!'

Whether he heard me above the din, I much doubt of. But he had got to his feet now, and I reached down and thrust the reins out to him. He looked up at me, and though his face was smeared with dirt, his eyes were clear. He took the reins and climbed into the saddle. He had lost his sword in the fall, and so I quickly gave him mine. Then as I turned, a lancer broke through, levelling at Tarleton. My pistol was ready in my hand, and I fired a ball into the fellow. He buckled and his horse veered away, carrying him like empty baggage into the fight. Defenceless now, and without uniform, I was as like to be killed in the confusion by one of ours as by any Frenchman, and so I did not hesitate to turn and ride off from the field. In the safety of the woods, I got down and reloaded my pistol.

It was possible that our best chance of taking Lauzun was gone; but in battles are many accidents, and Tarleton knew well how to use them. Once I had reloaded I remounted and watched as Tarleton disengaged a part of his force, and rode with them again as a body and straight into the French line, attempting a second time to break them. But Lauzun's line held, and Tarleton wheeled and tried again, but still they held, and by now it was clear that they would withstand any such hurried strikes.

Dismounted and wounded men now staggered from the fighting, and many loose horses, both on our side and on theirs. Before long there was a general disengagement sounded by the buglers, and both Tarleton and Lauzun sought to pull back their men.

More of our mounted Fusiliers then arriving along the road, Tarleton withdrew his men toward them. I came out from the woods and rode across.

'Dismount your men!' Tarleton shouted to the Fusiliers' captain. 'Form them to the front of the woods there with the 17th. Fire upon any French that follow after us.' Tarleton then led his cavalry around to the rear of that small wood where they might dismount in safety, put their tack and weapons in order, and generally make ready for another charge.

I dismounted and tied my horse. Then I went forward and soon found Calvert among the dismounted Fusiliers. He was loading a musket and had a wary eye upon the French in the field.

'Are they enough for you, Mr Calvert?'

'You should not be here un-uniformed, sir,' said he, casting an apprehensive glance over my attire.

'Eyes to the front, lad.'

Lauzun had regrouped his men; and though the first ferocity was gone out of them, yet they came after Tarleton now with some real vigour and purpose. And now it was that I had my own chance at Lauzun. At two hundred yards I picked him out from his fellows, for he was boldly to the front again. I made sure of my pistol, and then I waited. The whole line came on, and when he passed inside a hundred yards of me I raised my pistol. And then, for the briefest moment, I had him sighted – but only the very briefest – for the Fusiliers then fired a sharp, crackling volley. The French line veered, breaking into disorder, and Lauzun was instantly lost among his own cavalry.

Smoke drifted through the woods, and the smell of burnt powder.

'Did you get one, sir? I think I got one.' Calvert, his musket-butt already grounded, drew the rod for the reloading.

Out in front of us two French horses thrashed on the ground in their death throes. Beside them a lance was planted, useless, and the lancer lying motionless, face-up to the sky.

But the French quickly regrouped and came at us now aslant. There was no volley from the Fusiliers this time, but only a general heavy firing from both Fusiliers and dragoons, and pistol-shots from the Rangers in the first wood. The French advance turned sharply aside, and then wheeled away, their buglers sounding the retreat very sprightly.

'Stand, Mr Calvert,' said I; for in his eagerness to be at them he had made a move forward, which might have proven fatal both to him and to any who rashly followed at his heels. And very glad I was to the Fusiliers' captain then shouting the same order.

'Stand the Fusiliers! Make no advance!'

'But they are fleeing, sir,' Calvert protested to me.

'They are not fleeing so very far, Mr Calvert,' said I, and directed his attention north across the field to where the enemy militiamen were now arriving in number. Till then the press of Lauzun's cavalry had blocked our ears to the drums; but now we heard them beating, and saw the men marching forward onto the field.

Lauzun soon took his cavalry behind these fellows, and there the cavalry dismounted and commenced the same reloading and repair of themselves as Tarleton's men had already effected. When Tarleton and his men now rode from the wood, they faced a daunting wall of muskets, three ranks deep, kneeling and standing. In those ranks were both the motley of the Virginia militia, and the blue jackets of the Continental regulars.

Tarleton levelled his sabre, the bugles blew, and his dragoons rode hard at the rebel line. Such a charge must test even the most experienced infantry; for let but one man break and run, it is the first crack in a dam, with the trickle quickly a stream and the next instant a flood. But straight and hard though Tarleton rode at them now, the rebel line never wavered. Nor was there an early firing from their ranks, but their officer held his nerve and waited, and waited, and at last gave the order, 'Fire!' A great cloud of smoke went up from their muskets, and the next moment the sound of the crackling volley reached our ears.

Three horses went down, and several men fell or hung loose in the saddle. A few tumbled dragoons got sharply to their feet and retreated in haste, but others simply lay where they fell.

'They must go on,' cried Calvert, in quiet agitation to see our cavalry now veering away from the muskets. 'They have taken the shot. They must bear down.'

'They have taken not half the shot,' said I; for I had seen what Tarleton must have seen, but Calvert had not, that it was but the kneeling rank that had fired.

Tarleton gathered his men beyond the range of the muskets, and thrice more he rode in, but only as a feint, it seemed, to draw Lauzun out; but each time he was driven off by the muskets, Lauzun's cavalry remaining fast behind the immovable line of infantry.

On the next wheeling, Tarleton brought his men all the way back to the woods.

'Form up on the road!' he called to the officers. 'We are for Gloucester!'

I mounted and rode across to him. His face was red, and very freely perspiring. His white-lathered horse pawed the ground. Tarleton jerked his head northward, and there I saw yet another ominous dust-cloud approaching.

'They are too many,' said he, breathing hard. 'We cannot stay.'

The bitterest disappointment though it was to me, I must accept it. The numbers, and the day, were against us.

It was a most miserable and dejected ride for me the four miles back to Gloucester. We came there without trouble, Lauzun seemingly content to await reinforcement before coming down after us. Colonel Dundas and the laden wagons were already returned. As Tarleton's men dismounted, those fellows who had accompanied the wagons, and hence missed the fighting, now came forward disconsolate, but eager to hear the tale of the day.

We had brought some thirty wounded men back with us, and these were taken to the house set aside for a hospital. I did not speak with

Tarleton again for some several hours, for he kept with his men at the hospital (though himself unwounded). One officer had taken a shot full in the breast, and when the surgeons could do nothing for the fellow, Tarleton sat with him, only coming away at last when the man died in the night.

Tarleton reported this dispiriting news to me when he came down to my tent. He looked as if he bore the world upon his back, and when I offered him my condolences, he accepted them with only a curt nod.

Then he said, 'You should not have ridden onto the field.'

'Then you must learn to keep your saddle.'

'I might have taken Lauzun but for the fall,' said he, somewhat rueful.

'We might try again.'

He turned his head. 'They shall all come down here tomorrow. Lauzun, Choisy, Weedon. We shall be hemmed in then as tightly as we are at York Town.'

'They have not come down till now.'

He seemed about to answer me, but then only shrugged. He had neither the strength nor the inclination at that moment for either plans or debate. After he left me, I rose and extinguished the lantern. Then I lay on the camp-bed, and put my folded jacket beneath my head for a pillow. I listened to the distant pounding of the York Town guns and stared into the darkness. If Tarleton was right, if we were hemmed in on the morrow, I knew there would then be but one way remaining by which I might save the Morgans. A desperate throw of the dice. But Jenkinson was in London, and too far off to order me against it.

In the morning, Lauzun did come down just as Tarleton had predicted, and with him Choisy and Weedon, and every man they had upon the Gloucester side. In short order they drove our sentries and piquets from the woods, the sound of their heavy musketry sending every redcoat retiring in haste behind our palisades. From my place in the foremost redoubt, I scanned the treeline with my spyglass. The enemy soldiers were not in one section only, but across the whole wood, and we were hemmed in every bit as tightly as Tarleton had feared.

'Let the rest of our army cross, and we might still break out from here at a stroke,' remarked Tarleton beside me, scanning the woods with his own glass.

'But you shall not go out again.'

'No one shall go out again, Douglas, at least till the main part of our army come over. If you would find a prisoner, you must enquire once more upon the other side.'

CHAPTER 23

*T*he York Town guns were not half so busy as they had been upon the enemy's first arrival into the Pigeon Hill redoubts, which was as well; for a judicious restraint must be needed now, and not a shot wasted, if we were to maintain ourselves above a fortnight behind our entrenchments. And directly I was in the upper town I saw all about me the preparations being made to receive the enemy shelling whensoever it should commence. There were trenches and pits dug in many places, four and five feet deep, where soldiers might take cover from any bombardment that caught them beyond the protection of the earthen ramparts of our line. Nor was this work finished, but there were soldiers and blacks even now engaged with shovels and picks, and carpenters putting down wooden edges to the finished pits to prevent their collapsing. Only the stone houses of the town remained standing, and also the stone chimney-breasts of the dismantled wooden houses. For the rest, every plank and timber of every floor, wall and roof was gone to do service now as palisade or fraising, or as a reinforcement of our entrenchments. At the sight of all this I understood instantly the reason of the many townsfolk I had just seen down by the beach, digging new caves and hollows into the bluffs.

Here above, the engineers were supervising the construction of short earthen walls jutting out perpendicular from our ramparts into the town; which walls must be intended to confine the lethal shredded metal of the enemy shells. In the faces of the soldiers, and the sappers and the blacks who laboured on these walls, there was a strain and a tiredness I had not seen before. And in the shouted orders of the engineers there was an irascibility and frustration at the tardiness with which the work was done.

Mrs Kendrick's house being one of the primary stone-and-brick houses of the town, it remained largely untouched, but for the loss of its wooden porch. When I entered the house I paid no call upon the women but turned directly in to the library and found ink and paper.

My dear Cordet,

Here is a voice from across the years that I trust you shall neither ignore nor put by for consideration at your later convenience.

I find myself within the British line here at York Town from such circumstances as I shall better explain to you in person. In the briefest terms, my service with our Board of Trade and Plantations in the Indian country has by chance delivered me here to the coast at this inopportune moment and I am now one with the civilian townsfolk of the place. By a more fortunate chance I have discovered your presence on the other side of the line with General Rochambeau, and so I now make this appeal to you, that you will see me at once, and grant me a safe passage to you through your lines.

There are men's lives depend upon your positive answer, and I rely upon my memory of you that this appeal shall not be lightly received. You may consult your own memory of me that it is not lightly written.

I await your prompt answer by that same agency through which this letter is delivered.

Yours in expectation,

Alistair Douglas (Bengal)

Though I blotted and dusted the letter, I did not seal it, but folded it thrice, to the size of a man's breast pocket. And as I put it into mine, I heard Mrs Kendrick's voice outside the library door. 'Mr Douglas, is it you?'

I unlocked the door to her.

'You are returned safely then,' said she, and her wryness but a poor veil for her relief, which was something that I had hardly expected. Stepping back to let her in, I asked after news of her patient, and whether the illness was in any wise abated.

'To carry a child is not an illness,' she answered without thinking; but then she quickly checked herself, as if she regretted the words, and truly wanted no argument of me. She then added in a measured way, 'She does as well as we might hope, Mr Douglas. You may come up to her now, if you wish.'

'I must first see Lord Cornwallis.'

'They say Tarleton has been badly hurt in an action.'

'He is bruised from a fall, that is all. It is only his pride that is injured.'

She remarked that Tarleton seemed to her one who would sooner be shot than bruise his backside. I smiled at this, for it was no less than the truth. And offered her that I should tell him so when next I saw him. 'And yourself, Mr Douglas?' said she. 'You look still in one piece. And where is Calvert?'

I assured her that neither I nor Calvert had taken any harm, but that Calvert had crossed back with me, and had now gone to report to the Fusiliers' redoubt. I then noticed behind Mrs Kendrick the blonde locks of Lizzy Morgan as she peeped in at us around the library door. I lifted my chin, and Mrs Kendrick turned and saw the girl.

'Bring her in,' said I quietly. She called the child, and Lizzy came tentatively and pressed herself into the protective folds of Mrs Kendrick's dress. Lizzy kept her eyes upon me, not afraid but uncertain. I sat down upon the edge of my chair that I not tower over the poor child.

'Do you understand why you are here, Lizzy?'

She raised a finger, pointing upward. 'Mama is here.'

'And I see that you are not afraid of the guns.' She shook her head, and both her shoulders turned. 'Well, I think then that you must be as brave as your mother.'

'I am.'

'Yes,' said I, and not daring to glance up to Mrs Kendrick. 'Yes, I am sure of it. And we must ask you to be brave a little longer, Lizzy. It is not for ever you must put up with the guns, but only a few days more. And then you and your mother shall cross the river in a boat.'

'And Mrs Kendrick?'

'Yes. Mrs Kendrick too. Should you like that?'

'David has a boat.'

David, her brother. Any words more that I might have spoken turned at once to stones in my throat. All the last days bore down upon me. I looked at Lizzy, and she at me in her innocence; and I wished then that the ground might swallow me entire. My eyes clouded, and I quickly looked down that I not frighten her.

'Come, Lizzy.' Mrs Kendrick took the girl's hand and led her toward the door. 'Mr Douglas is very tired just now.' When I lifted my eyes, Lizzy was craning round to look at me with a frank and puzzled curiosity as she went.

After a minute, Mrs Kendrick returned. She found me upon the same chair, but slumped back, and gazing now through the window at the jacketless soldiers digging the trenches and pits in the street.

'I have left Lizzy with the maid. She will not trouble you again.' I nodded, but said nothing. 'Is there aught I might fetch you?' said she.

'No. Thank you.'

She hesitated, and then said, 'Her father and brother . . .'

'You would like to know if they are alive.'

'I would.'

'I believe so. But that is only to say that I have heard no different.'

She had been standing near the door, but now she crossed the room, though unsurely. She sat upon the sofa near to my chair. I looked at her, expecting some remark, but she made none. She sat quietly, her hands resting in her lap, and I turned from her and gazed through the window again. I own, I was not sorry of her quiet and unquestioning presence those next minutes. But when my strength at last returned to me, and my will, I rose, and she after me. She excused herself then, and no word spoken about those few quiet minutes. She went up to Mrs Morgan, while I crossed to the headquarters.

Lord Cornwallis had gone down to consult with Symonds about our fireships, and so it was General O'Hara that I met with in the main drawing room. I was not the first to bring him a report of the clash of cavalry outside Gloucester, and so I soon moved on from that to give him my assessment of the enemy's strength outside the Gloucester entrenchments. But when I began to rehearse to him Tarleton's continuing recommendation of a direct crossing of the army, and a breakout and rapid march north, O'Hara cut me short.

'Tarleton's preference is well known, Mr Douglas. If he chafes that the army's direction is not in his hand, what must we do? He shall bear it better if he accepts it sooner, and uncomplaining. Pray, no more of it now. What we have had from your Indian fellows has given us quite enough disturbance. You have seen our new trenches?'

'Aye.'

'If Washington has the siege guns that your fellows say – which I should tell you my Lord Cornwallis yet doubts of – then it is an uncomfortable wait we shall have now for General Clinton.'

Surprising as it was to hear that Cornwallis should even yet doubt of the siege guns, it was more surprising still to hear that Clinton's arrival continued to be expected with such certainty. I understood then that there was almost nothing by way of argument that might change Cornwallis's decision to stay rooted in York Town. I held my tongue. O'Hara then asked me when I intended to move Mrs Kendrick and Mrs Morgan down to the bluff-caves.

'I shall move them to the Gloucester side, General. It were as well, I believe, that all the townsfolk should cross.'

'They have most of them already made caves for themselves below.'

'If de Grasse come upriver from the Bay—'

'It is exactly the prevention of such a manoeuvre that my Lord Cornwallis and Captain Symonds are now discussing. You must allow us some understanding of our position, sir.'

I was in danger of antagonizing O'Hara now, which I sincerely had no wish to do. Indeed my presence before him was but a necessary preliminary to my true purpose at the headquarters. And so when an ensign then entered the room with a message for the General, I quickly took the opportunity of O'Hara's distraction to enquire, offhandedly, whether I might pay a call upon Secretary Nelson upstairs. O'Hara answered with a lift of the head and a flourish of his hand toward the door.

Upstairs, and seated outside Secretary Nelson's rooms, I found that slave who was Nelson's manservant. He was a young man, dressed simply but cleanly, in white shirt and dark breeches, and with buckled shoes on his feet. But for all that he sat there quietly, and made no obvious interference to the work below. That such a fellow was tolerated to observe every coming and going from the headquarters was exactly that madness of civility toward Nelson against which I had repeatedly warned Lord Cornwallis. But now I was here upon another matter, and so I put that by. Indeed, at that moment I had every reason to be grateful for Cornwallis's negligence. I gave the fellow my name, and was soon taken in to his master.

'Should I call this an unexpected pleasure, Mr Douglas?' said Nelson, waving the black from the room. 'Or have you come now to evict me from my own house?'

'I believe it is your own General Washington now working to that end,' said I with a nod toward the window. There was a clear view over our entrenchment, and across the several hundred yards of no-man's-land into the woods and the Continental army lines.

'He shall succeed, you know.'

'That is yet to see.'

'You have not beaten down the revolution in five years. Is there no lesson for you in that?'

'I am not come to discuss politics, Mr Nelson. But however the war might be finally ended, I confess myself surprised that you should on this occasion, upon the eve of a siege being established against us, have any desire to remain within our entrenchments.'

'This is my home, is it not? I have not sold it to the King. I have lent it to Lord Cornwallis, who asked it of me as a gentleman.'

'I doubt that the French gunners shall note the distinction.'

'Huh,' said he, very merry; and then hauling himself up from his armchair, he leaned upon his cane and looked at me from beneath his bushy grey eyebrows. 'You have no fondness for me, Mr Douglas. But that is no matter. I have lived enough to know that I may yet deal with a man though he have no fondness for me, nor I for him. In better circumstances, I think that we might find ourselves quite capable of doing some fair business together.'

'I cannot think what manner of business that would be.'

'Will you take a claret with me, sir?' When I declined, he limped to the table with the aid of his cane and poured himself a glass from the bottle. 'I understand you are a much travelled man. You have spent time in the West Indies.'

'It is no great distance.'

'General O'Hara has some idea you have been in the East Indies also. Your superiors in the Board of Trade and Plantations give you no rest it seems.'

This was an unsubtle probing, and I turned it upon him, saying that I doubted he had been always in Virginia.

'No, no,' said he, and hobbled with his glass and his cane back to his seat. He dropped into the armchair and sipped his claret. 'Not always, but for many years now. I have buried my wife here, and I mean it for my own last resting place.' One of the nearer guns on our line then firing, the sash-window rattled loudly. He glanced across, and then back. 'Though that rest shall not come for several more years yet, I trust,' said he.

'I have a message I want taken into the French lines.'

His glass paused on its way to his lips. Behind the merriness of his eyes was now a calculation that he could not properly hide. At length he sipped again, and then held his glass perched upon his blue waistcoat, on the uppermost part of his ample belly. 'Have you indeed. A message.'

'It is a private message.'

He avoided my eye. 'I do not understand you sir.'

Taking the folded letter from my pocket, I placed it upon the side-table by the arm of his chair. When he looked up at me, I said, 'It is for one of Rochambeau's officers. The man's name is Cordet.'

'What is that to me?'

'It must go to him directly.'

'Lord Cornwallis might send it across behind a drum.'

'It is a private letter.'

'Of which Lord Cornwallis may not approve?' When I made no answer, he said, 'Why you should bring it to me I cannot conceive.'

'I have not time, sir, for the luxury of persuasion. And so I shall tell you very frankly that to my belief you have kept up a communication with your nephew all the while that Lord Cornwallis has been in your house. And in spite of your solemn word.'

'Sir—'

'Nor do I doubt that even now the communications continue, and that you have yet some secret means of their conveyance. You shall have my letter conveyed by the same means, or you shall answer for it to General Rochambeau, and to your own people.'

'Nonsense.'

'Fail, and it shall hang about your neck the remainder of your days.'

'Take it away.'

'It is not sealed. You may read it,' said I, turning for the door.

'Take it away, sir.'

'It is yours.'

'Douglas!' he cried, and I stepped out and closed the door at my back.

CHAPTER 24

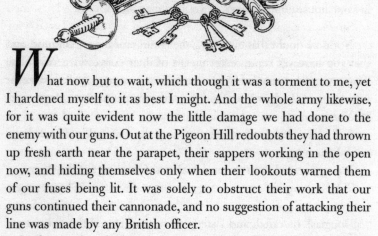

What now but to wait, which though it was a torment to me, yet I hardened myself to it as best I might. And the whole army likewise, for it was quite evident now the little damage we had done to the enemy with our guns. Out at the Pigeon Hill redoubts they had thrown up fresh earth near the parapet, their sappers working in the open now, and hiding themselves only when their lookouts warned them of our fuses being lit. It was solely to obstruct their work that our guns continued their cannonade, and no suggestion of attacking their line was made by any British officer.

In the evening the heavy cloud that had built throughout the day seemed to press low, and a light rain started. From the mouth of Stuart's cave I looked out through the rain at the ships, and at the faint lanterns upon the Gloucester shore. Stuart had told me that the Pamunkey would be down soon, before the turn of the tide. There being a message I must send to Campbell now, I stayed to be certain that the Pamunkey would take it directly.

'You are sure they mean to come down tonight?' I asked Stuart again.

'I am sure, Mr Douglas.'

He sat on the floor of the cave, his back resting on the wall, and with a lantern in a niche by his shoulder. In his hand was that same manual of siege-warfare that I had first seen him reading out at the Pamunkey reservation. He studied it now with the attention of a scholarly monk. When I turned from the rain and went and sat by him, he showed me some illustrations from the book, and questioned me upon their meaning. Though I answered him, I think he had sensed my distraction ever since my arrival at the cave, and it was not long before he set the manual aside.

I know not the reason that it should happen then, at such a place and hour, but after a time we found ourselves talking of his father. He enquired of me how it was that I had spent so long travelling about the Indian country, and how it was that his father and I had first met. These questions, and many more, I answered as best I could; for there was no guile in him, but he asked only that he might know, and from the only man he knew that might tell him. Nor did I refrain from mentioning Campbell's father; for without I mention Donald Campbell, the story of Jonathan's own father was not complete. And Jonathan, at last, seemed ready to listen.

'Why does Campbell remain here to help us now?' said he when I was done.

'Because I have asked him. You will not hold that against him.'

'I have been thinking of the time you stayed with us. When I almost split your head with the tomahawk.' I smiled, and he said, 'Was Campbell there also, in the village?'

'No. He was with his mother's people in Chota.'

'Did he ever come to our house?'

'Everybody came to your father's house.'

'And everybody must have known it, I suppose, when my father took in a Cherokee woman.'

I nodded. He seemed more accepting of it now.

'Campbell must have known it,' he said, and I nodded again, though not liking now where this tended. 'And Campbell must also know the woman,' said Stuart, and by the way that he looked at me now I knew

233

that he suspected something. And how he suspected, whether it was from my words, or from something Campbell had said, or by the piecing together of his own memories and the grievances of his mother, it scarcely mattered. I did not dissemble.

'He knows her. The woman is a cousin to Campbell.'

It checked Stuart a moment; and then he said bitterly, 'It seems that I have more family than ever I knew.'

I could not stop myself. I did not want to. 'Campbell is not of your blood, Jonathan. But if you knew him, you would regret that he is not. And whatever the supposed sins of your father, he was a man. He could recognize another man, whatever the blood. And if you cannot, you are the lesser for it.'

The bluntness of my rebuke silenced him. And I think it was a welcome sound to us both when we heard the owl cry on the river.

Campbell's message was to the point. He had sent estimates to me of the enemy forces ranged against us, and confirmation that the siege guns were now arriving in the artillery parks behind their southern entrenchments. He reported a rumour of the second line of entrenchment being commenced the next night. Finally, and what concerned me most nearly, the Morgans had been seen again. Both were alive, inside the Williamsburg gaol.

It was left only to reply. I went and penned my own enciphered message at Stuart's table in the cave.

Campbell,

It is now my intention to go voluntarily into the enemy lines. There is consequently no further service you may do for me here, but you must now take those Pamunkey who would go with you down to the Indian country. Send the others back to safety at their reservation.

I cannot think that there shall be British soldiers march in any good time to the aid of the Cherokee. You must look to yourselves alone in your defence against the settlers. My respects to Dragging Canoe. God give you strength.

Douglas.

This I gave into the hand of that Pamunkey who had waited all the while with Stuart down by the river. The canoe slid from the beach, the paddlers bent their backs, and in a minute were disappeared completely into the darkness.

The following day (which was the 5th of October), two French ships-of-the-line entered the York River, anchoring two or three miles below the town, out of range of our guns. I went out to the *Charon* with Major Ross to get a better view of them across the water. The first alarm caused by their sudden arrival in the river was by this time passed. They made no nearer approach, and our batteries now stood ready to give them a mauling should they advance any higher. But when I descended from the topgallant where I had gone with my spyglass, I found Ross on the quarterdeck discussing with Captain Symonds the merits of loosing three fireships downriver upon the tide.

'You would not wish to captain a fireship, I suppose, Mr Douglas,' said Symonds jovially.

'I wonder, sir, that you can spare three vessels.' I gestured out to the ring of scuttled boats and sloops below the town. 'You have already sacrificed a good many to the town's defence.'

'More than I should like. But it is three fireships or none. At least three shall be necessary to do any destruction.'

The expense seemed to me to outweigh the reward; but I made no dispute with him. After we had taken a sparse meal with Symonds and his officers, Ross and I were rowed ashore.

The tide had in the past days done a mischief that no one had allowed for, bringing up the swollen bodies of the slaughtered horses to the York Town beach. These bodies were now putrefying, and the redcoats and townsfolk in the caves had fixed kerchiefs about their noses and mouths to keep off the stench. Several boys had found poles, and now as Ross and I disembarked the boys played a raucous game relaunching the bloated bodies onto the tide. Further along, the blacks' largest encampment was now but charred wood and ash; for it had been burnt to halt the smallpox. The whole southern shore, in fact, was a scene quite dismal, and we quickly went by. As we came up from the beach into the valley, Ross mentioned the fireships again, saying that they were no extravagance but a necessity if we were to keep the French in the lower river. I could restrain myself no longer on the matter.

'Every vessel sacrificed is one vessel that cannot be used to ferry us to Gloucester.'

'His Lordship has no intention of ferrying the army across.'

'When the French siege guns are firing upon us, we shall see then the firmness of his Lordship's intention.'

'You are too free with your opinion, Mr Douglas,' said Ross hotly. 'Were you an officer, you might be broken for it.'

'It is not officers who fear to be broken that his Lordship is in need of at this moment, Major. Colonel Tarleton's advice was sound. I have tried the same advice upon General O'Hara, and failed. If no one can now persuade my Lord Cornwallis to a crossing, I much fear the consequence.'

'That is your opinion only.'

'It is the opinion of a good many of the officers. And I believe, sir, that it is your opinion.'

'I have not said so.'

'You are the man closest to my Lord Cornwallis. There is a great deal of good you may do here, Major. But there is little time that you now have to do it.'

'Do you school me in my duty?'

'I did not speak to offend you.'

'Then perhaps better you had not spoken at all.'

'And then I should be as guilty as any other.'

'Lord Cornwallis expects my full loyalty, sir, and he shall have it.'

'Major—'

'I will hear you no more,' said he, and threw out his arm in anger as he went up the main valley, striding out to put me quickly behind him.

The deep booming of our guns grew ever louder as I slowly climbed the valley after him. I was in annoyance with myself, for I had handled Major Ross very poorly.

When I came into the upper town I did not trail him to the head-quarters, but turned my step toward the Hornwork, thinking to observe from there the progress being made by Washington's sappers on the enemy line. But as I crossed the main street, I glanced toward Mrs Kendrick's house and stopped upon the instant. Nelson's man-servant was sitting upon the step of the house. He stood when he saw me. My heart hollowed at the sight of the note in his hand.

CHAPTER 25

'*I*f you keep coming out here, Mr Douglas, we shall have to enlist you in the Fusiliers.'

'Where is Captain Abthorpe?'

'In the redoubt,' said Calvert, and I thanked him and waved him back to his breakfast with his fellows at the campfire. I found Abthorpe by an embrasure of the parapet, surveying the open ground to the front of him, and the pinewoods beyond. In the pines was where the main body of the French troops lay hid. I told Abthorpe what he should expect to see in the next ten minutes, which was a French officer coming out from the woods, under a white flag.

'I am to go out to parley with him.'

Though surprised, he gave his gunners the order to cease their occasional firing. He instructed the Fusiliers upon the ramparts to hold their muskets ready, but discharge no shot unless ordered. 'You shall need a drummer and flag yourself, Mr Douglas,' said he, and sent his ensign to arrange it.

Ten minutes later, at just that time given me in Cordet's note, a drum sounded in the distance, and a French drummer lad came out from the woods. A blue-jacketed officer came with him, and also a soldier bearing a white flag. The officer was not Cordet.

'How long shall you be out there?'

'I cannot tell, Captain,' said I, lowering my spyglass. And before Abthorpe might question me further, I came out from the rear of the redoubt and met with my appointed drummer and flag-bearer. The flag-bearer, to my consternation, was Calvert; but not wishing to make a difficulty now, I proceeded with him around to the front of the redoubt.

Captain Abthorpe called down from the parapet. 'You are under Mr Douglas's command. But you are to advance no further than their flag.'

We set off, the drum beating for a parley, and Calvert came beside me.

'Keep the flag high, Mr Calvert. I should not like us to be shot in error.'

'What shall you say to them, sir?'

'I daresay I shall think of something.'

We were soon past the abatis of felled pines, and when the French party stopped two hundred yards off we continued our brisk advance till I called a halt right before them. Our drum, like theirs, fell suddenly silent.

'Monsieur Douglas?' said the French officer, a short, stout fellow with cheeks like red apples.

'I am he.' I then turned to Calvert. 'Go back now. I must now go on with this gentleman.'

'Sir?' said Calvert.

'You are witness that no threat is offered to me here. Both of you.' I looked from Calvert to the equally perplexed British drummer. 'Now do as I say.'

'Sir, we cannot leave you.'

'You shall leave me, Mr Calvert. Or would you disobey the order of Captain Abthorpe? I go willingly, as you see. And I would not keep this gentleman waiting.'

'Have you some trouble with this fellow, sir?'

'I am in no difficulty, Mr Calvert. Nor shall I be, if only you do as you are ordered.' I directed him with a jerk of my head back to the redoubt. The drummer turned, beating as he marched; and Calvert, throwing me a last unhappy glance, turned and followed the drum.

'You have no weapon, Monsieur?' said the French officer.

'No.'

'Then let us go.'

There were two horses saddled and waiting in the woods, and we mounted and crossed to the Williamsburg road. We followed this west a short way before turning onto a track southwards. Several riders passed us upon this track, both messengers, and officers and engineers, French and Continental. It was evident to me that this must be the main communication line between the allied armies. This track lay parallel with our inner line in York Town, but a mile or more distant, and hid from the town by the pines. The British guns, which now sounded but faintly, were here of no consideration, much less a danger.

Several smaller tracks converged on this main one, most of them freshly deep-rutted, which must be from the many transports accompanying the army. After a time we met with a wagon loaded with shot, the wagon bogged to its axles in the sand. The wagoner was busy reorganizing his team as we passed, and would not hear of any help being sent out to him, or listen to my escort's offer to take a message to Knox, Washington's chief of artillery. As we rode on, the French officer remarked in no complimentary manner the stiff-necked pride of the local people.

There soon appeared in the woods to both sides of us a great number of Continental soldiers and Virginian militia, wielding axes and tomahawks as they moved about collecting branches and sticks. By the track were a number of small carts being filled with stones that must be used to strengthen their entrenchment. To my observation, this work went on with an enthusiastic industry that was nothing like the exhausted sullenness and resentment of our sappers in York Town.

At length, the wood ahead opened into cleared farmland.

On the left hand was evidently the French artillery park, with two rows of tents facing a great collection of field-pieces, mortars and siege guns. The guns were ranked very orderly, with carpenters working upon the carriages, and gunnery officers going among them to make sure of the work. There were just as many heavy guns as Campbell had reported, and more. When the enemy line was finally established, and these guns were taken forward, there must be the havoc of Hell then loosed upon York Town.

On the right hand were a number of larger tents, which my escort now informed me comprised General Rochambeau's headquarters, and our destination. We halted by the nearest of these tents. As I dismounted, Cordet himself came out. He had still that same upright military bearing that I remembered. And when he stopped short of me and clasped his hands behind his back to wait, that too seemed strangely familiar. He wore no wig, so the silvering of his hair was plainly visible, as was the new scar upon his left temple. Apart from the scar, his face was little changed, though matured with a small deepening of the lines. My escort took the horses, and I walked over to Cordet and stopped before him. He studied me just as closely as I studied him.

'Monsieur Douglas.'

'Major Cordet.'

Turning, he led me into the tent.

'It is a long time.'

'It is.'

'You look not too badly.'

'And you have been a little careless,' said I, with a glance at his scar.

'Your navy marksmen were not as useless as I hoped.' He smiled then, and directed me to a chair. He sat himself by his campaign desk and leaned forward, his fists resting upon his knees. 'There shall be time enough for us to speak later. But you will understand . . .'

'Of course,' said I, no less eager to speak now than he to hear the reason of my note and get back to his duties. I began just as I had rehearsed. 'I believe that I mentioned my position with our Board of Trade and Plantations.'

'Yes. But you did not say what it is that you do.'

'I am an agent for the Board in a general way. I go where I am sent. Usually it is to restore some equability between those gentlemen who must enforce the Board's directions and those who must comply with them.' He nodded as though accepting the necessary vagueness of the answer. 'Inevitably I have been in the colonies here very frequently these past years.'

'Inevitably.'

'But it has been some while since I was on the Chesapeake. Years, in fact. But when I was last here I made the acquaintance of a local family. They are good people. The Morgans.' I paused, expecting now some intervention from Cordet. But he made none. He looked at me equably and gave no sign of recognizing the name. But it was simply not possible they had been kept by Lasceaux at the French head-quarters in Williamsburg, and yet Cordet not have heard the name Morgan. I continued, but with considerably greater caution; and, I own, sudden self-doubt. 'It was hardly a month ago that I came here to the coast from the Indian country.'

'With Lord Cornwallis.'

'No. I came alone. That is, with one other – but that is no matter. What matters is that when I arrived here, I met again with the Morgans. At my request – and it was only at my request – the father and son of the family sailed me out to a British ship that was in the Bay.'

He asked me the name of the ship. I told him.

'The *Guadeloupe* is a ship-of-the-line,' said he.

'She was for New York. I needed letters carried to London, and she might have been a ketch for all that it mattered to me. It was but a convenience to me that she might take my letters speedily to New York, thence to the Board in London.'

'I do not see your trouble.'

'It happened that the Morgans took me out to her almost the same hour that Admiral de Grasse arrived in the Bay. He came at the *Guade-loupe*. The Morgans took fright and fled. And whether it is by a report of the incident in the French fleet, or by someone ashore, the Morgans seem to be now held on account of it. But their whole actions were only done at my bidding, as friends to me. Their actions have been misconstrued. And misconstrued by some malice, I fear, and therefore cast in the darkest colours imaginable.'

'Are they accused?'

'I have it by report that they are held.'

'Such a misunderstanding may soon be put right.'

'Not if they are hanged first.' His head came up, and I said, 'When I learned of it, I wrote to you.'

'But how should you know that I was here?'

I told him it was the deserters come over to us. 'And you are an aide to General Rochambeau, they say.'

Leaning back, he rested one arm upon his campaign desk, watching me all the while. 'You fear that you have brought a false suspicion upon these Morgans.'

'I am sure of it.'

'And you appeal to me to release them?'

'Yes.'

'I cannot.'

'They are innocent men.'

'I make no judgement upon that. When I say that I cannot release them, I mean that it is not in my power.'

'Your word must count for something.'

'Perhaps. But if it does, that is only because I use it carefully.' His look now was disconcertingly direct. 'It is something strange that Cornwallis has permitted you to cross over to us.'

'I did not come here under his authority. But what problem I have made for myself does not signify. My concern is the Morgans. If you would see two innocent men hanged and do nothing—'

'You shall not goad me to argument, Douglas.'

'I would goad you to justice, and to the preservation of their lives.'

His eyelids drooped, and he smiled to himself. 'I wondered how much the years might have changed you. I see now it is very little.'

I remarked that I had trusted that the man I once knew in Bengal should hear me.

'I hear you very well,' said he, rising from his chair. 'It is another question what I should do with what I hear.' There arrived two captains at the opening to the tent. Cordet gestured for me to stay seated while he went out to speak with them.

There seemed nothing for it now but to continue as I had begun, for I could make no open challenge to his pretended ignorance of the Morgans. In spite of his pretence, I must continue to throw a different and better light upon the Morgans' actions, appeal to Cordet's sense of honour, and by my presence stand hostage for the truth of my words. To falter now was to fall. But to maintain every point of a lie is no slight undertaking; and so I was not sorry when Cordet came back to tell me that he must cut short our conversation and return to his duty on the line.

'I shall send word to the gaol that there is a witness will speak for these Morgans. If the Morgans are being questioned by our people, there may be other concerns. It may be that you shall be questioned.'

'I am ready to go there.'

'You shall stay here with my man. Do not go about the other tents. If you would take some exercise, you may walk the main track that you came by. But go no nearer our entrenchments. I shall return in the evening.'

About the immediate encampment, and in the artillery park across the track, there was a remarkable calmness reigned. Indeed were it not for the distant firing of the York Town guns – albeit this steadily decreased all the while – it was a scene might be found in any English county, with the local militia turned out for manoeuvres. But this sight, I well knew, was as deceptive as may be; for in the woods to the south were ten thousand and more troops assembled, awaiting the completion of the siege line, the sending forward of the guns, and the final order to attack.

In the late afternoon, the clouds that had thickened and darkened for some hours at last broke into a light rain, and so I retreated to Cordet's tent with my keeper.

The lanterns were just being lit when Cordet finally returned. He handed his wet cape and tricorn to his man, ordered hot water for his bath, and then enquired sternly why no wine had been poured for me. Not waiting an answer, he went to the small cabinet by his desk and brought forth a bottle and two glasses. I asked him what news from Williamsburg.

'I have concerns other than your friends, Douglas.' He handed me a glass. 'No message has come back. Do I presume that you shall wait?'

'Yes.'

'It may be that we shall not hear before tomorrow.'

'However long, I shall wait.'

He quaffed his wine then told me he would have a camp-bed brought for me into this outer quarter (his own lying behind a canvas curtain behind his desk). He said that I should ask his man for anything that I might need.

'I intended no intrusion upon you.'

'It is exactly what you intended. Though I do not blame you for it, Douglas, you might spare me the empty civilities.' There was amusement in his eye now, and I hesitated, then tipped my glass to him. A hip-bath then arriving, and buckets of steaming water, I would give him his privacy. Cordet told me that there was more work that he must do that night, and that once he had bathed and slept a few hours, he must go out again. 'We shall talk tomorrow.'

His man then took me to the mess tent, where I had the first fresh meat I had eaten for many days.

I did not wake when Cordet went out again after his rest, but some time after midnight I opened my eyes and heard the rain, and the booted tread of many soldiers going along the track. There must be sappers too, for there was a soft clinking of metal tools touching on the ground as they went by. Turning, I found Cordet's man slouched at the campaign desk, a candle burning beside him, and his head lying upon his arm.

'Reveille?' said I.

'No,' said he, but offered no explanation of the movements outside. A heavy fatigue was upon me, and so I thought no more of it but turned and slept again, dreamlessly, all the way to morning when I was startled awake by a tremendous volley of guns. I sat bolt upright. It sounded the heaviest firing there had been, and I dressed and was still pulling on my jacket as I hurried out from the tent. Cordet was seated by the campfire, a pannikin in his hand, and with his face turned toward the sunrise and the distant booming of the York Town guns. He looked tired, but very satisfied.

'What has happened?'

'Your Lord Cornwallis has woken up.' He poured the dregs of his coffee upon the ground before he rose. It then came back to me, the movement of those soldiers and sappers in the night.

Cordet called up two horses and we rode through the woods, and soon came to the Pigeon Hill redoubts. Climbing onto the ramparts we looked over; and a more astonishing sight I never saw. For midway across that no-man's-land, there was now a deep entrenchment and an earth wall where twelve hours previously there had been only open ground.

'Great God.'

'Now you may see how I was occupied.'

From our vantage at the rear of the new-made line, we could see how the digging continued yet, and the raising up of the earth-bank in every part. At several places were more substantial diggings, which must be the redoubts for the guns.

And the firing from York Town was now furious upon this new entrenchment which was but six or seven hundred yards off from the British line. But all too late. A single night of secret Herculean labour had been enough to establish the new line. The enemy soldiers and sappers now had protection while they worked, and whatever the firing from York Town, however accurate or fierce the shelling, the work would proceed steadily now till the French siege guns were at last brought into play. I studied the new entrenchment, and then raised my eyes to the British line. I saw with some disquiet that after Lord

Cornwallis's headquarters, it was Mrs Kendrick's house that was the best target for the French guns.

'You are fortunate, Douglas, to be out from there.'

I answered Cordet nothing, much less said what I thought; which was that once the Morgans were safe, I must make no delay but return at once into York Town.

CHAPTER 26

*I*t being a Sunday there were to be services held in both the French and the Continental camps, which when Cordet told me of he added that I was at liberty, if I wished, to join the Virginians. Though I knew this was at least partly to avoid any embarrassment to the Catholic priest, I accepted it as a courtesy. There was a pair of Virginian militiamen came up for me, and Cordet instructed them in my presence how I was to be treated as a guest among them, adding that a guest should not overreach the bounds of hospitality and that I was to submit to the order of any officer.

'You may let Mr Douglas pray as long as he will,' he called after us as we departed. 'For he is a very great sinner.' This brought cheerfully profane rejoinders from my companions, which I was relieved to hear; for there is in the colonies a strain of righteous religiosity will have any sane man soon reaching for his pistol and his whisky.

My two fellows had each done several hours' service at the new entrenchment during the night, and very keen they were now to show me the rawness of their hands and to share their delight at the terrible shock they had given Cornwallis. None of this, I must say, was to taunt me. For Cordet had introduced me as a functionary of the Board of Trade, and so the men set no account by me. To them I was just some lucky fellow who had got himself clear of York Town, which good fortune they congratulated me upon several times as we made our way to the Virginian encampment behind Wormley Creek.

We passed yet another artillery park, this one manned by Continentals. My companions told me that this was Colonel Knox's command, and much superior to the French (though it looked to me smaller, and somewhat disordered). Beyond this was an encampment of several hundred souls that I took for militia at first, only that when we neared I saw that they were many of them women and children. These were the familiars and camp followers of the Continentals and militia, and shocking it was to see the miserable state they were in. Almost every foot was bare, their clothing hardly better than rags, and their faces sallow and pinched. There was an utter exhaustion hung over their whole encampment. Some must have followed their menfolk up through the Carolinas, and others come down from the north. And God knows for how many years of the war they had trudged after their men. There were blacks among them too, which made me wonder at the fate of those blacks of ours turned out from York Town, and whether some had perhaps resubmitted, in their starving desperation, to their chains.

But so familiar was the sight of these people to my companions that they seemed scarcely to notice the encampment, and were even a little annoyed that I should remark the wretched condition of the women. I held my tongue after, till we came to the creek, and then I expressed a frank surprise.

'Yonder barn is the church,' said one of my fellows, lifting his head toward the barn in the field. But near the barn, and what had surprised me, was the congregation. Apart from the many Continental and Virginian officers (all in their best tunics and breeches) were a good number of women; and these women as unlike those dejected camp-followers we had just passed as might be. They were, so my companions informed me, the officers' wives, most of whom had come out from their billets in Williamsburg the previous evening. They would now attend the morning service with their husbands, take a meal with them, and then return in their buggies back to the town. There were perhaps a score of these women, and all in colourful crinolines and silks, and thirty or more officers mingling with them. The congregation looked more like patrons outside a theatre than people but a mile distant from a siege line. My two fellows guided me to one of the officers, who stepped apart from the others to greet me.

'Mr Douglas,' said he, extending his hand. 'I am Nelson, and charged by Monsieur Cordet with your care.'

I took his hand, and glanced at his epaulettes. General Nelson. In civilian life, the pretended Governor Nelson, the political leader of the Virginian rebels. He must be almost thirty years younger than his uncle, Secretary Nelson, and he had nothing of the older man's girth. But in his face was a definite resemblance: his eyebrows very full, and a quick intelligence in the eyes beneath.

My glance did not trouble him. 'And how fares my uncle? I trust he is treated well.'

'He dines regularly at my Lord Cornwallis's table. He is certainly not mistreated.'

'Your lordship is a gentleman. I shall be sure to tell him so once we have blasted him out from there. But come,' said he, putting his arm through mine, 'there are others here have friends in York Town. They shall not forgive me if I fail to introduce you.'

There then followed a most uncomfortable round of introductions, during which I must confess how very few of the York Town civilians I had met with, much less knew. To each person I now gave a general assurance that none of those within the British line were detained against their will; indeed, that it seemed to me it was only an excessive concern for their property kept them within the town. I explained that most of these civilians had now withdrawn both themselves and their chattels down to the safety of the caves, but that a further opportunity would certainly be offered them to leave should a bombardment seem imminent.

'How much more imminent could it be?' muttered one bluff captain, which amused his wife but drew a stern look from Nelson.

A drummer boy then came out from the barn and rang a handbell, and very glad I was to break off from the enforced mingling to go with the rest of the congregation inside.

There were camp-chairs and benches placed in rows in the otherwise empty barn, and I sat by Nelson. A frock-coated priest at the front took the service, and though I kept my eyes upon him and stayed silent, which is the custom in those parts, I paid him no mind. For all through the service my thoughts turned on Cordet. Not only had he deliberately lulled me the previous evening, and kept from me any hint of the astonishing work to be done that night, but now he had put me beneath this man Nelson's eye. Governor Nelson, who was undoubtedly the first recipient of every communication sent out by Secretary Nelson from York Town. But more than that, this pretended Governor of the colony must know very well of the accusations brought against the Morgans as spies in his territory. And he must likewise know of their confinement in his own prison.

He was a sandy-haired fellow of middling height, and his face fair, though reddened by his summer campaigning with the Virginia militia. He looked physically a tougher man than his uncle, but equally shrewd. I was in no doubt but that he knew very well my purpose in coming into the French lines; and yet he had not mentioned it once. I was therefore in considerable perplexity whether I should myself make mention of the Morgans to him directly. But by the time the service ended, I had decided that I should not. Better, I thought, to allow him the lead of me, that I might see his own mind the more clearly.

'If there is nothing calls you back to the French at once, sir,' said he as we came out from the barn, 'you must stay with us awhile.' He beckoned my two escorts, who had seated themselves by the door during the service, and told them that I would stay an hour or two more, and that they should not harry me but hold themselves off at a discreet distance. He would have taken my arm then, but that I stepped away and moved with all the others of the congregation across the field toward the creek. By the creek was an open-sided tent, like a summer pavilion, with a long trestle-table beneath. Nelson came up beside me.

'It is a wonder to us all how Lord Cornwallis has blundered so badly.'

'And has he?'

'You cannot think the British situation very comfortable, Mr Douglas.'

'I am not a military man.'

'He is well thought of by the French officers. But I may tell you, it was not taken kindly by my men how all the fresh water here was poisoned.'

'I shall not attempt to excuse it.'

'That is something, at least.'

'Nor shall I fling in your face all the savage brutalities that I have witnessed of your own people these past years. There have been evils enough done, I think, by both sides in this war.'

'I meant no personal accusation of you, Mr Douglas.'

Nearing the tent, we were passed by footmen and blacks hurrying with the chairs and benches from the barn. To one side of the tent, cooks laboured at giant pots suspended over the campfires. There were neither trees nor bushes lining the creek in that place, and the pavilion was set back only twenty yards from the water. Directly down the creek, the two blockading French ships below York Town were visible out on the main river.

The women were much taken by this view of the ships. Spyglasses were passed from hand to hand, and very sobering it was for me to see how sanguine and even light-hearted they were, and how that the distant firing of the York Town guns was nothing to them. The pavilion being by the creek and not the river, the slaughtered horses and the floating refuse and rubbish of York Town were all hid from us. A light westerly breeze ensured that the pastoral scene was not marred by any stench. A lieutenant then approaching from their line, Nelson turned aside from me to speak with the fellow.

And then it was that I saw Caesar, the Morgans' slave.

He was bringing wood for the campfire, and it was at first a vague recognition I had of his fleshy face. But then a cook called him by name, and I saw him instantly then, standing in the Morgans' upper field watching Tarleton and me go by. My stomach turned over, and I turned my face to the pavilion. I cudgelled my brain to recall every time I had seen the damned fellow at the Morgans' farm, and every time I might have spoken in his presence. And was he here now by chance? It did not seem possible. Nelson finished with the lieutenant and turned back to me.

I said, 'Sir, I hope you shall not think me disobliging, but my breakfast sits poorly on me. And even the smell of the mutton is uncomfortable to me now.'

'It happens that I am called away myself to the line,' said he, lifting a hand after the retreating lieutenant. 'And if you would not stay and eat, nor disoblige me, then you must come forward and admire our works.'

Without awaiting my reply, he called my two escorts to follow us. I did not at first question my good fortune, but gratefully left the creek, the congregation and Caesar. I accompanied Nelson northward out of the open field and onto a sandy track through the pines. The night's rain had wetted the mat of fallen needles, and the day's heat was now drawing the pine-scent into the air. We came to a series of clearings where Virginia militia and sappers were encamped; and here the smoke drifted from their fires and hung like a mist among the trees.

One small camp was set apart from the others. There were bearded fellows occupied this camp, with ragged coats made of deer hide. Most were without boots, some were barefooted, but others wore moccasins. I recognized these fellows instantly as mountain men; and, by the look of them, only recently come down from the edge of the Indian country. They would be mostly Scotsmen and Irish, but native now to the Appalachians; and it was the likes of these, I well knew, now fought Dragging Canoe and the Cherokees with such an unbridled savagery.

'If you would be advised, Mr Douglas,' said Nelson quietly, 'do not stare at them so. If they take against you, they shall not be restrained by my orders.'

'Who has brought these here?'

'They are volunteers. Some fought at King's Mountain. Come away now.'

From this point onward there were no more idle encampments, but the infantry that we met with were very purposefully engaged with the business of carting forward the gabions and fascines, and readying themselves to go out and take their places in the new entrenchment. At the end of the woods was a small redoubt, and here the Virginians very proudly welcomed Nelson onto the rampart.

From this redoubt, a few hundred yards inland from the York River, I took my second view of the enemy's new entrenchment. It lay four or five hundred yards to the front of us, and though it was not now the astonishing sight it had first been to me, yet I think it filled me this time with a greater trepidation. For I could now see the great advance made with this new entrenchment toward those two British redoubts to the south of York Town, nearer the river. Both those redoubts, when the rebel positions were finally ready, must be well within range of Knox's guns.

Nelson sent an ensign forward to the new entrenchment with a message, and then he gave me his spyglass. He said what I had heard already, and more than once, that day. 'You are well out from there, Mr Douglas.'

'It shall be more than guns needed to take the town.'

'There would be no shame in a surrender now. And it might preserve a great many lives.'

'If General Washington is minded to surrender, I am sure my Lord Cornwallis shall hear him.'

After some minutes there came a sudden sound of drums from the new entrenchment. The York Town guns, whose firing had become less frequent through the day, now fell silent; and it seemed that the British gunners paused to await the meaning of those drums.

'If you will look there,' said Nelson pointing ahead, 'you shall see Colonel Hamilton's colours.'

Upon the new entrenchment, a flag was now carried onto the wall, and the drummer went up after. And then – and much to my amazement – a few score Continental soldiers followed. Once atop the wall they were in plain sight, and exposed to the York Town guns. When I turned to Nelson for some explanation of this swaggering bravado, he directed my attention forward again.

And then I saw a foolishness that I never had expected. For these infantrymen of Colonel Hamilton's then commenced a number of parade-ground drills and manoeuvres, marched up and down, shouldered and grounded their muskets, and generally behaved with a complete contempt for the British guns. Somewhere in the new entrenchment a piper began to play a merry air. From all about us now huzzahs and whistling broke out from the Virginians as they watched their comrades' outrageous display. At last – at long last – the British gunners seemed to recover from their astonishment. They recommenced their firing, but could not quickly find the range. Hamilton's infantrymen continued their taunting drill a minute more; and then with not a man hit or even scratched, they retired leisurely into the safety of their trench.

'It may be that we shall need more than guns to take the town. But as you see, Mr Douglas, we have the men.'

'You have the men,' I conceded. 'And if they continue in that fashion, my Lord Cornwallis has the bayonets shall make them wish they were not only men but also soldiers.'

'You would not begrudge them their small celebration.'

'Their discipline is not my concern, sir. But by your leave, I would return now to my host, Cordet.'

'Colonel Hamilton has offended you.'

'Say rather, he has instructed me,' said I, coming down from the rampart.

'Major Cordet thought you might have some appeal to make of me.'

'He was mistaken.' Beckoning those two fellows who must now be my escort back to the French headquarters, I thanked Nelson for his care of me. He was thrown by the suddenness of my withdrawal.

'Shall you come down here again, Mr Douglas?'

'When I have completed my business with Major Cordet, my time shall be my own,' I answered, which was truly no answer at all. And why should I answer him who had brought me down upon a

Christian pretence, but only to be identified by a slave? As to any appeal to him, I never considered it, for it would only be to aid him in my own entrapment. I had taken Colonel Hamilton's instruction very well. Though I had rashly presented myself to the guns, those guns had now fired, and I must make a timely withdrawal before I was hit.

CHAPTER 27

'The Morgans have much to thank you for.'

'Are they released?'

'No,' said Cordet, putting aside his pen and turning from his campaign desk to face me. 'But neither are they hanged. Though had you not come over – had your appeal not gone down to the gaol—'

'They are sentenced then.'

'They are convicted as spies. Their execution is stayed only by your intervention. I must warn you, the stay may prove but temporary.'

It was all my worst fears made manifest with their conviction; and the stay of execution but a single thread of hope. I was in some small shock at the suddenness of Cordet's announcement, and I crossed to my camp-bed and sat down.

My two Virginian companions lingered without, and Cordet (I think to allow me a moment to collect myself) then went and sent them back to their own encampment. Once returned inside, he poured a glass of watered wine for me and retook his seat.

'It is one of our colonels has the authority over the Morgans. I expect he shall want to question you.'

'I shall go at once.'

'He has made no summons of you to Williamsburg. He knows that you are here.'

'Am I to wait?'

'Yes.'

'While the Morgans have yet the rope about their necks?'

'It did not come there by accident. And remember, the stay may be but temporary. You must prepare yourself for that.'

What I would prepare myself for was the Morgans' freedom, and to countenance any less must be to go down before despair. I dare not think that they might share a common fate with Major Andre. So I drank the watered wine in quietness and calmed the hard beating in my breast. I made no congratulation of myself for this first reprieve of them, for it was only the smallest part of my work done. Soon would come the larger part, which was my submission to Colonel Lasceaux's questioning (I had no doubt that the colonel with charge over the Morgans was he) and the maintaining against all the world, and in the face of the truth, the absolute innocence of my connection with the Morgans.

Cordet was to and from the tent all the afternoon, but his man stayed with me as my servant and my guard. Though the York Town guns continued firing, the fresh-roused ferocity of the morning was past; and certainly there was no attention paid by the French officers to each distant cannonade. Here at the far rear of the line, beyond the range of the British guns, every man went about his business in perfect safety.

In the early evening I walked out with Cordet's man along the northerly track through the woods, thoroughly absorbed with my own thoughts, and the fellow's taciturnity now a blessing. Nor was it only Cable and David Morgan that I thought on, for the sight throughout the day of the French artillery park had been a constant reminder to me of the awful firepower that must soon be unleashed upon York Town. And there Mrs Kendrick still was, and Mrs Morgan lay. And if they or Lizzy Morgan were to be caught by any shot, how then might I forgive myself that I had not moved them to a cave or over to Gloucester?

Behind this disturbance of my mind was another, which was all in a single name, Lasceaux. It were a desperate measure indeed to place myself into the hands of such a man. Though I knew that I must do it for the Morgans' sake, yet I could not pretend it was a decision would be supported by my superiors in London. In fact Jenkinson would be appalled to discover the risks I had already taken since my arrival on the Chesapeake, and this last one to crown them. And appalled, I suppose, with some good reason; for his responsibility was to the whole of the Deciphering Department, and the Morgans were not even names to him, but only coded entries buried in a dusty file. As to the questioning I must face from Lasceaux, it loomed beyond these nearer concerns like a threatening storm that might drive me to shipwreck. In short, I was so much distracted by these thoughts, that exactly how many times the owl hoot sounded before I heard it, I cannot say.

But certainly it was more than once, for when I broke from my thoughts I glanced directly to the left side of the track, and into the woods. It came again, but the undergrowth was very thick there, and such that any Indian might disappear into very easily. I could see nothing. Cordet's man was a little to the front of me on the track, his own attention engaged by several approaching riders. And though I considered some ruse that might allow me to step aside into the woods, I then saw that one of those approaching was Cordet. I therefore chose prudence and stayed upon the track; and when their horses slowed to a walk, and Cordet greeted me, relaxed and in good spirits, I must turn and fall in beside him.

The French officers with Cordet proved to be from St Simon's regiment to the north, and now sent down as envoys from St Simon's headquarters to meet with General Rochambeau's staff. (And to plan the annihilation of the British line, though they were too gentlemanly to say so in my presence.) Cordet soon dismounted, clearly intending to walk with me the last few hundred yards. He gave his horse to his man, who then rode on after the officers.

'He has taken care of you, I trust?' said Cordet, watching his man ride away.

I said that I had no complaint of my treatment. I then asked after Lasceaux, and when we might expect him.

'You are not the Colonel's only concern, Douglas. Indeed, I believe you are not even his main concern. We cannot expect him tonight.'

'In the morning, then?'

'It is possible.'

'I might as easily ride to Williamsburg.'

'You are not invited to Williamsburg.'

There was firmness in this, and I knew that any appeal must be waste of breath. The evening air was cool now, and the shadows of the pines slowly merging with the fading daylight. From the hidden creeks and waterways in the wood came the sounds of insects and frogs, all undisturbed by the distant guns. And those guns seemed to fire less frequently now, which I was glad of; for Cornwallis's munitions must be depleted very fast if that first rate of fire had continued. And to what little effect they had till now been expended, I knew only too well.

'Have you a wife?' said Cordet of a sudden.

'No,' said I, and to cover my startlement at the question added some feeble jest that I had hardly gathered more than a mistress or two. And then, but only because it seemed that I must, and despite that I knew the answer, I asked him the same question.

'A wife, and a son,' said he. 'My wife, I think you know.' I looked at him, scarce knowing what I should reply; but he straightaway continued, 'She was a Beauchamp. Mademoiselle Valerie Beauchamp.' Now he studied me. And though he could not possibly understand all that was in my mind, yet he seemed satisfied that it was the supposed revelation had struck me into silence. 'Quebec?' said he, as if I should need some reminder of the first place that I had met her.

'Mademoiselle Beauchamp.'

'Surprising, is it not?'

'And a son.'

'Five years old, and a tyrant,' said he. I offered him my belated congratulations. He inclined his head, but would not be put off from what he would say to me. 'Do you recall Chandernagore?'

'Of course.' Chandernagore had been the French stronghold on the Hugli River in Bengal, and the place where I had first met Cordet. I added, now, that I hoped I was not so ungrateful as to forget the refuge offered me there by the French after the Nawab's sacking of Calcutta.

'And do you recall,' said he, 'as we went downriver from there, that you made a sketch? It was of a lascar. You signed it, and I took it for a souvenir. After I was married – perhaps a year – I was turning out a trunk that I had kept from those days. By chance, I showed my wife the sketch. I told her of the young British fellow who had done it.'

'Dear God—'

'Yes. It was a great shock to her, I think. Naturally, she told me at once of her acquaintance with you.'

Acquaintance? The word was a cut to me: but was the word Valerie's or Cordet's? And why was he now opening himself to me so?

'It was some while before I tried your name upon her father,' said he.

'The Vicomte was never a friend to me.'

'So I understand.'

'Is he still alive?'

'Oh, yes. And he was quite unhappy that she had told me of you.'

I shrugged. I remarked that many years had now passed, and as for myself I did not dwell upon those days. Which though it was true, I confess that I had thought of Valerie more than once since first seeing Cordet in Williamsburg; and the news that they were now parents to a son had given me a painful jolt that I had not expected.

'Valerie shall be surprised by our meeting again, Douglas. As am I.'

'Let it only lead to the Morgans' freedom, and I shall not be sorry for it.'

'And otherwise?'

'I do not allow of otherwise.' I would not continue in this line, and so I asked that he might send my respects to his wife, and remember me to her.

'But of course,' said he, and held my look as he bowed his head

261

graciously. I understood, then, the reason why he had told me of Valerie: it was to break the power of my own silence. For I had no doubt now but that he must have known already (perhaps by Buffon) that I was previously aware of his marriage to Valerie. With a simple directness, and, I own, a delicacy I had not expected in him, he had brought my earlier acquaintance with her into the light where it might be visible, and so make no weapon to either one of us. I respected him for that. I might say I even admired his courage.

After, our talk went the easier; and not of Valerie now, but of those we had known in Bengal, which was a more comfortable subject to us both, at that moment, than the American war. We talked of Monsieur Law, still alive, and Mr Watts and Colonel Clive, both of them now dead; and so many other lives then joined, but now scattered upon the wind. He had heard of Mrs Watts's return to Bengal, and condoled with me upon the death some years past of her daughter Amelia; for he saw how it saddened me to mention it.

'I remember her. A pretty girl.'

'Her child survived. He is a godson to me.'

'It is something,' said he, which though he meant it for sympathy came to me as a sword stroke. As how could it not, coming from him who had got Valerie Beauchamp for a wife, and through Valerie, a son.

Ahead of us now there were lanterns being lit, the servants hanging them from poles outside the headquarters tents. I was not sorry when Cordet was called away to attend upon General Rochambeau. It was the last I saw of him that night. But late the next morning he came to say that Colonel Lasceaux had arrived from Williamsburg and was now ready to question me.

CHAPTER 28

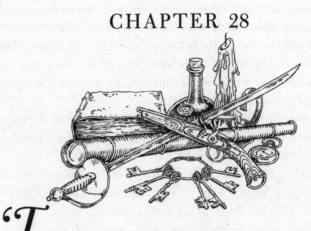

'*T*he paper is rather worn, Mr Douglas.'

'I believe it is legible, sir.'

'Oh, yes. It is quite legible,' said Colonel Lasceaux, keeping his head down and inspecting my credentials from the Board of Trade and Plantations. He was an older man than I had expected. He must be more than fifty years, and though wigged and uniformed he had nothing of the soldier about his bearing. His whole appearance was loose, from the heavy rings beneath his eyes to his slumped shoulders, his ill-fitting jacket and the muddy boots which were crossed at the ankles and jutting out from beneath the table. He looked as though he might be some impecunious officer, discharged with dishonour, and now drinking his way to the grave. 'And your business has been in the Indian country, you say.'

'Yes.'

'A long while?'

'I travelled down there in the winter.'

He lifted his eyes. 'Down from where?'

'New York.'

'A bad time for travel. What business had you in New York?'

'My business there is not material to the Morgans' confinement.'

'I am sure you are right, Mr Douglas. And once you have told me what that business was, I may in good conscience pass over your time in that place.' He looked at me quite affably, and with no hint that he had himself been there on the Hudson with Washington and Rochambeau at the time, much less that he had questioned Major Andre before the execution. I glanced at Cordet, who sat quietly to the side of the table as an observer. But he spoke no word, nor gave me any sign of sympathy, and I turned back to Lasceaux.

'There were troubles between the merchants and our Customs House. I was sent to make an enquiry of it. Whilst there, I received a further instruction to travel south.'

'They had small consideration of you who sent you over the mountains in winter.' To that I made no reply, and he said dryly, 'There is no Customs House, I think, in the Indian country.'

'There had been a sharp decline in our trade with the southern tribes. I was to report the cause of it, and to propose a remedy if I could find one.'

'And could you?'

'The cause is the war that the Cherokee are now engaged in with the unlawful settlers from Virginia and the Carolinas. Peace is the remedy.'

'By which you mean a forced expulsion of the settlers.'

'Sir, this is very far from the Morgans.'

'You then left the Indian country to join General Cornwallis. Is that a correct understanding?'

'I left the Indian country to come to the Chesapeake. My intention was to take a passage to New York.'

'But you knew that General Cornwallis was here.'

'Yes.'

'And you travelled alone?'

'I have not crossed into your lines, sir, to make an explanation of my every action these last months. Nor to bring yet more innocent men under suspicion. What I have to tell you, if you would hear it, is how your people have made a misapprehension concerning the Morgans.'

Lasceaux rested his forearms on the table and interlaced his fingers. 'Am I to take it, then, that you did not travel alone?'

This was so very far from the Morgans that I had not the slightest reason nor inclination to answer it. And to name Campbell as the companion of my journey must be to repay his loyalty with a treacherous ingratitude. I folded my arms and held Lasceaux's steady gaze. We were like this some moments before Cordet spoke.

'Had those with whom you travelled any connection with the Morgans?'

'No,' said I, very firm. 'No connection whatever, upon my life.'

'It need not come to that,' said Lasceaux; and though he smiled as if it were a jest, I felt a small constriction in my throat. 'But as you are so very anxious to correct our misapprehension concerning the Morgans, perhaps we should hear you.'

'I arrived at the Bay—'

'One moment please, Mr Douglas. This is not the first time you have been upon the Chesapeake.'

'No.'

'Nor the first time you have had dealings with the Morgans.'

Now we were come to the point that I had expected should make the commencement of my questioning. And having, since sending my first appeal to Cordet, reflected long and hard upon the possible questions, I was ready to answer. That is to say, I was ready with my several answers; for I must choose extremely carefully those times that I had been in the Morgans' company in all innocence, and about which I might say nothing that could be used as an entrapment to Cable and David Morgan.

For fifteen minutes then, or perhaps more, Lasceaux questioned me upon the Morgans. But his questioning was quite leisurely, and he frequently allowed me to expound upon my answers, by which means I suppose that he hoped I might inadvertently hang them. But how might they hang for the mere mischance of sharing meals with me, or allowing me to travel in their wagon or making a pleasure expedition up the James River?

'You first met them in the time of Governor Dunmore.'

'I did.'

'And were they in sympathy with the Governor?'

'They must tell you their own minds. I sat down with them in friendship. I do not recall that we discussed the Governor.'

'That strains credibility.'

'Nevertheless, it is the plain truth.'

'You must know that the Morgans have been long suspected as Loyalists by their neighbours.'

'Do you tell me so?'

'Neither father nor son is enlisted in the militia. Their neighbours have died in the cause of liberty while these two kept themselves apart.'

'I shall not debate with you the cause my American brethren die for, sir. As to the militia, I believe enlistment is voluntary. The lad is barely of age, and the father must look to his farm. He is not the only Virginian farmer to have declined to take up arms.'

'Their neighbours are quite decided against them.'

'If you would take the loose talk and suspicions of a man's neighbours as evidence, then none but a hermit may be safe. Consult your own village or town, sir.'

Lasceaux's gaze continued languid upon me. He was untouched by my words.

'So, Mr Douglas, it is August. You have arrived at the Bay.'

'I was upon the Portsmouth side, on the James River. I must needs cross over to the peninsula.'

'To General Cornwallis in York Town.'

'To the ships there, and thence to New York. Learning of the Morgans' presence on the Portsmouth side, I beseeched a favour of them, that they might carry me across.'

'They did more than that.'

'And I am sure they have told you the reason. It was done at my request, that I might be put aboard the British ship I then saw in the Bay. It was done as a favour to me.'

266

'They ran before the French flag. Admiral de Grasse came, they fled.'

'Would you not flee, sir, were it a British frigate bearing down upon you, and you circumstanced as were the Morgans? Could they explain themselves to the frigate's guns? De Grasse's ships did not arrive there as doves of peace. The Morgans fled to preserve their lives, and you cannot tell me that they were wrong to do so.'

At that moment an ensign arrived. After hearing the fellow's whispered message, Cordet did not scruple to keep it private but straightaway told Lasceaux that there were British deserters come across, and that Lafayette had requested the Colonel's instant attention to them. There passed a flicker of annoyance over Lasceaux's face, which made me think him no friend to Lafayette.

'You must excuse me,' said he, and he rose and went toward the tent-opening.

'Shall the Morgans now be released?'

'We are not done, Mr Douglas,' he replied; and as he departed the tent he called back to Cordet, 'We shall resume here when the others have been brought up.'

Somewhat surprised by this last, and more than a little concerned, I asked Cordet if it was the Morgans who would now be brought up from Williamsburg. But Cordet gave me no answer, only refolded my credentials and handed them back to me with due courtesy across the table.

If the Morgans were to be brought up from Williamsburg there must be only one reason, which was to allow Lasceaux to move the more easily between me and them in his questioning. I knew the practice well, and likewise knew the near-certainty that it must quickly discover some small discrepancy between our answers. And from this small discrepancy, and by further close questioning, Lasceaux would then make an entanglement and a deadly snare for each one of us. Already there seemed a suspicion of me quite particular, the cause of which, after some reflection upon Lasceaux's questions and my disquieting Sunday call upon the Virginians, I was inclined to lay at Secretary Nelson's door.

But whatever the cause, if the Morgans now came up I should have them within barely a mile of the British line and safety. My mind turned at once to the possibility of reinforcement. I must only await the moment.

It was after some hours, and Lasceaux having made no return to Cordet's tent, that I at last saw my opportunity. I put aside my book and rose from my chair, saying to Cordet, 'I would stretch my legs, if you would join me.'

But of course he would not join me. A pair of captains had just arrived at the tent-opening, and when Cordet looked about him he found what I had already seen, that his man was gone out.

'Keep yourself to the northerly track, Douglas. Go no further than the nearest creek. I shall send a man after you.' He then turned his attention to the captains, and I went quickly away.

Cordet's man would not be long behind me, and so I walked briskly along the track. At a hundred yards from the headquarters tents I whistled, but made no pause in my walking. Every twenty or thirty yards I whistled again into the woods, though keeping silence when any rider went by.

I was soon gone two hundred yards, and then three hundred, glancing back all the while to discover if any fellow came after me yet. At last a white-uniformed infantryman come from the tents and started toward me along the track. I was another fifty yards further on, and still no answer to my whistling, when I looked back again. The fellow was closing upon me. A French rider then approached from the north, and I hailed him, asking that he tell that infantryman that I had turned aside a minute into the pines to relieve myself. As he rode on, I stepped from the track, making as if to unbutton my breeches.

Beyond the first trees was a narrow path used by the wild boar or some such woodland creature, and there I turned north toward that place whence the owl's cry had come the previous evening. At my next stopping I made no whistle but instead cupped my hands to my mouth, like the Cherokee, and made that same cry. I paused a moment to listen, got no answer, and raised my hands again.

'Enough,' said a voice. Turning, I found Campbell coming toward me through the pines, with his musket held across his chest. I was never so pleased to see him, which is to say something indeed. I warned Campbell quickly of the infantryman on the track. Then I told him that I was neither entirely free nor entirely prisoner, and that the Morgans might soon arrive at Rochambeau's headquarters from the Williamsburg gaol.

'We have canoes to take them,' said he.

'Where?'

He lifted his chin. 'South, on the river. A mile below the militia.'

'Could we get the Morgans down there, and then up to York Town?'

He thought we could, but only in the night. I asked him how close he might safely come to the French headquarters.

'Their latrines are by the wood,' said he. 'I have watched their camp from a place there in the trees.'

'If they catch you they shall hang you with the Morgans.'

'And with you,' he added mildly. He asked me if the Morgans would be chained, which I answered was very likely.

I gestured to the knife at his hip, and he put down his musket and gave me both the knife and its leather sheath. These I tucked safely into the inner pocket of my jacket, beneath my left arm. 'I shall try to get them down to the latrines. A single whistle, and you must come out to fetch them. Two whistles, and you stay hid. If there is no sign of me before daybreak, withdraw to this place here again, that I may find you tomorrow. Are you alone?'

He answered that he was, adding that though he could fetch up the Pamunkey from by the river to our aid, he would rather not have the concern of them.

'Very well. I cannot stay here longer.'

He had picked up his musket by this time, and his only leave-taking now was to turn his back before retreating silently into the pines. As for myself, I retraced my step along the path and then cut across to the main track. There I met the French infantryman just arriving, slowing from a jog, and visibly relieved to see me coming out from the wood.

*

In the French artillery park there was considerable activity all the afternoon, with some of the lighter guns now hitched and taken forward to the line, and the remaining gunners dry-drilling. And, I confess, dry-drilling with a formidably precise and instant obedience to their officers' orders. To one side of the park, and under the direction of the French carpenters, blacks now loaded the carts with planks and timber which would be taken forward to make platforms for the guns in the line. This work, like the drilling, was done efficiently and well, and very different from that wearied labour of our own blacks in York Town. Throughout, I kept a careful eye on the wagons arriving along the Williamsburg track; but there was no sign of any gaol-cart or any prisoners.

It was now, and for the second time, that I saw the two allied generals together. I was seated beneath a mulberry tree near Cordet's tent, a book borrowed from Cordet opened upon my knee, when I glanced over at the track and saw General Washington ride up in company with his portly artillery chief, Knox. No ceremony was made of their arrival. They dismounted and went directly into General Rochambeau's tent. A short while later, Washington and Rochambeau emerged side by side, their officers trailing after them. They then crossed to the artillery park and made a tour of the guns.

As they went upon this round, Rochambeau summoned forward various gunnery officers to answer Washington's questions. And these French officers displayed a marked deference toward Washington, a thing most singular and surprising from this class of Frenchman. And the reason of this deference I only properly understood after the party was returned from the artillery park, and Washington and Knox had remounted. For then it was that General Rochambeau himself removed his tricorn and made a distinct bow of his head to General Washington. It was simply done, and Washington acknowledged it with a simple nod of his own before turning his horse and departing.

The smallest of actions, and over in a moment; but in this leave-taking was all the strength of their united armies. For here was no jealousy of command. In despite of the French fleet in the Bay, in despite of the preponderance of professional French soldiers, in despite of the greater firepower of the French guns, the French general had yet the wisdom to openly bow his head to the American and so maintain Washington's final authority. What a lesson was there for our own generals, Cornwallis and Clinton.

A light rain then starting, and no sign of the Morgans upon the track, I snapped shut my book and left the mulberry tree for the better cover of Cordet's tent.

Whether Lasceaux was all these hours engaged in questioning the British deserters I much doubted of; but that he was nowhere about the French headquarters was a thing certain. Cordet several times came and went upon Rochambeau's business; and each time that he came into the tent he with increasing puzzlement remarked Lasceaux's continuing absence from the headquarters. At last I asked if I might go and seek out Lasceaux directly from among Lafayette's regiment. Politely but firmly, Cordet refused me permission.

So it was that dusk found me again beneath that mulberry tree, and Cordet's man forty yards distant at the opening of the tent. He had been going in and out very frequently, carrying messages for Cordet, and now he did so again, turning his back and walking off this time toward General Rochambeau's pavilion. As he went, there came from the other direction, that of the Williamsburg track, the sound of a buggy nearing. And from the buggy came a Virginian voice vaguely familiar. Though I could not instantly place the voice, some instinct made me withdraw myself a little behind the mulberry tree.

Scarcely had I done so than the buggy came into view, and by it a mounted French officer, whose tall loose figure I recognized at once as Lasceaux's. In the buggy was a driver and his passenger, a uniformed French soldier. The driver's was evidently the Virginian voice I had heard, for he was talking yet. This fellow was neither soldier nor militia. And the nearer they approached, the greater my confusion. It looked that Lasceaux had indeed returned to Williamsburg during the day, though fetching back with him not the Morgans, but only these two in the buggy.

Moving myself about the tree, I kept myself hid as they went by me. But as they passed I recognized both the men in the buggy, and my heart seemed instantly gripped by a hand of ice. The passenger was that young Frenchman we had shot, the fellow we had nursed in Mrs Kendrick's library and with whom I had travelled under the white flag into Williamsburg. How he was well enough to even sit upright, I know not, unless it be he was forced to it by Lasceaux. And the driver, the talkative Virginian, was that damnable merchant Traherne who had pestered me whilst I was aboard the *Auguste*, and then again in Williamsburg near the gaol.

My breath stopped. I stood a few moments petrified, with one hand upon the mulberry trunk. I was scarce able to think, much less to quiet the clamour within my breast.

Lasceaux had said that he would resume his questioning of me when the others were brought up. The others. But it was not the Morgans that Lasceaux had meant, it was these two. Nor was it any further enquiry into the Morgans that Lasceaux had in mind, but only the proper trussing of me by the evidence of this deadly pair. I heard Traherne say now that he had harboured a suspicion of Danby from the very first, at which Lasceaux gruffly silenced him.

The buggy went by. I turned from the mulberry tree and forced myself to walk as calmly as I might past the tents and down across the open ground to the latrines.

'Where are the Morgans?'

'Your pistol, quickly. We must get to the river.'

Campbell gave me his pistol without further question. And still without question he turned and ran, and I after him, south through the woods, away from the tents. He carried his muskets one-handed, low by his side, and we moved swiftly along the path. Every yard, every second, I readied for the shout to go up behind us. But minutes went by, we ran without stopping, and still no cry rose from the French headquarters.

We slowed but once, Campbell looking back and signing to warn me of an encampment of soldiers in the clearing near the path; but once the clearing was behind us we ran again, and for our lives.

Campbell might continue an hour or more at that relentless loping pace, which I could not, and so I set myself to stay with him till either my chest burst or my legs gave way beneath me.

Four minutes, and five, and still no hue and cry came from the French.

On, on through the woods, with the light failing now. Then I caught my foot upon a root and stumbled. Campbell at once slowed, I think from fear that a worse accident might happen and stop us completely. Soon after my stumbling, we came to a broad creek and waded over thigh-deep in the water and mud. Then up through the bank of reeds the other side and onto the dry ground, and running again, till after a minute we veered east toward the river.

We were now far beyond earshot of the French headquarters; but to the north of us we suddenly heard the drums of the Virginians beating in their camp, for dusk was just turning to night. We said nothing but moved more swiftly till at length we came to the river. Campbell went along the bank, crouching down by the reeds. He cupped a hand to his mouth and made the call of an eagle. Twice more he made the call, and then the reeds away to his right parted, and the Pamunkey came out from their hiding place, drawing their canoes through the shallows.

Six Pamunkey and three canoes. Campbell climbed into the first canoe, and I into the last, and we paddled slowly and soundlessly out to the edge of the reed-bed. Those two French ships blockading York Town were anchored out in the river a few hundred yards to the front of us, so we clung to the reeds to stop from drifting while we waited for the protective darkness to come fully down.

When the ships were visible only by their lanterns, we finally let go the reeds and paddled out. And as we rode the tide up to York Town, all my hope of the Morgans' rescue fell away into the blackness of the river behind.

CHAPTER 29

'Doubt, my Lord? There can be no doubt. Rochambeau has siege guns in plenty, and their first batteries near ready. I am myself witness to their guns being taken forward.'

'Yes, you have said, Mr Douglas,' Cornwallis interrupted testily, but he turned not from the map upon the wall. The line of the enemy's first parallel was already drawn upon the map when I came into the main room of the headquarters; but in the past hour I had myself made many new marks upon it to indicate the positions of the redoubts, communication trenches, magazines and suchlike that I had seen the other side. And these marks, as I made them, Cornwallis seemed to take as an impertinent rebuke of him; and yet he could not now take his eyes from the map.

General O'Hara stood near him, and Sutherland and two captains of our artillery. They had all of them talked very freely before this, and questioned me upon all that I had seen behind the enemy line. But at Lord Cornwallis's testy interruption of me they fell silent.

'The first parallel we cannot prevent them completing,' decided Cornwallis at last. 'But if we allow a second parallel forward of it, then they shall have us by the throat.' He asked had I seen any signs of preparation for such a second line. I admitted that I had not.

'But nor was there a sign of the first before it was done,' I said.

O'Hara spoke up, saying that our two outer redoubts to the south, near the river, were well placed to observe any new entrenchment being made. There was a general assent to this by the others, everyone seeming content to follow Cornwallis's lead in underestimating the enemy's preparations. Further protest from me must be useless, an idle pissing into the wind. For with Tarleton gone over to the Gloucester side, gone too was any honourable and credible opposition to the strategy of immobile perseverance to which Cornwallis and Clinton had committed us.

When I came away from there near midnight it was with no good hope for our army's position, but with an absolute determination that the women must now be removed from the town.

'But we are not fired upon, Mr Douglas.'

'You shall be, Mrs Kendrick, and soon. Do not oppose me in this.' Having come down to find me already at breakfast, Mrs Kendrick had crossed to her chair at the far end of the table. She had not yet sat down, but stood with a hand now upon the chairback and looked at me. She was evidently not pleased with the direct instruction I had just given her. I said, 'I have already spoken with Captain Stuart. He has one of his caves empty now, and is content that you, Mrs Morgan and Lizzy shall be accommodated there till I have a boat ferry you to Gloucester.'

'Mrs Morgan cannot be taken to Gloucester. Have you not heard of the sickness there?'

I told her that O'Hara had mentioned it to me. She expressed a great surprise to see me so sanguine. And I confess, what she then told me of the sickness in Gloucester was quite alarming, and of a different order to O'Hara's offhand remark to me. Half the officers and men there were stricken with fevers, and some had died. If true (and I had no reason to doubt her), Gloucester was plainly no place to be taking a woman with child.

'Lieutenant Sutherland says Washington shall commence his first fire upon our entrenchment, and only come to the houses after,' said she, more confident now in her opposition to me. 'So we shall have fair warning before we need to leave here.'

'Sutherland is reading to you from the book of siege-warfare. Your house is clearly visible from the enemy redoubts. Their guns are being mounted as we speak. And you are not Sutherland's responsibility, but mine.'

'You take very much upon yourself.'

'If you would ready Mrs Morgan, we shall leave here at nine o'clock. If not to Gloucester, then as far as Captain Stuart's cave.'

She looked down the table at me, and I returned her level gaze. At length she seemed to understand that upon the question of leaving the house, I would brook no further argument. She dropped her eyes, drew up her chair and sat down. When she looked up again, she said, 'I have not bade you a good morning, Mr Douglas.'

'Good morning, Mrs Kendrick,' said I, somewhat wary.

'I am pleased you have come back safely to us.'

'Thank you.'

'If you are wondering where Francesca might be, I have sent her with those townspeople who left yesterday for Williamsburg. She has been given a place with a good family.'

'That was well done.'

'Major Ross was not so pleased at your crossing out from our lines.'

'I have made my peace with Lord Cornwallis.'

'Would I be wrong in supposing you were attempting some aid of the Morgans?'

'You may suppose what you will. It is enough for you to know that I would have both you and Mrs Morgan out from here that you be not blown to pieces.'

She had taken a spoon into her hand; but now she put the spoon down. 'Mr Douglas, what troubles you have faced these past days are no doubt beyond my imagining. But let that be. I have all this while been a nurse and a listener to Mrs Morgan. The guns have not paused more than a half-hour, both day and night. I am very tired, and you evidently think me very unreasonable. But do not treat me as a child.'

She had yet the command of herself, and she faced me with an admirable boldness. A woman less like a child I never saw.

'I was unable to effect an extenuation of the Morgans' circumstances,' said I; but this sounding even in my own ears very hollow, I put down my cup and made a sharp movement of my hand as if I might brush those first evasive words away. I raised my eyes to meet her look directly. 'The Morgans remain in the Williamsburg gaol. They are sentenced as spies.'

She made a sound of dismay. But after a moment's consideration, she said, 'As spies yet to be tried, or are they already convicted?'

'Convicted. As to any trial they have had, I cannot say. It is the French military has charge of them. I had thought to speak for them. I was not able.'

'Shall they be hanged?'

'Yes.'

'You must not tell her,' said she in sudden agitation. Rising from her chair she came toward me. 'She must not know.'

'She cannot help but know.'

'They are not hanged yet. And if you have a true concern for her, and for the child she carries, you must not tell her. You have been honest with me, Mr Douglas, and so I shall be so with you. Her body is sufficiently frail, but her mind is worse. She is in torment.'

'Aye.'

'It is more than that. There is something not right in her. It is beyond medicines. Doctor Gould promises me it is only her nerves and her condition. But I have sat with her too many days now. Gould is wrong.'

This came from her so sudden and with such quiet force that I was some several moments in gathering myself. Then I made to rise, declaring that I must go up to Mrs Morgan. But Mrs Kendrick put a hand on my shoulder to stop me. There was a sweet scent upon her sleeve.

'That would not help. I shall have her ready to go down to the cave. But please. You must not tell her.'

Our guns kept up a rain of shot and shell, but with so little damage done to the enemy's works that our gunners got no encouragement. Indeed, the only time I saw our men properly enlivened that morning was when one of our bulldogs got loose. This guard-dog was kept apart from the others of the pack as being too savage, and a positive danger to them. But now he had somehow slipped his chain, and he scrambled over the fraising and the ditch, and then in a maddened frenzy chased our ricocheting cannon-shot toward the American line. The Americans sportingly held off from shooting him; and after a minute of cheering and whistling from our gunners at the ramparts, the dog returned, two blacks being sent out with rope and chain to fetch him in. Apart from this incident, the loading and firing went on relentlessly, the drudgery of the gunners' work equal to the continuing hard labour of our blacks and sappers upon the walls.

I was in the Hornwork when Major Ross found me. He had been absent from the headquarters the previous night when I had marked the map for Cornwallis, but Ross had seen the map, and the new marks I had made upon it, and as we came out from the Hornwork and went to a quieter place above the southern valley, he showed a clear understanding of what those marks must mean.

'How long, Mr Douglas, before they open upon us?'

'It must happen within hours.'

His face showed a great strain, but I think my judgement came as no shock to him. After a moment more thought, he took a letter from his jacket and handed it to me. The seal upon the letter was broken. I glanced up at him, curious.

'It came up through the French blockade this morning with Major Cochrane,' said he. 'It is from General Clinton.'

I hesitated at first to open it; but Ross confirming with a nod that I should, I did so. It had been written in cipher, but the decipherment was clearly legible in the inter-line.

New York, 30th September, 1781.

My Lord,

 Your Lordship may be assured that I am doing everything in my power to relieve you by a direct move, and I have reason to hope, from the assurances given me this day by Admiral Graves, that we may pass the bar by the 12th of October, if the winds permit, and no unforeseen accident happens; this, however, is subject to disappointment, wherefore, if I hear from you, your wishes will of course direct me, and I shall persist in my idea of a direct move, even to the middle of November, should it be your Lordship's opinion that you can hold out so long; but if, when I hear from you, you tell me that you cannot, and I am without hopes of arriving in time to succour you by a direct move, I will immediately make an attempt upon Philadelphia by land, giving you notice, if possible, of my intention. If this should draw any part of Washington's force from you, it may possibly give you an opportunity of doing something to save your army; of which, however, you can best judge from being upon the spot.

 I have the honour to be &c.

 H. Clinton.

Stunned, I looked up. 'He has not yet sailed?'

'Major Cochrane has expressed a private doubt to me that this new schedule is any more to be relied upon than the first.'

'Surely we must now cross over.'

'It is Lord Cornwallis's decision that we should remain. And I must be content with that. But that is by the by. I have not shown you the letter to make an argument, but rather as a testament of my own neglect, or folly, or what you will.' He seemed in some embarrassment. He screwed up his courage now to speak. 'Cochrane brought the letter up at an early hour. I had reason to be in and out from the room. To be brief, Mr Douglas, I have a suspicion that Nelson's man has had some access to the letter.'

Ross's face went quite pale as he made this admission. And I must work now to contain my anger. I asked, with some asperity, had he questioned the man.

'My Lord Cornwallis forbids it. He thinks it would be as much as to accuse Nelson.'

So it would. And a very just accusation, in my estimation. But when I thought on it a moment, I could not perceive any great help the knowledge of Clinton's delay might be to Washington. Nor, since the increase in our patrols and piquets, and the increased watchfulness of our sentries, would it now be so simple a matter for Secretary Nelson to get the information out from our lines. But when I said as much, Ross answered me, 'Nelson might take the information with him. It is arranged that he shall go out from our lines tomorrow.'

'He should have been put out long since.'

'You do not think then that we should detain him.'

I raised an eyebrow. Ross knew as well as I that Lord Cornwallis would never stoop to holding Nelson by main force. 'It cannot do us good that Rochambeau and Washington shall know so clearly our situation, Major. But I believe it must make little difference to the actions they shall certainly take against us. The harm might have been worse.'

I returned the letter into his hand. He seemed affected much beyond the pallid reassurance of my words. 'It was only that I thought you should know of it,' said he.

I thanked him for the courtesy, and made no mention of the unspoken doubt he had revealed in Cornwallis's judgement upon the whole matter.

I was at the campfire behind the Fusiliers' redoubt, watching Calvert brewing tea, when the first French gun opened upon us.

'Mother of Christ!' cried a startled captain, jerking forward in his chair and spilling his drink into the fire. A rain of dirt showered down. The roar of the exploded shell rang in my ears as I ran with Calvert into the redoubt. But though there was now a barrage from the French side, no second explosion followed that first.

'It is the ships,' shouted Calvert upon the ramparts. 'They are shelling the ships.'

On the river directly alongside of us the *Guadeloupe* and the sloop *Formidable* lay at anchor; and between them now three great plumes of water went up, the last of these breaking like a wave across the *Guadeloupe*'s deck.

The Fusiliers with their muskets commenced to blaze away in the general direction of the French, while our artillery officers set their guns. I came out from the redoubt and ran back to the town.

'Mrs Kendrick!'

'We are above,' she answered. I looked up from the foot of the stairs and saw her upon the landing, and Lizzy by her skirts. 'We are almost done. Are we attacked?'

'We are under fire to the north,' said I, marvelling at the calm of her. 'And "almost done" will not do. You must be from here at once.'

She told me that Mrs Perkins, the Commissary's wife, had gone to fetch four men, that Mrs Morgan might be stretchered down to the beach. 'When she has brought the men, we may go.'

'Go directly they come, and do not wait for me,' said I. She nodded, took Lizzy's hand and withdrew.

Out at the Hornwork our guns continued firing in that same steady but uninspired fashion of the morning. General O'Hara was come there now, and hearing from me the situation at the Fusiliers' redoubt, he expressed a mild wonderment that all the enemy guns had not opened upon us together.

'It cannot be long now,' I answered unhappily, whilst tracing my spyglass over the broad line of the enemy's entrenchment.

'After you had crossed into their lines, Mr Douglas, I admit that I had supposed you should be disinclined to make any return to us. You must forgive me my doubt of you.'

'Your doubt of me was quite just, General. I am very disinclined to die without cause. I mistakenly believed that my word as to the enemy's siege guns should be heeded, where the word of Campbell was not.'

'We do not set our compass by barefoot Indians, Douglas. As to the siege guns, we need not fear what Rochambeau may have, but only what he may use.'

'What hope, sir, that you might now urge upon Lord Cornwallis a crossing to Gloucester?'

'It is a private advice that I owe his Lordship, and none of your affair.'

This pointed bluntness was very unlike O'Hara, and so too the fierce glare with which he momentarily fixed me. But by both these outward signs I at least understood the impotence he felt, and his fear of the possible consequence of Cornwallis's strategy. As O'Hara went down from the rampart, I raised my spyglass again. And then I saw that which sent my heart into my throat. For at every enemy battery and redoubt, the embrasures were being broken open, and within a minute I looked into the mouths of a hundred guns.

'General O'Hara!' called the captain beside me in alarm.

I did not wait for O'Hara's return. Leaping back off the rampart, I ran out from the Hornwork and toward the Kendrick house.

Mrs Kendrick was just from the front door with Lizzy. Before them, and carried upon a stretcher, was Mrs Morgan. Mrs Kendrick called out to tell me that the trunks and beds were already gone down to the cave, but her words were barely spoken when came the distant clap of Rochambeau's first southern gun. And in the next instant the first ball smashed through the Commissary's shed not thirty yards from where Mrs Kendrick stood. It was a dreadful tearing of timber, followed by a brief but awful silence.

Then from within the pile of smashed timbers a woman cried out. Mrs Kendrick understood at once.

'Oh Lord, it is Mrs Perkins.'

'Get Mrs Morgan and Lizzy below.'

'No,' said she, and swayed a little as she stared at the shattered timbers.

I took her by the shoulders and turned her from the shed. 'Take Mrs Morgan down. I must rely upon you.' I fetched Lizzy from where she stood petrified a few paces distant, brought her back and thrust her hand into Mrs Kendrick's. 'Go.'

'Mrs Perkins—'

'I will look to Mrs Perkins. Now go, before any more of their guns open.'

Pale with shock, she at last gathered herself enough to follow Mrs Morgan's stretcher, which was being carried swiftly away, toward the path to the beach.

Mrs Perkins wailed now, and I went over to the half-destroyed shed and went in, fearing what to find. I discovered her kneeling. The blood was all about her on the earthen floor, and soaking her dress. Her husband's body was beside her. He had been torn almost in two by the shot, which must have killed him instantly. Though Mrs Perkins appeared completely unhurt, she kept clutching her husband's face as though she might look there but no lower. Lying to the far side of her husband's body was another fellow, writhing silently in the dirt. His teeth were clenched, and perspiration ran over his face, but no sound came out from him. His hands made jerking movements in the air above his thigh, which was but a bleeding stump. He looked up at me in naked terror.

A scabbard and belt lay by Perkins's body. I freed the belt and wrapped it about what remained of this other fellow's thigh. And even in his terror he seemed to understand what I did, for his head came up and his hand grasped my shoulder like a claw. Then I cinched the belt tight, and he threw back his head and screamed to the heavens.

CHAPTER 30

*A*ll night the siege guns played upon the town, and not even Lord Cornwallis could mistake them now for carronades or light artillery. In the caves below, the sound of the shelling was muted, but the vibrations came through the ground, shaking free the loose dirt and stones. What sleep the women had I cannot say; but in our cave just by theirs we slept very little, for Stuart was several times called away by his men, and Campbell by his Pamunkey helpers, who had wrapped themselves in blankets upon the high beach.

In the morning Stuart brought word of a trial crossing to Gloucester, and a flanking manoeuvre to be practised against the enemy positions there. I greeted this news somewhat sceptically, my doubt of it further increasing when I saw the single barge and the few flatboats got ready for the purpose, and the forlorn body of tired soldiers and marines mustered for the embarkation. They returned from the crossing in the late morning, the barge lost along with some several of the men. The survivors made no muster when they came ashore but dispersed in disorder to various places of safety below the bluffs.

'Have they failed, then, Mr Douglas?' asked Mrs Kendrick, coming down to the water from the cave in time to see the last marines wading ashore from the flatboat. They held their muskets high above their heads to keep dry their flints and powder.

'Aye. Failed utterly.'

'I had no notion it should be like this.'

'They were ill-prepared.'

'Not these. All of it. The guns. Mrs Perkins. One moment a normal woman, the next a widow. What is it for?'

'The guns are opened, Mrs Kendrick. It is too late to question the reason.'

'How long must we endure it?'

'Till General Clinton arrives. Or till my Lord Cornwallis comes to his senses and crosses us over.'

'We might surrender.'

'Do not repeat that to any other,' said I, lowering my voice and giving her a glance of warning. There were marines about, and almost within earshot.

'But surely it is no more than common sense.'

'It is not a soldier's common sense, Mrs Kendrick, I do assure you. If you would be advised, you will keep the thought private.'

'You must think me weak-minded.'

'No. I think you a woman.'

'Obstinate, you mean to say.'

'I mean to say that you have too much good sense to properly fathom the idiocy that has brought us here. And, indeed, which now keeps us here.'

'And is that not a thought, Mr Douglas, that you yourself would be well advised to keep private?'

My glance stayed upon her perhaps a moment longer than it ought. She turned aside then, shielding her eyes against the sun as she looked out at the ships. And though as we returned up the beach she took my proffered arm, she released it just as soon as we were across the soft sand to the caves.

Outside each cave entrance, Campbell and Stuart now worked with the Pamunkey to make protective walls of stones and driftwood. Several enemy shells had by this time overshot the town and fallen into the river, and one had even exploded upon the southern beach. This last had sprayed splinters of metal, and cut down an infantryman. Our entrance walls now stood waist-high, a yard out from the entrances, and must afford us some measure of protection from any stray shell.

Within the women's cave were two beds, one to each side, and trunks that were now being used as tables, to the back. Upon the right-hand bed lay Mrs Morgan, and she just as disquietingly still when we now entered as she had been the first time I had looked in upon her. Though her eyes were open, they seemed to see nothing. She stared straight up at the wooden prop wedged across the earthen ceiling above her bed.

'Mrs Morgan?' said I.

She neither moved nor answered me. I exchanged a glance with Mrs Kendrick, who went closer and knelt by the bed.

'Mrs Morgan,' she said. 'It is Mr Douglas come to see you.'

There was no response. On the other bed, Lizzy had spread playing cards upon the quilt. She carefully put them into lines and paid us no heed. Mrs Kendrick tried once more, and was answered again with only the same staring silence.

'Perhaps she cannot hear.'

'She can hear, Mr Douglas. But for the present, she does not choose to talk.'

'Mrs Morgan?' I said. 'Sally?'

Nothing. Vacancy. Mrs Kendrick made to rise, but as I turned to go, Lizzy jumped unbidden from her bed and darted across and shook her mother. It was so quickly done that Mrs Kendrick could not prevent it. And neither could she prevent Mrs Morgan's hand, which instantly flashed out and struck the girl hard across the face.

Lizzy gave a startled cry, and there was such a look of bewildered pain in her eyes that it cut me. Mrs Kendrick instantly bent forward, putting her arms about Lizzy to shield her from her mother. But Mrs Morgan made no second movement. She was still again and both her hands lying motionless beside her. Lizzy then covered her face with her own hands and pressed into Mrs Kendrick's breast. The child was weeping. After a time Mrs Kendrick raised her eyes from Lizzy's head, and with a sympathetic glance directed me to leave. I came away, and went straight to Stuart's table in the neighbouring cave and composed a letter.

> *Cordet,*
>
> *I will go directly to the point of this missive: I hereby, and most solemnly, offer myself as a prisoner to General Rochambeau in exchange for the prisoners Cable and David Morgan.*
>
> *Only preserve their lives, and, when the siege is ended (either for or against us), I shall not remove myself but at once put myself into your custody upon condition that the two Morgan men be then released and thereafter left in peace.*
>
> *This is very likely the last communication we may have before we then shall meet. There is no more to write, but it remains only to put my signature to these few words, and to own myself under an eternal obligation to you should the exchange be successfully effected.*
>
> *Yours in trust,*
> *Alistair Douglas*

'Mr Douglas?' Turning in my chair, I found Mrs Kenrick at the cave entrance, and Lizzy at her skirts. 'There was a medicine left up in the house,' said she. 'Mrs Morgan has need of it.' But as she spoke she saw the letter. And perceiving something from the expression of my face, she said, 'What is that?'

'Secretary Nelson is to go out from our lines the next hour. It is a private letter that he shall carry for me.'

'I have explained to Lizzy that it was not her mother struck her, but the illness.' She put her hand tenderly upon the child's head.

'Mrs Kendrick is right, Lizzy. And if it is a medicine your mother needs, I shall go up now and fetch it down for her.'

I blotted and sealed the letter while Mrs Kendrick told me where I might find the medicine. She watched me closely as I sealed the letter, for she had an intuition of something, I know not how. But neither was I her first concern, for she had the child to look to, and Mrs Morgan; and when I came out, she returned to the other cave with Lizzy.

In the upper town the destruction wrought by the enemy guns was upon every side. For though most of their fire was concentrated upon our entrenchment, yet the gunners had additionally amused themselves with a peppering of the brick houses further back, so that many walls were holed now, and most of the roofs at least partially collapsed. No greater damage had been done anywhere than that to the Nelson house, whose windows appeared every one of them broken, and one corner of the house was now more fallen masonry than wall. Lord Cornwallis and his officers had abandoned the place, removing themselves to the cave prepared for the purpose in the southern valley of the town. And I had come up not a moment too soon, for Secretary Nelson was now following their example and leaving. He descended the steps with a cane to aid his gouty legs, and with his other hand upon the shoulder of his black. This black had a bundle slung over his other shoulder, which must contain Nelson's best possessions.

'You have come to bid me farewell, Mr Douglas,' said the impudent old fellow. 'That is a rare civility, and one I had never expected of you.'

'I would have you deliver this into the hand of Major Cordet,' said I, presenting the letter.

He thought but a moment before he took it. 'I shall not bid you farewell, Douglas. I am certain that I shall be but a short time away.'

'You may believe so.'

'Sir?'

'It shall need more than guns at a distance to breach our line.'

'No doubt. And no doubt our generals have considered that.'

One of our 18-pounders then fired nearby, and Nelson flinched. I saw that he did not like that I had seen it. Major Ross then appeared at the southern gate with a drummer and a corporal bearing the white flag under which Nelson must go out. Nelson thrust my letter into his pocket. Then clutching the arm of his black for support, he left me without another word.

The shelling continued through the day, and there being little that I could do on the line, I kept to Stuart's cave where Campbell and the Pamunkey now sheltered with me. They were strangely detached from the firing above, and their conversation was mostly of Dragging Canoe, and of the Cherokee war beyond the mountains. Though Campbell several times attempted to involve me, I offered neither opinion nor advice; for I was in those hours much quieted by the decision I had come to, and the offer I had made to Cordet. So quieted, in fact, that when their talk of the Cherokee war at length grew too tedious for me, I left them and went to look in at the other cave where I might find company more amenable.

Mrs Morgan was sleeping. Mrs Kendrick and Lizzy played at cards upon the left-hand bed.

'The medicine has greatly calmed her,' said Mrs Kendrick.

'Has she spoken?'

She turned her head. 'Shall you join us?'

'I would not disturb you.'

'It is no disturbance.'

'Please,' said Lizzy, though without looking up from the cards. I glanced to Mrs Kendrick, who then reached and put a pillow against the headboard that I might sit there.

It was night, and Mrs Kendrick now seated on a chair by Mrs Morgan, and I lying on a blanket on the cave-floor. Lizzy was seated next to me, reading by the lantern-light. And I must marvel at their calm, for the crump of the explosions in the town was almost continual now. When Stuart put his head in to call me away, I rose and went out; and on the river to the north of us a small boat was burning, the orange flames like a bright beacon on the water.

'Hot-shot,' said Stuart very grim; and in the same instant there blazed above our heads a red ball trailing fire like a comet. It arced and fell, plunging useless into the river. But another glowing ball followed moments after, and this one struck through the *Guadeloupe*'s rigging, sending sparks and brief flames flickering along the ropes. The sight filled me with dread.

Hot-shot, which is shot baked to a red heat, and the greatest danger to our ships there might be. The *Guadeloupe*'s guns opened broadside upon the hot-shot battery (which was French, and to the north of the Fusiliers' redoubt), and the flash and noise were tremendous. But the French had her range now, and the next glowing ball smashed down directly upon her deck. Campbell and the Pamunkey came rushing out onto the beach, and Mrs Kendrick put her head over the protecting wall of her cave.

I pointed at her. 'Stay there! Keep Lizzy inside!'

More red balls ripped overhead like comets, and not raining only upon the *Guadeloupe* now, but also upon the *Charon* half a league off from her.

The *Guadeloupe* cut her lines, the wild shouting of the seamen audible from the shore, and she was soon drifting toward the protection of the bluffs. She fired, and fired again, but the hot-shot continued.

'She will ground,' cried Stuart in my ear.

But she did not ground. Within minutes she was beneath the bluffs, and the hot-shot passing harmlessly over her. But hardly was the *Guadeloupe* safe than the *Charon* was hit. Hit amidships, and there must be powder touched, for an explosion tore out from her and she was instantly burning.

'God in Heaven, they are hundreds,' said Stuart in horror at the thought of all the men aboard.

'Get the canoes,' I told Campbell; and he ran with the Pamunkey up the beach to fetch the canoes from where we had put them by the caves.

A burning ship-of-the-line is a horror beyond imagining. Every part of her is fuel, and every corner suddenly a death-trap. In the kegs and in the magazines is enough powder to explode the hull to Hell, and send every man jack aboard straight to his Maker.

I waded into the water with Stuart as the Pamunkey brought the three canoes down to the shore. When the canoes were launched, I clambered into the first.

'Go no nearer than seventy yards,' I called across to Campbell. 'There shall be men jump. Let them come to you who can, but go no nearer the ship.'

The *Charon* had at last cut her cables, and was drifting; but being further out than the *Guadeloupe*, she drifted now in a direction her captain had not allowed for. Shouting broke out from the frigate and transports anchored below her. The confusion and terror went before the drifting ship, and the hot-shot fizzed overhead as we paddled out to the burning vessel.

The first sailor to jump was alight, and burning very brightly. He hit the water like a torch and went out; and though we scanned the dark water we saw no more of him.

Seamen rushed in disorder about the upper deck, beating the flames with sacking and canvas; but the fire was strong now, and never faltered. The *Charon* nudged up against the welter of vessels whose anchor-lines seemed now entangled, and the first of these, a frigate, began to burn. Then, and absolutely astonishingly, there came the flash and roar of guns from the *Charon*'s lower decks. It was surely ignorance, and not courage, kept the gunners at their stations; for they must have no proper notion of the terror above. By the light of the *Charon*'s flaming deck, I saw an empty flatboat lying at anchor well apart from the confusion.

'There!' I shouted to my two Pamunkey, pointing to the boat. In short order they had me alongside, and I climbed from the canoe into the boat. Campbell and Stuart, in their canoe, had followed me.

'Collect up any who jump,' I shouted to them. 'Bring them here. Tell the others.'

They turned their canoe and paddled away, Campbell shouting his orders to the Pamunkey.

Smoke rolled across the river, and the sound of the fire was now a steady roar, loud enough to muffle the sound of any guns. It smelt like a forest fire, and blazed just as high and strong.

The terrified seamen began jumping into the water.

We were about the business the next hour, the Pamunkey drawing their canoes up to the floundering seamen, and the seamen grabbing at the canoes in desperation and being towed back to me in the flatboat. There was no general abandonment of the ships, but at times the men dropped from the *Charon* like ants from an opened mound. And though she finally detached herself from the conflagration she had caused, by then there were seamen everywhere in extremities, and many yet who must choose to leap or die.

But with the *Charon* at last drifting alone toward Gloucester, and the worst danger gone with her, Campbell sent the Pamunkey to work closer in. The hot-shot had ceased to rain about us, and the canoes darted now with certain swiftness to gather the men before they drowned.

We had pulled upward of forty seamen from the water when that happened which I had most feared.

'Back!' I heard Campbell suddenly shout, and I looked up from the waterlogged fellow I was just then hauling aboard to safety. Campbell was standing in his canoe and shouting fiercely at a Pamunkey canoe gone in too close to the burning frigate. He shouted in Pamunkey, and then English, 'Come back!' But the Pamunkey went further in yet, to where a seaman struggled to keep himself afloat. Campbell then let fly at the disobedient Pamunkey a fearsome oath in Cherokee.

There was no warning of the explosion. It ripped out through the stern of the ship and instantly swallowed the canoe in a ball of fire and torn timber. The fireball shrunk back, and nothing remained of the two Pamunkey paddlers or their canoe, or the struggling seaman. The thunderous blast had deafened me; and in the painful silence that followed I saw Campbell's figure standing silhouetted against the flames.

At last he knelt in the canoe, and then he came back to me with Stuart. With the canoes alongside, I ordered the flatboat's anchor to be raised, and we returned in strange and silent convoy to the shore.

Sorely shaken by the loss of their fellows, the four surviving Pamunkey carried the canoes up the beach and then retreated into Stuart's cave. I stayed without, and Campbell by me. We looked with stricken wonder at the dreadful scene upon the river. The water shimmered golden with reflected flames, the burning vessels moving now like drifting bonfires, the sparks spouting into the red-fringed smoke above. Now and then came a small explosion from out of the burning fleet.

I said, 'There is no reason more of the Pamunkey should die.'

'They went too near.'

'This is not their fight. I should not have brought them here.'

Campbell watched the burning a minute more. 'It is their fight,' said he, and then he turned and went up to join the Pamunkey in the cave.

CHAPTER 31

*D*aybreak showed us the full extent of the destruction; the smouldering hulls clung together in the river with their cables ravelled, and over by Gloucester the *Charon* listed helpless beneath a plume of black smoke. The smell of burnt tar and timber hung in the air. There were yet some few sloops and flatboats remaining to us, and the *Guadeloupe*, and some small boats near Gloucester; but this depleted fleet was now hardly enough to ferry the army over. And so I was astonished and appalled when shortly after daybreak an undamaged sloop was brought to the protective ring of sunken vessels just out from the shore and promptly scuttled. I hurried across to the wharf to enquire the reason of this folly.

'It is Lord Cornwallis's order, sir,' answered the presiding lieutenant; though he seemed as little pleased with the waste as I.

In the southern valley, I soon found Major Ross. He was alone in that cave dug for Cornwallis's headquarters, and awaiting his Lordship's return from the Hornwork above.

'The burning of our ships has made an attack by de Grasse's fleet the more likely,' said he in answer to my terse enquiry concerning the scuttled sloop. 'But Captain Symonds let three fireships loose upon them in the night. That is something.'

'That is less than nothing against what we have had from their hot-shot, Major.'

'What would you have of me? Am I to rebuild the *Charon* with my own hands? What has happened we must accept of. You as well as any other.'

'I am prepared to accept of what has happened. What I am not prepared to accept of is that we should be sinking the few good vessels that remain to us.'

'It is a reinforcement to the river palisade.'

'It is a destruction of our only means of retreat to Gloucester. You may come down with me to witness it.'

'I need no excursion to the river to show it me, sir. It was I who sent the order down.'

'You sent the order down, and yet made no question of it?'

He rounded upon me. 'Whether I agree with you or no, Douglas, that signifies nothing. I am his Lordship's aide. What he has endured from the procrastination, the interference and the downright obstruction of lesser men – men whose opinions he is obliged to respect though they face not half the dangers nor responsibilities of his situation – what he has endured from them, I cannot begin to tell you. And now when we are reduced to these straits, and in no small measure by the heedlessness of these others, am I to join myself to them and become yet one more obstruction to him?'

'It is no obstruction for his aide to proffer an honest advice.'

'He has advisers enough, I think. And perhaps too many.'

'Your silence is the very worst advice he may get.'

'He shall have my loyalty, sir, which is everything.'

'Loyalty has a voice that speaks clear, Major Ross. And it does not always say "yes".'

The colour flamed into his cheeks. And then behind me I heard people approaching down the path, and soon they arrived at the cave-mouth, Lord Cornwallis to the fore. Entering the cave, he brushed by me and tossed his tricorn upon the table.

'There is nothing you may do for us now, Mr Douglas, but just to stay clear,' said he. 'If you look for an acknowledgement that you and your Indians were right about the siege guns, you have it.'

'My Lord, if I may be some help with the guns on the line or in the redoubts, I am at your service.'

'I am obliged,' said he; and that with no churlishness, but sincerely. 'Having just now seen what officers and gunners I have lost in the night, it may well come to that. But for the moment I am more concerned for the repair of our walls.' He asked me had I been up into the town, and whether I had seen the damage done there by the shelling. When I said that I had, he enquired my expectation of a second enemy parallel being dug against us. I told him that it seemed to me a certainty that this would happen. 'I know it shall happen, Douglas, but how soon? Saw you anything behind their lines that might give us any near apprehension?'

'My Lord, I should be surprised if they made no beginning either this night or the next. Our rate of fire is noticeably diminished. That must tell them the success they have had with their shells. And they may see very well what their hot-shot has done upon the river.'

'They may likewise see our protection there,' said he, meaning the boats that he had so injudiciously ordered to be sunk, and that he was sinking yet. I exchanged a glance with Ross, who stood silent with O'Hara by Cornwallis's table. 'I am told your Indians behaved very creditably in the night, Douglas,' Cornwallis continued as he drew up a chair. 'You must congratulate them for me before you put them out.'

'They are willing to stay.'

'They are mouths that we cannot afford.'

Lieutenant Sutherland then arriving with a report upon the damage to our walls, and the number of sappers killed in the night, I saw that I was not needed and so came away.

By now there were fifty to a hundred of our men killed on the line, and many times that number wounded. And the doctors having been forced from the Courthouse hospital above by the enemy shelling, they had now only some few small caves near Cornwallis's to work in. But as I came down past these caves the opposite side of the valley, I saw how cramped they were, and rendered almost useless by the crowding. The cries of agony were something shocking to hear, with many of the wounded lying out in the open, and the dark caves a tight and bloody Bedlam. So I was not surprised when later that morning many of the wounded were brought down to the wharf and ferried across to Gloucester. Stuart was put in charge of the crossing, and he took over two flatboats filled with wounded, and returned in the evening with the same two boats now filled with Dundas's men, who went at once up to the line.

'Every house in Gloucester is like a hospital,' Stuart told me when I met him upon the beach. 'Simcoe has a fever that may kill him, and these' – he waved his hand up after Dundas's disembarked men – 'these were only too happy to come across, and that in despite of the wounded they saw me bring over.'

I asked him if there might yet be a place in Gloucester for Mrs Morgan.

'No doubt they would make provision for her in one of the houses, Mr Douglas. But my advice would be that you do not send her. She is better to stay here.'

'But it cannot be so bad there.'

'It is.'

This was an unexpected thwarting of my intention. And as I stood pondering how best to proceed, Mrs Kendrick came to join us from the cave. She asked Stuart just as I had, after the situation in Gloucester. He repeated to her what he had told me, and then he excused himself and went up to the cave. She followed my gaze to the boats at the wharf.

'You would not be so ungentlemanly, Mr Douglas, as to arrange a shipment of women as though they were cattle. You would speak to them first, I trust.'

'You shall not be crossed over. But neither should you be from the cave without reason.'

'I saw the reason and came,' said she. 'And if you would come now, Mrs Morgan has a little recovered her senses. She asks that she might speak with you.'

'Alistair,' said Sally Morgan, which was the first time she had called me by my Christian name since I had arrived this season on the Chesapeake. 'I think that I have spoken to you as I had no right to speak.'

'You have not been well.'

'It is no excuse. Though truly, I do not feel myself well, even now.'

'Then you must rest.'

'Is that the guns?'

'Yes.'

'Mrs Kendrick says that we are by the river.'

'It is a cave in the bluffs. We are a short way north of the wharf. You are quite safe here.'

'The guns have been firing a long while. But they were louder, I think.' Her hand drifted from her pillow, and she touched her fingertips to her temple.

'They were louder when we were above,' I told her, for she was still in some confusion. 'In the cave here, the sound is muffled. You are safe here. Both you and Lizzy.' At this mention of her daughter she raised her head, but weakly, to look about her. I touched her shoulder to ease her down. She made no resistance. 'Mrs Kendrick has taken Lizzy into the next cave. She thought that you wished to speak to me privately.'

'Yes. Yes, I told her so.'

She was very much wasted by her illness. The cheekbones stood sharp in her face, and she lay still now, with her hollowed eyes fixed upon the roof of the cave. Her breathing was shallow, and in the quietness it seemed that she gathered her strength. I waited patiently. I knew not what she might say, except that it likely be some judgement against me.

'You would not lie to me, Alistair.'

'No.'

'Are they hanged?'

'They are held as prisoners.'

She did not close her eyes. After a few moments they glistened, and she turned her head to brush away the tears. Then regathering herself, she said, 'Mrs Kendrick says that you have tried to help them.'

'I am not done with trying.'

'I have been thinking on it all the while I have lain here. Listen,' said she, and her thin hand reached out to me. I gave her my hand, and though she clasped it, there was no strength in her. I let our joined hands rest by her side on the bed. 'I have thought on this,' said she. 'I have some right to speak. It is my son, and my husband.'

'No one shall silence you.'

'They must not hang David.' Her voice came almost without breath; but her intensity held me fixed.

'Neither one of them must be hanged.'

'David is innocent.'

'Both of them—'

'Please listen, Alistair. Please.' She squeezed my hand again; she had barely the strength of a child. 'Cable knew what he did. And I knew what Cable did. Though it was done at your asking, I do not accuse you. I did accuse you. But I was wrong. What Cable did, he did freely, as a man. And I helped him, as his wife.'

'I know.'

'But David is a boy. While I have lain here, when my mind has not wandered, I have thought on them. And I have thought what Cable must need of me now. He needs that I tell you this—'

'Sally.'

'Listen, Alistair. I have a right. I have thought . . . Cable needs me to tell you. If any one may be saved, it must be David.'

'I shall strive for them both.'

'If David be hanged, Cable shall want no more of life. Nor I.'

'That is your illness speaks,' said I. And what a dreadful sickness was in my heart now at what I had wrought; for she had tried all her strength upon the awful question, which one of them to save, and so tortured herself almost to madness. 'You must rest now.'

'But you have heard me. Promise me that you have heard me,' said she, and again with that disconcerting intensity, and the fixed gaze of her eyes.

'I have heard you.'

Unclasping her hand from mine, I bent and wiped her brow and then I sat with her till she slept.

Though I had told Campbell in the morning of Cornwallis's decision to send the Pamunkey from the town, yet they must wait till nightfall before they might depart upriver. They expressed a curiosity now to see our guns, and the entrenchments above, before they departed (for they had stayed all the while in the caves or on the beach). And so in the evening I took them briefly into the upper town. But what they saw of the destruction of the place, the houses mostly destroyed, killed soldiers hauled out from the trenches and lying upon the open ground, and enemy shells falling continually, all this was sufficiently unnerving to them, and we did not stay long but soon retreated to the river. Upon our return to the beach, I overheard them asking Campbell if the Appalachian settlers had any such guns. They seemed very relieved to hear that there were no such cannon beyond the mountains.

When the tide turned in the early hours of darkness, they went to fetch their canoes down to the water. Campbell told me then that he had instructed the Pamunkey to make camp two miles upriver, and wait for him there.

'There is no need for you to remain in York Town,' said I. 'Take them now, back over the mountains.'

'This is not finished here.'

'Your obligation is to the Cherokee.'

When Campbell looked at me now, there was challenge in it. He had not forgotten that promise I had made to Dragging Canoe, that I would do my utmost to bring redcoats to aid his people against the settlers.

'My first obligation is to the Morgans, and then to Cornwallis,' said I. 'I shall think on the Cherokee after.'

He seemed to accept of this; but he would not depart with the Pamunkey. He gave them some final instruction and they waded out, stepped into their canoes, and pushed off into the darkness upriver.

CHAPTER 32

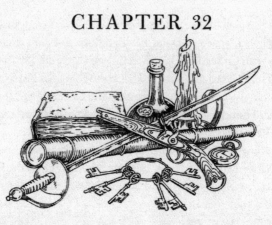

*A*t first light there came a sudden increase in the firing of our guns, and I went up with Campbell to discover the cause. It was not far to seek; for after mounting the southern rampart we saw the second siege line made by Washington's sappers and engineers in the night. It stretched like a deadly necklace a mere four hundred yards out from us. And though but a few feet high, it reached almost the entire length of our southern line, though kept back from the river by our two outer redoubts.

Campbell remarked its small height.

'It shall be high enough in a day or two,' I said. 'And then their siege guns, from that small distance, shall pulverize our walls.'

Though many of our guns were by this time dismounted or destroyed by the accuracy of the French artillery, those that remained to us were now turned upon this second siege line with a will. But the enemy was secure in the shallow ditch behind their low wall, and we might fire now till the Judgment and not dislodge them. Their sappers were working yet, hidden like moles, and only the new-shovelled earth to make a target for our guns.

'But this must be the finish then,' said Mrs Kendrick when I reported what we had seen above, and the meaning of the second siege line. 'Surely now Lord Cornwallis must surrender.'

'We shall see soon enough,' said I; though in truth I had but small hope of it.

And what small hope I had was quickly dissolved in the late morning when I went up to the headquarters cave and found Lord Cornwallis with General O'Hara, and they in conference with Colonel Abercrombie, Sutherland and one of the German officers. To my dismay, they were earnestly debating the security of the outer redoubts, and how best they might throw off an infantry attack should it come. There was no talk of any surrender.

I went above but once more that day, and twice the next, and nothing changed in what I saw but only the height of the enemy's front line and the numbers of our wounded and dead. There was a hospital now made aboard the *Guadeloupe*, and wounded men were taken out to the ship every hour, both day and night. And the cries and screaming they made as they were ferried were so dreadful that Mrs Kendrick must distract both herself and Lizzy with singing and playing at cards, and in the night she hung a blanket over the mouth of their cave.

On the lower slopes of the two valleys leading up into the town, the blacks dug shallow pits for our dead. Mortars now fired upon us from the enemy's front line, making an occasional random slaughter in our trenches behind the main wall. But so tired now were our men that no Christian burial was even thought of, but the severed and shattered limbs were bundled indifferently with the bodies and at change of guard carried down in canvas sheets to be emptied into the pits. This all happened at some distance from our caves, beyond the sight of Mrs Kendrick and Lizzy, which was the sole thing about it to be glad of.

We suffered desertions each night. Some men sent out by Cornwallis on short patrols to give warning of enemy infantry simply never returned; others, when no officer was near, clambered over our parapets and fraising, and then risked the enemy guns to make their way directly across. But these desertions, I knew from Major Ross, were many fewer than Cornwallis's expectation. My own frustration to hear of these crossings was very great; for I would myself be over to the enemy lines to exchange myself for the Morgans, but that I could not act till I had Cordet's formal agreement to my proposal. Without that, to cross into their lines again must be to surrender my life to no purpose. But a much worse trouble than these desertions was our want of working guns. Our emplacements had by now taken such a heavy and sustained fire that most of our cannon lay dismounted in the batteries, useless smashed metal, beyond any hope of repair. This want of guns compounded every difficulty; for the less we fired, the less we worried the enemy; the less we worried them, the more accurate and heavy their own relentless fire upon us.

What I might do in these straits, other than offer myself as a target for the enemy, was very little. And so I frequently visited Calvert out in the Fusiliers' redoubt, and otherwise spent time in both caves, the morning with Campbell, and the afternoon and evening with Mrs Kendrick, Lizzy and Mrs Morgan. Stuart went to and fro between the upper town and the wharf, arranging the constant traffic of wounded. And it was from Stuart that I received the unhappy news of Major Cochrane's decapitation by an enemy ball; and nor was Cochrane the only man to be so lost to us.

On the third evening after the night of hot-shot, and I reduced to a frustrating idleness, and playing at cards with Mrs Kendrick and Lizzy, Stuart looked in upon us.

'Sir, I am sent by Major Ross. You are wanted above.'

The large cedar close by Nelson's ruined house had been hit by the shelling, and its upper trunk was now toppled over, gone down like a broken topmast amidst its torn branches. Major Ross stood to one side of it, awaiting my arrival, his face strained and ashen.

'I shall not dissemble, Mr Douglas. We have had a rebellion by the sappers. They are refusing the order to repair our walls.' He turned on his heel and took me directly across to the line.

Our earthen walls, I could quite clearly see, were badly mauled, and not nearly so sturdy as they had been even that same morning. The shelling had broken the parapets in many places, and a light smoke drifted over them from outside, which must be the pines of our abatis, burning. Their balls and shells were coming in ten to our every one. In the trenches some several hundreds of our infantry huddled useless with their muskets, and scarcely a man visible upon the ramparts.

'This cannot go on,' said I.

'Without the walls be repaired, we must fear the worst when their front-line guns open. It is my Lord Cornwallis's direct order that the sappers have refused.'

I did not wonder at their refusal; for to go onto the face of the wall at such a moment must be to make a lottery of one's own life.

'Mr Douglas,' said Ross, pausing now to speak to me confidentially. His voice was by no means steady. 'I would myself lead the sappers out onto the wall to make the repair. Only that I hesitate to give the order for a fear that they shall not follow me. But I think that they have some regard for you.' At this, my heart almost stopped in my breast. 'If you would join with me,' said he, 'I believe they might do it.'

'It is madness.'

'Yes. Quite possibly. But we must hold fast while there is any hope of General Clinton.' He then assured me that there were fascines and gabion baskets already prepared, and that the labour of an hour at dusk would secure the walls a day or more against the siege guns. And all the while that he talked my eye ran along the broken parapet, and along the lines of dejected redcoats in the trenches. The wall once down, these miserable fellows must inevitably become a bloody fodder for the guns.

'A day or more shall not signify, Major Ross, if his Lordship only continue to sit in his cave below and ponder.'

'He knows it, Mr Douglas. But shall you help me?'

'An hour only, sir?'

'A half-hour only, Mr Baker,' said I. 'And Major Ross and myself alongside of you.'

Baker being the leader of the sappers, I had put it to him directly, and with no equivocation, nor any futile deprecation of the danger. For the sappers were weary to their very bones, and in no obedient temper after the sharp and threatening words they had so recently had from the officers. Baker now withdrew along the trench that Ross and I had stepped into, and we watched as he put my proposal to his fellows. But while they discussed it, there came a piece of sheer good fortune to us, which was that a pair of infantrymen climbed out from the next trench and came across to volunteer themselves (the sappers' disobedience having become, I now gathered, a matter of general disgust among the soldiers). These two redcoats told me that they had rather die like men than like rats in a hole, and making light of the intended work they called along the trench to demand tools of the sappers. Encouraged by this unexpected turn, Major Ross went along the other infantry trenches calling for more volunteers; and by this means got a dozen or more redcoats. With this example before the sappers, and they feeling, I believe, somewhat slighted in their pride, there were a score of them now came out after Baker to join us.

We made two parties, Major Ross's to repair the Hornwork and the line south, and my party to concentrate upon the northern section of the line.

And for once the infantrymen and sappers made no distrustful division between themselves, but worked together in raising the gabions and fascines onto the ramparts. This was not only work but distraction, for many times the wall was hit very near to them. And when darkness began to fall, and the time to go out onto the wall approached, there was many an anxious look thrown over the parapet.

'We must use the last light now,' I called at last; and, to say true, there was more fear in me than I might then admit to, and certainly more than I might show them. 'Put the gabions and fascines over the parapet. Courage, and with me now, lads.' I set my hands upon the parapet, and the sappers and redcoats watched me. My every fibre rebelled against the foolhardy action. A most powerful rebellion it was, for it was nothing less than the deepest instinct of self-preservation. But to hesitate now was to lose all, and set them in flight

306

back to the trenches. So I willed my arms and legs to movement, climbed over the parapet, and stood upon the face of the wall.

'With me now!'

Baker was next over, bellowing at his sappers, and these could not disgrace themselves now but clambered over. The fascines and gabions were passed out by the redcoats, and the sappers set to work fixing the fascines against the wall with wooden spikes, and pouring rocks and earth out from the gabion baskets into the holes nearest the embrasures.

We were like insects upon the wall-face, and the enemy gunners like boys throwing stones at us for their malicious amusement. The failing light was our only protection, and a much lesser one than I had hoped for. The enemy shells mostly went over us into the town, but some slammed into the wall, shaking us to our knees. Worst of all were the shells that smashed hard into the wall, burying themselves deep upon impact, and then exploding with a force that rocked the earth. I was half-deafened from the very first.

'Keep them at it, Baker!'

He replied with an oath and carried on with his spiking.

I sent his men both north and south that they be not clustered for a slaughter. Then I moved along the wall giving encouragement and help, and also because the blood coursed so fiercely in me (I own, from mortal fear) that I could not easily keep still. With no hope to repair all the extensive damage to our wall, I had the men concentrate near the embrasures of our few remaining guns. And I will say of the sappers that not a man made a single murmur or complaint against any order I gave them now, but their only speaking was to call up to the redcoats for more baskets of earth and stone.

I lost one infantryman killed, who took a shell almost directly, and a sapper who was struck by a ricochet and had to be dragged up the wall, unconscious, by his fellows.

It was more than half an hour we had been out, and the darkness grown more an impediment to us than friendly cover. At last I went along the wall and ordered the sappers in, and they needed no second order but made haste to obey.

Once I had counted them safely over the parapet, I clambered up there myself and scrambled over. The feel of the wall at my back, when I dropped to the rampart, was more welcome to me than all the gold of Croesus. I sat there a full minute, collecting myself, before I went to find Major Ross.

'Two killed, three wounded,' Ross told me when I joined him in the Hornwork. He looked wild-eyed and strangely exhilarated. Though he had come in from the wall, the fear was still upon him. I told him of my own dead and wounded, and then we got down into the communication trench that ran back toward the headquarters valley. Word of our going out onto the wall had spread among the redcoats, and there were both officers and men congratulated us as we went along the trench. But we were from the trench and walking down toward the lantern-lit headquarters when Ross turned aside suddenly from the path. He bent and clutched his knees and spewed into the bushes.

I let him be a moment. When he was done, I enquired if I should go on without him.

He shook his head, wiping his sleeve over his mouth as he stood upright. 'I am well enough, Douglas. But God strike me dead if I am ever such a fool again.' He was not in the least exhilarated now, but very sober; and we carried on down the path to make our report at the headquarters.

Lord Cornwallis was there, and in conference with General O'Hara, Captain Symonds and a few more of his senior officers. After interrupting them to make our report, Major Ross and I stood to one side and listened to the several proposals then put forward for the further maintenance of our defences. But the first disobedience of the sappers appeared to have given some wound to Cornwallis's easy self-belief, so that nothing now was quickly decided. Nor, it seemed to me, was there any true and frank acceptance of the straits we were in. Each officer gave his advice tentatively, and as though awaiting some clearer direction from Cornwallis.

But Cornwallis, for all that he did not rail at his officers, or blame them, yet he seemed to have lost any capacity to decidedly lead them.

All his folly in trusting to General Clinton, all his error in refusing Tarleton's advice, all his confident holding still while Washington and Rochambeau put the noose about him, these seemed now fully present to him. Indeed, he sat like an aged man, hunched at his table, and his head sometimes in his hands. Though his was the only uniform there neither marked nor torn, his collar lay open, and there was a creasing and wear on his jacket matched his face. At length he rocked back in his chair, pinched distractedly at the flesh on his throat, and lamented the too-rapid depletion of our shells.

'It wants only a better supply of them, which I think we may get from Gloucester, Major Ross?' This Cornwallis said almost without thinking, as though Ross must make his familiar echo, and so be a bolster to him in this lonely hour.

'I think not, my Lord,' Ross answered evenly.

Cornwallis looked over. He seemed more puzzled than affronted by Ross's reply. It was as though he had put a hand blindly to a familiar prop and found it inexplicably removed from his reach. 'Do you really think, then, that we have enough shells this side?'

'My Lord, we have neither the shells nor the guns – nor even the walls – to hold Washington off much more than a few days longer. There is only one action may save us now, and that is to cross over the river and attempt a breakout through Gloucester.'

There was not a man spoke. Cornwallis looked at Ross with the bemusement of one who has taken a rebuke from his own footman.

'It is shells I want, Major Ross.'

'Yes, my Lord. And if that is your order, I shall apply to Colonel Tarleton to find what more he may spare us.'

'Thank you.'

'It does not alter my advice, my Lord.'

O'Hara, Symonds and the others peered at Ross, and, I think, in some admiration; but none dared openly to support him. And now Cornwallis, though somewhat bemused, stiffened in his chair and looked hard at Ross as though to quell him back to his place; but Ross held his Lordship's gaze, which needed a courage at least the equal of that he had shown upon the wall. For a few moments, an explosion threatened which might dislodge Ross clean out from his commission. But at last Cornwallis said nothing to his aide, but dropped his eyes to the map and called the engineer Sutherland forward to explain how the Hornwork might be refortified on the morrow.

CHAPTER 33

One day more the ceaseless guns; one day more the wanton waste of life. Then in the early evening Stuart was called to the outer redoubts to replace an officer lost to the shelling. When he came to the women's cave to tell me, I rose to go with him.

'But surely you are not wanted there,' said Mrs Kendrick; and Lizzy put a hand up from the outspread cards of our unfinished game to tug at my sleeve.

'It is but to see their line,' said I, touching the crown of Lizzy's head as I went. 'I shall be returned within the hour.'

Outside, I discovered Campbell already come from the neighbouring cave to join Stuart, and the three of us then went by way of the headquarters valley into the southern part of the town. (Though what might warrant calling it a town by this time was very little, for it was but smouldering rubble, cratered earth, and trenches.) Once through the southern gate we ran the first fifty yards in which was the greatest danger from the enemy shells. Beyond our abatis was a path trod into the dry grass and leading to the outer redoubts. We followed this path till we came to the Rock Redoubt on the southern bluffs.

But Stuart reporting there, the major turned him away, saying that it was the second redoubt, to the west of him, that was in need of officers, and that we should be much welcomed there by Major Macpherson.

And so, indeed, we were; for in spite of the internal buffering walls made of sandbags, and casks filled with sand, there had been many officers killed in this westerly redoubt.

'You must take charge of the second gun, Captain Stuart,' Major Macpherson directed, and then he turned to Campbell and me. 'You and your fellow may do me some good service if you are willing, Mr Douglas. I have had the German marksmen at their posts all the day. If you would spare me a few hours, I might relieve them in pairs, with you replacing them while they eat.'

Upon my agreement, he took us to the German station on the ramparts. Two of them came down, and we went up. The half-dozen remaining Hessians gave us neither advice nor welcome; and after some minutes it seemed to me that these fellows put their heads above the parapet rather less frequently than any self-respecting marksmen ought. But after I had myself looked over several times, and fired once or twice, the reason of their desultory work was the clearer to me. Two hundred yards to the front of us was the very endpoint of the enemy's second parallel. Our muskets might gall the position, but it must need an accurate fire from our 16-pounders to do them any real harm.

With nightfall came a sudden coldness in the air, and the change brought up a soft fog from the river. The men who had put off their jackets in the day's heat now donned them again, and some luckier fellows drew blankets about their shoulders. I had my own shoulder against the parapet, and was silently cursing the tardy Hessians that they took so long over their meal, when Campbell jabbed a finger into my side.

He then pointed over the parapet.

'What is it?' said I.

But in the next instant Major Macpherson cried out, 'Cease firing. Cease your fire!' Stuart and the officers quickly stopped the guns.

With our own guns quiet, I now understood what Campbell had been the first to perceive: the enemy guns had already fallen silent.

Fifteen seconds went by. And then thirty. And then a full minute. One-by-one, our remaining guns in the town's entrenchment fell silent. In the redoubt, not a man spoke. I put my head above the parapet. There was nothing visible but the fog.

Macpherson climbed up beside me and looked out. The enemy's second parallel, which had been so clear the hour before sunset, was now invisible. 'Heard you of any stratagem, Mr Douglas, that my Lordship means to practise against them tonight?'

'No, Major.'

'Nor I,' said he, and he looked a moment longer into the fog. Then he made up his mind and turned to face his men in the redoubt. 'Fix bayonets, the Guards! Fix bayonets, and to the ramparts!' Leaping down, he continued shouting his orders. The men were now in alarmed and rapid movement about him.

Stuart came up to join me and Campbell on the rampart. He brought with him three cutlasses from by the guns. Giving one to each of us, he looked over the parapet into the fog. 'Shall they try us now?'

'Very likely.'

I felt the balance of the cutlass in my hand, and then I rested it against the wall by my musket. While I loaded my pistol, there came the sound of distant firing.

'Fusiliers' redoubt,' said Stuart.

'Gloucester,' said Campbell.

But after a minute, and the distant fire waxing and waning, it sounded to me that they were both of them right. But whether these were determined attacks or only feints to distract us, we could not tell. My pistol finally loaded, I wedged it between two sandbags on the parapet near my shoulder. Then I raised my musket; rested it on the bags, and looked over the barrel into the fog.

We were fewer than a hundred and fifty in the redoubt. Somewhere in the fog and darkness lurked an army of several thousands. A ball of fear came into my throat and I swallowed it down, and breathed steadily in and out.

There was a solid line of redcoats and Hessians by us on the ramparts now, all watching the German sentries out to the front of the ditch. The waiting seemed endless, and only Macpherson's occasional order to hold his men from firing. Then there came from somewhere behind Washington's line a series of six distinct shots from their cannon.

'Signal?' said Stuart.

'Aye. A signal.'

A minute more, and then a sudden barrage of musketry and shouting sounded from the Rock Redoubt by the river, two hundred yards behind us. We looked back there and saw the musket-flashes through the fog. They were under attack.

'Eyes open, lads!' called Macpherson. He climbed onto the ramparts and strode boldly about, so that no man should think of flight.

From the other redoubt, there now came shouts and cries, and the clash of bayonets. It was no feint, but an attack in very earnest. To my left, Campbell kept his eyes upon the darkness. To my right, Stuart stayed watchful, and when I touched his shoulder he nodded to assure me of his readiness.

Then down to the front, near the ditch, one of our German sentries cried into the darkness, '*Wer da? Wer da?*' He waited, but receiving no answer, he cried out a third time, '*Wer da?*' – Who goes there? – and then he fired into the fog.

Though no answering shot came back, all our sentries then scurried to the rear of the redoubt. And moments later we heard from the fog a sound that I can only liken to the stir of leaves before a wind. Then it was as though the wind gently rose and carried the leaves nearer. Our bulldogs, on their chains behind the redoubt, started up a ferocious barking. At last, from out of the fog, the enemy came slowly walking. One man, and then two; now a dozen, and suddenly a score. To the front, and left and right of us. French pioneers they were, wielding axes. They fell upon the abatis before the ditch to hack a way clear for their infantry.

Macpherson shouted, 'Fire!' and a volley of musketshot smashed into them, the powderflash throwing a bright flare into the fog. And what the flare of light showed was a scene that might make the bravest man quake. For the French infantry were in hundreds behind the pioneers, and coming forward, and not a man of them firing, nor even pausing to help their fellows hit by our first volley.

I sighted a French officer and put a ball into him. Then crouching to reload, I called to Stuart, 'If they break over the rampart, stay by us.'

'The fraising shall stop them,' said he; to which I said again, 'Stay by us.'

There was a crackling fire from all quarters of our ramparts now, and yet still the French muskets stayed silent. The only sounds to the front were the axes and the screams of the wounded. And so firm appeared the discipline of their infantry that I had no doubt now their resolve to carry our redoubt or die.

They finally broke through the abatis after their pioneers and came pouring forward into our ditch, shouting like madmen. I picked out another officer and shot him.

More muskets were brought up to the ramparts by the Hessians, and what with our bayonets, cutlasses and axes, it was a fearsome armoury the French must now confront if they broke through our fraising. The pioneers were upon the wall now, and working frantically with their axes and with bare hands to tear up our fraising. And so great was the surprise in the redoubt at the enemy's dauntless advance, that few took proper aim, but instead hastily pointed their muskets over the parapet and fired blind toward the French.

The first pioneer broke through the fraising. He rushed onto the upper wall, brandishing his axe and crying wildly, '*Vive le Roi!*' and Campbell put a ball through his heart.

But the first breach once made, their infantry scrambled from the ditch, clawing more openings in the fraising. Up they came, onto our wall like a rushing torrent. Campbell was upon one knee reloading when a Frenchman appeared on the parapet over him. I snatched my pistol and fired upward. The fellow's jaw splashed from his face and down he went into the ditch. I put the discharged pistol into my left hand for a club, and, with my right, grabbed the cutlass.

They broke on every side now, screaming blue murder, an unstoppable tide rushing over the parapet. Some fired, but most came slashing and stabbing with their bayonets. Our marksmen had held their fire till now, waiting in the centre of the redoubt. Now they sent a volley into the Frenchmen; but the enemy wave was checked for only a moment, and then it rose up and again broke over us.

The screaming was the screaming of berserkers, and I one of them. It is not steadiness at such a time, but only surrender to mad fury will preserve a man's life. I hacked the legs from under one fellow and split the head of another. I saw Stuart tear an officer through the bowels with a bayonet.

The powder-smoke was thick, with only the flashing crack of pistol-shots to fitfully illuminate the hellish scene of slaughter.

Slashing with the cutlass, I kept clear the parapet before me. But from the right side of the redoubt there came suddenly cries of '*Vive le Roi!*' and Frenchmen were now down on our rampart there, and more yet flooding over.

I shouted to Campbell, 'Where is Stuart?' for he had suddenly gone from my side.

'Centre!' he cried, jerking his head toward the midst of the redoubt.

A Frenchman then hauling himself onto the parapet just by us, Campbell swung down his cutlass. The fellow toppled backward, gaping in dumb horror at his half-severed arm.

'They are over us! We shall not hold them!' I shouted. 'Fetch Stuart, and to the town!'

Campbell leaped from the rampart. But before I could follow him, there was another Frenchman came over. He fired into the face of the redcoat who had taken Stuart's place next to me, and then he thrust down at me with his bayonet. I swerved, and parried the bayonet with my cutlass. Unbalanced, he fell head-first upon me, the weight of him tumbling us both from the rampart onto the ground. Luck landed me atop of him, and he with his face in the dirt. I smashed my pistol into the back of his head, and the skull burst, and I left him.

The berserk hand-to-hand fighting had spread across the redoubt, and the musketfire and pistol-shots had died almost to nothing. It was now a moiling cockpit of purest savagery.

Even as I saw Stuart he took a blow from a swung musket that dropped him to his knees. Campbell stepped up to protect him. But what then happened I never saw, for a fellow charged me with his bayonet and I leapt smartly aside. I hacked down with my cutlass, and his bayonet caught in a sandbag. As he struggled to free it, I made a sweep with the cutlass and opened his belly. His musket dropped, he clutched at his innards and fell to his knees.

The French were too many. There must be little time now to get clear. I leaped over a wall of sandbags and found Stuart and Campbell to the far side. Now it was Stuart protected Campbell, who was on all fours upon the ground behind Stuart's legs.

'Bayoneted!' shouted Stuart to me in desperation.

I knelt and raised Campbell, and my hand and arm were instantly soaked with his blood. His legs barely supported him, and I must hold half his weight.

'Out from here! Now!' I shouted to Stuart, and he cut a path for me and Campbell toward the rear of the redoubt. But though Stuart slashed left and right, our greater aid was the general confusion; for so many of the enemy were now within the redoubt, and such a similarity was there in the darkness between their uniforms and those of our Hessians, that I saw enraged Frenchmen now engaged with their own fellows to the death.

Breaking from the rear of the redoubt with fleeing redcoat comrades both before and behind us, we retreated pell-mell from the slaughter.

Stuart put his shoulder beneath Campbell's other arm, and on we went, with Campbell's legs weakening beneath him, and he growing ever more heavy between us. After a hundred yards, Campbell's legs gave way completely, and he was a dead-weight now, and barely conscious. 'On, and quickly,' said I; and we each of us lifted one of his legs, and held his arms about our shoulders, and so carried him the rest of the way to the town.

*

'You will get no miracles here, Douglas. The man is dying.' I looked past Gould to the table where Campbell lay. Where Campbell lay dying? It seemed a thing impossible.

'There must be something.'

'There is nothing. You may see the wound as well as I. He was stuck clean through. His guts are carved like mutton. He cannot properly breathe. The staunching we have made of his blood shall prove but a temporary relief to him. I have administered an opiate that should keep him peaceful.'

'But there must be more—'

'There is no more can be done, I promise you, Mr Douglas. He shall not see this hour tomorrow. You may take him ashore or leave him on deck, as you will. But do not tarry. I have need of my table.'

Behind Gould, the loblollies were already moving Campbell onto a stretcher.

There had been a considerable difficulty in bringing Campbell aboard, and it was with an equal difficulty that we now got him down from the *Guadeloupe* and into a boat to be rowed ashore. Once the seamen had brought him into the cave they left us, and then Mrs Kendrick came in with a lantern. I took the lantern and put it into a niche in the wall. Campbell's eyes were closed, and in the pale light his skin looked grey, as though he might be already dead, only that his chest rose and fell very shallow.

'Stuart has not come down, then?' said I.

Mrs Kendrick turned her head, but her gaze stayed upon Campbell.

'It is a bayonet wound,' I told her. 'The doctors cannot help him.'

'I am sorry.'

I explained that the southern redoubts were taken, and that I had sent Stuart to Major Ross to make a full report of it.

'Captain Stuart is unhurt?'

'Yes.'

'And you?'

'I am unhurt. I mean you no discourtesy, Mrs Kendrick, but I would not talk now.'

'Of course,' said she. Her gaze dropped to Campbell and lingered a moment, and then she went out from the cave.

When she was gone I drew up a chair and sat quietly.

Stuart came down an hour later. He told me what was happening above, which was that there had been neither counter-attack from Cornwallis against the captured redoubts, nor any general attack launched by the enemy against our own main line. Our guns were now turned upon the lost redoubts to hinder the enemy's joining of them with their front siege line. Stuart held but little hope for any success. He remarked that the enemy's siege line must soon be closed against us on the south, all the way to the river. 'There is a plan afoot for a sortie against their nearest guns,' said he.

'It shall take more than a sortie and a spiking of guns to save us now.'

'I have volunteered.'

'You need rest.'

'The sortie shall not happen tonight.' He had his eyes upon Campbell all this while, and now he lifted his chin. 'He is lying there because he saved me.'

'It was the chance of war.'

'Will he live?'

'No.'

Upon the bed, Campbell stirred; and whether he had heard us, or simply shifted now to ease the pain, there was no telling. We talked no more then, but allowed him what peace he might have. We slept by turns through the night, that Campbell should be looked to whensoever he wakened.

Campbell did not pass in the night. But so very still did he lie in the morning, and all through the day, that I must several times put a hand to his face to make certain of him.

In the afternoon Major Ross came down and gave me a report of the enemy siege guns being brought up into our two lost redoubts, and the near-completion of the enemy's front line. His face was grave, and he then brought a letter from his jacket. 'Once I have ciphered this, it shall go out by a log-canoe or a whaleboat tonight for General

Clinton,' said he, putting the letter into my hand, 'Captain Symonds has a fellow believes he can slip by the French ships.'

The letter was not sealed.

Sir,

Last evening the enemy carried my two advance redoubts on the left by storm, and during the night have included them in the second parallel, which they are at present busy perfecting. My situation here becomes very critical; we dare not show a gun to their old batteries, and I expect their new ones will open tomorrow morning. Experience has shown that our fresh earthen works do not resist their powerful artillery, so that we shall soon be exposed to an assault in ruined works, in a bad position, and with weakened numbers. The safety of the place is therefore so precarious, that I cannot recommend that the fleet and army should run great risk in endeavouring to save us.

I have, &c.,
Cornwallis

When I looked up, Ross said, 'There shall be another council tonight. They may listen now. And I would be grateful, sir, if you would support me there.'

CHAPTER 34

*I*n truth, there was but the smallest listening done by Cornwallis or any other when I went up to the council that night. Fatigue and exhaustion were writ on every face, and on Cornwallis's most of all; the last of his confidence was vanished, lost with our southern redoubts. Now he must look full square upon our dire position, and bear the weight of it if he could. The word 'surrender' was not spoken, yet it hung behind almost every other word that was said; and this unspoken word was the reason that my support was not needed: as the only remaining alternative to surrender, Major Ross's appeal for an attempted breakout through Gloucester was accepted with neither protracted debate nor any serious dissent.

But if there was no dissent, there was likewise no great enthusiasm from Captain Symonds, the depletion of whose fleet by the enemy hot-shot and our own scuttling had made any ferrying of the army now a perilous undertaking. 'It might be tried after dark tomorrow, and with a squadron of small boats to begin,' he conceded. 'But we are under their guns now, and I cannot answer for the consequence.'

I cannot answer for the consequence. A remark, indeed, that might have stood as a fitting motto for the most senior British officers throughout the siege. For no man, neither Cornwallis nor Clinton, nor Germaine back in London, had taken on his shoulders the full responsibility of it, nor responsibility for the actions leading up to it; and it seemed equally certain to me that no single one of them would now directly answer for the consequence.

There was one other action decided, which was that the proposed sortie under Colonel Abercrombie must now happen before daybreak. Though the declared intent of this sortie was to wreak havoc upon the enemy's front line, it was in fact a point of military honour that such an attack be made, and was more like to the mechanical playing out of an empty hand than an action of any real purpose.

Returned below, I called briefly on Mrs Kendrick and told her of the planned crossing. Lizzy was sleeping, and with her head very peaceful in Mrs Kendrick's lap.

'And what would you have of us then, Mr Douglas, that we should cross over?' she said; and there was no contention in it. She had been now a number of times from the cave by necessity, and she knew from the great numbers of wounded going out to the ships how deplorable a state the men above must be in. And nearer at hand, the carcasses of Tarleton's slaughtered horses washed ashore now on every tide, and the stench was constant. Whatever the sickness in Gloucester, it must soon be no better here. I think, therefore, that my answer surprised her.

'There is no point in your crossing now, Mrs Kendrick. Even if the breakout succeeds, Washington must then pursue our army through Virginia. Mrs Morgan has not the strength for that. You are better to stay here and wait.'

'And you?'

'I shall stay also.'

'But how then shall you avoid to be taken?'

'That is not your concern,' said I, for I would not tell her of my offer to Cordet. I asked after Campbell. She said that she had looked in upon him and Stuart an hour past.

'He is no different. But Captain Stuart is sunk very low.'

322

'Did he speak with you?'

'I believe he blames himself for Campbell's wounding.'

I looked to Sally Morgan where she lay upon the bed. Her wasted hands rested to either side of her upon the linen sheet. The pallor of her skin was scarcely better than Campbell's.

'If you stay this side of the river, Mr Douglas, then surely you shall be taken.'

'We are all taken in the end, Mrs Kendrick. Let it be in a just cause, and I shall not fear it.'

Campbell died before morning. He went so quietly that I only understood that he was gone when I reached my hand over from my book to make sure of him. But the moment that I touched his face, I knew. I put down the book and knelt by him. His eyes had come half open in death, and I closed them. Then I lifted his hands and set them together upon his chest. I rested my own hand upon his, and I said a quiet prayer for him. To the far side of the cave, Stuart woke and sat up; but he made no interruption of me. The prayer once finished, I reached to the foot of Campbell's camp-bed and drew up the sheet to cover him.

'He went peaceful, then,' said Stuart.

'Aye.'

'We should bury him properly.'

'In the morning, after sunrise, I shall find a place.'

Stuart could not take his eyes from the sheet a long while. We sat quietly an hour, and it was not yet light when Stuart buckled on his sword and went up to join Abercrombie's sortie.

I was left to my own thoughts then, which were all of Campbell and his people, and the great mourning there would be among the Overhill Cherokee when they learned of his passing. Though he had travelled often, and far, he had been always with them in his spirit, and they with him, both his clan and his family; and now he was with them eternally, and with his father. Men have lived and died much worse.

The sun rose, and the next hour Stuart returned. There had been a spiking of some enemy guns, and hand-to-hand fighting, but the only sign Stuart showed of it was the flush upon his cheeks. Honour satisfied, Abercrombie had withdrawn, Stuart told me, with only a few of his men lost. We wrapped Campbell's body tight in the sheet, and then carried him along the beach northward, away from the common burial pits. There was a slope leading up toward the Fusiliers' redoubt, and partway up that rise we found a level place of dry summer grass. Here we made a shallow grave and put Campbell's body in. We said the Lord's Prayer over him before I picked up my shovel to begin covering him. But I had hardly begun when Stuart took something from the pocket of his jacket and tossed it into the grave. I almost asked him what it was; but then I saw the black ribbon tied in a bow, and recognized with a start that the bow was tied about golden hair, a bloodied flap of skin binding it like a bouquet. My head came up sharply.

'Campbell may rest easy now,' said Stuart. He kept his eyes lowered to the bloodied offering he had thrown there. For that it surely was, an enemy scalp, the traditional Cherokee offering, which must help Campbell's spirit on its journey. Stuart must have taken it during the sortie with Abercrombie.

What to say? I said nothing, but only bent again and shovelled the dry earth into the grave. Stuart soon did the same at the other side, and so we buried Campbell. But while we buried him there was a sudden change in the sound of the enemy guns. They were louder; and the close-following boom of the shells now shook the ground where we stood. We looked at each other across the grave, knowing at once the reason of the change; and then we continued our work in silence, but with more hurry.

The enemy's front line was completed. Their siege guns had now opened upon us with a final vengeance.

'Captain Symonds does not like how the wind has turned, my Lord,' Major Ross reported as he came off from the wharf onto the beach. 'He believes it may come on to rain.'

'That can make no delay to us,' said Cornwallis. 'And it may be as much help as hindrance if only it distract the French gunners. Was that the extent of Captain Symonds's doubt?'

'Yes, my Lord.'

'Then give the order to embark the men, Major Ross. And once these are from the beach, you may bring down the next muster.' Ross bowed his head and hurried to carry out the order. It was intended that the fleet of sixteen vessels should go over to Gloucester, and then return to ferry two more cargoes of the remaining able-bodied red-coats. I had no doubt but that a general disorder must descend by the time of the third crossing, which disorder I trusted should disguise the fact of my own failure to embark. But when I made toward the wharf now, Cornwallis called after me, 'You shall put yourself at Tarleton's service when you reach Gloucester, Douglas.'

'I shall stay this side till the last crossing, my Lord. But I would now see Captain Stuart away.'

He dismissed me with a nod, and turned up the beach with O'Hara.

The first muster of a thousand men had come down at eight o'clock. They had not gathered together on the beach, but strung themselves out below the bluffs, that they make no accidental target for the enemy guns. But it was now gone ten o'clock, and the men cold and impatient to be into the boats, and the main trouble of their officers now to prevent a general stampede onto the wharf. Stuart's band of a hundred had been the first taken forward, and I jostled my way through them on the wharf till I emerged just by him.

'If you have changed your mind, Mr Douglas, there is a place for you.'

'Not this time Jonathan.' I glanced up to the dark clouds.

'It is a storm coming,' said he.

'Aye. And you must waste no time in getting over.'

'We are to go in convoy, by Captain Symonds's order. We must stand off from the wharf and not cross, but wait till the others are embarked.'

What purpose there might be in this I could not see, and so must presume it was some good naval reason outside my ken. I asked after Calvert. Stuart pointed into the bow of the flatboat alongside, and I soon found Calvert seated on the bow-locker amidst his fellows.

'Are you coming with us now, sir, or after?' he called upon sight of me.

'No, Mr Calvert. I have come to thank you for your aid of me till now, and to wish you good luck.'

'Thank you, sir.'

'I have commended you to Lord Cornwallis. You must not make a fool of me by getting yourself killed.'

A broad smile broke upon him, and he raised his hand to acknowledge the warning.

When I returned to Stuart, he was busy loading the last of his men. There was no time for any proper farewell, and so I briefly shook his hand, which surprised him, though he made no question of it, and then I wished him luck as he climbed into the boat. The wind was rising now, and as I moved back through the press of men and onto the beach I felt the first drops of rain.

By the time all the boats were loaded it was raining in earnest. From where I watched upon the beach, I could see the small waves being whipped up by the wind, and the difficulty the men had with their oars. But once the convoy was finally set out upon the crossing, I ran up to the cover of the cave and put off my wet jacket. Stuart had left behind a trunk, for the order had been to take no baggage; and so I fetched out a dry shirt and breeches from his trunk, and a cloth to dry myself.

But wet and cold though I was, this must be nothing to what our infantrymen and sappers now endured in the trenches above while awaiting the order to come down and cross to Gloucester. Soaked through, and cowering beneath the shells, they must be in a constant fear that the pummelled wall might be breached at any moment. And they must know that the Americans and French soldiers who would then come pouring through were men properly rested and fed, and ready to give no quarter.

My shirt and breeches changed, I was sitting on the camp-bed and drawing on my boots when Mrs Kendrick came hurrying into the cave. She had her own small jacket held over her head as protection against the rain.

'Has Lord Cornwallis left us?'

'He shall go with the senior officers in the third crossing.' I finished pulling on my boots. 'Mrs Morgan should not be alone.'

'I would ask you something that I would not have Mrs Morgan hear.'

Rising from the camp-bed, I turned my back on her. Then I went and closed Stuart's trunk.

'I think you know what it is,' she said.

'You wonder why I stay.'

'I have a fear why you stay.'

'One man's actions at such a time must signify very little.'

'It must signify to that one man, or he would not perform the action.' I heard her step further into the cave. When I turned, she was by the foot of the camp-bed on which Campbell had died. 'And in this case,' she added, 'it might signify to me.'

'That is only to say that we are different people, Mrs Kendrick.'

'Not so very different, I think, Mr Douglas.' Her look was direct. But then a fierce gust blew in, stirring her hair and her dress, and making the lantern-light flicker, and so I took the opportunity to turn from her and I reached to shield the top-hole with my hand. When the lantern flame steadied, I went by her to the cave-mouth and looked over the wall of stones into the darkness. The rain was lashing now, the squall quickly rising to a storm. Nothing was visible upon the river; and invisible, too, the lights of Gloucester, which Stuart's convoy had struck for. The rain seemed a solid curtain against the world.

'Shall it make a great difficulty?' said she, coming up by my side and looking out.

'The rain hides our boats from their guns. But the wind is a curse, and what Cornwallis had not looked for. Yes, it makes a difficulty.'

We were a time watching the rain; and impossible to say now if those dulled claps of sound without were the enemy siege guns or thunder. The boats must be in midriver by this time, or a little further on. And the wind and the waves must buffet them hard.

'You did not answer me,' said Mrs Kendrick at last. 'You did not say why it is that you shall remain here. It is the Morgans, I presume, that keep you.'

'It is hope keeps me.'

'Does Lord Cornwallis know that you shall remain?'

'My Lord Cornwallis has responsibilities other than the Morgans.'

'And I should think that you are one of them. You cannot plead for the Morgans with no authority but that of your own tongue.'

'We shall see.' I kept from facing her, though I felt her eyes upon me. I continued to watch the rain.

'When you crossed over to Gloucester with Tarleton, you wanted a prisoner—'

'Mrs Kendrick—'

'You wanted an officer, a high-ranking officer, who might be exchanged for the Morgans.'

'Lizzy should not be left,' said I; but as I made to step out from the cave, she put out her hand to stop me.

'It is you. You have made yourself your own prisoner. That is the plain truth, I think. That you mean to exchange yourself for the Morgans.'

'That is a fanciful speculation.'

'Shall you deny it to my face?' It was but half a moment I hesitated. But that was half a moment too much. Her eyes filled with a fierce and sudden anger. 'You are the most arrogant man.'

'Well—'

'You meant to sit here and wait, and tell no one.'

'You must allow that I have some experience in these matters.'

'I do not see that your experience has been any great help to you.'

'Madam—'

'No. I will not be so lightly put off.'

'I trust that you would not go to Cornwallis with any such fanciful speculation.'

I saw by her look that she considered it. Then she lowered her eyes. When she raised them again, there was less of anger and something of weary and bewildered acceptance. 'You would find a way, just the same. I shall not tell his Lordship, if that is what you fear. But if I cannot alter what you intend—'

'You cannot.'

'Then you must come now, and keep company with me and Lizzy.'

'I am content here.'

'I never thought you a dishonest man, Mr Douglas.'

With a parting look, she lifted her small jacket again to make a cover for her head from the rain. Then she hurried out, and along to the other cave where Lizzy must be awaiting her return.

It was an hour before I followed her.

Mrs Kendrick was seated on her bed, with Lizzy beside her, and Sally Morgan on the bed opposite, sleeping.

'You may come in, Mr Douglas.'

'It was only to bid you all goodnight.'

'It was to be sure that I had not gone with some speculation to my Lord Cornwallis,' said she. 'But you must come in anyway. Lizzy has forgotten the card-trick that you showed her.'

'This one,' said Lizzy, splaying the cards in her hand as she turned toward me.

I looked over the girl's head at Mrs Kendrick. In the other cave was nothing now to take me back; neither friend nor companion, nor any human feeling. And so at last I went in, and sat myself down in that place become my own these past several days, on a blanket, with my back propped against the cave wall. Lizzy came at once and knelt by me, and then I showed her how she must shuffle and order the cards.

We played a half-hour before Mrs Kendrick came down and joined in with us, and a half-hour more before Lizzy grew tired and climbed onto the empty bed to sleep. Then it was only Mrs Kendrick and me, with the wavering light from the lantern throwing shadows that swung and dipped with each gust of the storm. We spoke hardly a word to each other. Indeed, she seemed to play at the cards the more intently that she might hold off from any speaking. But after a time, and while that she dealt the next hand, I said, 'It has been the greatest help to me that you have taken care all this time of Lizzy and her mother.'

She glanced up. 'I would not betray your intention to Lord Cornwallis. But I would ask you that you reconsider what you do.'

'It is past consideration. But I am truly obliged for your concern.'

'It is more than concern, Mr Douglas,' said she, and she held my look a moment more that I be in no doubt of her; which when she saw that I was not, and that I yet made no answer, she lowered her eyes again and finished dealing the cards.

'Mr Douglas?' called a familiar voice into my sleep, and I stirred; and when the voice called again, I slowly opened my eyes. The wind had died. The storm was past. I saw that it was daybreak. I was not returned to Stuart's cave, but remained with the women. Mrs Kendrick and Lizzy still slept together on the bed. I lay propped against the blankets by the wall, but my hand rested near Mrs Kendrick's face upon her pillow. Withdrawing my hand to keep from waking her, I put off my blanket. Then as I rose, Stuart appeared at the cave entrance, with Calvert at his shoulder.

Soaked to the skin, they looked half-dead with exhaustion.

'But what has happened?' said I.

'The boats are scattered. The army cannot cross,' said Stuart.

Calvert made a despairing gesture with his hand. There was the pain of defeat in his eyes. 'It is finished, sir. Lord Cornwallis means to surrender.'

CHAPTER 35

*A*t ten o'clock, and in the presence of Lord Cornwallis and his senior officers, one of our drummer boys – with no small courage – mounted the ruined parapet of the Hornwork to beat the chamade, signifying our capitulation. It is impossible that the enemy gunners should have heard the lad, for their weight of fire was something tremendous now. But certainly he was seen, and slowly their firing slackened, till after a minute his drumming sounded distinct between each shot. A minute more, and their firing stopped altogether, and then the drumbeat came clear. An awful sound it was to us, though glorious it must be to the enemy, as it rolled out from our wall and across to them in their siege line.

'Major Ross,' said Cornwallis, with both hands upon the parapet, and staring now into the awful stillness before him. Ross ordered forward the selected captain, who carried Cornwallis's request for a parley with Washington. This captain climbed up to join the drummer lad, and then raised a white kerchief and waved it over his head. It was a pathetic sight, and almost harder to endure than the sound of the drum. Then the lad and captain went down from the wall, across the ditch, and out toward the enemy line.

I glanced at Major Ross. Though tight-lipped, he seemed stoical, as if he had hardened himself to face this terrible humbling. General O'Hara, just beside him, appeared almost relieved that the end had finally come. But Lord Cornwallis looked neither stoical nor relieved. He stared like a man stricken, with his hands still braced against the parapet for support.

From the trenches behind us, our common soldiery now dared to lift their heads and come out; and though slowly at first, there were soon scores of these fellows climbing up onto our ruined ramparts and wall. And on the enemy line too, there were some of their soldiers appeared, watching the drummer lad and the captain.

An enemy officer finally came out to meet Cornwallis's envoy. He sent the drummer lad back to us, and took the captain with him into their line.

'My Lordship shall now go below,' Ross said to me, pausing at my side as the senior officers departed the Hornwork. 'He invites you to join us while we await Washington's reply.'

For the first time in days we might walk as men though the ruined town, and not scramble about the communication trenches like rats. The quiet was something extraordinary, and likewise the scene of devastation all about; for now that we had no fear of the enemy shells we could make a calm observation of the wreckage both on our line and to the rear. There were craters everywhere about the pits and trenches, and the bodies of those men killed that morning, waiting to be taken down for burial. The remains of Mrs Kendrick's house were smouldering from a recent shell, as were the remains of the Nelson house and several others. Hardly a one of our guns remained mounted. No one spoke to Lord Cornwallis as we passed through all this and down to the headquarters cave. And he, for his part, stared straight ahead, as if it were too much to take in the bare fact of the over-whelming destruction.

Once in the cave, he gave an order for the scuttling of our last ships to prevent them making a further supplement to Admiral de Grasse's fleet. After this, there was some discussion of the terms of surrender. Major Ross suggested the example of Burgoyne's surrender at Saratoga as the best we might hope for; but others frankly feared that General Clinton's recent imposition of unreasonably harsh terms upon the surrendered Americans at Charleston should now be returned upon us. But in truth, all this talk was idleness till we received Washington's reply; and when General O'Hara excused himself to get some air, I went out with him.

'An awful day, Mr Douglas. But no other choice was left to us. To wait further must have brought only butchery.'

'I make no question of it, General.'

We walked a short way along from the cave, and then propped our backs against the sloping bank. With the guns silent, we heard now, and for the first time in many days, the sound of birdsong. Down on the river, it appeared that Captain Symonds was already preparing to receive the order to scuttle; for there were laden boats coming away from the *Guadeloupe* and the two other remaining ships, and rowing toward the beach. O'Hara offered me snuff, I declined, and he took some for himself.

'In London they shall blame us, you know,' said he. 'Five years of bad policy, but they shall throw everything upon today.'

I remarked that Mr Jenkinson, our Secretary at War, knew only too well the difficulties that the ministry's policies toward the American colonies had made.

'And as little good you have done with your correspondents in London as I with mine, Mr Douglas. The ministry has steered toward this as surely as if they had set their compass to it. But now that we have arrived, you shall see there is no one shall confess himself the pilot of the wreck. If America be now lost to us, the army shall get the blame. Every hand in Whitehall washed clean. Mark me, Douglas, and tell me in a year if I was wrong.'

But I had no doubt that he was right; and the only surprise to me that he should so openly countenance the complete loss of our American colonies, which must be the worst possible outcome of our army's surrender here. His weary and somewhat cynical acceptance of this final unravelling silenced me awhile. But then, for myself, I found that when I considered of our defeat I was nothing so shocked as I had thought that I should be either; for it was true, as O'Hara said, that we had been steering toward this wreck since the war began, and not in the past months only. But though there might be no shock, yet there was painful regret. So much might have been done differently, and better. There had been too many sacrifices made. Too many lives had been lost, Major Andre but one of them.

O'Hara attempted to engage me in some conversation concerning the political consequences of our surrender for North and his ministry, but I found myself disinclined to talk. All my thought was now upon the Morgans and Cordet. And when that same captain who had gone out to request a parley now appeared on the path above, I made no hesitation but returned at once to the cave. Lord Cornwallis received the sealed papers from the captain, turned them over in his hand, and to my considerable surprise called me to him.

'What is this?' said he, holding out to me one of the two sealed papers (which, now that I was nearer, appeared more like a package). It bore my name, and the name of the sender, Cordet.

'I do not know, my Lord.'

The other sealed paper was undoubtedly Washington's reply. Cornwallis gathered himself a moment, and then broke it open and read it. And as he read it, the weight of the world seemed to descend upon him. He turned quite pale. Though he said nothing, by his face we saw that Washington had not forgotten Clinton's severe treatment of the surrendering Americans at Charleston.

'Open yours, Douglas,' Cornwallis told me at last. 'It cannot be worse.' And while his officers gathered about him now at the table to read Washington's note, I stepped aside and opened Cordet's package.

My Dear Douglas,

I confirm receipt of your appeal to me regarding the Morgans on the 10th day of August, by the hand of Secretary Nelson.

It is with regret that I must inform you that Cable Morgan and

his son David Morgan were both hanged on the 9th of August in the
Williamsburg gaol. I can therefore make no acceptance of your
offer, nor can I give you any safe passage into our lines.

I enclose the letters written to Mrs Morgan by her husband and
son before the execution.

Yours,

Cordet.

Down near the wharf, I put Cordet's note into Mrs Kendrick's hand. She read it in silence, but with a hand at her breast. When she was done, she lowered the letter and looked at me. I took the letter and slipped it into my pocket with those other two, yet unbroken, from the Morgans. Tears stood in her eyes. I turned aside a moment that she might collect herself.

'It is too dreadful,' said she.

'There is a cease of hostilities for tonight. But tomorrow there shall be a negotiation over the terms of surrender. When that is completed, there shall be Virginians then come into the town. Some, I must suppose, from Williamsburg.'

'But what shall you do?'

'I must tell her, or someone else certainly shall.'

'Of course. But I had meant yourself. Now that you cannot be exchanged, you must be in some danger of apprehension.'

'That is nothing for the present,' said I. Further along the beach, Lizzy was come out from the cave. She was drawing patterns in the sand with a stick, and appeared to be talking to herself. Her mother remained within.

Mrs Kendrick said, 'I could tell them, if you wished.'

She was in earnest. It was no false courage that she possessed. 'You know that is not possible,' said I. Then as I turned toward the cave she touched my shoulder briefly, in compassion.

Sally Morgan made not a sound after I had spoken. She lay propped on her pillows, and I sat on the chair that I had drawn up beside her; and I could not bring myself to look upon her face. Instead, I stared at those letters from Cable and David. She had not opened them, and they rested now beneath her hand on the linen sheet.

It seemed an hour, which must have been only minutes, before she said, 'You have not told Lizzy.'

'If you wished—'

'No, I shall tell her.'

At last I dared to raise my eyes. Thin and wasted, but strangely still, she gazed toward the mouth of the cave, indifferent to my presence. Indifferent to the world.

'Sally—'

'I do not blame you, Alistair. But you must leave me now.'

'I might sit with you awhile.'

'No,' she said, and with a voice neither pleading nor emphatic but quietly unanswerable. And so I rose. At the mouth of the cave I looked back. She had not moved, and her eyes had not followed me. 'Mrs Kendrick is without, if you should want for anything.' She answered me nothing, not a word or sign, and I hesitated but a moment before I left her.

CHAPTER 36

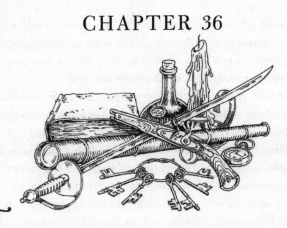

*T*he cease of hostilities extended into the next day (which was the 18th of October), when Major Ross and Colonel Dundas were sent out by Lord Cornwallis to negotiate the terms of our surrender. They went to the Moore house, a mile out from our lines, and very near to where I had attended that Episcopalian service in the barn.

But for all the importance of these negotiations, Sally Morgan continued my main concern; for though she had allowed Mrs Kendrick to be with her, and though Mrs Kendrick had assured me that I could do nothing more for the present, yet I had now a considerable doubt for Sally Morgan's future, and for Lizzy's, once the surrender was signed. (And I own, to concern myself in this way gave my heart and mind a necessary distraction from my own grief and guilt.) Her husband and son had been hanged as Loyalist spies, and she must surely be branded the same by her neighbours. The Morgan farm was already made forfeit by Cable's execution, and would certainly be sold to help pay the Continental soldiers. And how then might she and Lizzy continue to live on the Chesapeake?

'She is not the only Loyalist still with us,' said O'Hara when I

337

stopped him outside the headquarters cave and told him of my concerns. 'I expect that there shall be some provision eventually made for all of them in the articles of surrender. I know it is discussed.'

'Is there some difficulty in it?' said I; for his tone suggested as much.

'They shall not be forgotten, Douglas.' He gestured into the cave. 'There is a captain here rides over shortly with our latest instructions for Major Ross. If you have a mind to go with him, you may speak with the Major directly. You must excuse me now.'

Tarleton had by this time sent over twenty horses from Gloucester for the use of our officers, and I went and claimed one, and waited at the southern gate. Our redcoats were fully established upon our ruined walls, with hundreds of them now loafing about there. Some, for their own amusement, played fife and bagpipes, which music was answered by occasional piping from the enemy line. It was one of our own pipers now played as the captain and his flag-bearer rode up to the gate. O'Hara having told them of me, the slip-rail was opened and together we rode out to the Moore house.

After tying our horses we went into the orchard, a place somewhat apart from the French and Continental officers standing about the farmhouse. Ross soon came out to us. I had the answer to my concerns very quickly, for Ross assured me that there was an article of the capitulation already agreed which allowed of our sloop-of-war, the *Bonetta*, sailing from York Town unexamined by either the Americans or the French.

'The *Bonetta* shall take Lord Cornwallis's private communication to General Clinton,' said Ross. I expressed a doubt that she should truly be allowed to leave unexamined. Ross lowered his voice. 'It shall be a convenience to both sides, Mr Douglas, if we can take off any who wish to go. Both our Loyalist soldiers and any townsfolk. Washington wants no trouble between these and his Virginians.'

'And if the sloop is full?'

'Mrs Morgan and her daughter shall both have places aboard. You have my word upon it.'

It was a more certain answer than I had hoped for, and I thanked him warmly. I then withdrew myself from the orchard whilst he received Lord Cornwallis's instructions from the captain. And I was but halfway back to our horses, when a French officer broke off from the others near the house. He removed his tricorn and put it beneath his arm as he came toward me. His other hand rested upon his sword-hilt. He did not need to hail me, for I recognized him at once and stopped.

'You received the letters?' said Cordet, halting before me.

'Yes.'

'There was nothing could be done.'

'You owe me no apology.'

'Would that I might say the same, Douglas. But now that we have the victory, I find that I am almost able to forgive you your deceit.'

'As you say. You have the victory.' I dipped my head to him, and turned; for I would not engage in recrimination, nor make measure of the deceits we had each of us practised against the other. But he checked me with his hand, and fixed me with his eye.

'I have not come to accuse you, but to warn you,' said he; and when I looked at him warily, he opened a hand toward the tied horses, saying, 'Please,' and then we walked on together, though I still unsure of him, and of his purpose. 'You have made a fool of Colonel Lasceaux.'

'I do not believe so.'

'He believes so, and that is enough.'

'He would have done the same.'

'That may be. But he does not forgive you. And after the surrender you shall have no protection from him.'

I shrugged. I remarked that I did not look for Lasceaux's forgiveness, nor feel the need for any protection.

'Lord Cornwallis, I suppose, means to give you a brevet commission, that you be paroled back to England with the officers?'

'It is possible,' said I, though it was much more than only possible; for I had received my brevet commission that very morning. Upon the army Return, I was now Major Douglas, and attached to Lord Cornwallis's headquarters as an aide.

'The legitimacy of any such commission shall be challenged. Lasceaux works even now to get evidence that you were acknowledged a spy within York Town. And that it was as a spy that you crossed into our lines. You have met Secretary Nelson, I understand.'

'I have met him.'

'Lasceaux has no intention of allowing your parole, Douglas. He shall get what evidence he needs, and he shall overturn your commission.'

'And has he first sent you to tell me so?' At this, Cordet threw me a hard look, and I added, 'Why should you warn me?'

'Why should you allow my escape after Plassey? The siege is finished. And very likely the war. Your arrest now can change nothing.' We arrived at the horses. The captain was coming out from the orchard, which when Cordet saw he asked me quickly had I heard of the sloop *Bonetta*, and the permission she had to sail, unexamined, to New York. I said that I had some knowledge of it. 'Be aboard of her after the surrender,' said he, 'or Lasceaux shall certainly hang you.'

A hand resting upon his sword-hilt, Cordet dipped his head to me. Then he put on his tricorn, turned on his heel, and went back to join his brother officers.

Upon my return to York Town I went directly out to the *Bonetta* and arranged with her captain that Mrs Morgan, Mrs Kendrick and Lizzy should be allocated a small area outside his cabin for the voyage north. He promised me that hammocks should be slung there, and a curtain of sail hung up for their privacy; but having only just been told of the part his sloop was to play in the evacuation of the Loyalists, he was anxious to be at his work.

'The crew must make her ready now, Mr Douglas. And I should be grateful if you send no one aboard till the morning.'

I then went to report the news of the *Bonetta* to Mrs Kendrick. She was much pleased to hear that those Loyalists who had joined our ranks were not to be abandoned to the avenging mercies of

Washington's men. She told me, in her turn, that Sally Morgan had been up from her bed, and had even come out from the cave a short while to watch Lizzy upon the beach. This was unexpected, and an encouragement to me; but Mrs Kendrick having some doubt that I should yet look in on Sally Morgan, I made no insistence upon it. I spent the remainder of that day and a good part of the night, up in the town and about our lines, giving some assistance to Carruthers and Gould, whose hospital and patients must all be brought ashore again to allow the scuttling of the ships.

On the morning of the 19th, Major Ross and Colonel Dundas finished negotiating the Articles of surrender. When I went up to join the senior officers at the headquarters cave, they were all of them turned out in their best uniforms, which were washed clean (there were campfires burning again, and hot water in plenty). The only sign on their persons of the brutal siege was now upon their faces, which were drawn, and in their eyes, wherein was clearly written our defeat. There was almost a score of men present, and every one of them silent when Major Ross placed the Articles on the table. Behind the table sat Lord Cornwallis and Captain Symonds; and though both commanders must now sign the surrender, it was Cornwallis that every man watched.

And he looked now hardly the same man that he had been at the siege's commencement. However fine might be his gold-braided red jacket, and however carefully powdered his wig, it was his sloping shoulders and his haunted eyes that told the truer story. Whatever the fault in Clinton's inaction, or Germaine's in London, it was from himself that Cornwallis could not conceal his own part in bringing us to this moment.

He who had the greatest reputation for decision and bold action, he to whom the greater part of our army had been entrusted, he to whom his men had committed their lives; he had vacillated, faltered, and finally gone down before a generalship superior to his own. He knew it, every man present knew it; and every man present knew also that when he signed, it was not only York Town's surrender would be effected, but that the King's hold upon our American colonies must finally be broken.

How heavy the pen that Cornwallis at last took into his hand. Without a word, he dipped it into the ink and signed.

CHAPTER 37

*T*he Union Jack was struck from our line, and our drummers beat the withdrawal.

Cornwallis had sent out by his officers a message of gratitude to the soldiers and sappers for all their efforts during the siege; yet this counted for nothing against the sight of the enemy soldiers who, at our withdrawal, came forward to stand sentinels upon our own ramparts. They raised their colours, both Continental and French, and our men must watch the banners flutter there and yet make no opposition. Most of our redcoats then did as they were ordered, and made clean their uniforms and boots, to be ready for the ceremony of surrender; but there were others, I confess, found grog (I know not where, unless from the seamen), and these soon compounded our defeat with a more personal disgrace.

I borrowed Major Ross's second jacket, that I might take part as a brevetted officer in the surrender. But when the moment came, and I mounted with the officers, my ire was as great as that of many others to find that it was General O'Hara and not Lord Cornwallis who would lead us out.

'My Lord Cornwallis is unwell,' Major Ross answered me; but he would make no further defence of his commander. And in truth, what defence might there be? It was an absence beyond either excuse or reason. And just what might have prompted Cornwallis to stand aside from his own army at such a moment it is almost impossible to conceive, unless it be an absurd and hollow pride; but certainly it was a misjudgement, and unmanly; and the officers were fully as dispirited as the common soldiery by his inexplicable absence from our head.

With the men assembled (whom death, injury and sickness had now winnowed to half the number they had been at the siege's commencement), O'Hara looked over the column, and then over the ruined town. And then he said to those of us mounted near him, 'It is but a short way to the end now, gentlemen. Let us get there with what good order we may. Major Ross, have the fife and drums lead us out.'

And so with the fife and drums playing before us, our column left by the southern gate. The rebels had made a way for us through their first and second siege lines, filling their ditches to the breadth of a track, and collapsing their walls. But beyond these we met with a sight that might quell the pride in any British heart; for up ahead of us was prepared a uniformed avenue. To the west side of the track were the French; the Americans to the east side; and each army standing in three ranks. The uniformed avenue stretched some hundreds of yards, and all the way to the field where we must formally surrender our arms.

Nor were the soldiers to be the only witnesses to our ceremonial humbling, but there were many wagons drawn up behind them, and these bearing local farmers, and townsfolk come out from Williamsburg. Men, women and children, and they dressed as for a fair, standing now on the trays to get a better vantage of us. At our approach toward the uniformed avenue there were taunts and jeers from some of the civilians, but such insolence was no more than we had expected, and so we paid no mind to them. Our drummers beat steady, and our fife-men now played a melancholy air, and with such sad spirit that the memory of the whole war swelled up then in my heart. But I kept my head up and my eyes to the front, for the Morgans' sake, and for the sake of Major Andre.

As we came near to the uniformed avenue, we found all their senior officers mounted there. General O'Hara called us to a halt.

'His Lordship's sword, if you please, Major Ross,' said he; which when Ross had given it him, O'Hara took the sword forward to make the surrender. Whether what followed was O'Hara's own unworthy notion, or done at Cornwallis's order, or merely a misunderstanding (which O'Hara later claimed), I cannot say. But O'Hara made directly for General Rochambeau, and no doubt but that he meant to make our surrender to the Frenchman. But Rochambeau, seeing the intention, at once sent an officer forward to block O'Hara's way. And then Rochambeau made a sign very clear that this junior Frenchman should now escort O'Hara to the opposite side where General Washington, mounted upon a fine white horse, waited calmly. O'Hara had no choice then but to cross to him.

Major Ross leaned toward me. 'Who is that French colonel looks at you?'

'Lasceaux.'

'The fellow you told me of?'

'Yes.'

'You need not fear a man who cannot keep his jacket buttoned.'

He was very wrong, but I made no answer to him. Cordet, mounted just behind General Rochambeau, gave me no sign of recognition.

To the opposite side now, O'Hara and Washington spoke a few words together, which seemed some apology by O'Hara for Lord Cornwallis's absence. Then O'Hara attempted to surrender the sword; but Washington would not receive it. Instead he beckoned up one of his junior officers to take it from O'Hara's hand, which was a clear return of that snub Cornwallis had made by his failure to come out and surrender in person. This formality being completed, and at a nod from Washington, the sword was then returned very courteously to O'Hara.

So it was concluded, and much after the same manner as the entire

345

siege; with Rochambeau and Washington cooperating together, and so maintaining ever the upper hand over us, while we stood upon a misplaced pride all the way to our inevitable capitulation.

General O'Hara then summoned us forward to the field of surrender, and on we rode down the uniformed avenue, the longest march of the war.

Our officers were permitted to keep both swords and side-arms, and were granted the freedom of the peninsula; and so after watching the first sullen piling of the Fusiliers' muskets in the field of surrender, I returned alone to the town. I had not in the least liked how Lasceaux had fixed his eye upon me. And now I put aside my first suspicion of Cordet's warning to me; for I saw that my brevet commission would make but a flimsy protection against a man such as Lasceaux in anger. To stay longer than necessary in York Town now was to invite my own destruction.

Going through our southern gate, I dismounted, thinking on the *Bonetta*. But while I thought, I heard a woman call my name. I looked up, and it was Mrs Kendrick hurrying toward me, with her skirts gathered in her hands. She called out, and in distress, 'I cannot find her. I cannot find Mrs Morgan.'

We searched the upper town, I spoke to the French sentries at every gate, and to the French soldiers on our walls; no one had seen her. But at my asking, and reading in Mrs Kendrick's distress the genuineness of our plight, they promised to detain the missing woman if she attempted to depart the town.

Mrs Kendrick apologized to me again as we went from the gate, and again berated herself as we left the upper town and went down the valley toward the beach.

'I will not hear it more, Mrs Kendrick. The fault was not yours,' said I; and indeed, it was not. For she had told me by now of the whole unfortunate happening. The *Bonetta*'s captain having sent two boats to fetch the Loyalists out to him, the women had been separated at a lieutenant's order for some convenience of the loading. Lizzy had gone with Mrs Kendrick. But though Mrs Kendrick had seen

Sally Morgan into the other boat, and though both boats had then set out for the *Bonetta*, yet the vessel which carried Sally Morgan had turned back to pick up another passenger. It was only when this second boat finally reached the *Bonetta* that Mrs Kendrick had learned of Sally Morgan's disembarkation ashore.

'She may have gone back to the cave by this time,' said I when we reached the foot of the valley. The beach both north and south of us was empty.

We went along toward the caves, calling her name, and looking into the several smaller caves now abandoned by the soldiers and towns-folk. She was in none of these. Our final and best hope was in our own pair of caves; but arriving there, and making a glance into each of them, the hope was dashed.

'Another boat may have come in for her,' said I; though in truth, I did not think it likely. Nor would Mrs Kendrick allow herself any such empty consolation, but she started along the beach toward the northern palisade, and the track leading up to the Fusiliers' redoubt.

'She would have no reason to go up there,' I called.

'She has no reason to go anywhere,' Mrs Kendrick threw back over her shoulder. 'But it might be that she has put herself on the road to Williamsburg.'

This thought was no bad one; and the Williamsburg road passing hard by the Fusiliers' redoubt, it could do us no harm to go up and make enquiry of the French sentries posted there. As I started along the beach after Mrs Kendrick, there was an eagle opened its broad wings where it perched on one of those half-sunken boats near the palisade. With a few powerful beats, it lifted away from the river. This movement first caught my eye, but what then held my gaze were the several bodies of the horses collected by the tide against the sunken boats and the palisade.

'Mr Douglas?'

'Go on,' I told her. 'I shall be a minute behind.'

She did not go on. As I turned my step toward the palisade, she came down from the redoubt track to join me, and both of us hurrying forward over the sand now, neither one of us speaking, but our eyes fixed upon the yard of white lace settled alongside one of the dead horses.

I made no stop at the water's edge, but waded directly in till it was over my boots and then my waist, and it was almost to my chin before I might finally clutch the white lace in my hand. I gathered it, and it was joined to a length of plain cotton sunk deeper, and I gathered this in like heavy rope and drew it to me. The weight of it shifted, and I felt it move against me. I dropped my arms and put them about her, and she was so slight but as heavy as the world, and in an agony of soul I turned her from the horse and brought Sally Morgan's life-less body in to the shore.

In the evening we buried her in that grassed level ground overlooking the river, just a few paces from Campbell. Having taken her own life, she must have no proper ceremony but only the prayers of those few of us gathered at her graveside. I found the letters from Cable and David Morgan, and these we interred with her, and also some flow-ering reeds that Mrs Kendrick had tied as a wreath. As we came away, I fell behind with Stuart while Calvert and Mrs Kendrick walked on ahead with Lizzy between them. When I told Stuart what I required of him, though he was taken aback he agreed without hesitation.

'Tell no one,' said I, and he nodded and we went on in silence.

At the wharf, I got into the boat with Mrs Kendrick and Lizzy. That junior French officer who had but distantly shadowed me the past hours now stood upon the beach. He made no pretence but that he watched me.

'Mr Douglas.'

'I have seen him, Mrs Kendrick.' I took her hand to help her into her seat in the boat. 'He cannot come aboard the *Bonetta*.'

'What does he want of you?'

'I believe he is the aide of a certain Colonel Lasceaux. And Lasceaux is a fellow should like to hang me.'

We shoved off, and the *Bonetta*'s boatmen rowed us out to the ques-tionable safety of their ship.

CHAPTER 38

*T*hough no enemy soldier might rightfully come aboard the *Bonetta*, that same fellow of Lasceaux's came out at sunset the next evening to confiscate the ship's boats. He told our captain that in future these boats might be used during the daylight hours only, and that they must not go over to the Gloucester side, or indeed to any place other than the York Town wharf.

We were now the solitary British island upon the river; for the two blockading French ships had earlier come up and anchored off the town, and their men had claimed our few small unscuttled vessels and dispatched the last British seamen into captivity with the redcoats ashore.

After dark, the sound of the continuing French and rebel celebrations, the pipes and the singing, came to us very clear across the water from both sides of the river. And most grateful was I not to be ashore, and a witness to their revels.

Instead the *Bonetta*'s captain obliged me with pen and ink, and also the brief privacy of his cabin.

York Town, 20th October 1781.

My Dear Jenkinson,

    By the time that you receive this letter you shall have had the first news of our surrender here at York Town. And no doubt you have received likewise the first excuses, and seen the first manoeuvrings to make the shame of it fall on parties deserving of the blame and others quite innocent. I shall not make addition to the tales that you must now most certainly have from every quarter. Enough to say that it is no lack of courage in our soldiery has undone us, but our strategy was at fault throughout (Lord Germaine, Lord Cornwallis and General Clinton having between them made that strategy, you must know better than I the likely success of any enquiry into it).

    However, you shall hardly be surprised if I give it as my observation that though our strategy was flawed, and our defeat very bitter, yet these have been but the final consequences (and almost inevitable outcome) of the ministry's ill-directed policy toward our colonies these past several years. We have attempted to compel by force what we could not get by a peaceful consent, which vain efforts we would never have embarked upon had we only deigned to hear and understand our American brothers the better. But the higher road is long since behind us, and we have taken the lower all the way to its end, and nothing to do now but endure the consequence.

    As to myself, I have suffered no physical injury, only grief, but that in such plenty, and so recent, that I am even now in the midst of it. The half-Cherokee Campbell is dead, killed during the siege; and two Chesapeake men have been hanged for their assistance of me. Yesterday (which was the 19th of October, and the day of surrender) I buried a woman of the same family, and now I am aboard the Bonetta *with some hundred others (mainly Loyalists and some blacks), which ship by the terms of our surrender shall remain uninspected by the enemy, and have safe passage to New York when she is ready.*

Like every British man here, I am now impatient to put York
Town far behind me; but all things being here in such a state of
disorder as you may imagine, I can give no certain promise where
the next months shall find me, though it must be very doubtful
that I shall make any near return to London. You must trust to
me that I shall continue to look to the King's interest, howsoever
it be without benefit of your direct guidance or instruction for
some months at least. To this end, you would greatly oblige me
by ordering a bill written to my favour to the sum of that £200
sterling owed me by the department, and drawable upon the usual
House in New York.

What more is there to say? Our worst fears have come to pass,
and no consolation to be had. To pretend otherwise must be the
merest casuistry.

It remains only to fulfil our avowed duties here with what
honour is left to us, which you may be certain I shall now strive to
do, and to the utmost.

My respects to Willes, and to Sir Joseph.

Yours,
Alistair Douglas.

I wrote but one more note, very brief, and then I sealed them both
and took them with me from the cabin.

Boats came and went from the *Bonetta* all the next day, the crew
fetching supplies and bringing out carpenters and sundry other men
to assist in making her ready for the voyage. Though it was not
expected she should leave inside the week, yet the captain pressed
his men hard that there be no delay in the departure.

Mrs Kendrick and Lizzy kept mainly below, for the upper deck was
both crowded and busy, and to move about was only to inconvenience the crew. Nor could I be of any help to the seamen, and so I
found myself for some hours doing much as I had whilst in the cave,
distracting the child with card games, and conversing with Mrs
Kendrick. What Lizzy felt or understood concerning her mother's

death was difficult to discern. Though she had wept at the burial, she had hardly mentioned the great loss since, and then only in passing. It was as though the finality of it was not yet real to her. Sally Morgan had evidently not told her of the deaths of Cable and David Morgan; and Mrs Kendrick had asked me not to do so either, saying that she would watch Lizzy carefully, and await the proper time, which might not come for some days or weeks. In this, I must bow to her better womanly understanding; and I had no doubt but that she had a deep feeling for the child. Now while Lizzy had her head in Mrs Kendrick's lap and slept, I sketched them both, which was but a poor distraction of myself.

'You must make a portrait from the sketch when you arrive in New York,' said Mrs Kendrick, her hand stroking Lizzy's head. 'It shall ever remind me of her.'

'You must know it may happen that no one of her family here shall want her.'

'The loss would be theirs.'

'You have thought of it.'

'Yes, I have thought of it.'

I kept my eyes down. 'You might not then need the portrait,' said I, wondering if this was too bold, or whether I had misjudged her.

'I should like it anyway. It would be a memory for her when she is grown.'

It was simply said, as if it must be the most natural thing possible that Lizzy might now go to New York, and Mrs Kendrick raise her. But when I looked up, there was something unspoken in Mrs Kendrick's glance which I did not acknowledge or return; and Major Ross then coming down in search of the captain, I took the opportunity to join him.

From Ross I had confirmation of those disorders ashore that I had expected, with our men resentful of their surrender, and many of them in drink. But the good sense of Washington and Rochambeau, he assured me, had done much to keep off any violence; for the American troops were kept back from York Town, and only the French had been allowed to stand as guards and sentries around our battered line.

Though Ross was satisfied by this, it seemed to me a final and dismal ignominy. The fraternal bitterness between us and our American brethren had apparently sunk us so low that we must now be grateful to be kept from each other's throats by the French.

'Washington treats us all very civil. Lord Cornwallis shall dine with him at the Moore house tonight.'

'His Lordship is over his illness then,' said I.

'That is too hard, Mr Douglas. Our position here was impossible.'

'I meant no contempt of him, Major. In truth, I expect he now regrets that he did not surrender his sword in person. I shall take it for a warning, and a guide to myself.'

Ross told me that Tarleton had now crossed over to York Town from Gloucester, and intended to come out and see me on the morrow. I made no correction to him, and soon after that we parted without ceremony, for the *Bonetta*'s captain would go ashore with him. My brief farewell to Ross I made as a matter of course, and fully as though I expected to see him again the next day.

A half-hour before sunset, I was at the rail, and waiting with some anxiety over the imminent withdrawal of the ship's boats, when Stuart was at last rowed out from the wharf to the *Bonetta*. He could not stay long, for the boat must now be taken ashore by that order of Lasceaux's aide; and so Stuart quickly told me how it should be, and the time.

'If there is aught else I might do, sir—'

'There is nothing, Jonathan. Only that perhaps you would beg my forgiveness of Calvert that I could not see him. And I must not give you my hand now lest it be remembered against you.'

The crew had by this time hefted aboard those provisions brought out with Stuart in the boat; and so now he made only the briefest nod to me and then he re-embarked without calling attention to our parting. Neither did he look back to the ship, but kept his eyes upon the shore: his own father could not have done it any better. This last boat once returned to the wharf, the night darkness descended and then I went below to wait.

*

It was long past midnight, and most everyone aboard sleeping, when I felt the gentle sway of the sloop beneath me, and heard the new strain upon the anchor-rope. Past the slack, the tide was going out. I put off my blanket and sat up slowly. Lizzy was in the hammock, and Mrs Kendrick, just along from me, was very still upon the thin mattress given her by the captain. Taking great care to make no sound, I took my satchel from beneath my pillow. But as I opened it, Mrs Kendrick said quietly, 'Mr Douglas?'

I turned sharply and put a finger to my lips.

A few moments she lay there watching me; and then she sat up. Again I pressed the finger to my lips, warning her to silence. Then I picked up my boots and my jacket and beckoned her to follow me above. She came out from beneath the hammock and stayed close to me, putting one hand upon my back to keep herself from stumbling in the dark. Though there were many people below decks, a passage had been kept open to the steps. And at the steps, I gave her my hand and helped her up to the open deck. The crew slept before the mast, and only one midshipman was now awake and at the watch.

'Give us no disturbance, lad,' said I as we went by him; and he no doubt wanting to think himself a man, said nothing but only nodded to me. Then I led Mrs Kendrick back into the narrow darkness at the stern rail. There I crouched, and she beside me; and I opened my satchel.

'Whatever are you going to—'

'Quiet now. Take these two letters. The first is addressed to a fellow in London. You must give it to the captain.'

'But you might give it to him yourself.'

'Tell the captain he must put it with those other letters that he shall carry for Lord Cornwallis. This second is a note to an accompting house in New York. It is an authority for you to draw two hundred pounds against my name, which money you may need for Lizzy. It shall be good in a few months from now.'

'You might do it directly,' said she; but in her voice now was a dawning understanding that I might not do it directly, and perhaps also the reason.

'I shall not be in New York,' said I, to end any doubt. 'And so I must do it through you.'

'But you cannot stay now in York Town.'

'I do not mean to stay.'

She looked over the water toward Gloucester, and then back to me. 'But you are safe here on the ship.'

'I do not go in search of better safety.'

'Lizzy—'

'I have been an angel of death to her. I have destroyed her family, and I cannot now remake it. Her best hope is in you.'

'In time, she would understand.'

'It cannot be.'

'It could, if you wanted it so.'

'It cannot be.'

'You have decided.'

'I have.'

From upriver came the faint call of an owl. She looked toward it; she had heard the call before, while she had been in the cave. And now I saw the full understanding of my intention come to her. She faced me. 'If I had not wakened—'

'I would have woken you.'

'But only to say . . . what you have said.'

'Only that. And to give you the letters.' I propped my back against the bulwark and pulled on my boots. 'You were not made for a widow, Mrs Kendrick. But neither was I made for quiet.'

'That is not the reason.'

Just out from the ship, a Pamunkey canoe came sliding from the darkness. There were two paddlers, and they let the canoe drift the last ten yards on the tide before turning to lodge silently against the stern.

'I must go now.'

Still crouching, she reached and clasped my hand between hers. 'Lizzy shall know that you did everything a man could to preserve her family. She shall not blame you.'

'She does not need to.'

'Then you are truly decided.'

'I am.' She looked at me intently, and then she dropped her head to hide her face from me. Now I took both her hands in mine. 'I know that if it happen, you shall care for Lizzy as your own. She has chosen you. And she could not have chosen better. I must be for ever grateful to you.'

It was some moments she was silent before she raised her eyes. 'You take too much upon yourself, Mr Douglas,' said she; and then she smiled, though I saw that she would have wept.

I did not trust myself to say more, or stay longer; and so I bent and kissed her forehead and then I released her hands and climbed over the side and down into the waiting canoe. The paddlers pushed silently off, and we slipped away from the *Bonetta* and into the darkness. After a minute the second Pamunkey canoe joined us, and together we went on down the river, wide of French ships, and York Town fell away behind us, and I did not look back.

We stopped sometimes in our paddling to listen, and twice we drew near to the reeds to avoid some French vessel in midriver; but always we moved on the tide toward the Bay. And once we had passed out from the York we saw in the far distance the lanterns of de Grasse's great fleet, which had stood guard there, unchallenged, throughout the siege. We hugged the shore around Old Point Comfort, and at last entered the James River. The tide was moving against us here, and so we stayed close to the bank for some few miles. But when the Morning Star showed bright, and the tide at length slackened, I gave the order to cross to the far side.

It was that same stretch of water across which the Morgans had first carried me. And when the pale light of early dawn revealed the southern bank, I guided us to that same cove where Campbell and I had waited after our journey over the mountains.

The two canoes finally slid onto the muddy beach of the cove, and we stepped ashore. The four Pamunkey had each of them a musket, a powder-horn and a knife, and that was all. After walking up the beach a short way, I turned to face them. They were as they had ever been, dressed half-European and half-Indian, and with broad swarthy faces, and near unreadable in their silent placidity. Against the wave of American settlers that would now break over the mountains and through the King's Line, they would be nothing. They never moved, but stayed by their beached canoes and only watched me, till I said, 'I cannot hold you to any promise that you made to Campbell. You must choose your own way.'

Then they talked among themselves a few moments. And next they dragged their canoes from the beach and into the shallows, and I thought they meant to embark and return to the reservation. But there in the shallows they weighted the canoes with stones and sank them, and then they waded from the water and came up the beach, and I understood now that they would stay with me to the end.

The sun was up, and shining on the face of the river. I looked my last upon the tidewater before turning my back, and the Pamunkey with me. Together we put the Chesapeake behind us, and struck out for the Indian country.

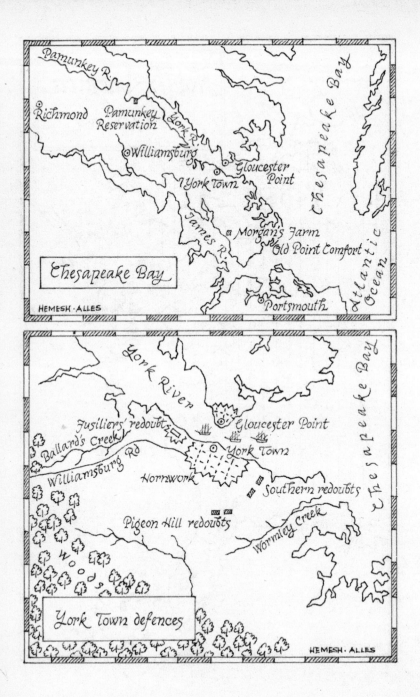

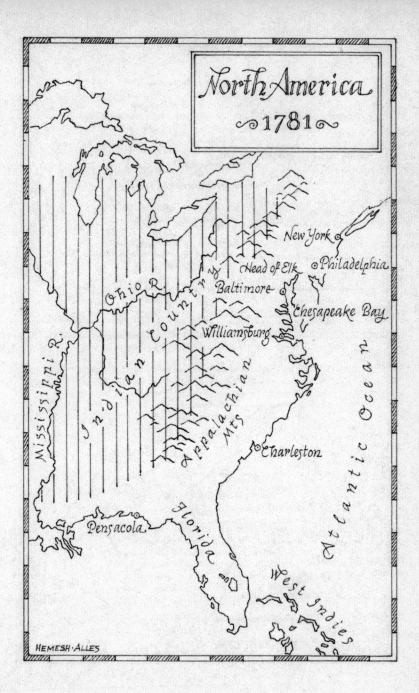

North America
1781

New York
Philadelphia
Head of Elk
Baltimore
Chesapeake Bay
Williamsburg
Ohio R.
Indian Country
Mississippi R.
Appalachian Mts
Charleston
Atlantic Ocean
Pensacola
Florida
West Indies

HEMESH·ALLES